BEING

MICHAEL

SWANWICK

OTHER BOOKS BY ALVARO ZINOS-AMARO

Traveler of Worlds: Conversations With Robert Silverberg
When the Blue Shift Comes
Equimedian (forthcoming)

Praise for Alvaro Zinos-Amaro and
Being Michael Swanwick

"Michael Swanwick shows a rare, writerly combination: He's articulate about his own work and also one of the kindest people I've ever met. What can I say other than I thoroughly enjoyed this book and felt privileged to have read it."
— **Samuel R. Delany, SF Grand Master and author of *Babel 17***

"I've watched with admiration and envy as Michael Swanwick has published story after celebrated story over the years. How does he do it? Alvaro Zinos-Amaro has stepped across Michael's keyboard to find out. Here's a tour of four decades of science fiction history as told by someone who was always near the center of things. Not only is this a treasure trove of craft secrets, cultural insight and just enough gossip, but Michael also offers answers to those pesky FAQs we writers always get asked. Where do we get our ideas from? How do we make them come alive? Michael knows—and now he's telling."
— **James Patrick Kelly, Hugo, Hugo, Nebula, and Locus Award winner**

"Some authors refuse to talk about themselves or their work. Others do so, but run out of new things to say. Only a few have the fertility and the mental legs to go deep and long. J. G. Ballard and Samuel R. Delany and Robert Silverberg are three who've done so, at great length: but the books containing interviews with them, which take up hundreds of pages, end too soon. And so it is with Michael Swanwick. The 300 pages of *Being Michael Swanwick* are not enough. It is only the beginning of a fractal journey into the art and artifice and accident and fatedness inspiring his work that make almost every story Michael's written over the near half century of a brilliant and prolific career so much worth talking about. The more we read, the more we want. The more we want from him, the more we gain."
— **John Clute, author of *Science Fiction: The Illustrated Encyclopedia***

"Whether you're a longtime Michael Swanwick fan or just encountering his work for the first time, this book is a treasure trove of advice, insight, and gossip, as well as a major contribution to the oral history of science fiction."
— **Alec Nevala-Lee, author of *Astounding: John W. Campbell, Isaac Asimov, Robert A. Heinlein, L. Ron Hubbard, and the Golden Age of Science Fiction***

"The sorcerer reveals his secrets and his magic becomes all the more powerful for this telling. To read *Being Michael Swanwick* is pure joy!"
— **Henry Wessells, author of *The Private Life of Books***

"*Being Michael Swanwick* is a delightful book. The reader is drawn directly into Alvaro Zinos-Amaro and Michael Swanwick's enthralling conversation. Alvaro's insightful questions and Michael's perceptive responses provide an intriguing introduction to the thoughts of one of SF's most distinguished and creative authors. The interviews provide a master class in writing, and they are invaluable historical documents that offer reflections on a large slice of science fiction's history."
— **Sheila Williams, editor of *Asimov's Science Fiction Magazine***

"Michael Swanwick is one of the most interesting, important, and imaginative writers of his generation. He can 'think around corners' to conceive and create stories and novels that are truly astonishing. *Being Michael Swanwick* is insightful and—dare I say it—revelatory. My advice: read this book, and then read or reread all the work mentioned therein."
— **Jack Dann, author of *Shadows in the Stone***

"An intimate deep dive into the creative process, Alvaro Zinos-Amaro's *Being Michael Swanwick* can be equally enjoyed by devotees of Swanwick's work and those looking for deeper insight into the craft of writing."
— **Jacob Weisman, publisher of Tachyon Publications and**
  co-author of *Mingus Fingers*

"Theodore Sturgeon taught us to ask the next question—but equally important is asking the right question. Alvaro Zinos-Amaro does both in this collection of interviews with one of our very finest sf writers. Few writers have been as central as has Michael Swanwick to both modern science fiction and fantasy literature and the communities from which it springs. *Being Michael Swanwick* offers detailed insights into both Swanwick's individual works and those literatures and communities. An invaluable resource and a fascinating read."
— **F. Brett Cox, author of *The End of All Exploring: Stories***

"A fascinating collection of insightful interviews from a very sharp critic, of one of our smartest fantasy writers."
— **Farah Mendlesohn, author of *A Short History of Fantasy***

"This absorbingly insightful conversation reveals not only what makes Michael Swanwick tick, and how his stories came about, but how the world of science fiction ticks, coping with and encouraging change and keeping science fiction fresh and vibrant."
— **Mike Ashley, author of *The History of the Science Fiction Magazine***

BEING

MICHAEL

SWANWICK

ALVARO

ZINOS-AMARO

FAIRWOOD PRESS
Bonney Lake, WA

BEING MICHAEL SWANWICK
A Fairwood Press Book
November 2023
Copyright © 2023 Alvaro Zinos-Amaro
All Rights Reserved

First Edition

Fairwood Press
21528 104th Street Court East
Bonney Lake, WA 98391
www.fairwoodpress.com

Cover art © Dusan Stankovic, Getty Images
Cover and book design by Patrick Swenson

ISBN: 978-1-958880-14-2
First Fairwood Press Edition: November 2023

For my mother, Alicia Amaro Roldán, who once wrote down the secrets of life for me in a Spider-Man notebook, and later taught me the true meaning of the words *alea iacta est*

CONTENTS

11   Introduction by Gregory Frost

15   Chapter One: 1980-1984

51   Chapter Two: 1985-1989

83   Chapter Three: 1990-1994

114   Chapter Four: 1995-1999

157   Chapter Five: 2000-2004

191   Chapter Six: 2005-2009

225   Chapter Seven: 2010-2014

265   Chapter Eight: 2015-2022

300   Chapter Nine: Caprichos & Series

314   Chapter Ten: Collaborations

324   Afterword by Marianne Porter

INTRODUCTION

BY
GREGORY FROST

Some years ago I was in the audience at Temple University where Samuel R. Delany (at that time a professor in Temple's writing program) was introducing author Kelly Link. The first thing Chip said was "Great writers break rules." It was an appropriate curtain-raiser for her fiction, and I think, if anything, even more so for Michael Swanwick's body of work—the subject of the book you have here.

Michael will no doubt credit two stellar writers and friends of his—Jack Dann and, especially, the late Gardner Dozois—for taking him under their wings after he arrived in Philadelphia (this would be late 1970s-early 1980s). He and I have talked about this period in his career over glasses of wine and cups of coffee. Jack and Gardner were the Penn & Teller of science fiction, who showed him how the magic worked, impressing upon him the idea that no story's shape is ever immutable, that you can, in effect, pull a rabbit out of a hat without there being either a rabbit or a hat.

Even intuitive "pantser" writers start with some notion of what the final form of their composition will be, however indistinct; but Gardner and Jack drew back the curtain on the explosive idea that the story as conceived could be warped and reshaped, re-imagined and even explored from the opposite side from whence you began . . . and that if you could hold on to it, you could produce something amazing. Amazing like "Ginungagap," or *Stations of the Tide*, or the two incorrigible con men, Darger and Surplus, who in their perambulations very nearly take down the whole world.

Gardner and Jack guided him to his own school of magic.

Now jump forward a few decades. Michael was creating brilliant flash fictions spun from a variety of influences, including a series of images by Goya called *Los Caprichos*. He had by then completed a couple of flash series, including one based on the Table of the Elements, and I recall asking how he was accomplishing this. He answered that he first imagined himself doing it to the point that he could almost see the finished work, in effect verifying for himself that he could. And as a result he simply sat down and did it.

That ability to see a story in progress from many angles with fresh eyes is also something he willingly shares. His past Clarion students know this. And from years of associating with him, I know it, too. I have for some time argued that every story and novel we write is in a dialogue with some other story or novel. Michael is probably the poster face for this notion, except that a story or novel of his might be engaged in a dialogue with Vladimir Nabokov, Guy Davenport, Roger Zelazny, and Hans Jakob Christoffel von Grimmelshausen's *Simplicius Simplicissimus*—and all at the same time. His points of reference and layers of influence can be dizzying. It's no surprise that he is a voracious bibliophile. Books are everywhere in his house.

Michael's novels can seem to be entirely intuitive in construction, but they are not. This is another bit of his magic. He slides in those layers with a structuralist's precision, testing and considering, turning and shaping them until they lock into place. Take for example the opening sentence of *The Iron Dragon's Daughter*: "The changeling's decision to steal a dragon and escape was born, though she did not know it then, the night the children met to plot the death of their supervisor." There in a single sentence is a situational opening that provides you with two mystery hooks. Look at the careful wording: "The changeling's decision to steal a dragon and escape" doesn't tell you whether she does escape, only of her intent. That's a mystery hook that won't be answered for a third of the novel. Likewise "the night the children met to plot the death of their supervisor" doesn't say that they kill him, only that they *want* to. And that's a hook for the opening chapter to pull you right into the story. Structurally, the sentence maps precisely upon the much-celebrated opening sentence of Gabriel Garcia Marquez's *One Hundred Years of Solitude*. Nothing about this is accidental, but at most a reader might think "nice sentence" and flow right along to the next. But we have here an opening chapter that's immediately in a dialogue with Garcia Marquez, not to mention with Charles Dickens and Mayhew's *London Labour and the London Poor* (a text Dickens often referenced). He reveals still more influences in the pages to follow. For *Being Michael Swanwick* is modeled on a book he compiled some years back from a series of interviews with the late Gardner Dozois, in which Gardner self-deprecatingly broke down his processes, experiments, failures and intuitions. Similarly, Michael here both reveals hidden influences and connections, but he also proffers for the careful reader that same magic system that Gardner and Jack showed him. In talking about his specific choices, he is drawing back the curtain on such choices as they might apply to your own fiction.

One final aside. Way back in the early aughts at a party at his house, he asked me what I was working on, and I described for him this world of interconnecting bridges. "No continents or major landmasses; everything interesting that happens, happens on the bridges." But I hadn't quite figured out what to do with it yet. Michael looked at me very sternly and said, "You have to write that. If you don't, I'm going to steal it." He was absolutely serious. I wrote *Shadowbridge*. And that's the other thing about M. Swanwick: He is ridiculously generous with ideas and assistance, almost as if he were compelled to pass along and share all of this magic in his charge. We have collaborated on one story, and he insists parts of that story that I am sure he wrote were in fact written by me. I don't believe it, but I don't have the evidence to disprove him, and he knows this.

So, if you are interested in hearing how stories get assembled, what synchronicities and insights come into play in their development, how an intuitive-structuralist process might be unpacked, then you have here the rare luxury of inhabiting the uncanny world of Michael Swanwick. Try not to fall off.

—*Gregory Frost, July 2023*

CHAPTER ONE
1980-1984

Alvaro Zinos-Amaro: "The Feast of Saint Janis" (*New Dimensions 11*, ed. Marta Randall and Robert Silverberg, 1980) was your first published story, though not your first story sale.

You've mentioned that you started writing when you were sixteen, and that you finished your first story when you were twenty-eight. Gardner Dozois helped turn on a switch in your creative process in terms of figuring out how to write stories to completion. Before that time you'd been starting them but not finishing them.

Michael Swanwick: That was a streak of luck, though it didn't feel so at the time. I was unable to finish any of the slum of bad stories that most writers start their careers with, so none of them saw print. By the time I was publishable, my stories were a lot more accomplished than those of most beginning writers.

I had known Gardner for years. At first he was wary of me because he was afraid that I'd try to inflict my undoubtedly terrible fiction on him. I was one of those people who let you know they're a writer on first meeting. I never did show him my stuff. Finally, after five years, he broke down and said, "Show me your dreadful fiction." So I did. At that time Jack Dann, who was Gardner's best friend back then, would periodically come down from Binghamton, New York. When he did they would plot out stories, plan anthologies, and talk big and talk art. Somewhere along the line they started inviting me over to Gardner's apartment. One hot summer evening—Gardner was living in a cat-and-cockroach-infested two bedroom apartment—the talk was really, really good, and Gardner took this story I was working on and gave it to Jack to read. Jack read it and then they went over the story with me line by line, paragraph by paragraph, showing me what I'd done wrong, what I'd done right, what changes should be made, and how it could be reshaped and turned into a story. And I understood it. It was like a chiropractor grabbing you and resetting you and all of a sudden your posture's good again. I got it! I understood it perfectly. I went home that night, at two or three in the morning, drunk on Gardner's really bad cream sherry, repeating to myself over and over, "I'm a writer now." And I was. From that moment I was. And it doesn't get easier, but the difference between impossible and possible is so huge. From then on there were things I could not do yet, but there was nothing I couldn't do eventually.

Zinos-Amaro: Was "Saint Janis" one of the first pieces you returned to after that evening?

Swanwick: Yes. I was fascinated by Janis Joplin and Gardner and I used to talk about her sometimes. She was kind of a saint for our generation. Gardner had this whimsical observation that in the future people would worship Janis Joplin, which I thought was a great image.

Zinos-Amaro: Gene Wolfe's "Seven American Nights" (published in 1978 in Damon Knight's *Orbit* 20, reprinted the following year by Gardner), in which an Iranian man named Nadan visits a decrepit Washington D.C., does drugs and falls for an actress, has some parallels with "Saint Janis."

Swanwick: I read Wolfe's story and was knocked out. Wonderful story. Everybody knew that story, we all recognized its greatness. The underlying theme was environmental chemical degradation. The image of America becoming a Third World nation, while not new to Wolfe, was a very powerful one. I put that together with the observation of Janis Joplin and I could see the story. I went around for about a month, enormously frustrated that I couldn't do it because I didn't want to rip off Gene Wolfe. Then one day I said, "You know, someone had to have written the first post-nuclear holocaust story, and today we all feel free to write post-nuclear holocaust stories." I realized that post-environmental degradation stories can be written by more than one person too. So I wrote it.

My agent sent the story to *Orbit*, but it was rejected with a really kind note by Damon Knight saying he would have bought it, but he'd already published "Seven American Nights."

Zinos-Amaro: Do you know if Wolfe ever read your story?

Swanwick: I never spoke with Gene about "The Feast of Saint Janis," alas. He must surely have read it—we all read *New Dimensions* back then. But I never had the stones to ask him about it.

Zinos-Amaro: Tell us a little about this late-twenties Swanwick.

Swanwick: When I made my first sales, I was twenty-nine. I was working as a clerk typist. I had very cunningly majored in English in college, so there was no proper way for me to make a living other than writing. When I was twenty-nine, before any of my stories came out, I lost my job, went into a nine-month long writer's block, and I got married. Turning thirty was nothing!

It was a very terrifying time. During my writer's block, I'd sit down at the typewriter everyday and work and not a word of it would be usable. I was trying to move the two stories that would eventually become part of *In the Drift* forward, and nothing ever happened. I would try to make things happen, like introduce a character with a gun, and someone would say, "Oh no! He's got a gun!" Then the characters would keep talking about it. It was as if your friends had come over for a party and then stayed, just hanging around and talking and doing nothing useful. Eventually I got out of the block by continuing to sit and write every day. After nine months my hindbrain got the message that not giving me ideas was not going to get it out of me sitting there writing. So it said, "All right, you win. You can have ideas."

Of course my greatest concern was to be an adequate husband to Marianne, which entailed having a job. The background of my first few stories was pretty bleak.

Zinos-Amaro: After your breakthrough with Gardner, did you go back to other earlier unfinished stories and apply what you'd learned? What's the longest you've set a story aside until you felt ready to finish it, and what story was that?

Swanwick: I have a story called "Robot," about a man who believes he's a robot, which I started after I wrote a collaboration with William Gibson called "Dogfight." At the end of this, I had some things that hadn't made it into our joint story and I wondered if I could use some of these. I started another story. It begins really well, and it proceeds well for a while. But then it stalls out. Every now and then, every few years, I'll look at it and say, "This is really good," and I'll try to write it again, and fail. This story was begun in '83 and I'm working on it right now. That's forty years.

Zinos-Amaro: By the time we finish these conversations, your story might be completed!

Swanwick: Maybe. We're a lot closer to that world now than we were when I began writing it . . .

Zinos-Amaro: Brian Aldiss, you've shared, was an early inspiration. Do you recall, in your pre-publication days, what about his work resonated with you? Are there any specific Aldiss stories or novels that struck a deep chord?

Swanwick: I was struck, particularly in his short fiction, by the fact that his work was high literary and at the same time very core science fiction. "Old Hundredth" is kind of a touchstone for me. That's a beautiful story with a great deal of science fiction ideation and creation. He did some wonderful robot stories too. He managed to combine being humorous with being dark. Mostly it's that everything he wrote was very, very good, and he did not concern himself with creating a brand. He didn't repeat himself. And then he wrote the Helliconia books, which I thought were dreadful, but were the most profitable things he ever sold.

Zinos-Amaro: Walter Miller Jr., in the anthology *Beyond Tomorrow*, calls your story "The Feast of Saint Janis" an "underworld myth." Were you thinking of the cyclical death of the Janis Joplin impersonators or avatars in mythological terms?

Swanwick: He identified that correctly. I'm very big on mythology and I've done a lot of unstructured reading in it. I probably got the idea for the mythological subtext from Philip José Farmer, from his novel *Flesh*, in which an astronaut returns to an entirely new culture on Earth, and he's given antlers and turned into a priapic god. The novel was a romp, and I was fascinated by the use of mythology, by his embedding that into a hard science fiction story with no mysticism at all.

Zinos-Amaro: In "Saint Janis" America exports its poisons ("chemicals and pesticides and foods containing a witch's brew of preservatives") and there's been a global Collapse. In "Mummer Kiss," another one of your early stories, the United States has done great environmental damage to itself. Keith talks about how "the toxic chemical wastes from one dumping would combine with those from previous dumps, and strange alchemical interactions would take place. The ground would burst into flames or weird orange worms crawl out of the earth. There was a site he had seen in upper Bucks County where the ground actually crawled, boiling and bubbling year-round." Was this inspired by environmental concerns on your part?

Swanwick: At the time there was a great awareness of environmental concerns. The awareness of the problem was relatively new then. It was only at the end of the sixties that people became aware of the damage that we not only *could* be doing to the Earth but *were* doing to the Earth.

I have a friend who grew up in Delaware, which is a wholly owned property of the Du Ponts. He had stories about playing around as a kid in what were essentially unlicensed Du Pont chemical dumps. There were ponds that were bright blue and gave off poisonous fumes, and so on. I don't think I exaggerated much there.

Zinos-Amaro: The character of Ajuji says: ". . . hard-core technology, that's all it was, of a piece with the kind that almost destroyed us all. If you want a measure of a people, you look at how they live." In the same story Wolf states: ". . . if a major thrust is made, we can clean up the gene pool in less than a century. But to do this requires professionals—eugenicists, embryonic surgeons." Do you consciously try to offer varied views on technology and science in your fiction, or is it simply the function of a story's dramatic requirements?

Swanwick: I was imagining that in post-American Africa they had come up with different social understandings of how to deal with technology and how to use it as a positive force. I was imagining that in Africa they'd come up with a more responsible way of dealing with all the issues, while at the same time they're still human beings, and therefore they still say snarky and offensive things about people they consider their inferiors, such as Americans.

I'm on both sides of the fence on this issue. I love science. I'm a strong believer in knowledge and in the good that science can do, and I could come up with an enormous list of benevolent things that science has done for me in particular. But anybody can see the damage that's done when you just don't care about consequences.

Zinos-Amaro: The character of DiStephano is referred to as the "Spider King"—where did this come from?

Swanwick: That's a term that's been around since Louis XI; it was just a useful image, a nice shortcut to tell you who and what he was.

Zinos-Amaro: Maggie, who performs the Janis Joplin cover songs, is found through a computer search, which interestingly pre-dates Internet and social-media born stars. Your notion of representing decadence by glamorized, and ritualized, nostalgia, seems to have come to pass.

Swanwick: It was funny. I wrote this story and sent it out and before the story was published I ran across a small article in the *New York Times* about somebody who was on tour impersonating Janis Joplin. I felt responsible. I felt like I created this.

Zinos-Amaro: Maggie describes her generation of artists as "just echoes, man," and later calls herself a "goddamned echo." She uses the word "dead" a lot, describing Dead music, a town as dead, saying "this place is fucking dead." Does she know her own fate? Were you planting it in the mind of the reader with this word choice?

Swanwick: Yes, she knows how she's going to end up. It's part of the deal. She gets to be Janis Joplin for a year, and then she dies. The Dead music was Grateful Dead music. I am an apostate on this one. I've never been a fan of them, though I think very highly of their fans; they're lovely people. Maggie is living in a dead country, in the wastelands. Everything really is dead, to the degree that she is drawn to living for a year as Janis Joplin, who is *alive*—and that was the emphatic thing about her, how alive she was. I have a line in the story "When The Music's Over . . ." that states this explicitly: ". . . she [Janis] was so alive that she made the rest of us look like we were walking around half dead."

When I was writing the story I read every biography of Janis Joplin I could get a hold of. There were a surprising number of them. I got her voice caught in my head. Everyone else's dialogue was very difficult to write, while her words would just come flowing out. She had such a beautiful, vivid voice. Ever since, I've been hoping to find more people to base characters on who have really good voices like that.

Zinos-Amaro: DiStephano's closing words about this post-Collapse U.S. society having "nothing to lose" speaks to a kind of desperation. Was that part of a zeitgeist you were tapping into and transposing to an imagined future, or was it derived from your world-building?

Swanwick: I'm afraid I'm going to have to say half and half, really. The times have been dark on the environmental front for a long time, to such a degree that I find myself forced to be optimistic just because the alternative is imposed upon us. When my son was a little boy once he said he felt bad sometimes thinking about the future because the world wasn't going to be nice ever again, it was just going to get worse. I said, "No, no, no. There's hope. We know what the problem is. We can do things to undo the damage." In fact, we *have* undone some of the damage. When I was a kid, eagles were extinct in the lower forty-eight states. Large birds were almost gone. Then they made a wonderful comeback. Places where people take action, they can have enormous effect.

We've been teaching children environmental education and not realizing that what we've been telling them through this is that everything is bleak and hopeless. This is exactly the opposite of what we need. We need to have hope, and we need to have optimism in order to undo the damage that was done when we didn't realize what we were doing.

Zinos-Amaro: Is this something you think science fiction can help with?

Swanwick: I honestly don't know. Way back when, we were writing anti-overpopulation stories, and I can't see that we did much good. Maybe we did, and we didn't notice it. I try to maintain my optimism. My wife thinks I'm doing a terrible job of it, though!

Zinos-Amaro: I compared the text of this story in its first appearance in *New Dimensions 11* with the version in *Gravity's Angels*, and there are some subtle edits. I found the same to be true when comparing "Mummer Kiss" in *Universe 11* to the reprint in *Gravity's Angels*. Is this part of your normal process when a story is reprinted, or did you tweak these stories in particular because they were early work?

Swanwick: It's a normal part of the process. You go over the work and look for errors that have crept in that you missed the first time. Style is a part of it too.

Nowadays when I finish a story I put it in the pie closet for a couple of weeks, until I've lost that fever of creation. I come back and re-read it and find myself making lots and lots of little changes. I don't remember revising those stories, but I suspect that's what was going on there too. I had gotten some distance from them and when I put the collection together I cleaned them up a little bit.

Zinos-Amaro: Let's move on to "Ginungagap" (*TriQuarterly* 49, ed. Elliott Anderson, Jonathan Brent, David G. Hartwell, and Robert Onopa, 1980), which derives its title from the primordial void in Norse mythology. As a young reader, did you differentiate between mythology, fantasy and science fiction?

Swanwick: Oh yeah. The difference is huge. I started out wanting to write fantasy. I read Tolkien when I was sixteen and it changed my life forever, made me want to be a writer. I wanted to write specifically fantasy. I read everything published in fantasy—which didn't take very long, back in the late 60s. I got deeply into science fiction because it gave a fantasy-like kick, in large part because for a long time if you were a fantasy writer, you had to find something else to do with your talent. Some people wrote Arthurian fantasy. Some people wrote historical novels. And some people wrote science fiction. If you look at, say, Leigh Brackett, or C. L. Moore, one of their novels will begin with the hero riding away from the spaceport on a Martian eight-legged horse and it gets startled by a Martian eight-legged rabbit, he falls off, loses his blaster and can't find it, so from now on he has to fight with his brawny fists and his sword. And the Martians are all too proud to use energy weapons. You look at that scene where he loses his blaster, and it goes from science fiction and turns into a fantasy novel in a single sentence. There's a lot of fantasy DNA hidden in science fiction. As I progressed as an unpublished writer, my loyalty switched over to science fiction because it's more difficult to write than fantasy, and writers are drawn to difficulty! I had all this reading in mythology and fantasy, and it inevitably affected my science fiction. There's a certain amount of fantasy feel running through all the science fiction, and a lesser degree of science fiction feel running through the fantasy. But they're still separate things.

I gave this some thought a while back, and I decided that science fiction is set in a knowable universe. People might not be able to figure it out because we're not smart enough, but somebody smarter than us could understand anything in the universe. It all makes sense. There's an explanation for it. But in fantasy, the very core of it is mystery. That mystery is close to or akin to religion. It's the numinous. Essentially fantasy is set in an unknowable universe. You never will know exactly what the rules are, in part because, as Farah Mendlesohn has pointed out, any sufficiently explained fantasy tends to become science fiction.

Zinos-Amaro: When do you recall identifying science fiction as having a particular flavor that appealed to you?

Swanwick: When I was doing my peak reading it was the New Wave era. That was all very exciting. People were doing new, interesting literary things with science fiction. Meanwhile, in the mainstream they were writing novels about men with unfaithful wives who take sabbaticals and go off to live in the country for six months with a graduate student. There was a great deal of mainstream then which was of no interest to anyone with serious literary ambition. Meanwhile science fiction was the place where interesting things were happening all the time. I was entranced.

Zinos-Amaro: In the anthology *Before They Were Giants*, you explained that "Ginungagap" ended up appearing in the special science fiction issue of *Triquarterly* because David Hartwell was guest-editing it. You went on to say, ". . . my agent, Virginia Kidd, sent the story in. How I happened to have an agent and why she was handling short fiction are stories for another time." Now is a great time for those stories!

Swanwick: I had written a mystery/crime short story. After Gardner and Jack taught me how to write that one evening, I finished the story and sent it off to *Ellery Queen's*, and they rejected it. I sent it to *Alfred Hitchcock's*, and they rejected it. That used up all the markets for it. Gardner said, "I'll send it to my agent, Virginia Kidd, and see if she can do anything with it." She read it and saw potential in the story. She wrote a letter back directly to me saying "Welcome to the agency." So I had an agent before I had sold *anything*. I had an agent who was the last agent on Earth to charge ten percent, and the last agent on Earth to handle short fiction. Virginia was intensely interested in everything. By that time she didn't get around very much—in her later years she was bedridden. Mostly she stayed in her house. But she was a fantastic letter writer and advice-giver. I loved Virginia. When many years later it became necessary to fire her as an agent it felt like getting a divorce. I walked around saying, "I do not feel guilty. I do not feel guilty. This was the right thing to do." I have only good things to say about her.

Zinos-Amaro: Did you ever return to mystery and try to write other stories in that genre? Does it tempt you in some way?

Swanwick: Not really, no. In fact, at a certain point I stopped reading mysteries. Not that I have anything against them, but my reading time is limited, and I know that if I started reading mysteries now I would read nothing else for at least two years. I was doing a reading once with Lawrence Block and he had a stack of these remaindered hardcovers to sell, so I bought one so I could get his autograph. I read it on the train on the way back and thought, "This is great! I'm going to read more of his stuff." But then I told myself, "Stop, Michael. You're going to read *all* of his stuff. And then you're going to go one by one through the rest of the mystery field, because there's a lot of fantastic writers out there." Only, I really do need to keep up with science fiction and fantasy. I need to be reading new stories, so I know what's being written now and I don't end up writing old-fashioned 1980s science fiction and fantasy.

Much later in my career I did write a fantasy story that was a locked-room mystery, "A Small Room in Koboldtown." I like it, but purists say it didn't really play by the rules, which is to say, give the reader enough clues to figure it out. But I think readers will who are smart enough!

Zinos-Amaro: Terry Carr said that "Ginungagap" was one of the best stories to seriously consider what the psychology of aliens might actually be. What are some of your favorite stories that tackle alien psychology?

Swanwick: "Alien Stones" by Gene Wolfe is a good one. *The Left Hand of Darkness*. "Strangers" by Gardner Dozois, the novel and also the novella before it. It's all about the difficulty of reaching across the otherness to communicate.

Zinos-Amaro: You mentioned not wanting to be stuck writing 80's sf. Jerry Pournelle wrote of "Ginungagap" that it was a "highly plausible action and adventure in a detailed future of marvels" and said it reminded him of an earlier era in science fiction. To me, the story's inventive density and use of language have kept it fresh. When you look at it today, do you feel that it's reminiscent of an era of science fiction that predates the time when you wrote it?

Swanwick: I was aware of the fact that it was in a tradition of space wonders; you know, stories where you go out into the Solar System, filled with exotic and very different cultures and people. I was trying to capture that same kind of excitement. But I was not trying to write a retro story, or an homage. I remember being surprised by the glee with which people seized upon it. It was only decades later that I could look back and see that what it was, was that I was bringing in a lot of new stuff from the streets. I had space environments painted with supergraphics, for example. I had a lot of interest in off-the-wall things because I was young and alert and involved with the culture. At the time I couldn't see that these were actually positive additions. When I find a new writer now that's exciting, I can definitely see that in their work.

Zinos-Amaro: Speaking of bringing things in from the streets, Gardner wrote that you were sometimes unfairly judged to be derivative of William Gibson, despite the fact that your early work preceded Gibson's. About this story specifically Gardner said that it "prefigures many of what would later come to be considered cyberpunk tropes, as well as a few postcyberpunk tropes."

Swanwick: I wrote an essay called "A User's Guide to the Postmoderns," which was about the cyberpunks and the "humanists," my contribution to nomenclatural confusion. It was very clear to me that there was this new generation that came in all at once, over two or three years, just one after another, and there were all these strong similarities between them, especially their influences. They belonged together in one group. Taking half of the best writers and labeling them cyberpunks was really doing a disservice to the rest of us.

Zinos-Amaro: On the topic of influences—Gardner cited the following as some of yours: Samuel R. Delany, Alfred Bester, James Tiptree, Jr. and John Varley. We mentioned Brian Aldiss earlier. Who would you add as some of the heavy hitters that can help us frame up the context of your early work? No doubt others will appear when we get to latter stories.

Swanwick: My generation was the last to come into the field having read almost literally everything, almost every major writer who had ever lived, and a lot of the really bad ones too. To your list I would add a name. When I was writing that "Postmoderns" essay I got in touch with almost everyone of my generation, and the one writer that they all praised specifically was Philip K. Dick. That's an interesting thing, because at that time his star was still rising. A generation before that, his name wouldn't have been on the list at all. That was kind of fascinating.

I'd also add Roger Zelazny to the list. What all these writers have in common is that they're very highly colored. Very brightly entertaining. Also, simultaneously pop and literary.

Zinos-Amaro: If I understand correctly, the bits about black hole mechanics in "Ginungagap" came out of a long chat with a Ph.D. candidate named Bill Franz.

Swanwick: I worked with his wife in the National Solar Heating and Cooling Information Center. It was a government subproject and we were all sweatshop intellectuals. A poorly paid, highly motivated, very positive group. Bill told me about things his mentor had speculated about regarding black holes. None of it was published at that point, so I couldn't actually cite anything or name names.

Zinos-Amaro: You were also inspired by a *Star Trek* novelization. Do you remember what it was and how you came to read it?

Swanwick: Yes, it was one of James Blish's *Star Trek* novelizations! I read it because I read everything back then. I look back and I cannot imagine how I had all the time, or all the speed, to read as much as I did.

It might have been a short story adapting an episode. Blish did a very good job with those. He had Spock and Bones arguing about what happens when you go into the transporter, and whether in fact you were destroyed and killed and a copy of yourself was created. I came down on the side that this kills you. It was perfectly obvious to me. For years I had conversations with people about this and they would not concede the point. They felt that something identical to something else *is* that exact same thing. So I wrote this story in part because it was very frustrating not to be able to put my own point of view across to them. In the course of it I think I balanced off both views. They're incompatible, but I wanted to examine it fairly.

Zinos-Amaro: I think the story does a beautiful job with that. What was your relationship with genre television and film growing up?

Swanwick: I grew up at a time when most science fiction television and film was terrible. It was astonishingly awful. I remember when they first aired ads for *Star Trek*. Just a poster of the characters, and a little bit of music: "*Star Trek* is coming!" One of the people there had pointed ears! My God! It seemed astonishingly daring. I loved *Star Trek*. Much later on, when *Star Wars* came out, I was there in line with my friends, an hour before the movie opened on the first day. When the movie began, after the crawl the spaceship went right overhead and my jaw fell open and I did not close it until the end of the movie. I was so delighted. You have to keep in mind that immediately prior to that I'd seen *Buck Rogers*. That was a terrible movie, when it came out, the high point of which is Buck teaching a cute little robot how to play football, and also disco dancing.

Zinos-Amaro: It wasn't all bad. Had you watched *The Twilight Zone*? How about Stanley Kubrick's *2001*?

Swanwick: I watched the *Twilight Zone* and it terrified me. It's brilliant and the best of it still holds up. Amazing little fables. As a technical matter, a screenwriter once explained to me that that little opening where Rod Serling stands there with a cigarette and says, "Portrait of a man who . . .", saved them fifteen minutes of exposition, so they could do a whole story in a half hour.

2001 came out my senior year of high school. I borrowed the family car. I was living outside of Richmond; my family had moved there at the beginning of the year. I moved away, went off to college the next year, so I had very few friends, no real connections. I went to the theater alone late at night and I saw this bleak and wonderful and magical and positive movie. I came out feeling like the entire universe had changed. So, I'm not entirely a book snob!

Zinos-Amaro: Garble the cat—is there a backstory there?

Swanwick: There's a front story. As I was writing this story every so often I would bring it to Gardner, and he would read it and he would give me his thoughts. He did this with all my stories up until he became the editor of *Asimov's*. When that happened, it was a piece of good fortune for the rest of science fiction, and a piece of bad fortune for me. He was the best story doctor in the world. He had read the first section of "Ginungagap," and I went to visit him one day and he said, "How's that story of yours coming along Michael?" I said, "It's going all right. I just wrote a scene where a cat hijacks a starship." He said, "Oh you did not!" But I had. Ever since then, for the rest of his life, I kept trying to astonish him again, and I never succeeded. But I did manage to astound Gardner Dozois once.

Zinos-Amaro: There's a sequence in this story in which Abigail recalls her space suit shooting "her full of a nerve synesthetic." This allows you to write things like "With a sick green feeling in the pit of her stomach." At the start of that scene, you say that the "lab's geodesic dome echoed white clouds to the north," so you're already conflating sound with color—was this deliberate foreshadowing on your part?

Swanwick: No, that was just good luck, I'm afraid. I can tell you one thing interesting about that though. When I first started writing the story, the main character was male. I kept grinding to a stop because the character was not believable. Finally I said, "Who is this guy? He's me. Where does he come from? He comes from Schenectady, New York. Why is he behaving like this? Because he's a space hero." So I changed the character to a woman. Thinking of her as a woman, the character made sense, because all the women I've known have had good reasons for everything they did. Or at least reasons for everything they did. They weren't like me, a creature of whimsy and folly. I found that by making the character female, it gave me the distance from the character to let that character be realistic rather than a fantasy figure. The synesthesia section you mentioned is a classic science fiction hero moment—she's in a tight spot that would kill almost anybody else, but because she's smart and because she's tough she's able to do what needs to be done and rescue herself. You don't get more heroic than freezing your arm and smashing it in order to escape a trap. But she is, I think, a *believable* hero.

Zinos-Amaro: In the story there's a debate about whether, if oxygen is limited, to save a human, a spider, or neither. Abigail immediately asks "What's the point of this debate?" Besides the straightforward narrative function of that scene, were you making a kind of meta-textual commentary on Tom Godwin's "Cold Equations" and the Campbellian school of problem-solving stories?

Swanwick: No. Your source is so much better than mine. At the College of William & Mary, where I went to school, they had an annual raft debate. The premise is that there's three people and only enough room on the raft for one person to survive. Somebody from the sciences argues that he or she should be saved because the sciences are more valuable. Someone from the humanities argues that he or she be saved because the humanities are more valuable. And then you have a trickster who argues that nobody's worth saving, they should just scuttle the raft. I had some exposition to embody in the story and I thought of that raft debate and thought it would be an interesting way to do it. In my early fiction there's a lot of exposition, and I'm trying very hard to find entertaining ways to do it. I may be the only person who's ever used Michael O'Donoghue's article "How to Write Good" and taken it seriously. He had a section on exposition and he suggested that you throw the exposition into a sex scene to hold the reader's interest. I thought, "Well, why not?" I did it again in "When The Music's Over . . ."

Zinos-Amaro: The next story, "'Til Human Voices Wake Us," was your first sale. It was accepted by Jim Baen for publication in *Destinies* but ended up appearing in the anthology *Proteus: Voices for the 80's*, edited by Richard S. McEnroe, along with other pieces originally purchased for *Destinies*. How did this begin to shape your opinion of the publishing world?

Swanwick: As you said, that was my first sale. At that time *Destinies* was a monthly paperback magazine that Baen did. It was a noble experiment. I made the sale, and the next month the magazine came out, and I knew it wasn't physically possible for my story to be in it but I went out and bought it anyway. I wasn't in the table of contents, but I went through the whole issue anyway just to make sure they hadn't included the story and forgotten to put it in the table of contents. I did this for over a year. Rather a long time. Then at some point the "publish date" on the contract passed, and they sent me a note that they were putting it in *Proteus*, which was a collection of stories they regretted having bought for *Destinies*. I wrote to them and said, "Actually, you don't have the right to publish that." They replied that they'd give me something like twenty-four bucks as a republishing fee, and told me if I wanted to publish it elsewhere for the first time before the book came out, it was fine. By that time my first story had come out, so it was no longer such a big deal. It was just amusing—I hope.

Zinos-Amaro: There are some interesting illustrations by Broeck Steadman that accompany "'Til Human Voices Wake Us." Later we'll discuss stories of yours inspired by paintings, but can you talk about your relationship with visual art? When you write, are you seeing the scene you're in?

Swanwick: I love visual art. I cannot draw at all. But when I'm working on a novel I'll make little drawings of things that are going to appear in it, even of the characters. They're all dreadful.

Ironically, I'm a very visual writer. I have to find a way to express in words what I cannot say in drawings. I visualize how things go. I do see the scene, not with perfect clarity, but pretty well.

Zinos-Amaro: In your introductory comments in *Proteus* you mention that you were in a trolley that caught fire midway through the Schuylkill River.

Swanwick: I was in this very crowded trolley. In the side wall of the trolley smoke started coming out, like three feet away from me. This tension among the people nearby who saw it spread out. People in the back started asking, "Excuse me, Mr. Driver? Sir?" in the most polite, calm way possible. We could all feel that if anybody panicked we would *all* panic. The driver looked annoyed, and he stopped the car, slammed the doors open and said, "Everybody out." We walked the rest of the way through the tunnels. It was a wonderful experience, actually. Especially in my early work, I used as much of my own personal experience as possible, whatever was there to be used that would make the story more interesting.

The very opening of this story starts with the character drowning. When I was twelve or so I was in Burlington, Vermont, where my father worked in General Electric. The employee's association bought an old resort hotel, a pleasantly run-down place, and kept it as a facility for the employees. In the summer my mother would take us there every day we'd go swimming in the lake. It was really quite lovely. One day I decided to see how far I could swim, so I went out as far as I could. Then I turned around and started back, and about halfway back I realized that my plan was flawed. I fell *through* the water. I struggled up, gasped for air, went down again. I came up a second time, then went down for the third time. I remember thinking that the whole going-down-for-the-third-time thing was superstition, that it was mere coincidence that I wasn't going to come up for a fourth time. And then I saw a black wall—this is in one of my other stories too. This black wall was right in front of me, stretching to infinity on either side. I could almost reach out and touch it. I realized that I was about to die. I was about to pass through the dark wall. When I did, I would know, or else not. At that instant an arm wrapped itself around me and this guy pulled me up to the surface and in life-saving style he got me to the shore and asked me if I was all right. Then he went back to his girlfriend. He wasn't the life guard, who was still sitting in his chair. He was just some guy who'd noticed me drowning. I said, "Thank you for saving my life."

Zinos-Amaro: That's not the only dream we see in the story, since Calvin, the narrator, has "recurrent precognitive nightmares." In "Ginungagap" we experience one of Abigail's intense dreams as well. What's your attitude these days toward dream passages?

Swanwick: They're extremely useful. They're a great way to put in alternatives and possibilities and explanations. They're of course not at all like real dreams. For about two years I kept a dream diary. I taught myself to remember my dreams, which you can do for about five minutes after you wake up. Whenever I had a vivid one, I would write down all I could remember of it. At the end of those two years I read what I'd written for the first time and found that dreams are very fluid and that they occur in a variety of media. Some are like movies, and others take more abstract forms. There was one I remember that was in the form of black and white manga. You'd have a still picture in manga style, and then all the lines would move and blur to the next panel. I learned a great deal of interesting things from this, none of which I think is applicable to writing, although I did get some good images out of some of the dreams, which I then bundled into my stories. I'm always on the lookout to make a story more interesting.

Zinos-Amaro: "'Til Human Voices Wake Us" is the first of your stories with a first-person narrator, but I feel just as close to Wolf or Abigail, maybe more so, than to Calvin, because he is confused about his experience of the world. Did you deliberately choose the first person to make it harder for the reader to differentiate between Calvin's perceptions and the ways he might be changing reality itself?

Swanwick: When I wrote the first draft of that I was unpublished and unpublishable. I was trying everything at that time. I tend to avoid first person whenever I can—sometimes it's unavoidable. This story could have probably been told in the third person.

Zinos-Amaro: Let's turn to "Mummer Kiss" (*Universe 11*, ed. Terry Carr, 1981).

Swanwick: "Mummer Kiss" came about because I was in Philadelphia when Three Mile Island melted down. My wife and I left town because it was the responsible thing to do. Luckily it did not go to a full meltdown, but it was such a significant event that of course I wanted to write about it. I combined that with my fascination of the Philadelphia Mummers, and it became a story.

Zinos-Amaro: In "Mummer Kiss" one of the main characters is the reporter Suzette Fletcher, whose discovery that Philadelphia is actually in a contaminated zone can upend the local status quo. In "Walden Three," which we'll discuss next, the reporter Maude Bataleur also shakes things up. Both of these stories feature female journalists who discover something important about the worlds they're investigating, and neither comes to a good end—Fletcher is killed, while Maude lives the rest of her life with regret.

Swanwick: That was just a function of the plot that was necessary. I was looking over them in preparation for this, and I was struck by how much more interesting, complex and believable the women are than the men in my early stories. I wish I'd made that observation then. I would have had made more of the protagonists female. It would have made for more work for me but it would have made for better stories.

Zinos-Amaro: How soon after writing "Mummer Kiss" did you decide that you'd want to expand on this material and turn it into what would be your first published novel, *In the Drift* (1985)?

Swanwick: Very famously there had been the Milford workshop, in Milford, Pennsylvania. Gardner and a group of his friends—Jack Dann, Joe Haldeman and his brother Jay, George R. R. Martin, and I think George Alec Effinger may have been a part of it too—had a similar workshop in the house of one of them in the Guilford section of Baltimore. When Gardner decided to resurrect this workshop it made sense to call it "Philford." I took "Mummer Kiss" to the workshop. All the workshoppers basically explained to me how to turn this into a novella. But you can't sell a novella with basically the same plot as the novelette. So it had to be the opening of a novel. The novel was a fix-up. I was so desperate to write a novel at that time, I was willing to do anything, including a fix-up. I plotted it out and planned it out from that expansion. I saw it as being a triptych: this story, along with "Marrow Death" and "Boneseeker," and two short hinges in between. "Boneseeker," by the way, never had independent publication. I was very close to done with it when Virginia Kidd sold *In the Drift* to Terry Carr. I hadn't wanted to sell an unfinished work but she assured me that the money and the exposure justified it. She was certainly right about the exposure. The New Ace SF Special line got tons of it, particularly after *Neuromancer* came out in 1984. So I signed. But my reluctance to do so was justified too. Writing those last several pages was like clawing a tunnel in granite with my fingernails. My hindbrain got the message that the novel was done and shut down by refusing to give me any ideas.

Everybody recognized that *In the Drift* was a fix-up, and I caught a fair amount of heat for that from reviewers. Especially from the Brits. They were really very morally indignant about the idea.

Zinos-Amaro: At one point in "Mummer Kiss" Fletch is exposed to a kind of procession of "men in feathers, in sequins, dressed as clowns, as Indians, as playing cards, strutted by in organized disarray." There's also "a female impersonator" but Keith explains to Abigail that women were banned from this shortly after the Meltdown. Tell me more about this sequence.

Swanwick: The Mummers are a real thing. I came to Philadelphia and discovered the Mummers. If you see them on television, you won't get it. But if you're standing there on the street, where these men in elaborate costumes that signify nothing but are spectacular combine with bands and clowns and such, and it goes on hour after hour after hour, you notice that some of them who have completed the parade take off their big capes that fit on their backs but they're still in their Mummers garb, faces painted, cans of beer in their hands, cruising down the sidewalk. You also notice that some people who have showed up to watch the parade are in costume. Other people have a feather boa or a funny hat. And at some point you can't determine if someone is dressed in a Mummerish way, or if they're just eccentric all the time, and then there comes this magical moment when you realize that *everybody* is a Mummer to some degree or other. It's an immersive, extraordinary experience. At the time I first came to Philadelphia, which would be 1974, women were not allowed in the Mummers. By the time the book came out there were a couple of women in the Mummers and more and more joined in. Now, currently the Mummers have gotten a lot glossier, a lot glitzier, a lot more pop entertainment-ish.

With the women being banned, I was indicating that with the collapse of the economy you get a collapse of social freedom too. Women lose a lot of their rights, gays lose a lot of their rights, blacks go down to the bottom of the social scale: all hard-earned and deserved rights go away and the world becomes a nastier, more brutal place.

Zinos-Amaro: Speaking of style, "Mummer Kiss" seems to me more restrained than "Ginungagap" and certainly than "'Til Human Voices Wake Us." It has a more down-to-earth descriptive approach that serves to heighten the horror and the misery of this world. Were you learning how to modulate your style by this point?

Swanwick: I couldn't be said to be modulating yet, but I could tell it was the proper voice for that tale. I knew it was a story that didn't call for flamboyance.

Zinos-Amaro: Let's talk about your reception in the field at this point. "Saint Janis" and "Ginungagap" both ended up on the 1981 Nebula ballot in the Novelette category. "Mummer Kiss" appeared on the 1982 Nebula ballot, same category. This is indicative of the high regard in which in your peers immediately held your work. Did this affect your confidence as a writer, or your literary ambition?

Swanwick: Nothing could have affected my literary ambition, because at that time I wanted to be much greater than Shakespeare! I was amazed and delighted and I was really encouraged by it. To start with two stories *losing* the Nebula is the best way you could possibly go. I've known people who won their first time out, and it blighted things for them, because from that point on anytime they didn't win they were failing to live up to their earlier promise. For me, my first story was published in 1980 and I didn't win anything of great significance until 1990, by which time I felt I deserved it. All the awards lost felt great—it made me feel like I was an active part of something important. Looking back now, I realize that a lot of the awards go to young people. Science fiction is always looking for what's new and exciting. It's idea fiction. We want new ideas, and new ideas tend to come from new writers.

Zinos-Amaro: Did you realize at this time that your work wasn't having the same popular appeal as it did among your fellow creatives?

Swanwick: David Hartwell once wrote that the purpose of awards was to encourage people who couldn't make a living at it to keep writing science fiction anyway.

I went into this business with my eyes pretty wide open. Part of my plan was poverty. I was talking with Chip Delany not that long ago and he said that when he started out, his artist's plan was poverty. Once you decide that you're never going to live as well as a Certified Public Accountant that makes a lot of things possible! One of the things it makes possible is that you get to write whatever you want. I chose freedom over money.

There were several points in my career when I could have done the commercial thing. After I wrote "Dogfight" with William Gibson there was a certain amount of encouragement from the fans of cyberpunk stuff for me to become a William Gibson lite. I recognized that this would probably be financially advantageous, but at the same time I really didn't want to be the second-best William Gibson in the world.

Zinos-Amaro: In "Walden Three" (*New Dimensions 12*, ed. Marta Randall and Robert Silverberg, 1981), as in "Mummer Kiss" and "Saint Janis," you return to the idea of society under existential pressure. Terry Carr called this one a "fascinating portrait of a colony in flux."

Swanwick: B. F. Skinner's *Walden Two* was the main influence here. I was raised Catholic, so I have a lot of training in the theological side of free will. I'm definitely on the side of free will. Determinism horrifies me. The idea that you could turn people into indistinguishably interchangeable units to make them happy I found horrifying.

When I look at this story now I'm really not happy with it. The Waldenites, the people with the little device inside of them to make them happy, they're not seen as real people. They're the bad guys. They're the Man. They're everything that a teenage boy dislikes and abhors. It didn't really feel fair. It's a kind of self-pitying story.

Maude Bataleur was modeled after Maggie Kuhn, who was the creator of the Gray Panthers. She was fighting for old people rights, basically. She was this wonderful, radical, plain-spoken woman who just went around telling people true things about being old. She insisted that she wasn't a senior—she was an old woman. She was really great. When I was working as a church secretary in West Philadelphia she had an office kitty-cornered across from us at the intersection, so I got to see her occasionally. Maude was a grumpier version of her.

Zinos-Amaro: Speaking of fighting the Man, "Walden Three" and "Saint Janis" both feature behavioral modification—the mental implants in Saint Janis, the "ceramics" in this tale. To some degree "'Til Human Voices" is about manipulating human beings also, and in "Ginungagap" they try to turn Abigail into a bomb. Was this thematic strand in your work born out of a kind of skepticism of the world around you?

Swanwick: Marianne observed to me, at some point maybe ten years into our marriage and ten years into my career, that everything I wrote was about identity. I went back and looked and by God she was right. It's about integrity of identity and fluidity of identity. I believe I've moved on to more themes since then but it pops up in story after story after story. I think it's a very productive theme. You can go on writing stories about that forever and never have to duplicate yourself. These things happen. They're part of your makeup and one has no say over them.

Zinos-Amaro: Coming back to the Waldenites as the baddies: the phrase "Happiness is Contagious" and the preponderance of viewing screens in "Walden Three" are very Orwellian touches.

Swanwick: Yes. Orwell had been around for a really long time, and science fiction had been absorbing his influence for a really long time. I think that was just part of the science fictional toolkit at that point. But I will say, I do find Skinnerism to be awfully, awfully Orwellian.

Zinos-Amaro: "Walden Three" engages with some of the same notions of conformity as Jack Finney's *The Body Snatchers* (1956), but in a more rigorously justified manner.

Swanwick: I never read Finney's novel, though I saw a couple of the movie versions.

I had read Skinner in college, and I had this visceral dislike of everything in his work, in addition to which I thought he was wrong. *Walden Two* was a novel, but there was also a real-world commune that was named Walden Two in his honor, and they tried to live by his precepts. He visited them at one point. They were in awe of him but at the same time they asked, "How do you get people who don't want to do the work to do their share?" He said, "Treat them the same as everybody else, and they'll all fall into place." In his theoretics it worked perfectly; on their actual farm, when you put it to the test, it didn't work so well.

I'm afraid I let my visceral dislike into the story. The people are just machines, meat puppets manipulated by themselves and others.

Incidentally, the original title for "Walden Three" was "The Clown of Dead Lady Town." This was a play on Cordwainer Smith's "The Dead Lady of Clown Town." My agent and whoever bought the story told me that was a terrible title! I couldn't get away with it. So it got named "Walden Three."

Zinos-Amaro: The final section of "Walden Three" jumps to an omniscient viewpoint and encompasses a great passage of time. A few lines, like "The broken land was patched and restored, and the thousands came up from Earth to people it," have a kind of King James Bible cadence.

Swanwick: I wanted to pull the camera back and put the story back into its context. The real issue of course was that the Waldenites, all being happy all the time, offered a very seductive possibility, and the fear was that as human beings left the planet they'd all have to be made into human automata. What would go out into space and to the stars wouldn't be human beings any-more but another species really. By adding that section at the end, where the camera pulls back, that's to show that it's people who went out, with all their flaws and glories.

Zinos-Amaro: The story's final line refers to the beginning of a philosophical and moral conflict. Were you ever tempted to go back and see what came of Dickens and Walden?

Swanwick: No, no. As I've indicated, I ultimately wasn't re-ally happy with that story, so it's not a world I wanted to go back to and draw more attention to. Also I had other stories to write.

Zinos-Amaro: Indeed. It's interesting that the first five of your solo stories are all technically novelettes.

Swanwick: At that time 11,500 to 12,500 was my natural story length. Over the decades it's gotten a lot shorter. Part of it is that my craft has gotten very tight, so I can tell a story in fewer words. But back then that was the length I was comfortable with. It was the size of the ideas I got. There's the old saying, "Write to length." If you have a 12,000-word idea, and you either try to write it in 5,000 words, or turn it into a novel, it's going to be too short or too bloated. That was just what I could write back then. So it's not a coincidence that my first novel was made up of shorter parts. I couldn't yet go the length. Like being a sprinter as opposed to a marathoner.

Thinking back on these early stories, I remember it was a very exciting time to be writing. It was just at the beginning of a new generation of writers who came in, people like Kim Stanley Robinson and Pat Cadigan and Bill Gibson. There really was a feeling that we were doing stuff that was new and exciting. We were storming heaven as it were. Stan Robinson wrote a story called "Black Air," a story set on the Spanish Armada. It was so good I got really upset! How dare he write something this good! I should have written a story that good! So I sat down and wrote "Covenant of Souls," which we'll talk about later. Stan had a scene where there's a St. Elmo's fire in the masts of the ship, and the character dances to them. So I had a scene where there was a St. Elmo's fire in the church and the character dances in the organ, which I'd climbed high up into for research. I threw that in to acknowledge Stan's influence. Stan, of course, saw that immediately.

Zinos-Amaro: How long do you feel that that sense of newness and excitement lasted?

Swanwick: I'd say a decade. The 80s. That was a really good time. Most of the best stuff was coming out in *Asimov's*, and in *Omni*, especially after Ellen Datlow became the editor of *Omni*. She was really good at spotting hot new writers.

Zinos-Amaro: This leads nicely to our next story, "The Man Who Met Picasso" (*Omni*, September 1982). This story was inspired by an actual story told to you by a repair specialist working on a chandelier-related component called a bobeche—is that right? What led to you being out in the world getting a bobeche repaired?

Swanwick: The church of Marianne's parents—the church she grew up in—bought the house next door. They used it as office space. There were these very nice Victorian chandeliers. Marianne's mother snatched one of them that was surplused, and we hung it upstairs in my office. It's a beautiful Victorian purple chandelier inside an office with the walls painted an emphatic green. My office is really quite an extraordinary place.

Zinos-Amaro: How did you embellish or modify the basic material?

Swanwick: I came home and I told Marianne the story this man had told me. It took me about twenty minutes to tell. It was a remarkable story. Picasso gave this young artist money to go to the Prado to look at one painting and then come back and tell him what he saw. Then I saw a friend and I told her this story. Then there was someone else and I told *him* the story. I realized that at twenty minutes at a time I was losing a lot of my life, and it occurred to me it was awfully good, so why not just modify it?

A lot of the dialogue in the story is word for word what he said. I added the bit about him calling Picasso a wizard and at the end Picasso turning out to be a literal wizard. There were a few other things: his female friend misbehaving, for example, that was added to give the whole thing a more story-like shape and keep the pacing right. But really this was a true story except for those parts of it that were impossible. It came pretty fast, and so of course I was delighted for it on that ground.

I have never known which actual painting it was. I thought it was "View of Toledo," but I've looked at reproductions of it and I don't see that orange roof.

Zinos-Amaro: Were you already familiar with El Greco and had you visited the Prado before writing this?

Swanwick: I was familiar with El Greco, of course, because he's El Greco. I've never been to Spain at all. Or France, for that matter. In those cases you're simply a little vague about the surroundings. I looked up the information about the museums so that it would be plausible enough. You just don't mention things you don't know whether they're there or not.

Zinos-Amaro: The opening line of "Ginungagap" references Toledo Cylinder. Was this an allusion to the same Toledo of El Greco, or was this the Midwestern Toledo?

Swanwick: That was the Midwest, to evoke an industrial city.

Zinos-Amaro: Though the story is anchored in realism, "The Man Who Met Picasso" is your first overt move into the fantastic. Did the fantasy element give you pause, given how well your science fiction was received?

Swanwick: No, not at all. As I've mentioned, when I was sixteen I had set out to become a fantasy writer. I didn't really switch over to science fiction until the mid-to-late 70s. I knew this was a fantasy story. There was no way I could make it science fiction. But that was all the thought that was really needed. It was a very simple choice. The market was there. I did not approach my writing career in careerist terms, but rather in artistic terms.

Zinos-Amaro: In a way, "The Man Who Met Picasso" pokes a little fun at the familiar "club tale" framework. In these stories an audience gathers and then the story begins as an account by the in-story narrator; in yours Franz's customer walks out partway, so that the teller of the tale is left speaking alone!

Swanwick: Everybody was familiar with those club tales back then: *The Tales from the White Hart*, Lord Dunsany and so on. There were lots and lots of them around, and I think that any well-read science fiction/fantasy reader was familiar with them. And they are kind of comic. You know how implausible they are, how artificial, and yet they are enjoyable. To a degree, they're a guilty pleasure.

Zinos-Amaro: Were you an admirer, for example, of the Jorkens stories by Dunsany?

Swanwick: I enjoyed them. I can't say that I admired them, because they weren't *great* club stories. Larry Niven's tales from the Draco Tavern are great. I think Niven is underappreciated artistically. He's really good with story structure. The stories from the Draco Tavern are club stories, they're short, but they're also real science fiction. That's a lot of different things to put together into one very short story. I always admired Niven's short fiction.

Zinos-Amaro: "The Man Who Met Picasso" also felt like an homage to the "magic shop" category.

Swanwick: Yes. "Shottle Bop" by Theodore Sturgeon of course comes to mind. Avram Davidson did a bunch of them. And there were those television anthology shows, like *Twilight Zone*, that had several of them too. It's a subgenre that appeals to the avarice of us all. You're in a junk shop and you're going to find a first edition of an H. P. Lovecraft hardcover or maybe the Holy Grail.

Zinos-Amaro: The protagonist of "The Man Who Met Picasso" is introduced to the reader as Franz Weil, and he speaks some German—I was surprised, in the flashback, when he talks about his American accent. Why the Germanic background?

Swanwick: Germans have been such a major part of America, from very early on. German immigration started in colonial times. Because of two unfortunate World Wars, their contribution to American culture has been downplayed. I wanted a character of German descent, who I figured grew up in a bilingual household. His parents probably had strong accents.

Also, we had German neighbors when I was a kid. My French teacher in college once said, "Germans are the nicest people on Earth, one or two or three at a time. But when you get them in a group they start marching and carrying weapons and taking over the world." My friends of German origins have all been very warm and positive.

Zinos-Amaro: When Franz returns to Paris, you reference the Rue des Grands-Augustins and write: "Balzac had lumbered ponderously down this very way, a walrus touched by divine fire." Where did that image come from? Were you a reader of Balzac?

Swanwick: I *was* a reader of Balzac, but not a deep one. I had read some of the Human Comedy and loved it.

The walrus image may have come from Rodin's statue of Balzac. Rodin did a striding nude of Balzac and then he sculpted around the body the bathrobe that covers him entirely. It was interesting because he submitted it to whatever group was considering buying it as a maquette, and one of the people on the panel criticized it, saying there was no way there could be a human body underneath. Rodin must have been seriously tempted to pick up a hammer and smash off the robe so they could see! But he had too much respect for his own work.

Zinos-Amaro: Picasso's primary lesson here is to support without touching, to support at a distance. How does that sit with your own personal beliefs about an artist's role?

Swanwick: I feel that as a writer my primary responsibility is to the work itself. I have to believe that the work is capable of achieving good. That's pretty much it. I've never really thought a lot about the role of the artist. I think a lot about the role of the story, but not so much the person who writes them.

I've always admired Picasso because he was a real hard worker. He was working all the time. All my heroes are hard workers.

Zinos-Amaro: This story appeared in September 1982 and your next, "Ice Age" (*Amazing Science Fiction*, January 1984) wouldn't be published until 1984. What was happening in your life during this gap in publications?

Swanwick: I think a lot of that was an accident. When you sell a story, it takes forever for it to come out in print. I was writing steadily during this time. I was writing more complicated stories, and they took longer to write.

Zinos-Amaro: "Ice Age" is very much, pun intended, a cool-premise story, with memorable visuals and several fantastic lines ("There was a wooly mammoth in his ice cube" and "There's a lost civilization in my refrigerator" are my two favorites). Rob and Gail are essentially stand-ins for the reader, which is another departure for you in your short fiction at this point. One gets the sense you wanted to have fun with this one.

Swanwick: To begin with, the International Harvester Refrigerator was in my apartment at that time. It had the motor on the top, so that the heat vented upward. I was defrosting the freezer part and came up with the image: I saw a wooly mammoth the size of a horsefly. At the same time, my friend Gail was about to get married to a young man named Rob. So I basically wrote the story as a wedding present to them. I started with the image and then just carried the idea through.

I was pleased with those lines. The story was recently made

into a cartoon for *Love, Death and Robots*. The adaptation was just wonderful. Tim Miller himself adapted the story and directed it. Every change he made was for the better. At one point I went back to look up something in the story and I came across the second line you quoted, "There's a lost civilization in my refrigerator." I stopped and thought, "Wait a minute. That should be '*our*' refrigerator, Rob!" I do not know if this was a lapse on my part, a mental typo, or if it was unrecognized sexism on my part. Given that we're talking about the early 1980s, unrecognized sexism is a very strong possibility. So that part embarrasses me a little bit. The rest of it, though, I loved.

In the adaptation, when they bury the mastodon Gail makes a quip, and Rob says, "Too soon." Oh, I envied that line. It was not a catchphrase when I wrote the story though.

Zinos-Amaro: "Ice Age" ends with the image of a tiny brontosaurus raising its head in the freezer, suggesting that pre-history and all that follows are starting over again. Were you trying to comment on the cyclical nature of events, or was it just a neat way to end the tale?

Swanwick: It was simply a neat way of ending it. It's a shaggy dog story, really. The importance of that story to me—aside from the fact that it made my friends Gail and Rob very happy—is that I could have just given it to them and not published it. At that time I was seen as a pretty serious writer. The times were kind of serious too. But I decided I would not limit myself by not writing or not publishing minor comic stories, "lesser" works or whatever. I decided I would write and publish everything, and this would give me the most satisfaction from my art. And it did. It has.

Zinos-Amaro: In a way, this is also a "Lost World" story.

Swanwick: I think about that periodically. There was a time, when Edgar Rice Burroughs was writing, when you could imagine that somewhere there were lost civilizations. But nowadays we have satellite photos of every inch of the Earth, so we know there aren't any. Things like that had to migrate from science fiction into fantasy. It's a pity that the world is so much less mysterious, and so much less varied, than it used to be. But there are advantages. The messenger RNA vaccine comes to mind!

The idea of a lost world story, as in Conan Doyle or Burroughs, is better than the execution almost always. If you conjure up a beautiful city out in the jungle the adventures that Tarzan is going to have there are not going to be half as good as the ones you can imagine in your mind.

Zinos-Amaro: The idea that time might pass very quickly in some kind of microcosm appeared in early science fiction stories from the 20s and 30s like R. F. Starzl's "Out of the Sub-Universe" (1928) or Jack Williamson's "Pygmy Planet" (1932), but for me "Ice Age" recalled Theodore Sturgeon's famous story "Microcosmic God" (1941). In that tale a scientist develops tiny beings called Neoterics who evolve at a vastly accelerated time-rate, and the end of the story suggests that their progress far surpasses current levels of human technology. Had you read that story?

Swanwick: More than once. Fabulous, fabulous story. I cannot pretend I hadn't read the Sturgeon. It was one reason why I had to go and take it in the comic direction. If I did it seriously, it would be an imitation. It being a gentle fantasy was my contribution to the whole thing.

Zinos-Amaro: What do you think of Sturgeon's work?

Swanwick: I believe I have read literally everything he ever wrote. That wasn't that unusual when I was starting out. I remember that I read the last paperback that I managed to find by him and realized there was no more. When this happened, I had read everyone of serious importance. I felt like Alexander the Great, with no more worlds to conquer! Sturgeon was a fantastic writer. One of many, but right up there at the top. *More Than Human* is a fantastic story, and original in the way it's put together. Sturgeon took and wrote wonderfully real lives and then moved them into science fiction.

Zinos-Amaro: We turn now to "When the Music's Over . . ." (*Light Years and Dark: Science Fiction and Fantasy of and for Our Time*, ed. Michael Bishop, 1984), your second first-person tale. Can you elaborate on what you said earlier about a story sometimes having to be in the first person, and how that applied here?

Swanwick: I'm not a fan of first person as a general rule because it's so easy to just slip on that mask and write in your own voice. It's like pretending that *you're* in that situation rather than creating a character who fits in that situation. Now, mind you, there have been lots and lots of brilliant works in the first person where the writers did not make that mistake. This is simply a preference of mine.

This one had to be first person because the narrator was two people. He was himself, and he was this other person who was unaware that the first person was inside him. Saying "I did this, and then I went under, and *he* did that" always made it clear who was on the surface and who was in control at that time.

Zinos-Amaro: This story shares a sense of disintegration with "Saint Janis." Here you're engaging with the idea of destabilizing Western Culture through time-travel agents who are trying to reshape historical patterns. What set you on this track?

Swanwick: I wanted to write about rock and roll a lot back then, in part because editors were very resistant to it. You could write a story about jazz musicians and sell it to a science fiction editor very easily but they really weren't interested in reading stories about rock and roll music. They were actively disposed against it. Rock and roll was the heartbeat of my generation. It was a part of everything we did. I felt it was very important, and I wanted to write about it.

The fact that so many of the best musicians of the era—Buddy Holly, Janis Joplin, Jimi Hendrix and so on—died horribly, tragically young, with a lot of accomplishment yet ahead of them, seemed almost like a curse upon rock and roll and upon the times. So I combined rock and roll with the times, the dark side of the 60s and 70s, and conflated the two.

Zinos-Amaro: For me this story's opening paragraph evokes New Wave science fiction: "The stubby-winged gray drone dwindled to nothing as soon as I jumped. There was a sickening lurch, and my stomach simultaneously queased outward and shrank inward. I pulled the one-ring, and watched it and an eight-inch length of cord bobble alongside me before darting away as the timechute opened. Great square boxwings unfolded, and I went tumble tumble tumble down through the years."

Swanwick: I can't remember exactly what I was thinking when I wrote that. I was on a panel once at a convention, the last panel that Virginia Kidd attended, and I said that to me the Golden Age of science fiction was the New Wave. She almost choked on her laughter. But it was true. I was reading the New Wave intensely, and with great excitement, as it came out! I was really,

really, really excited about it, and the excitement has not entirely left me, I'm afraid.

Samuel R. Delany was a huge influence on me, most particularly the first of his books that I really got into, *The Einstein Intersection*. He did something that was very clever of him and very useful to me: he put all the literary tricks of the trade he was using right on the surface. You could see them. You could see the way that he was structuring the words and the ideas in ascending or descending sequences. Usually we do that kind of thing and then smooth it over and hide it. He left it out on the surface, so that reading it carefully I learned a lot about how to write, the way that thought can be structured and how clauses can be joined together. Roger Zelazny was another big influence. He's probably a major reason why I got so hipped on mythology so early on. Of course, they were both in the American New Wave, which is entirely different from the British New Wave, which would not have either of them on a bet. Chip told me he wanted to be in the British New Wave, but Michael Moorcock didn't like his stuff very much.

Zinos-Amaro: What was it like working with Michael Bishop?

Swanwick: He was another one of my heroes. And a really nice guy. I met him before I was actually published. He was Guest of Honor at the PhilCon in 1978. Wonderful writer, and I admired him immensely.

I haven't had a lot of editorial feedback for my short stories. Usually they're just copy-edited and put into print.

Looking back on "When The Music's Over . . .", I'll say it's a very young story. My understanding of interpersonal dynamics was less developed than it is now—perhaps!

Zinos-Amaro: Speaking of interpersonal dynamics, there are some very complicated ones at work in your next story, "Trojan Horse" (*Omni*, December 1984). This is the first of your stories to explicitly engage with theological themes, and to reframe metaphysics in terms of neurology and programming. Were these topics something you'd been thinking about for some time?

Swanwick: Yes, especially questions of free will. The source for this story—credit where it is due—is John C. Lilly and his book *Programming and Metaprogramming in the Human Biocomputer*. Lilly was a scientist, a serious scientist, and best known for his attempts to communicate with poirpoises. Also I believe he invented the isolation tank. He went very far out in his exploration of human thought, starting with staying in the isolation float tank for eight hours at a time. Eventually the silence was so great that he could apparently hear the electrical workings of his brain. From there he went really deep into what is either astonishingly profound or completely wacko. It's impossible to tell which. But he did actually believe he briefly touched the state where he was aware of programming in the universe. The metaphysics was actually very good, and I borrowed heavily from it.

There was a lot of really interesting non-fiction about the brain and the mind and consciousness that was out there at the time. Pre-New Age, science-based speculative theology, I guess. There used to be a metaphysics bookstore in Philadelphia on South Street. Thousands of different titles—religious or theological or metaphysical, in one store. I would go there periodically searching around, looking for things where mysticism intersected with the physically real. A really good example of that was an article in the *Burlington Free Press*. A yogi was on tour who said he could stop his heart, and some doctors at the University of Virginia asked him if he would be willing to do that hooked up to an EEG and EKG. He said "No, because I'd have to fast several weeks before doing it fully. But if you want me to stop it for ten or fifteen seconds, I can skip dinner tonight and do it tomorrow." They said "Yes, yes!" And they wired him up to EEG and EKG machines and he stopped his heart. The electrocardiogram showed that what he did was not slow down his heart, he sped it up until it fibrillated. It spasmed. They asked if he'd known that's what he was doing, and he said no, that it was very interesting. He had learned to do that, but he didn't know *what* he was doing. That's the sort of thing I was fascinated in, where mysticism and reality end up as the same thing.

Zinos-Amaro: This brings me to the next question. The Star Maker project at the heart of the plot relies on the substructure of the human mind being in a "one-to-one congruence with the inherent substructure of the universe." Do you believe that such a congruence exists, or is even possible?

Swanwick: It might be! I do not know. I am in most things a skeptic. I'm an atheist, but I'm honest enough to admit that I could be wrong. I view the honest beliefs of religious people with respect. The same thing goes for mystics also.

Zinos-Amaro: What was it about the setting of "Trojan Horse" that made you want to return to it in *Vacuum Flowers*, which began serialization in *Asimov's* in late 1986?

Swanwick: My father was an electrical engineer. He worked for General Electric. In the 50s when I was a kid he would bring home handouts from GE. I have somewhere a chart with little drawings of various spacecraft charting out what the next fifty years of space travel would be like. For at least ten years, it hewed pretty closely to what actually happened. One of those handouts was about colonies on the Moon, and showed a lunar crater that they had covered over with a shallow glass dome. The inside of the crater had been terraced. People were walking gracefully through parklands with flowers and trees. I thought that was just a wonderful image. It always stayed with me. I used it in this story, and I used it again, and much later John Kessel borrowed it. He had the kindness to acknowledge that he'd gotten the idea through me, which was not necessary but was nice of him.

The image was new to science fiction. It's surprising how many writers tend to rely on previous science fiction for their visions of what the future is going to be like, what habitats are going to be like. I was trying very hard through all the 80s, and I hope after that, to imagine alternatives to the way that it had been imagined before.

I like how complicated "Trojan Horse" is. I like how all the little pieces fit together like a machine. I thought it was pretty well done on young me's part. It was a story that really fit the times well.

Zinos-Amaro: Right. Another Nebula novelette nominee, in 1985. Revisiting this story today, how do you feel about the cyberpunk language, like "wetware surgeon" etc.?

Swanwick: It was interesting stuff back then. I was working for the Franklin Institute. They had a grant to run the National Solar Heating and Cooling Information Center. One of the perks there was that you got to wander about in their library. Members of the Institute could borrow books from the library, but couldn't wander around. But if you worked there, you could. I did the old trick of going to the interesting subject part of the stacks and just pulling out books and looking at them. I found the word "wetware" in the introduction to a book that was something like half equations—I couldn't possibly follow them! But it explained what "wetware" was: a tool for thinking about the mind. It was not actually rigidly defined. That seemed to be a useful idea. Also from very early on it seemed clear to me that we were getting closer and closer to a revolution in cognition and in manipulation and reshaping of the brain. That's an interest that stayed with me ever since.

Zinos-Amaro: Yes, it'll come up again in "Wild Minds," for instance. Your next story was "Marrow Death" (*Isaac Asimov's Science Fiction Magazine*, Mid-December 1984). This was the big cover story. The cover also displayed, in smaller font, the name of Brian Aldiss and other writers. How did that feel?

Swanwick: It felt wrong. But I'm not responsible for the bad judgment of the editor! Aldiss was very good for a long time. I was scanning "Marrow Death" before we talked, and I barely remember it, which is funny, because so much work went into it.

It was in my first novel, and you don't go back to your first novel. I think most writers don't like their first novel very much. Sturgeon referred to his first novel *The Dreaming Jewels* as *The Drooling Genes*. Bill Gibson was speaking at the Free Library of Philadelphia and I went to see him. Somebody asked a question about *Neuromancer*, and he said, "Well, keep in mind that I wrote this a long time ago. I haven't looked at it in twenty years and I'm probably never going to read it again." I was sitting in the audience and said to myself, "Ah, you too Bill."

Zinos-Amaro: Did you already have your fix-up plan in mind when you conceived of "Marrow Death" or was the plan hatched afterwards?

Swanwick: The fix-up plan was already in mind. After the first novella, which was an expansion of the original novelette, I needed two more novellas, and I roughed out what was going to happen in the whole thing.

Zinos-Amaro: In this novella, Keith becomes the antagonist to the mutant Victoria and the reporter Patrick. This novella acts as the closing section of the novel, so I'm wondering if you were concerned about readers being "spoiled" (rather, than say, having them read the first two thirds or whatever)?

Swanwick: Well, I had been trying for years to write a novel, and failing. I had the beginning of one novel, that became a collaboration with Gardner Dozois years later. I had started a couple and could not finish them. I wanted to write a novel, in the worst possible way, and finally I did—in the worst possible way.

Zinos-Amaro: The character of Victoria strikes me as one of your most interesting and complex in your short fiction through this time.

Swanwick: I didn't particularly enjoy this story when I revisited it. I came up with ideas, and I gave it my all, but in the end it was written in order to have a novel, rather than written from a compulsion to get an idea down in physical form. "Marrow Death" is kind of alien to me now.

Zinos-Amaro: Shawna McCarthy was the editor of *Asimov's* when "Marrow Death" was published, and that year she won the Hugo for best pro editor. She edited the magazine 1983-1985. Do you have any recollections of working with her?

Swanwick: As with most of my career, I would send in a manuscript, I would get back an acceptance, and a while later they would send the copyedits. I would have to contain my natural urge to stet everything. That would be it. My main feeling about Shawna was that I admired the job she was doing with the magazine. She was getting really, really great people there. Fantastic stories. Under her, and later under Gardner, it was *the* place to get published. It was the first place you looked every month for new work, because it was the most likely place for something great to appear.

During this phase of my career I discovered who my peers were. They were the people that I wrote to impress. They were the ones who were the strongest influence on me. When Jim Kelly wrote "Glass Cloud" or "Mr. Boy" it was like a challenge: "I defy you to write something as good as this!" I would go to the typewriter in a fever to show that I could write something even better! It was a surprisingly large number of people, considering they were young and they were all working at the same time, who were doing stuff that good. Stan Robinson, and Connie Willis, and Nancy Kress, and so on. They were the stand-in for my audience.

People ask if you write to an audience. I've never been able to picture what the audience looked like, but these writers were the kind of readers I wanted to impress.

CHAPTER TWO
1985-1989

Alvaro Zinos-Amaro: Philip K. Dick died in 1982. Walk us through the creation of "The Transmigration of Philip K." (*Isaac Asimov's Science Fiction Magazine*, February 1985).

Michael Swanwick: Philip K. Dick was the single science fiction writer that everyone in my generation agreed was great and important. Everybody else, *someone* didn't like, but he was universal. Of course, after his death we were all thinking about him a great deal, and I had this observation that a lot of Dick's work was extremely funny. If you look at *Galactic Pot Healer*, which is probably my favorite of his books, there's a scene in which the main character finds himself in what is essentially a coffin. He feels around in total darkness and finds a radio, so he turns it on, and it's a talk show, and a guy is asking people to call in, if they have anything to say or if they don't have anything to say and they just want to talk. He feels a telephone and calls in and the guy says, "What question do you have for the audience?" He says, "I want to know where I am." The guy responds, "Don't worry, we've got a million listeners up and down the East Coast, somebody must know where you are!" The godlike alien power at the center of this novel calls up and says, "I know where he is. He's in a box in my basement, at 457332 Elm Avenue." The DJ says, "There you are! You're in a box in Mr. Glimmung's basement. All you have to do is get out." More things happen, and when he finally sees the alien, it manifests as a wheel of fire spinning inside a wheel of water, floating in front of a faded paisley-clothed backdrop and in front of that the vapid face of a teenybopper. It's like a hilarious tumble down the stairs, one ridiculous non-sequitur after another. I was talking about this with Stan Robinson and said, "Nobody ever comments on how funny Phil Dick's stuff is." Stan said, "Once you've said it's funny, what else is there to say about it?" So I thought let's take that and run with it.

I was basically seeing how many of Phil Dick's signature tricks I could rope in: the robots who give unfailingly bad advice, the guy upon whom the entire world relies but is sweating bullets because he thinks he's going to get fired, just one thing after another. I wanted to show how much fun Phil Dick could be. Of course, at the end everything resolves, and then the resolution dissolves underfoot, partly because that's what Phil Dick did a lot, but also because anytime he came up with an answer he was always, in the later years, questing for reality. After he came up with an answer he just moved on and came up with another answer. This story was my Master's thesis on Philip K. Dick.

Zinos-Amaro: Right. You have the humor. "The Transmigration of Philip K." pays homage to PKD's paranoia and reality-destabilization. You're also casting him as a kind of hero or anti-hero inside one of his own stories. What was the impetus for that?

Swanwick: Admiration for the guy. Phil Dick belongs in a Phil Dick story. He put a lot of himself into the stories. If a story doesn't have Phil Dick in it, it's not really a Phil Dick story!

I also deliberately employed a flat and unornamented prose in imitation of Dick's style. Delany once copyedited one of Dick's mainstream novels, which had been accepted and proofed before the deal fell apart, and he observed that the man had a very plain "whitebread" style but that every time he made an effort to rise above it, the proofreader took it out.

Zinos-Amaro: When you wrote "The Transmigration of Philip K." had you read *Radio Free Albemuth* or *VALIS*, in which Dick inserted characters named Philip K. Dick into the narratives? Were you slyly commenting on his own penchant for fictional self-depiction?

Swanwick: Well, I was. I had read those books. So yeah, that was there too. But it was all done in admiration of him. Also the thought that when we talk about Philip K. Dick we're always way too serious. We follow the most serious ontological approach to him. Sometimes reading about him is like reading about William of Ockham. This was a guy who liked to get stoned with his friends and then tell tall tales and see if he could take them in.

Zinos-Amaro: When you were coming up through fandom, did you have interactions with PKD? Would you discuss his work with Gardner Dozois?

Swanwick: I never met him. The divide between the East Coast and West Coast is so great, or was so great then, especially for me, since I had no money, that I tended not to meet most of the West Coast writers at all. I never met Phil Dick, and I never met Ursula K. Le Guin. I regret both of those things.

I did discuss his work with Gardner. Gardner was another admirer. I believe that Gardner felt that the last couple of works, where Dick was much more serious than in the earlier works, were not his best. But we both agreed that he was an interesting writer in that he didn't really have the standout novels the way that most writers have. He just had the oeuvre. The entirety of the work was the work. When you talk to people who really love his fiction, we've all got different favorite works. I never met anybody else whose favorite was *Galactic Pot Healer*.

Zinos-Amaro: I've never heard it cited as a favorite either. It's true about the body of work. When the Library of America decided to publish Dick, they ended up reprinting thirteen novels. What are some of your other favorite PKD novels or short stories?

Swanwick: He wasn't at his best in short fiction. He was at the best when he was writing a novel and he let it get out of control. *A Maze of Death* is quite wonderful. It ends with a literal deus ex machina. The protagonist is about to kill himself and everybody on his stranded spaceship when God walks through the wall and says, "Stop." That's an amazing moment! In retrospect you realize that he did quietly set you up for this. But it's an astonishing moment. *Counter-Clock World*, where time goes backwards, has a great moment in it when a group are gathered for a man to come back to life and they've dug up his coffin. He opens his eyes and says, "I saw God. Do you doubt it?" The atheist present says, "Do you dare to doubt it?" They go back and forth trading lines, and it turns out to be a poem by James Stephens called "What Tomas An Buile Said In a Pub." Let's see—there's also *Martian Time-Slip*. This guy is in a park. It's an ordinary day. He's thirsty, so thirsty he's feeling a little woozy. He sees a hot dog stand in the distance and he decides to get a soda. He walks up to it, and when he gets there the hot dog stand isn't there. He looks around and sees a slip of paper on the ground. He reaches down, picks it up, and it says, "Hot Dog Stand." Then there's little line break and he's looking at this cigar box that he has, and there are two dozen little slips of paper saying various things like that. That's astonishing. And then there's *Ubik*. *Ubik* is probably the one that stands out above the others. Just marvelous. I'm not as much of a fan of *The Man in the High Castle* as some of the others because I tend to like the funnier ones more. There's lots of good things to recommend among his work, and only a couple of novels that aren't terrific.

Zinos-Amaro: When I read Dick's early novels a few years ago, I was reminded of Robert Sheckley's work.

Swanwick: That's a good observation. They were very much like that. Again, it was that dark, paranoid humor. Sheckley is considered a major, major writer in Russia now. I was a Guest of Honor at Aelita in Yekaterinburg in the 90s. The city had only been an open city for a couple of years. They had a press conference at the beginning, with like six television cameras and a room full of reporters. Somebody asked about this year's attendance at the convention compared to the previous year's, in which Robert Sheckley had been the Guest of Honor. The organizer looked at the camera and said, "Swanwick is a writer. Sheckley is a god." Within a year, I saw him at the Worldcon. He looked kind of depressed, and I went up and told him that. That perked him right up.

Zinos-Amaro: With your next story, "The Blind Minotaur" (*Amazing Stories*, March 1985), we're back to Picasso. How did you encounter *Blind Minotaur is Guided by Girl Through the Night*, and what did you first make of it?

Swanwick: I probably saw it in a museum. The story is based on the Vollard Suite. I looked at all these etchings, at the primate patterning behavior, and said, "There's a story here." Of course Picasso didn't think in that way. He didn't come up with a story and then illustrate it. He put out these variants and different possibilities, all from some central I-don't-know-what, some notion or set of images. I bought a book of the Suite and constructed a story from it. Then I proceeded to over-write it extraordinarily, to see just how ornate I could make the prose without falling over into word-mush.

Zinos-Amaro: "The Blind Minotaur" represents a fascinating fusion of science fiction and mythology or fantasy, in a way reminiscent of Delany's *Einstein Intersection*, which you mentioned earlier you really responded to. Tell me about the world creation process here. For instance, how did you envision the Lords?

Swanwick: There's definitely a certain amount of Delany here. It's not a pastiche, but I was thinking of the way he used words, and I did something similar, or so I think. When you write something dense like that, you can suggest a world around it. I just made it up as I went along. I assumed that these archetypes had been created as a propaganda set of devices, as a function for keeping the populace entertained and amused and under thumb. The Lords are the ones who sponsored the engineering of this. They were the Lords because they had all the power. They were the one percent. They didn't make things themselves, they had people do that for them. But the people they had were good. As I went along, I introduced things like the people who were cohabiting with insects. The minotaur doesn't understand this, and there's no explanation given, because there was none. This would be my memory of the 70s. Everything was questioned; everything was up in the air. There were alternatives to everything. Some of them were noble experiments and some of them were noble failures. David Hartwell said that he thought of the 60s, as we called it—from the mid-60s to the mid-70s—as a massive failure of common sense. But there was something aspirational to it.

Zinos-Amaro: Now that you mention that, it reminds me that cohabitation with insects is the key reveal in "The Transmigration of Phil K."

Swanwick: I guess it is! That hadn't occurred to me. I do know that I was thinking of the Bob Dylan line: "There was music in the cafés at night / And revolution in the air . . ." I was going for as romantic—in the sense of Romanticism—a world as I could make, one that was just rich and dense with detail.

Zinos-Amaro: In Picasso's print, the Minotaur appears to be crying out in anguish, but in your story he is more controlled and resilient after the initial hopelessness. He is also a primal force of seduction. How much of Picasso the man, as you surmised him to be, did you put in the Minotaur protagonist?

Swanwick: I put a lot of him into it. You look at the etchings and it's hard not to see him empathizing with the Minotaur, projecting himself into it. That just seemed to be faithful to the picture.

Zinos-Amaro: We learn about three-quarters through that the Minotaur actually tore his own eyes out. Were you overlaying Oedipus on the Minotaur character?

Swanwick: This is me and mythology again. I like the idea of recurring patterns of mythology, reappearing but always different, always changed. This is sort of like a junior varsity version of Robert Holdstock's *Mythago Wood*. I've been rereading that recently. That is some fine work.

Zinos-Amaro: Freud famously saw the unconscious as a kind of labyrinth, and believed that psychoanalysis, by facilitating a synthesis of insights, could provide a thread out of that labyrinth. The flashback structure of "The Blind Minotaur" seems to suggest a synthesizing of experience for the Minotaur. Were you commenting on Freudian theory with this story?

Swanwick: I don't really know much Freudian theory. I'm more of a Jungian, which I think shows in the archetypal figures walking around the Earth. The labyrinth was definitely deliberate, because that's where you find a minotaur.

I also thought of him as being an exemplar of toxic masculinity. All that strength and power and seductiveness, which of course comes from the etchings too, are very masculine traits. But there's also the irresponsible, violent masculinity. That's his weakness, his flaw, his kryptonite. He can very easily fall into violence and do terrible things. So I was talking rather a lot about masculinity there.

Zinos-Amaro: In "The House of Asterion" Jorge Luis Borges tells a story from the perspective of the mythical minotaur; in "A Planet Named Shayol" Cordwainer Smith depicted a bull-man warden; and in *The White Bull* Fred Saberhagen reinterprets the mythological origins of the Minotaur in a science fictional way. Were any of these influences?

Swanwick: I haven't read the Saberhagen, I'm ashamed to admit. I read the other two, of course. They probably went into the mix. I would throw in *The Maze Maker* by Michael Ayrton.

Zinos-Amaro: I'm not familiar with it.

Swanwick: The critic Guy Davenport wrote about how Edmund Hillary, he of Everest fame, commissioned Ayrton to make a golden honeycomb. The lost-wax process, and possibly the invention of the lost-wax process, was involved in its creation. Ayrton made the honeycomb, and Hillary placed it on a column in his estate, as a piece of living sculpture. Bees came and filled it with honey and their young. That was Michael Ayrton. He was a sculptor first and a novelist second. *The Maze Maker* is about Daedalus. It's mostly a historical-mythological novel, but occasionally it gets very, very strange. When Daedalus has fallen from the sky, and he's on the rock and the sun is beating down on him and he's lying there helpless, an ant climbs up his face and crawls into his ear and begins to slowly traverse the maze of his brain. He feels this and he names the ant Daedalus. It's a lovely and strange novel. I'm a big fan of it.

Zinos-Amaro: This Minotaur ends up becoming a kind of Homer of his world. Were you suggesting that storytelling can be a redemptive act?

Swanwick: The story required a redemptive act at the end, and that's what I came up with! I do think storytelling can be a redemptive act. It's offering alternatives. Chip Delany has a theory that people were a lot crueler before the invention of theater, and books, and mass media of all kinds. Having sympathetic stories about other people has made us kinder and more humane. I was thinking about that. That's the way the Minotaur saves himself, through storytelling.

Zinos-Amaro: Our next story, "Anyone Here from Utah?" (*Isaac Asimov's Science Fiction Magazine*, May 1985), is short and exquisitely crafted. As with "When the Music's Over . . ." you lure us into a first-person narrator much different from what he first appears to be. You certainly didn't fall into the trap you described of putting on a mask.

Swanwick: That was definitely deliberate. This one began after I read this description of how television works, with the old CRTs. The scanner goes down two lines, and then skips two lines, all the way down and goes back up, filling in the blanks. It was an explanation for why television is so toxic, because it gets past your censors. You have to assemble it in your mind, so the normal screening that your brain does for you has been sidestepped. I was at a bar at a convention with James Morrow and I gave him this theory. Jim smiled in that genial, gentle way of his, and said, "Oh no, a television just has nice pictures, pretty colors. I think that's all that's going on there." I said, "Jim, stop looking at the television screen! You can't stop looking at it, can you? You're staring at it. Why are you doing that?" This is another case where I couldn't convince anybody of something I believed was absolutely true, so I put it into a story instead.

I recently looked at this and thought, "This is paranoid fiction now, but it's not *science* fiction." The little television that fits in your pocket—we all have one of those now. It shows you how fast science fiction can age.

This one was a relatively fast story for me. I don't think it has much more depth than what's on the surface. Mostly for me the fun part was putting together this paranoid picture of the world, where there is no Utah! It was just written for the fun of it, really. It's a dark story, but the details in it are a lot of fun.

Zinos-Amaro: The themes of identity endangerment, conformity and social control are very explicit in this tale, but this is your first somewhat humorous or satirical take. How did you land on the tone for this story?

Swanwick: It was just what the idea called for. It couldn't be done straight because the idea is a little bit silly. I think you could disprove that we're being controlled by television in the ways that I said by the mechanism rather than the content. When it's silly, it gets past your screening mechanisms.

Zinos-Amaro: So your chosen tone for this story is similar to your theory of what television does. Cool!

Swanwick: Yes, very much.

Zinos-Amaro: Moving on to "Covenant of Souls" (*Omni*, December 1986), what were the real-life experiences that must have surely informed this tale?

Swanwick: I was working in a church in West Philly. Part of my job was to go down every morning and check the boiler, which had a slow leak in it, and fill it up so that it didn't run out of water and explode. As I was writing this story I did a lot of work through all parts of the building. I was the church secretary. I set out to include as much of the church as I could in the story.

This one came out of nowhere, but it was very hard to write. One day I bought coffee and the little egg sandwich I describe in the story, and went to my office and said, "I'll do an exercise. I'll do ten opening lines." I wrote the first three and the fourth one was: "There was something ugly growing in the air over the altar." I thought that was a good opening, so I wrote the next line.

Zinos-Amaro: The samples of Peter's writing you provide, and his complaint lists, ground the narrative. The administrative and logistical aspects add realism too, which makes the supernatural aspects more believable.

Swanwick: When I was working at the church we had a mostly absentee minister. (He did preside at Marianne and my wedding, and he did a good job there.) A few years after I quit that job, he quit too, and went into insurance, I believe. So he really wasn't suited for that. There was a subplot about the sexton where the board of trustees fires him and writes down in their meeting notes that with the next sexton they should have a warm, loving relationship, like they haven't had with him. Those two notes were taken right from the board of trustees meeting. They were literally word-for-word the same. There was kind of a happy ending, in that before they could actually fire him he had a heart attack while working in the church on a Sunday. So he died not knowing that they were going to fire him. They were going to cut his hours in half, and they knew he would quit because he was a very proud man, whom I personally admired, I have to say. They resolved to have a more personal relationship with the next sexton that came in, but they didn't really, because they were never there.

Zinos-Amaro: You mentioned when we discussed "Trojan Horse" that you were an atheist. Were you already an atheist when you held this church job?

Swanwick: Yes, I was an atheist by then. I was a good kid. I was raised Catholic. Very sincere. Went to St. Francis Xavier Grammar School in Winooski, Vermont. I knew an enormous amount about the religion and when I was young I planned to become a priest. And then I hit puberty, and discovered the existence of young women. That changed my mind. In college, I was talking theoretically with a friend, the way that you do in college, about everything, and I said, "If there is a God . . ." She looked at me and said, "Michael, you know there isn't." I stopped and looked at myself and said, "I *do* know that! This is what I believe. Or fail to believe." I'm not agnostic at all. I'm an atheist. I don't make a big deal of it because I don't see that being an atheist is a positive val-

ue, and trying to convince somebody to believe in nothing seems
to me like a pointless occupation. But when you're educated by
nuns one thing that is emphasized over and over is that God hates
a hypocrite more than anything. So if there is a God, and I *pretend*
to believe in him, that's not going to get me any points.

When I worked at this church, anybody who cared knew that
I was an atheist. I have a friend in Mattapoisett, Massachusetts,
whose mother was a church secretary. She was working in Philadelphia and she'd go back home and tell her mother stories of
this atheist, science-fiction-writing, male church secretary, and
her mother was fascinated. She had a monthly meeting with the
other church secretaries in town. They would all get together
and have lunch. They were toying with the idea of inviting me
to come to talk to them at one of their lunches, but they couldn't
afford to pay carfare, so they never did. I wish I'd known, I would
have volunteered to come! I was so pleased to be a member of the
sisterhood of church secretaries. That, I felt, was a very positive
thing. Church secretaries help each other out. They're good to
each other. It's an occupation I respect.

Zinos-Amaro: Though some of your previous stories were
certainly grim, this might be construed as your first flirtation
with horror. We haven't discussed your relationship with the horror genre.

Swanwick: Ellen Datlow and I had a symposium on this once.
I told her that I didn't like horror because it scared me, and she
said, "That's why I love it." I thought about this and said, "Well,
we've covered the entire subject!"

I admire horror. I don't read it for pleasure. I recognize how
good it can be. I've read a fair amount of Stephen King—only a
small fraction of his work, but quite a lot by number of books.
Still, even as a kid I didn't like horror.

Horror is sold as a genre, but really it's a mode, an outlook.
That makes it incredibly pliant, applicable. You can write anything as horror: you can have horror romance, and horror science fiction, and so on and so on. There are some ideas that just
have to be told as horror stories. When I get them, I'm not entirely happy because it means I'm going to have to live in a horror
universe for the duration. But if the idea is good enough, then it's
worth writing.

Zinos-Amaro: This story has a truly explosive ending. It's like an exponential version of the engulfing flames at the end of "Marrow Death." Did you have this ending in mind for "Covenant of Souls" before you started writing it, or did you discover it along the way?

Swanwick: The story came very slowly, because I had no idea what was going on, but it came. There was always a little more I could write and I could make up. As I was going on things started to happen. The homeless people gathered on the lawn and started having religious services; there was a woman living underneath the church; a man from the government who might be a robot comes and says sinister things. I was enough of a writer—I had enough craft under my control—that I could recognize that this was all leading somewhere. The story was closing down possibilities and pointing up possibilities. But I had no idea where it was going. I took it to Gardner Dozois and Jack Dann, who as I keep saying were the two best story doctors in the business. They read it and said, "Just keep writing." I said, "Well, big thanks for that!"

But I did keep writing. And then my son was born. After we brought him home, and after a couple of days to recover from the primal experience of that, I looked at the story again and said, "Oh, right." I realized that the story was all about the fears that a pregnant woman or the partner of a pregnant woman have for their unborn child. It's a very common thing for people in that situation to have horrible nightmares. Once I recognized that this was all about the birth of our son, I knew that the story would have to end with a symbolic birth.

I should point out a detail. The character of Jennifer who comes out from under the basement and eats the crayons—that was an example of pica, the strange eating urges that a pregnant woman gets. In retrospect that was so obvious! How I could know enough to put that in, but not know what I was writing, I do not know.

Zinos-Amaro: For certain readers I think this story could feel like a precursor to *The X-Files*. I'm curious if as your career developed in this second part of the 80s, and then on into the 90s, you continued to watch sf shows and movies as you had done when you were younger.

Swanwick: I was still watching science fiction movies and television. I believe I've seen every episode of *The X-Files*. That's a lot. They stole from everyone, with both hands. I kept watching the best stuff, I would say.

Now I'm in an extraordinary situation where there's first-rate science fiction and horror on television and I can't be bothered to watch anymore. I feel guilty about that.

In 1979, Gardner Dozois, Tom Purdom and I were on a 3 am psychic world radio show and Gardner horrified the talkshow guy by saying that there wasn't anything of artistic merit on television and never had been. The guy said, "What about these wonderful shows?" And Gardner replied, "Well I haven't seen them." Now there's amazing, really good stuff on television. But it's hard enough keeping up with books. I can't do books and television both, so a lot of the television has to go.

Zinos-Amaro: You mentioned *Counter-Clock World* just recently. When you first conceived of the irresistible high concept behind "Foresight" (*Interzone*, #20 Summer 1987) did you set it aside until you found the right plot with which to marry it, or did the whole thing come to you at once?

Swanwick: It all came at the same time. I did probably get this one from *Counter-Clock World*. I read that and wanted to do a time-going-backwards story, but I didn't want to do an imitation of Philip K. Dick, so I came up with the idea that time still goes forward but consciousness has been reversed. That seemed to me to be a really, really rich-in-possibilities idea. I just began writing it and figured, "It has to end with his death, because he can see all the way to his death." So I wrote, "He died." Then I give you a moment before he died, and then a moment before that, going backwards.

I got only a couple of paragraphs in, and he's lying on the ground in the parking lot dying, and I thought, "What is he seeing?" I turned off my typewriter, went downstairs and went to the nearby parking lot. I looked around to make sure no cars were coming and I lay down on the ground, and I looked. There was an amazing amount of things to be seen: lots of broken glass, of course, a rusted spark plug that had been run over many times, weeds, flattened cans, and such. So I made a list of all of them, then went back and used the best details for that scene. That has actually been a technique I've used a lot ever since. It's easier to go out somewhere and look at something analogous to what you're writing of than it is to sit and make it up out of nothing. And the results are usually better.

As you can guess, this story was not easy to write. I was about two pages into the story when Marianne came home from work, and she said something and I tried to reply to what she was *about* to say. After a minute or so of talking back and forth like this she said, "You realize you're making no sense at all?" I held up my hand and said, "Wait!" I ran upstairs, grabbed the two pages and said, "Read these." She read them and then said, "Oh okay, now this makes sense." Within ten or fifteen minutes I'd returned to normal.

This is one of those stories where as you're writing it you figure out where it's going to go. By the time I was within a few pages of the ending, I knew how it was going to end up, but I certainly didn't know it when I began, and I didn't know how it was going to end exactly midway through, except that it would end with the beginning of his affair. What made this interesting to me is that it was a great way to explore whether it's possible to have free will in a deterministic universe. As I've said before, that's one of those things that concerns me greatly, probably more than it should.

Zinos-Amaro: By describing events backwards in time, you align the reader with the consciousness of the characters and make it a truly immersive experience. But you could have chosen to describe events in a forward fashion—the arrow of physical time isn't itself being inverted—while depicting their subjective memories of the future rather than the past, leading to an external dissonance for readers. Did you consider this possibility as a potential technical challenge?

Swanwick: I knew right from the beginning that I wanted to do it the way that I did, to put the reader in the same position as the protagonist, knowing everything that's going to happen from the next instant to the point of his death but not knowing what came before. I had to cheat a little bit, because each scene is played forward. Otherwise it would not be possible to make it comprehensible. I pictured it as basically walking down a set of stairs backwards. It's a short story idea. Imagine an entire novel written that way. It would be terribly tiring.

Zinos-Amaro: "Foresight" was published in *Interzone* in 1987; as far as I can tell, this is the first of your solo short stories to see original publication overseas. Do you feel like British readers were becoming more aware of your work by this time? Who were British writers of the day that you were into?

Swanwick: No idea if they were. I've never been really good at handling my career as a career. I forget even how I came to submit it to them. It was a nice place to appear, but it did mean that a lot of the people in the States, where I live, wouldn't see it, so there was a trade-off there.

We've talked about Brian Aldiss. Michael Moorcock was another of my heroes. I liked Moorcock because his work was varied: he did science fiction *and* he did fantasy. I was a big fan particularly of the Elric of Melniboné stories. He was willing to experiment. *The Dancers at the End of Time* trilogy—man, that's astonishing. Or *Gloriana*. He could be ravishingly beautiful when he cared to. That was something I aspired to. I also admired how fast he could write and in that I have not been able to emulate him.

I was also a big fan of J. G. Ballard. I'll say more about him when we get to the story "The Mask." In the 70s, before I got published, I was reading all the anthologies, all the New Wave stuff as it came out. Christopher Priest too. And Holdstock, of course. All those guys, all of them. John Brunner. I've got something like forty of his novels, which is only a fraction of what he wrote. I was resistant to Brunner for a long time in college, when *Stand on Zanzibar* came out. That was a huge, huge hit. All these people who didn't read science fiction were urging me to read it, so of course I didn't, because I was a science fiction snob. "If you've heard of this writer, he's sure not good enough for me!" But eventually I did read it and had to admit that, yes, he was amazing. He also wrote something that I really love: his Traveler in Black stories. They hit me very strong, because they are core fantasy and are absolutely original. They're not leaning on anybody else's work. It's strange how fantasy tends to be long, and there's not as many of the important works in fantasy that are short fiction— Lord Dunsany, and a few others, like Tanith Lee. But that was that strangest of all creatures: fantasy short stories that, put together, tell a much larger story. It was really quite wonderful.

Zinos-Amaro: Speaking of experimentation, in "Foresight," if you remove the misalignment of consciousness's arrow with the arrow of physical time, the story reads to me like the most mainstream piece you'd done at this point.

Swanwick: Yeah, it was a very mainstream story, really. Not that I could have sold it in the mainstream market. I was looking at "Foresight" recently and thought, "Hmm. There's a lot of strange sex in this one." It's the effect of having lived through the 70s. There was a lot of strange sex going on in real life there.

Zinos-Amaro: Between the publication of "Foresight" and the next story we're going to discuss, "The Overcoat" (*Omni*, April 1988), you published *Vacuum Flowers*, your second novel. Was there anything about structure or storytelling that you discovered during the writing of *Vacuum Flowers* that subsequently informed your short fiction?

Swanwick: Oh, I'm not sure. *Vacuum Flowers* was written in reaction to my first novel. By then I was not happy with *In the Drift*, so I went the other way. Instead of a dark and gloomy story I wrote a colorful, inventive story. I may have overdone it a bit, but I'm still happy with it because I love that kind of science fiction. Eileen Gunn made a remark recently about that being my cyberpunk novel, but in fact it was not written as cyberpunk, and since Bruce Sterling was the keeper of the gates, I was officially a class enemy. He had defined the group, and originally I think it contained just four people. David Hartwell said, "You can't have a movement with only four people, you have to open it up," and so in the *Mirrorshades* anthology, he included a few people who were technically humanists because it was hard to find enough good writers trying to write cyberpunk. I was definitely on the outside of the group. I'm actually glad about that, because they all found the cyberpunk label to be very annoying as they aged.

There *was* a scene in my novel where Rebel Elizabeth Mudlark goes to a memory shop. That was my cyberpunk scene. Later on in the novel I had another scene which was my nod to the humanists. But I had them at separate ends of the novel, so they would not fall together and implode.

Zinos-Amaro: Did you have personal dealings with Bruce Sterling?

Swanwick: I met him a couple of times. We got along well. He once recruited me to participate in a computer-human interface conference. He put together a panel of science fiction writers. It paid quite well, and it was a fascinating experience, because we got a little glimpse into the coming technology. There were these young people, and they were all incredibly privileged. They had set boards up with "offers to hire" and "looking for work," and the "looking for work" boards had one card on it: they were looking for something very, very specific. The other boards were just covered. One of the people on a panel had this little local network thing that you could use to check and see if your fellow employees were at their desks. If you wanted to talk to them, for example, you could check that they were there before walking over to their office. Someone in the audience said, "How do you prevent this from being used by your boss to keep track of you?" The person being asked looked baffled. He didn't even understand the question.

I've always been grateful to Bruce for that, and he wrote an introduction to one of my short story collections, *Tales of Old Earth*, that was the best introduction I've ever gotten. I have no complaints about that either.

Zinos-Amaro: With "The Overcoat," you return to horror, as part of the "A Handful of Horror" feature in *Omni*, or in the case of your piece, a pocketful . . . The story is creepy and effective in its own right, but also parodies Stephen King. You mentioned reading a fair amount of his work.

Swanwick: I wrote this because I was reading a collection of Stephen King short fiction. He's quite a good short fiction writer, but I noticed that he had this recurrent theme, where in stories like "The Crate" or "The Raft" somebody puts their hand through a hole, and then gets slowly eaten through that hole. At some point I said, "Boy, you've written a lot of this story." So I wrote a parody of it. You can't really a write a parody of something that you don't respect. I tried to make the character interesting. I was closely imitating what King himself would have done with the idea, and knew that when the eating started, you had to make it go on and on and on.

Back then I routinely sent everything to Ellen Datlow first because she had the best and most visible market. And this sold to *Omni*! I'll admit, I was a little surprised.

Zinos-Amaro: The character name of Weed sounds a bit cyberpunk, but I'm wondering if it was a reference to Stephen King's personal proclivities.

Swanwick: No, I was thinking that this was a guy who picked up this nickname for smoking marijuana, that he was a loser and this was his only accomplishment in life. He was a little weedy and a little seedy. That's all there was to it.

Zinos-Amaro: Considering how many of your preceding stories were novelettes and novellas, was it challenging to work at this very short length? Was this the writing experience that made you want to pursue micro fiction and flash fiction, which we'll be discussing elsewhere?

Swanwick: This had to be short and snappy because it was a short idea. If I'd written it out another couple of thousand words, it would have been too long and it wouldn't have worked. That's one reason why Weed realizes things! He sees this Burberry and realizes it must have been on an expedition to the arctic, and so on! He realizes things that he cannot possibly realize!

I think this was an early sign that I was learning how to do very short fiction. When I was writing unpublishable stuff, I tried to write flash fiction, or short shorts, as we then called them, and could not. I found it an almost impossible form. And then at some point I discovered I had a knack for it, and it's never gone away.

Zinos-Amaro: "The Dragon Line" originally appeared in *Terry's Universe*, edited by Beth Meacham. Did your relationship with Terry Carr inform the themes or settings of this story?

Swanwick: It didn't really. I was just finishing up the story when he asked me to contribute to the anthology and I thought it was a worthy story to send in. I would have felt really bad submitting anything that I'd phoned in to that anthology. I was on the Nebula jury several years with Terry Carr and Gardner Dozois and other people, and Terry wrote just wonderful letters. He was full of insight into science fiction and stories. I learned a great deal from him.

Zinos-Amaro: How was this story born?

Swanwick: I was driving through King of Prussia where there's like six lanes of really complicated traffic. I was stopped at a light, and it was sunset. I was able to concentrate for a second on something other than driving, so I looked up at the sunset on the horizon—and there was not a horizon. It was a dark area spangled with lights. It seemed so contemporary! I whipped up my notebook and wrote the story's first sentence: "Driving by the mall in King of Prussia that night, I noticed that between the sky and earth where the horizon used to be is now a jagged-edged region, spangled with bright industrial lights." I was writing it down furiously while the light changed! When I got home, I wrote the first paragraph.

This story took me a long time to write. I went back and read through all of Mallory, which is full of interesting material, such as the fact that when Arthur went to fight Mordred, the people of England sided with Mordred. He had brought them peace and prosperity and all Arthur ever brought them was endless war! So there was a great deal that went into there, including of course the dragon lines from Feng Shui and the ley lines from England, from my interest in the occult. The name of Shikra refers to an Asian and African sparrowhawk. I had that in because she's Merlin's great grand-daughter, and a merlin is also basically a sparrow-hawk. So that seemed like an appropriate name for her. I liked her character. She doesn't get a lot of lines, but she's smart and amoral, which is always a fun combination. It all came together, but it did not come together fast.

Zinos-Amaro: The unpublished manuscript to a novel called *Mordred* by Anna Quindsland played a role in your writing of "The Dragon Line."

Swanwick: When I was in college, Anna was a friend of mine. She was the one person I thought most likely to become a success-ful writer. She had genuine talent. She had written a story about Mordred. There was a contemporary frame about a woman and this man she knows in past lives: they were Mordred and a young woman who loved him. I had worked with Anna trying to figure out a way to make that story work, but I was maybe twenty-one, so I could not. I didn't have the stuff. A few years after college, she died. I've got two conflicting memories of it. One is that she had an aneurysm, and the other is that she was attacked and struck on the head. Whichever one it was, she was coming back from the library one night, and they found her body, and she was in a coma for maybe a week and then died. If Anna had lived, I think she would have ended up as someone like Mary Stewart, writing intelligent novels with romance in them that people loved. It really was a loss.

Zinos-Amaro: Once again, in "The Dragon Line" we have an emphasis on environmental damage. At first, this seems like an odd concept to fuse with Arthurian revisionism, but you integrate it well. What motivated the melding of these ideas?

Swanwick: Anna had put together Mordred's personality: he was an idealist, like his father. He came to court and he found it was all hypocrisy. He wanted to destroy Camelot because it was not what it should have been, and what he wanted it to be. I thought that would fit very well: the contrast between modern-day industrial America and Arthurian legend would be a very productive one.

The murder of the infant, by the way, that was mine, that was not Anna's. I felt particularly brilliant to come up with that.

Zinos-Amaro: When "The Dragon Line" was reprinted in *Asimov's* the following year, the introduction mentioned the influence of Jay McInerney's *Bright Lights, Big City*. Beyond the protagonist's substance abuse, and perhaps this sense of the world spinning out of control, were there other resonances for you? How much mainstream fiction were you reading at the time, and what in particular struck you about McInerney's work?

Swanwick: *Bright Lights, Big City* is not a great book, but it's got energy to it. It has this youthful, naïve vigor to it. After I read that book, I thought, "I know what happened. McInerney came home drunk one night, looked in the mirror and started lecturing himself." You can see that. I did it myself when I was that age.

I wanted to write about people behaving badly. That's why the story opens with the protagonist driving very badly and irresponsibly, emphasizing that he's putting himself in danger, and putting other people in danger because he's such a mess. I was looking for something for the story to be about.

I was reading a goodly amount of mainstream fiction at this time. In the 1970s, as we discussed when we talked about "Ginungagap," a lot of mainstream novels were pretty awful. But by the time I was established as an up-and-coming science fiction author, they started doing new and interesting stuff again. I didn't think that I couldn't learn from them. David Hartwell was always lecturing people of my generation to stop trying to write main-stream-ish stuff. He wanted us to focus on good, hard science fic-tion. But I don't think any of us took him seriously. I know John Kessel, for one, certainly didn't. We swiped everything we could from whatever was greatest. You just cannot argue with success. We entered the house, took the TV set, the jewelry, the silver, everything we could.

Zinos-Amaro: Even for you, you pack a lot into the ending of "The Dragon Line."

Swanwick: With the moral at the end, I was thinking of Kurt Vonnegut's *Player Piano*. At the end of *Player Piano* it's discovered that the priest knew all along that the revolution was doomed to failure. After all the suffering, Anita says, "Why did we go through all this then?" And he answers, "For the record." That's a brilliant conclusion, and it's essentially a religious conclusion. I swiped that. Mordred does not believe that there's a chance of saving the world, but has to do it because he's Mordred. He's an idealist; he does his devoir.

I was proud of the ending, when Heaven opens her legs to welcome us all in. It struck me that Hell is always so much more interesting and vivid than Heaven. I wanted to make Heaven fresh and shocking. I think that in its own weird way that's a lovely image.

Zinos-Amaro: Tell me more about Vonnegut.

Swanwick: I read almost everything he wrote. I'm not a sati-rist, so a lot of it I'm not really in sympathy with. But I admire good writing wherever I find it. I read an article about him once and it mentioned that on the back of the door to his basement he had a report card with a list of all his novels and a grade next to them. The reporter reproduced what the grades were and I said, "You know, those are exactly the grades *I* would give his novels." Including the ones that got pretty low grades indeed.

I really, really loved his *Mother Night*. What resonates with Vonnegut for me is the moralism. We're both moralistic writers, I'm afraid.

Zinos-Amaro: Vonnegut famously rejected genre identifi-cation.

Swanwick: At that time, you couldn't be a great writer *and* a science fiction writer both. You had to choose. A lot of science fiction writers were pissed at Vonnegut because of the choice that he made. I think he was right to do it. If he were the same writer producing the same work today, he could have pulled off the trick of being both.

I was at a SFWA function once, and I heard this "puff puff puff" at the back of my neck. I turned around and there was young Mr. Jonathan Lethem, who was very new then, and still a science fiction writer. He smiled at me and said, "I'm breathing down your back." A year later he was more famous than I was. And it has to be said, he did it clean. He did it fair and square. He never denied being a science fiction writer, but he was able to make it into the mainstream anyway. So kudos to him.

Zinos-Amaro: Regarding our next story, "A Midwinter's Tale" (*Isaac Asimov's Science Fiction Magazine*, December 1988), you shared these thoughts about its influenced with Marty Halpern when he reprinted it in the anthology *Alien Contact*:

> "So many different things went into 'A Midwinter's Tale' that I despair of listing them all. The chiefest of them, and the trigger for my writing the story, was a Marc Chagall retrospective at the Philadelphia Museum of Art. Chagall's art is so fabulous—in both senses of the word—that I immediately saw there was a story to be found in it. I went through the show several times, taking notes, and many specific paintings appear in the story. If I hadn't misplaced the catalog, I could list them by name. One became the birth scene, another the narrator's vision of death, and a third, (this one I remember; it's called *The Soldier Drinks*) showing a soldier and a samovar with himself in miniature sitting happily with a peasant woman on his knee, provided the story's frame. The narrative structure I borrowed from Jack Dann's autobiographical essay 'A Few Sparks in the Dark,' which described how, almost dying of an infection, he hallucinated wandering through wastelands of ice, how afterward the fever had left him with partial amnesia,

and the strange forms that amnesia took.

The prose style was not an attempt to pastiche Gene Wolfe but I did use his work as a kind of model in order to emulate a narrative richness which I felt would go well with Chagall's vision. Similarly, the Christmas section was written with Dylan Thomas's 'A Child's Christmas in Wales' firmly in mind. The larls are distant ancestors of the Coeurl in A. E. van Vogt's 'Dark Destroyer,' which later became part of *The Voyage of the Space Beagle*. Their means of serial immortality came from a now-discredited experiment in the Sixties, which I unsuccessfully attempted to replicate in high school, showing that planaria could acquire knowledge by eating other planaria. The harshness of the winter landscapes is rendered from life. Nobody who has ever gone hiking in the Green Mountains of Vermont when it is forty below will ever forget the experience.

The word 'larl' I invented forty years ago when I was working in the loading docks of a furniture factory and, out of extreme boredom, took my first halting steps toward publication. Proof positive that a true writer never throws anything away."

That's a wealth of contextual information. I'll admit, the van Vogt reference surprised me. Today he's hardly ever mentioned alongside folks like Clarke or Heinlein. What did van Vogt's work mean for you growing up?

Swanwick: I discovered him when I was eleven or twelve. I read "Recruiting Station." That is a story that will pop up in a later discussion. I read that story, thought it was terrific, and he was the first science fiction writer where I actually said, "I should remember his name, because maybe he's written other good stuff." At his best, he could be a visionary writer. He would just bring in astonishing things. He had a formula where he had to bring in something new every so many hundred words. As a formula, it's not successful, but when it's working, as an experience, it makes his stories electrifying. I know that as a result I've always felt that all of a sudden bringing in something that the reader wasn't expecting is not a bad thing. I suspect a lot of writers avoid that, so that their stories will feel consistent, but it's never bothered me.

Zinos-Amaro: In "A Midwinter's Tale" we have a concatenation of two unreliable narrators, the human who opens the story, and the larl within the second narrative layer.

Swanwick: This was not easy to write. The particular scenes that were based on the paintings were so vivid to me that they gave me the motivation to connect them. I imagined a rich universe, the kind that Larry Niven or Jack Vance would have, where there are hundreds and hundreds of worlds and people on them, and different cultures and societies in them. There's a lot of space in between planets, so there's room for strangeness to creep in. I think it was also the first time that I ever brought in the idea that the purpose of war is not to kill, but to create expensive damage to the enemy soldiers. Ellen Datlow gave me a magazine that Gucci's publications had started for the chemical weapons industry. It had a fantastic article on mustard gas, and what an effective weapon of war it was, because it didn't kill, it tied up a lot of enemy resources in hospitalization and at the same time provided a demoralizing example of what might happen to enemy soldiers. It was such a Machiavellian article, and such a Machiavellian magazine, that it sank pretty deep into me.

Zinos-Amaro: Yes. That appears in the second paragraph of your story.

On the Guggenheim website, Jennifer Blessing talks about the subjects of *The Soldier Drinks* and *Paris Through the Window* both figuratively mediating between "dual worlds"—was your two-unreliable-narrators structure related to this duality?

Swanwick: That I took straight from Chagall. The paintings are so hallucinatory as to be more visionary than reliable, but telling an important truth. Also, you can see in the way that they're unreliable that they're about memory, memory and dream and fantasy, and where all these come together. They're unreliable narrators in an unreliable universe. You don't even know for sure that the larl is telling the truth.

Zinos-Amaro: Technically we don't even know if the larl exist!

Swanwick: Right, they could be part of the brain fever. But my own theory is that they really do exist, because I like them a lot!

Zinos-Amaro: The human narrator's unreliability stemming from memory loss feels, as you anticipated, like a Gene Wolfe touch. But do you think on a deeper level it may also speak to your preoccupation at this point in your career with maintaining the self in the face of forces trying to dissolve it?

Swanwick: I'm sure of it. I was quite obsessed with the idea of identity back then.

Zinos-Amaro: You won the 1989 Asimov's Readers' Poll for "A Midwinter's Tale."

Swanwick: Yes. It's a crowd-pleaser. It's got the sort of things that science fiction readers like. It had a heroic woman with a gun. It had aliens. It had scary places you wouldn't want to go, and warm, pleasant places you *would* like to go. And it's a Christmas story!

In the Christmas parts of the tale I was trying for a Gene Wolfe-ish richness. The human narrator, as a boy, was given a cookie at one point, and that has to have been inspired by the coffee roll that was given to Tip in "The Eyeflash Miracles." Tip bites into it hoping for a raisin. What a good line! You can taste the raisin. It's so real.

There's also Nabokov in this story. Now I'm bragging! But the early sections of *Ada* have a lush richness to them that I think found its way in here too.

Zinos-Amaro: In "Snow Angels" (*Omni*, March 1989), you again take up the idea of modifying consciousness to achieve a kind of transcendence, as you did in "Trojan Horse." What was it about skiing specifically that helped inspire "Snow Angels"?

Swanwick: I wanted to write about mountains in winter. When you've been out on a mountaintop at forty below, it leaves an impression. It gets so cold that the nose hairs in your nostrils freeze. If you pinch your nose you hear them crackle. You've got a scarf around your lower face, and the outside of it freezes from the moisture of your breath. There's a great deal of physical effect in extreme cold weather, and I had these experiences and wanted to write about them. I did a fair amount of winter hiking when I was in the Boy Scouts. I was actually an Eagle Scout. I did make the coffee-can stove, as in the story, but I did not do the snow cave hike. I was not a big fan of winter! The snow cave was just a little too extreme for me. But all the other things I did. And skiing—

well, you had to meet *somebody* up there. Skiing is a big industry in Vermont.

Zinos-Amaro: Were you a skier?

Swanwick: No, I didn't have the money that requires. I finally bought a pair of ice skates during my last winter in Vermont, and that year there was an atypically warm winter and the ice rink never froze, so I never did learn how to skate. But at that time there was an Olympic skier named Billy Kidd who was a Vermonter, so he was followed religiously. Everybody read about his career, which is why I named my character Jessie James. I put that together with your basic exoskeleton equivalent, and they seemed to fit.

That was about the time when ecstasy first came into society. I never had any. I'd moved beyond my drug-taking days by then. I had taken a lot of acid in my youth, and psilocybin and such. I think you can see traces of it in my work. I was certainly trying to use the experiences in my work.

Zinos-Amaro: Were you yourself looking for transcendence?

Swanwick: I can't say that I was trying to achieve transcendence, but I was a seeker. An adventurer. I was trying to find out what could be learned and discovered. Essentially what happened was that at some point it was like with rock and roll: it stopped being meaningful. So I got off the bus. There came a point where it was nothing but hedonism. There was nothing spiritual to be discovered; I lost interest in it at that point.

When I reread "Snow Angels" recently, I was struck by just how long I managed to keep the story going before introducing a second character. You have to have self-confidence to do that. By that point I'd had enough award nominations and the like that I felt that I knew what I was doing. I think it also, at that point, makes it a surprise when the woman does show up and the mood changes entirely. It's entirely possible that when I wrote the line about her expecting him I did not know what was going to happen.

Toward the end the protagonist looks down the mountain and he sees a dragon down in the valley below. Again, I hope it comes as a surprise. That comes from being up on the mountain, looking down and seeing a snowstorm coming in, curving its way between the mountains like a dragon. It was quite a storm, actually, and it came up the mountain and swallowed up everybody on the ski lift. They had to wait for the storm to end until the rescue people could come with the harnesses and let them down. What he sees down below in the story is a troop carrier, and that's when you learn what's gone unsaid during the whole thing, that he's a fugitive.

I read this and I was surprised because I think this was a turning point for me in maturity. Particularly the fact that with the ending he's probably not going to make it to Canada. But that doesn't matter. He's in the same situation we're all in. We're not going to make it to the twenty-third century. All that really matters is what you do right now. There is the moment of transcendence you can have. It's just like in certain schools of Buddhism. They say you can achieve nirvana—but it'll only last for an instant. You have your nirvana, and then you go on.

Zinos-Amaro: The man in "Snow Angels" references a sculptor that a little research shows to be Larkin Mead.

Swanwick: I read about this in Vermont and I just thought that was the greatest thing ever, that there was a marble statue that was a *copy* of the snow angel. Just absolutely wonderful. That stayed with me for a long time.

Zinos-Amaro: At one point in "Snow Angels" the man admits that he's never done anything remarkable in his life, but he wonders if his encounter with Jessie is so that he can bear witness to something truly special. Have you witnessed any metaphorical snow angels in your own life?

Swanwick: Not really. I don't think that way. I tried to bear witness to Anna Quindsland's career, to what it might have been. And of course, Gardner Dozois. The whole purpose of *Being Gardner Dozois* was to preserve some of what he had done, and to bear witness to what he was like. I was talking about him with Marianne yesterday, and about some other friends who had died. "But Gardner's different," Marianne said. "Gardner was not like anybody else."

Zinos-Amaro: Definitely. Writing in *The New York Review of Science Fiction*, Alexander Jablokov noted the following: "A common mythic theme, or at least mythic character, runs through several of the works [. . .]; the magical woman who vanishes from our world through some sort of technological Assumption. This includes Elin/Coral in 'Trojan Horse,' Abigail in 'Ginungagap,' and Jessie in 'Snow Angels.' All the women reach their state as a consequence of some dramatic physical accident, a version of the crippling wound necessary to contact another world, common in legend. These wounds are all healed through the technological wizardry of the various civilizations the women live in, but their emotional consequences remain." What do you make of this Assumption interpretation?

Swanwick: Well, it sounds convincing to me. I would attribute it to being raised Catholic, and being very sincere about it when I *was* Catholic. There's a great deal of emphasis on transcendence in Catholicism. I would say that it being all women comes from that early realization that if I made an interesting character male, it would have a tendency to become me, and if I made that character female, I was putting enough distance between myself and her that she could be herself. These are probably my own fantasies of transcendence projected on other characters. The wound I cannot answer for, except that it might be an artifact of prose fiction, which needs to have bad things happen.

In the case of "Snow Angels," there's a little bit of Jack London. He did winter very well. Something like "To Build a Fire" is a beautiful accomplishment.

Zinos-Amaro: Add to that the solitary character we talked about.

Swanwick: Yeah, come to think of it. He was like a role model for how to use that material.

Zinos-Amaro: A form of loneliness informs your next story, "The Edge of the World." This is a wondrous, haunting tale that masterfully externalizes the uncertainties of youth. It appeared in the distinctive *Full Spectrum 2*, edited by Lou Aronica, Pat LoBrutto, Shawna McCarthy, and Amy Stout. What was the editorial remit for this submission? Had you read the first *Full Spectrum* published the previous year when you wrote this?

Swanwick: I think they were just looking for the best work you had, and that was the best work I had. I was aware of what they were doing with the first *Full Spectrum*, but I didn't have anything in shape to submit to them, or I would have. I was aware of the rapturous joy with which that book was received by the reading public, so I was of course happy to have something to submit to the second one.

This story took a long, long time. It began with the stairs. I live in a neighborhood of Philadelphia called Roxborough. Down below there's the Schuylkill River. Next to the Schuylkill River there's a neighborhood called Manayunk, which is an old mill town. It was in fact one of the first big industrial areas in the country. And then there's a cliff. Roxborough is up on the top. We're in the Piedmont region, and the people down below are in the Tidewater region, geologically. I know this because I used to live in Virginia, where the separation between the Piedmont and Tidewater is distinctive and everybody knows about it. Here in my neighborhood it's distinctive, but nobody knows about geological regions. When Marianne first bought a house here I was driving around with a map to see what the neighborhood was like. I went down a street and all of a sudden the street stopped, there was a little fence, and there was a set of metal and cement stairs going down a cliff face, and then the street started again at the bottom of the stairs. I'm sitting there in the car, feeling like God's laughing at me. He's just played a practical joke. I was fascinated by these stairs for years. There's at least a dozen of them, maybe twenty. When I came up with the idea for the story I spent a day going up and down every set of steps and taking notes from what I saw. If you think about it in abstract terms, it sounds like it wouldn't be very interesting, just going down stairs, but there are many surprising details, the best of which made it into the story. There's also being in the high spot, looking out over the town of Manayunk below, with the church spires and a pale moon floating in a blue sky—it was like spending a day in a children's book.

Zinos-Amaro: Talk to me about Russ' fate.

Swanwick: From the inception of the story I knew that it was going to be a story about teen suicide. When I was a teenager—you'll find this hard to believe—I was very unhappy. My senior year of high school in Seven Pines, Virginia, was not a joyous one. There was a lot going wrong at that point. My father had contracted early-onset Alzheimer's. We'd left our old life in Vermont behind and I was seventeen. Things got better when I went to college, but I swore that I would remember just how bad it was to be that age and that someday I would write about it. My hope was that somebody who was that age and feeling that way on reading the story would realize that someone else had felt exactly the same way and had somehow survived it, so there was hope. That was my intention. I've taught "The Edge of the World" at high schools several times, and as far as I can tell teenagers all hate the story, because it's dark and not optimistic. What they really want is a story that will tell them that life's going to be great. I can see their point!

Zinos-Amaro: Was the very specific psychological dynamic of Donna, Piggy and Russ inspired by any recollections from your own childhood, or classic works of literature? Were you referencing *The Lord of the Flies* with Piggy?

Swanwick: In part experience, like everything else. What kicked it off was a long article in *Philadelphia Magazine* about two teenage boys who committed suicide. They planned this out. They dropped acid and they had a tape recorder on, so they were recording all their feelings and thoughts. It was a really difficult thing to read. They were almost gleeful about it. It was kind of a weird adventure to them. I had three characters to create a dynamic that would prevent them from being able to communicate effectively. Donna is a teenage girl: she's sensible, practical, she's got a good mind, and she feels things too much. Russ is the kid we all wish we could be, and Piggy is the kid we fear we might turn out to be.

I probably picked up that name from *Lord of the Flies*. Like everyone else I read it and, well, *loved* isn't quite the right word, but I was productively horrified by it. The name is such an insulting one. It does a lot of the job of characterizing him. You know you should be feeling sympathetic for him, but he's got that name, so you don't sympathize as much as you should.

This story is also about Martin Luther King Jr.'s assassination. That year when everything was going so bad he was killed. The next day I stopped by my friend Steve's house, two doors down, so the two of us could go to school together. His mother was in her nightgown, watching television, the footage of Martin Luther King's funeral, saying bitter, cruel things about how Mrs. King was making fun of Jacqueline Kennedy by pretending to be heartbroken. She was using the N-word rather a lot. I put that scene right in. I remember Steve slamming around the kitchen and shouting, "Mother, where's my fucking lunch?" She said, "Don't you use that tone of voice with me!" It was then that

I understood a lot about Steve. Steve was a nice guy who nevertheless decorated everything he owned with swastikas and affected a German accent and made master race jokes. I realized then that this was his way of fighting back against his parents, who were just stone racists, terrible, terrible people. He could not fight back as a liberal, because that they knew how to deal with, so he was fighting back as a Nazi. At school, my friend Daphne told me that she and another friend had been out bowling and on the intercom they announced that King had been killed. Everybody cheered and then somebody began singing God Bless America and people joined in. She went out into the parking lot and threw up. That went into the story too. I was putting into that story all the horrible things about being a teenager in Seven Pines, Virginia, at that time.

Zinos-Amaro: Speaking of setting, when Nick Gevers reviewed your interview volume with Gardner Dozois, he lamented that because the focus was on Gardner, we didn't get to find out why in this story you placed an American Air Force Base in Lord Dunsany's Toldenarba. Why the hell did you do this, Michael?

Swanwick: It turns out in fantasy there hasn't been a lot of fiction about the edge of the world. Larry Niven did two stories and Philip José Farmer did "Sail On! Sail On!" and that's close to it. But Dunsany had stories set at the edge of the world—it was the edge of *our* world and another world. If you're going to have a literal edge of the world, that image was so good that I really wanted to work with it. It becomes a fantasy world, so there's a whole history of high fantasy hidden in there. There are references not only to Dunsany but also E. R. Eddison and several other fantasy works. In part there's also a comment on Orientalism, how we've been projecting this Arabian Nights fantasy onto the Near East through Western culture, and contrasting the fantasy with the reality: it's all old factory buildings, at lunch break the men come up and shoot a few hoops and smoke cigarettes . . . So there for your fantasy world, it's all gone. In a way this story is a comment on fantasy itself. I'm a strong believer in fantasy as a survival mechanism.

Zinos-Amaro: The existentialism of the infinitely descending steps in "The Edge of the World" reminds me of another short story I love, Thomas Disch's "Descending."

Swanwick: I've read "Descending" several times. It's a classic. Also one of Disch's best stories, which is saying something. It's definitely a *possible* influence. But I can't remember if it was one I was aware of when I was writing. Probably not. But influences don't have to be consciously remembered to be powerful.

Zinos-Amaro: This story earned you a Sturgeon Memorial Award in 1990, and was also in the running for the Locus, Hugo and World Fantasy awards.

Swanwick: I was very happy with that. To a degree, I think it deserved it. It was enormous amounts of work putting this story together.

Zinos-Amaro: I'm fascinated by the fact that this story was reprinted in Gardner's *Modern Classics of Science Fiction* as well in Mike Ashley's *The Mammoth Book of Fantasy*. Do you see it as more one than another?

Swanwick: Oh, I think it's definitely a fantasy because it's set in an impossible world. But as we've discussed, the DNA of fantasy is in science fiction, so the whole idea of any kind of genre purity is long lost.

Zinos-Amaro: In the intro to the reprint in the seventh *Year's Best*, Gardner mentions you had just finished work on your third novel, *The Drowning Lands*. I assume this was the working title for *Stations of the Tide*?

Swanwick: Yes. I was unhappy with *The Drowning Lands* from the start. It sounds too T. S. Eliot. The novel was almost published under the title of *Sea Twin*. I hadn't found the title when I sold the novel. I really should have waited to have a title before sending it in, but it was done, I wanted to see it in print, and I thought there'd be time to figure out a title. I only came up with *Stations of the Tide* when the book had begun to go into production. It happened that I had a friend at the publishing house, Don Keller, who, because he was a friend and a nice guy, went running up and down several floors, changing the title in all the production documents. If he hadn't done that, it would have been published with a sucky title.

Zinos-Amaro: To return to "The Overcoat" for a moment, it strikes me that in a way "The Edge of the World" shares space with Stephen King territory. You have youthful characters, realistically depicted in their embattled relationship with the world, in a cautionary tale in which a great power is unleashed through their minds and they alter reality.

Swanwick: We were drawing on a lot of the same resources, I think. This is also a three-wishes story, where of course the third one is the disastrous one.

Again, there's an unknowability. We never do learn why Russ wants to kill himself. You can't. You can come up with theories, but you'll never know.

I was thinking also when I wrote "The Edge of the World" about a friend of mine who told me that the time she'd tried to commit suicide was the bravest moment of her life. It took genuine courage. With this story I wanted to present suicide as something more difficult to deal with, not an act of cowardice or necessarily even of despair, but something very difficult to talk about.

Zinos-Amaro: We've covered twenty of your solo stories now over a decade, but I feel there's something special about this one.

Swanwick: I think so. I hope so. A lot of these early stories you can tell are written by a young man. I think that maybe toward the end here I'm beginning to grow up. Fingers crossed!

CHAPTER THREE
1990-1994

Alvaro Zinos-Amaro: When "U F O" (*Aboriginal Science Fiction*, September-October 1990) was published, were you handling your short story submissions directly, or was your agent, Virginia Kidd, still involved?

Michael Swanwick: She was involved. I know that because it was "Griffin's Egg" (*Legend Novellas* chapbook, Legend/Century, 1991) which caused me to leave the agency.

Zinos-Amaro: We're going to talk about that shortly. This story, meanwhile, seems to owe a debt to writers like Robert Sheckley and John Sladek. You're essentially doing surreal comedy, with some philosophical underpinnings.

Swanwick: They always tell you that if you're going to be a successful artist you have to take chances. On this story I took chances—and it really didn't work. It was not a great success. In fact, Jim Turner called me up to find out if I had completely lost my mind and thought that this was a good story, just so that he could write me off if I did.

What happened was that I read a story by, I believe, Lewis Shiner. It was a piece of punk humor. I thought that was really quite interesting, so I decided that I would try that myself. As you can see, this is a punk story. It's about bad art. It amused me, but pretty much nobody else. Around that same period there were a lot of writers in my cohort who tried strange, surrealistic humor and sort of got bit on the first attempt and walked away from it. Lucius Shepard's "The Fundamental Things," a story that I know he ended up hating, but I actually liked, begins with a man on a golf course falling in love with his golf ball. The world is going through a series of mutations, and the first one is a romantic one where everybody just falls in love with the closest person or thing that's there. Later on there's the world of Doomed, Romantic Men, where all men put on trench-coats and stalk through the fog moodily.

There was something in the air, and I took a flyer on it. I didn't think this was a successful story, and I certainly didn't follow in that vein anymore.

Zinos-Amaro: Assessing beings for sentience in this crazy test becomes quite serious, which makes things tricky tonally.

Swanwick: The question of whether or not we're sentient, and whether we would know it if we weren't, is a serious one, and quite interesting. I used that to give some ballast to the story. All the rest of it is taken from, oh, science fiction covers and UFO magazine covers. Why in all these science fiction covers are people always walking up and down stepped pyramids? Obviously this is what people in the future do for fun!

Zinos-Amaro: Right. In a way this story could be a forerunner to *Rick and Morty*, but with slower pacing.

Swanwick: It's also a pretty nihilistic story, so not really suited for me, because I'm not really a nihilist. I was faking it there. Mrkao, by the way, comes from James Joyce. It's the sound the cat makes in *Ulysses*.

Zinos-Amaro: Ah. After reaching the story's final lines, this felt to me like something that might have started out as a very long, elaborate bar joke, but which you turned into an actual story.

Swanwick: That's it. It's set, by the way, in Highland Springs, which is where I went to my senior year of high school.

Zinos-Amaro: The "asshole of the universe."

Swanwick: It was a very unpleasant place when I was there. There's no getting around it. I went back exactly once. My mother wanted to get a picture of the house we lived in there for a year. She had pictures of all the other houses she'd lived in. I went there, and the houses were identical. I'd forgotten the number, but I knew it was either this one or the one next to it. I took a picture of one and made sure the number didn't show up, because I figured she wouldn't be able to tell either. On the way out I saw two dogs crouched by the side of the road, their heads turned toward the car. I thought, "I'd better keep an eye on those dogs. They're plotting something," which is a very strange thought to find in your own head. As we drove past the dogs, they launched themselves forward, snapping and barking, and went *bam! bam!* and bounced off the side of the car. I drove on and said to Marianne, "It's exactly the way I remembered it."

It was a terrible place in a lot of ways. The day after we moved in, the guy next door was moving out and left his key with my father to give to the landlord. Ten minutes after he left the state police arrived and the FBI very politely requested the key. He was a neo-Nazi. He was a police officer, too, and had swastikas painted on the walls. I could go on for days about that part of the world . . .

Zinos-Amaro: You mentioned bad art. The sex stuff in "U F 0" was obviously deliberately over-the-top even back then, but how does it read to you today?

Swanwick: The same as it did then. It was bad sex based on bad girlie magazines that the character of Ron was reading. I was young and I wrote bad portrayals of bad sex—nothing you'd actually want to have. By my reading, all UFO-logy is bad thinking, wishful thinking, but the fantasies are not wonderful. Andy Duncan wrote a first-rate story about that called "Close Encounters," which won a Nebula for best novelette.

Zinos-Amaro: The title, we should specify, is not UFO but U F 0, which we eventually find out stands for "You Fucking Zero." What inspired the way that Emily communicates? It's like a precursor to modern texting.

Swanwick: I basically put that system together so that I could have the title. Instead of the "O" you have a "0" so you'd have to read the story to discover what the title was. It was kind of fun putting the language together. It wasn't as brilliantly clever as someone who creates crossword puzzles would have done, but it was fun.

I have a paragraph in this story with a lot of "nadas" in it; I stole this from Hemingway's "A Clean, Well-Lighted Place." That's because growing up in school they always taught that Hemingway's prose was perfect. It was everything that prose should be, and didn't draw attention to itself. Of course when you want to be a writer you don't want to write things that *don't* draw attention to themselves, you want to write things that *do*. I felt a little annoyed at the cult of Hemingway, not at him per se. The paragraph in "A Clean, Well-Lighted Place" with "Our nada who art in nada, nada be thy name thy kingdom nada thy will be nada in nada as it is in nada" is drawing attention to itself.

So there's some good jokes in "U F 0," but on the whole, no, it doesn't work. I have to be honest about that.

Zinos-Amaro: Around the time of this story and the next one, you published something that worked exceedingly well: your novel *Stations of the Tide*, a magnificent achievement. This was actually the first thing by you I ever read. I found the British paperback, put out by Legend, in a used bookstore when I was seventeen or so. I worked up the courage to write you a fan letter shortly after turning twenty, in 1999. In your response you said, "When I wrote that book, I was more than half convinced that nobody would understand a word of what I was trying to say. So it is particularly pleasant to have *Stations* both understood and appreciated."

Swanwick: As it turns out, it's been my most understood book! I think that it goes to show that you should just assume the best of your readers. I always assume that my readers are intelligent, rather suave people, who smile wryly at a hidden reference to James Joyce.

Zinos-Amaro: I'm again curious, when you won the Nebula for *Stations of the Tide* the following year, did this impact your confidence or sense of stamina as a short story writer?

Swanwick: Except for the Sturgeon award, this was the first major award I ever won. I'd been losing Nebulas for ten years. Mostly, I was thrilled. I came up through science fiction at a time when the Nebulas usually went to better literary works than the Hugos did, so that meant a lot to me. I felt that I had arrived somewhere. It was probably around 1990 that I began feeling that I had some kind of handle on fiction writing.

Zinos-Amaro: This shows in "Griffin's Egg," which was published as part of the Legend novella series. Had you read preceding novellas in the series, like "Heads" by Greg Bear or "Kalimantan" by Lucius Shepard? I'm particularly curious about "Heads," which is also set on the Moon and features a big corporation and a kind of mystery.

Swanwick: I read them both. I'm a big fan of "Kalimantan." "Heads," not so much. What one wants from Greg Bear is the science. Trying to reach ultimate zero, that was good. Accidentally going beyond, and what the heck does that mean, into I guess negative motion, that was good too. But his interest in the cult in this novella was not where my interest was. The Moon setting was a coincidence. I'd been wanting to write about the Moon for a long time. We talked about the GE handout that showed the doomed lunar crater when we discussed "Trojan Horse." I'd been wanting to use this and expand upon it. "Griffin's Egg" has the same initials as General Electric. That is not a coincidence.

When Legend decided to do this novella series, the editor, Deborah Beale, told me about it and said, "Let's meet at the Worldcon and discuss it." I went there with two ideas to pitch to her. One was "Griffin's Egg" and the other was what became *The Iron Dragon's Daughter*. At the last moment I decided to go with "Griffin's Egg" for the pitch, and she liked the idea. She said, "Okay, we'll send out the contracts." Time passed and I didn't get the contracts. I asked Virginia what was going on. Our British associate agent for some reason just wasn't bothering to do it. I told her, "Really, we've got to do this." They were offering me more money for that than I would have gotten for a novel. Virginia wouldn't put the pressure on the associate agent. Then I met Deb Beale at another convention and she said, "What's the problem? Why won't you sign this?" I told her to send it directly to me, and I signed it. When the accounting was done, and it was less twenty percent for my American agent and British agent, I said, "Why am I paying money for them to basically prevent this book from happening?" That's when I realized that Virginia wasn't doing the job anymore. I'd been with her from the beginning, and she was so smart and so fun and so funny and always on your side. So firing her was pretty terrible. But she wasn't taking care of business, and I had to find somebody else. It broke my heart.

Zinos-Amaro: This novella represents not only an inflection point in the business part of your career, I think, but also a summation of sorts. For example, Gunther has a German background, like the character in "The Men Who Met Picasso." You use the story about the Yogi who stopped his heart, which you had included in "Snow Angels." You talk about weapons, in the context of your "schizomimetic engine," as a way to inflict damage without defeating the enemy, a concept from "A Midwinter's Tale." One of the things the story deals with is understanding how the brain operates, and exploring the ability to change that. Krishna rewrites her own personality, which recalls "Trojan Horse." And so on.

Swanwick: Absolutely. When I set out to write this novella, I realized that after I finished it I was going to write my fantasy novel. So it would be several years into the nineties before I would be able to get back to writing hard science fiction again. I thought, "I don't want to be writing 1980s science fiction in the 1990s. So I'll use up everything I've got in this." That's why it's so dense with incident. I had a solar flare storm, a nuclear war on Earth, and so on and on. I think that contributed a great deal to its texture. I think there's probably enough plot in there for a full-length novel.

The techies in this story are all extremely privileged. They can't imagine bad things happening, because they never had before. I based this on the techies from the computer-human interface conference we talked about in connection with Bruce Sterling and *Vacuum Flowers*.

I realized that I've used the idea that in war injury is better than death because it ties up resources in at least three stories. I've never served in the military and so I try to avoid stories involving the military and/or war. When dealing with war, I ask myself what valuable thing I have to say. And *that* is valid. But I'm obviously going to have to do more research before I go anywhere near a fictional war again.

I had the little factory systems which were very much 3D printers—also 3D bio-printers. And again death is the black wall, which we talked about in our discussion of "'Til Human Voices Wake Us"—another thing I recycled!

Zinos-Amaro: How do you feel about the ending, specifically Gunther killing Ekatarina?

Swanwick: I don't really know. It was meant to be shocking. It was meant to be realpolitik. There are big issues at stake there, and at that moment he has to take a side, and he does. Really it's the first time that he's thinking with his head rather than his glands. I'm obviously not convinced that he made the right decision. Both sides were presented as honestly as I could, and I suspect that Ekatarina was right. The dangers probably outweighed the fates of a couple of hundred people. But I try to make that even out.

Throughout the novella, the sex is all pretty bad. Gunther

doesn't realize what he's doing, but he's just using other people and taking the course of least resistance. When he kills Ekatarina, he's not taking the course of least resistance. He's finally taking action. It's a *bad* action, but it's consequential. Before this, he's just been following in the wake of events.

Zinos-Amaro: You again explore environmental concerns and the threat of nuclear war.

Swanwick: When I was writing this, I came to the point where they had to have a nuclear war on Earth. At that time all political logic said that it had to be a confrontation between East and West, between the Soviet Union and United States, between capitalism and communism. I went to write that and I thought, "I can't do this. It's so bleeping boring." So I created a war where we don't know who's actually responsible, who started it. Everyone is on hair trigger, it happens, and the news cuts off. In between when I sent the manuscript in and when it was published, the Soviet Union collapsed. It fell in large part because so many of its citizens found the Soviet narratives so boring they couldn't stand it. So I really lucked out, because my novella was still a viable work when it was published, but if I'd done the East/West confrontation, it would have been a piece of Cold War nostalgia on publication. That was good fortune.

On the environmental front, I make a great deal about trash in the story. Gunther feels pleasure driving through the virgin land, but of course he's leaving behind tire prints.

Zinos-Amaro: In "Griffin's Egg" you also revisit the notion of free will. Krishna and Gunther have a discussion about whether or not we're "machines."

Swanwick: Yes. In the section where the researcher is on psilocybin. I did that myself. I was on psilocybin and I realized that a friend of mine was like a machine, in the sense that Timothy Leary said that people were machines, just acting out their reflexes. I was laughing at him saying "You're a machine!" He'd get mock-angry and I would laugh at that. Then he'd laugh. You could watch him shifting back and forth between the two strategies, trying to make one of them work. Just like a machine.

I should say a word about the suits in the story. I worked to do this analytical thing about how you dehumanize people. It's the people with the power who dehumanize those without the power. I've observed this a lot in life, that people with power and money are always feeling that those without it are inferior and also in some way an imposition upon them. I tried to bring that up. My observation is that most American writers, unlike the British writers, are not aware of class. I think I'm painfully aware of class—and resentful, too.

In the novella, they gossip about the mad people. Philadelphia had a mad woman uncharitably called the Duck Lady. She'd make these sounds like a duck quacking and then say, "Hey, Mac, give me twenty bucks!" You'd say "No" and she'd look at you with astonishment. It was a common rumor that someone had seen her being picked up in a limousine at the end of the day, that she was an eccentric old lady who was rich. When she died, it turned out she was homeless, and these were just myths that had risen up to protect us from the reality.

Zinos-Amaro: All that color certainly informs "Griffin's Egg," which was again nominated for all the major awards.

Swanwick: That was pretty nice. I wonder sometimes what would have happened if I'd gone the other way, and had written the beginning of *The Iron Dragon's Daughter* as a novella for Legends and taken "Griffin's Egg" and written it as a novel. But I think I made the right choice. I really do. "Griffin's Egg" works better as a novella, and fantasy tends to want to have more room to stretch out.

In terms of reception, I know that the new British space opera guys were in sympathy with me too. They understood what I was doing and felt pretty good about what they were doing at the same time. I was also reading their stuff. Lots and lots of it. So much of it is great: Paul J. McAuley, Colin Greenland, Ian M. Banks. What was really brilliant about it was that they were taking a form that Americans had given up on and resurrecting it and making it British without any of the qualities that we'd tagged the British writers with, unfairly I think. Their stories were being done without irony, without distancing. They were out-American-ing the Americans, beating us in our own territory.

With Banks, I'll admit that I was a fan of the Culture novels but preferred some of his so-called mainstream books. *The Wasp Factory* and *The Bridge* were two that knocked me out. They were so different and fresh.

Zinos-Amaro: When I think of possible influences on "Griffin's Egg," John W Campbell Jr's *The Moon Is Hell*, Clarke's *A Fall of Moondust*, Heinlein's *The Moon is a Harsh Mistress*, and Larry Niven's *The Patchwork Girl* all come to mind.

Swanwick: Guilty on all counts; Niven in particular. A friend of mine once said that what Niven is doing is basically writing cartoons, not cartoons like Sunday cartoons, but like the ones that artists make for murals beforehand. They're simplified, but the structure is there, the positioning is there. At his best, Niven is brilliant at plot. For essentially literary and political reasons, he's never really gotten full credit for his particular brilliances.

With "Griffin's Egg," this was a case of everything I'd read over the course of my lifetime influencing it. I'd read so many stories set on the Moon or on hostile planets. It all went in, your classic standing-on-the-shoulders-of-giants kind of thing.

If you look at the beginning, by the way, there's half a poem by Vachel Lindsay. I cut it in the middle, because in my experience the judgment of girls is always superior to the judgment of boys, and I wanted to make it a dark epigram. The part of the poem I left out is, "Yet gentle will the griffin be / Most decorous and fat / And walk up to the Milky Way / And lap it like a cat." If you include the second half, it turns the whole story into a work of mindless Campbellian optimism!

In the lunar system I developed, you have nuclear power because it's perfectly safe there. If a reactor melts down it's just a financial loss. There's no atmosphere to carry the radioactive material around.

Zinos-Amaro: That was one of my favorite details from the start of the story: "Fortunately, the occasional meltdown was designed into the system."

Swanwick: You know, writing hard science fiction is a lot of fun; building your own world, getting to play at being an engineer, only with the advantage that when *you* write it you can say, "And it works." With real engineering it doesn't work, it doesn't work, it doesn't work, and then you make it work, and when the boss comes in to see it, it doesn't work. Gene Wolfe told me that once: whatever you build will not work in front of the boss.

Zinos-Amaro: This is a nice in to your next story, "The Wireless Folly" (*Thunder's Shadow Collector's Magazine*, Feb 1992), a meta-commentary on the assembly of science fiction itself. How did this come to be published in *Thunder's Shadow Collector's Magazine*, and what kind of publication was that?

Swanwick: It was a half-magazine, half-catalog. A catalog with ambitions is what it was. A bookseller just approached me and said "I'd like you to write something for my magazine catalog." I thought about it and came up with this notion of science fiction/fantasy as a building. How much of the history of science fiction and fantasy, I thought, can I encode in the description of a piece of architecture? It's got John W. Campbell and his radio experimenters—

Zinos-Amaro: The "sincerely young men with skinhead crewcuts."

Swanwick: Yes. It's also got an entire room dedicated to H. P. Lovecraft. The member who goes through swinging an axe declaring that he's going to tear down the entire place, being pursued by the portly older members of the club, is Harlan Ellison. The rubber bands are the result of the American New Wave wars. The writer who takes an empty swimming pool and turns it into a pornographic theater is of course J. G. Ballard.

Zinos-Amaro: Tell me about this comment: "There is a certain nostalgia for those rough additions nowadays, perhaps because some few (fewer with each passing year, alas!) of the original members are still with us." What was happening in the field that prompted that observation?

Swanwick: When I first got into science fiction, just about everybody was still alive. You could challenge a fan to name ten significant science fiction writers who had ever died, and it would not be an easy game to win. Asimov was still there; Heinlein; Clarke; everybody was still around. And then one day in the 80s they all started dying off. It was almost like they were giving each other permission to die. I didn't want that. I just wanted them to scooch over on the couch and make a little room. Science fiction used to be like the village in *One Hundred Years of Solitude*, so obscure that death couldn't find its way there. It was a lovely little world.

Zinos-Amaro: This is your first solo story without a protagonist or central character. It consists entirely of descriptive narration.

Swanwick: As you can tell, I wrote this story with a great deal of affection. It's a very impressionistic history of the genre. I saw how much I could fit into that and stopped before it got bloated. It's all razzle-dazzle. With something like that, you have to know when to stop. I was perfectly content with it. It's not trying to be more than what it is.

Zinos-Amaro: Do you think the readers of that catalog magazine understood what you were doing?

Swanwick: I don't know. I have no idea. I never got any feedback about it at all. They might have, though. It was a science fiction magazine behind the scenes.

Zinos-Amaro: Later you chose this as the introduction for your collection *A Geography of Unknown Lands*.

Swanwick: That book happened because of Chris Edwards. He's a friend of mine, and a book dealer. He approached me and he said he had this idea to do a slim collection of my work. It would be slim so that he could price it properly. Earlier, *Pulphouse*, run by Kris Rusch and Dean Wesley Smith, had put out these little chapbook collections by science fiction writers of my generation, and they quit before they got to me. I was buying them with great avidity. But I found that the writers had included only their second-rate work, and were holding out their best work for their serious collections. I was talking about this with Jim Turner, who was then editing for Arkham House. He said very disdainfully that they could put anything in there, because he wasn't competing with *Pulphouse*. So when Chris proposed his idea, I gathered up all the best uncollected stories I had. They fit together very well, as it turned out. I've been delighted with that collection ever since. I have a particular fondness for it.

Zinos-Amaro: You worked with Jim Turner on your first collection, *Gravity's Angels*, which came out from Arkham in 1991. What was that process like?

Swanwick: Jim Turner got in touch with me and asked if I'd like to do it. We gathered most of everything I'd written, with a couple of the lesser stories left out. Jim made suggestions for changes within the stories themselves, but not many. Little things. In "The Man Who Met Picasso," for example, the protagonist was on the way to the opera; Jim suggested a particular opera. I said, "Fine." Changes like that that were all reasonable, so I didn't have any fights or trouble with them. Originally Jim's vision for the book's cover was to use Picasso's "Guernica" as a wraparound. He called me and said that he had to change it, because he found out the proportions were wrong. In order to make it a wraparound, he'd have to cut off parts of it, and he said, "You can't cut off parts of a great work of art." I bit my tongue. I wanted so much to say, "Oh, go ahead Jim!" Just to yank his chain. But he was a good guy, so I didn't do it.

I think Lucius Shepard was the one writer who Jim admired most. He did all the Lucius material he could.

Zinos-Amaro: The next story up is "In Concert" (*Isaac Asimov's Science Fiction Magazine*, September 1992). From the introductory note in *Asimov's* I gather that you had somehow committed yourself to setting one of your new stories in Sevastopol.

Swanwick: This story started with the image of Lenin striding up on stage, wearing slacks with the razor-crisp pleat in them, ripping off his jacket, grabbing a Stratocaster and bursting into "Workers of the World Unite." That was the moment I wanted to capture. These were the early days of the Web, and I was in communication with some fans in the Ukraine, specifically Sevastopol. I asked them, "If you had a rock concert in Sevastopol, where would that be?" They told me it would be in the Fisherman's Palace of Culture. I thought, "Dear God, now I have *got* to write this story in Sevastopol!" The first thing I did was to try and find a map of the city. I went to the University of Pennsylvania, which has a huge library, and found a little tourist book about the city. It had descriptions, but no map. There were no maps anywhere. I was asking around on various bulletin boards like GEnie. That was new and exciting technology then. Another General Electric thing. They'd offered science fiction writers free memberships of the bulletin board as a draw for other people. I got in touch with the people in Sevastopol, but still no maps. I considered asking the CIA, because I knew they would have maps, but I didn't. Finally a guy who had been a jet pilot for NATO, stationed in that part of the world, sent me a copy of the map he had. So the only people who had maps of the place were people who were prepared to drop bombs on it.

I found out that the reason there were no maps was that the Black Sea Fleet was quartered there. So Sevastopol has been a military secret since before the Crimean War. During the Crimean War, somebody found a tourist picture, one of those bird's eye views of the city, and they used that when they were attacking the city. That was the best information they could find.

Zinos-Amaro: Paul Park, Mike N. Korkin, and Andrei Chertkov were the three folks you thanked in *Asimov's*. Do you usually look for maps when you're writing about places you haven't been to?

Swanwick: I try to learn as much as I can, and a map is certainly the easiest way to get your head into a locale. For "In Concert" I did as much research as I could and covered it up where I couldn't.

When I was in college there was a 5th Dimension concert in the big music stadium that they built. I did not have a lot of money in college, so I very rarely could afford a ticket. I'd sit outside and listen to the spillover. There was this outgoing black guy who set up a blanket and several of us students gathered around him because he was charismatic. We sat drinking cheap wine and talking before the concert, and then when the concert started we decided to try to sneak in. We did manage it. So I threw this incident into the story.

I had a friend, Bob The Musician we called him, who once told me that he'd worked up a slow-dance version of "I Am the Walrus" just because he liked the thought of yuppies slow dancing while he sang, "Yellow Matter custard, dripping from a dead dog's eye."

Zinos-Amaro: When we discussed "Snow Angels" you talked about feeling that after a while rock and roll became all about hedonism. There was a burnout.

Swanwick: That definitely feeds into "In Concert." It might have been Lucius Shepard's influence. He had a story in the early 80s where there's a musician who I think is a cyborg with heart-shaped pupils in his eyes, which is something that he despises. Lucius wrote this story all about how rock was dead and I thought that was just brilliant and wonderful. I wanted to write that too. Rock and roll was so very important to me in my life: it was like Radio Free/Liberty, news from the outside world at a time when I was rather hoping an outside world existed. For a long time it was extremely meaningful to me. It kept building and building and

building. And then at one point—for me it was about the time
that Southern Rock came up—it just stopped going anywhere. I
wanted to write about that. I deliberately referred to Lenin as the
Boss early on because I wanted people to think that I was talking
about Bruce Springsteen.

Zinos-Amaro: You certainly tricked me. Tell us about the
name Misha Cyberpunk.

Swanwick: That's an inside joke. If you look at my name in
Cyrillic, the way that they spell Swanwick looks a lot like the
word "cyberpunk." Misha was the endearment for Michael. The
Russians loved cyberpunk. I thought, "Misha Cyberpunk, what a
great name that is." For a while I had a story I was ideating, mus-
ing on, dreaming up, called "Red Star," about a Soviet hacker in
the United States. It just never reached the point where it turned
into something important to say, so it never got written. "Misha
Cyberpunk" was the character's nom de Web.

A certain amount of alienation went into "In Concert." I
moved around a couple of times when I was young, as do almost
all of us. The experience of being somewhere where we really
don't feel at home or belonging went into it.

Zinos-Amaro: The ending of the story is notable for its take
on alienation. In the course of two pages you take us from Tex
thinking that the event is "horrible" to feeling "a joy as would be
impossible to describe." This transformation to me is suggestive of
the power of a communal experience; there's almost a kind of Dio-
nysian ecstasy at work. But it's also a warning about indoctrination,
whether by communism, religion, or anything that buries the self.

Swanwick: Hopefully all that is in there. That's what I wanted
to get at. Also a sympathy for those generations of people who
gave their hearts, their souls and their loyalty to communism and
were betrayed. For a time there it looked to them like they were
building something worthwhile. When Sputnik went up, people
were hugging strangers on the street in Moscow. For the first time
they had this physical sign that they were winning, that all their
sacrifices had been worthwhile. You have to feel sympathy for
them. At the end of the story Tex achieves an understanding of
everything that's been lost, of how beautiful the promises were
that nobody was ever going to deliver on. The last line of "In Concert" is supposed to be unspeakably sad: "It could have gone on

forever." No, of course it couldn't have. I've always wondered what the Russians make of this story.

Zinos-Amaro: Have you heard from any Russian fans?

Swanwick: Not specifically about this story. But they appear to like my work there. I'm actually a much bigger name in Russia than I am here.

Zinos-Amaro: You were guest of honor at the Aelita and won the Aelita Award, the first American writer to do so.

Swanwick: I had one Russian critic, very drunk, of course, because this was in the evening, who told me he thought the two greatest American writers were me and Faulkner. I thought, "How can your perception and mine be at such variance?"

Yes, I was the first Westerner to win it. But it's because they just changed the rules of the award this year to allow that to happen.

Zinos-Amaro: Probably just so that they could give it to you!

Swanwick: There's a certain amount of that. The people running it are my friends. I think I'm popular there because of *The Iron Dragon's Daughter* mostly. Russians identified with it. It begins with this girl who's been stolen and is working in a factory, doing hard labor and being mistreated. That speaks to the Russian sense of what's been happening to them, I think, for the last few hundred years.

Zinos-Amaro: I can see that. We're going to get to "Cold Iron" soon, but first up is "Picasso Deconstructed: Eleven Still-Lifes" (*Asimov's*, May 1993). In the magazine introduction to this story you said that "mostly writing isn't fun."

Swanwick: Yes. It's hard work. And my first drafts all suck. You know, writing bad prose isn't fun, but it's a necessary first step to writing good prose.

Zinos-Amaro: But this particular story was fun.

Swanwick: It was. There was a show at the Philadelphia Museum of Art full of Picasso still-lifes. I went to see it and thought, "I may as well get a story out of this." I took a notebook and a pencil and jotted down thoughts as I looked at specific works. The best ones I worked up into little flash fictions. As happens when you work with flash fictions, when you put them together they begin to relate to each other. The eleventh one was not based on a specific painting but was a way of tying them all together and making them into one coherent story.

Zinos-Amaro: Each of those ten original flash pieces has a powerful hook and can serve as a plausible story opening. How did you decide which of these potential openings would go last?

Swanwick: It was the one that was all about Picasso and what sort of person he was; how we should judge him. Whereas the others are all things that spin off from his work. This one spins back *into* Picasso.

Zinos-Amaro: Tell me more about fragment number four.

Swanwick: That's from the Wallace Stevens poem "The Planet on the Table." In a way, I like that one the best because it doesn't come from a still-life, but from "Visit to Picasso," a film by Paul Haesaerts. You can find it on YouTube. It's a really fascinating document. They rigged up a big pane of glass. Picasso took white paint and painted a drawing on the glass. When it was done, he paused for a second to look at it and admire it, then took a sponge to clean off the paint, destroying it. He was making fauns and all these romantic images and then obliterating them. He was so full of craft. They were really good drawings, one after the other after the other. For the second part he did a painting, and it was a collage painting. You get to see clips of it. You don't see it in real time, but you see things added and subtracted. When it's finally done he looks at it and says, "C'est mal. C'est très, très mal. But now I know how to fix it." So he strips it all down and starts again and turns it into a painting he's satisfied with. I loved that and threw that in.

Zinos-Amaro: How did you land on the specific order of the eleven fragments?

Swanwick: I think I started where I started because it was short and flip. The mission from van Gogh is a joke, a change on being on a mission from God. The story begins trivial, and builds.

In the second fragment there are references to Ophir and Mu. This is one of my signature tics. I keep dropping in references to fantasy literature and the occult in my fantasy—whether it belongs there or not.

Near the end of the story, I bring in the Spartans. I have this longstanding fascination with Lycurgus, who created our Sparta. Sparta was originally known for its licentious, unruly self-indulgences. Lycurgus turned it into the Sparta that we know and admire, in a horrified way, in one generation. I've always been fascinated by the fact that you really can create an artificial society and make it work. It was done thousands of years ago. It's one of my enthusiasms.

The story is a collage. I was doing what Picasso would have done: put the pieces down and move them around until the order feels emotionally satisfying.

Zinos-Amaro: I also wanted to touch on fragment number six and the influence of the daily American comic strips. You ended that with Guernica!

Swanwick: Picasso really was fascinated by comic strips like Toonerville Trolley and Krazy Kat and supposedly collected them. If you look at the etchings, like the Vollard Suite—which we talked about in connection with "The Blind Minotaur"—you can see an influence on his line coming from things like Toonerville Trolley and the early, very wild comic strips. It *is* irreverent of me to tie that into Guernica, I have to admit.

Zinos-Amaro: We owe this story to Gardner, who enjoyed some fragments you put up online and encouraged you to turn them into a story.

Swanwick: Gardner was always trying to find ways of tricking writers to write stories which he would then buy. He was great at that! I remember that Neil Gaiman once posted online that he had this horrible experience because he'd promised Gardner a story for an anthology and he somehow couldn't write it. This was a shock for Neil, because he could always write everything. But for some reason he couldn't write this one story. Gardner said, "That's okay. Write a story for one of my other anthologies." And Neil was so grateful for this, he posted online about how wonderful Gardner was. I'm thinking, "Neil, you're a big name!"

Gardner, by the way, was never impressed by your name, he either loved your fiction or he didn't.

Zinos-Amaro: Are there other stories or novels that you remember as being distinctly fun to write, like "Picasso Deconstructed"?

Swanwick: "'Hello,' Said the Stick" comes to mind. It was a lot of fun. I'll explain why when we get to it. I think the fun ones were all the ones that came fast. They happen periodically. Nobody knows why sometimes you can write something in a flash, and sometimes it'll take you years.

Zinos-Amaro: Speaking of long gestations, we should talk about "Cold Iron" (*Asimov's*, November 1993), which is really the first five chapters of *The Iron Dragon's Daughter*. You spent a long time developing this world. You've mentioned being inspired by the ruins of an old ring fort during a trip to Ireland all the way back in 1982. When was this specific story conceived?

Swanwick: This was the novella that I did not pitch to Deborah Beale. I was driving to Pittsburgh with Marianne one day, with Sean in the back seat, and we were talking about fantasy and steam locomotives. I made a joke about the Baldwin Steam Dragon Works and Marianne laughed. About a mile later I asked her to write that down for me because I recognized that it was a story idea. By the time we got to Pittsburgh I knew I had a story there. I then accumulated tons and tons of notes. I went to all the abandoned factories I could, climbed around on old steam locomotives. I found in the Free Library of Philadelphia a booklet that contained photographs and descriptions of every building in the Baldwin Locomotive Works Eddystone plant. I Xeroxed the entire thing. It included a map. Anywhere in "Cold Iron," whenever they're traveling from one place to another, I give the actual places you have to get through. You'll get through the iron shop to get to the hammer shop, and so on. That was enormously useful to me.

I went back and looked at Dickens again, because I had a child working in a factory. I realized that when Dickens was dealing with an unhappy child, his formula was to make the child suffer over and over and over again, until the end of the novel, at which point he would pick him up, dust him off, give him an ice cream cone and say "Good boy." That's kind of the ending of "Cold Iron" and also the ending of the novel.

Zinos-Amaro: When you structured the novel, did you plan to publish the first quarter as a standalone story? Did a clean narrative break just happen to occur five chapters in?

Swanwick: By the time I started writing, I knew that it was going to be structured in gyres, Yeats's gyres, where everything comes around full circle but keeps moving upward. So it's cyclical but never returns to a place it's been before. When I was getting ready to pitch the idea to Deborah Beale, I thought about how the opening of the novel would work as a novella. I had the overall shape of the novella, from beginning to end, with her escape, and

I knew that the rest of the novel would go on from there. Jane would escape and part of the story would come to a close, and then she'd have to pick up again somewhere else. After I sold the novel, I knew the novella could be sold, and I asked the publisher if they'd have any objection if I sold it to *Asimov's*. They said it would be nice exposure. Whether it helped sell any books or not, I don't know. Not my department.

Zinos-Amaro: I wanted to touch on the humor in this piece. When Jane breaks in to the overseer's office, for example, she sees a SAFETY FIRST poster. She also notices a naked mermaid calendar. Later she thinks about how overseers must have a "benefits package" that protects them from certain wards, and so on.

Swanwick: The situation is so horrific—you have enslaved children being worked twelve hours a day, and very unhappy with their lives—that it needed little bits of humor to make it bearable, to give you something to enjoy.

Zinos-Amaro: Jane seeing Tilt ageing because of the Time Clock was a fantastic moment.

Swanwick: When I was in college, I worked summers at the Johnson-Carper Furniture Factory in Roanoke, Virginia. I worked forty-eight hours a week: four ten-hour days, and Monday, which was an eight-hour day. When they hired you, your first day was always on a Tuesday so that week they did not pay you a penny of overtime; it was very carefully constructed. Oh my God, but I hated that time clock. If you got there and put your card in one minute late, you were docked a half hour pay. The time passing more quickly in the story—that's just my science fiction and fantasy training. It's almost a pun.

Zinos-Amaro: But it also captures a deeper truth about growing up.

Swanwick: It cuts close to this feeling that we all have that we are, after all, the prime victim in this world. All the world is against us. Well, we at least have that feeling when we're adolescents. The novel and the novella are emotionally honest to that feeling.

Zinos-Amaro: You use a number system to identify the dragons, which adds industrial flavor. Was there any special significance to 7332?

Swanwick: It was originally 7334, and all of a sudden I thought that number looked familiar. I made the connection with Thomas

Disch's novel *334*. I had to change it, or else people were going to assume some linkage there that does not exist, and it would drive them mad! Other than that, the number had to be meaningless, that's why it's an even number, because I wanted to avoid primes and because odd numbers always sound cooler.

Zinos-Amaro: We were talking about fantasy and science fiction before, and I think "Cold Iron" is a wonderful example of a fantasy aesthetic infused with science fiction elements. You play with other genre conventions too.

Swanwick: There was a point when I was about halfway through *The Iron Dragon's Daughter* when Marianne said to me, "You realize that Jane is a spy." I went, "Huh?" She said, "She's totally opaque to all the people around her. Nobody knows what she's thinking or why she's acting the way she is. She is as baffling to them as they are to her." This is, I think, the key to why that book works.

I found a strong influence on this, which especially shows when Rooster is experiencing the *awen* and he's channeling semiotic garbage from our world, from M. John Harrison. I read Mike Harrison's *Viriconium* works way back in the day, as they were coming out. There was one story, "The Lamia and Lord Cromis," that really hit me strong. Lord Cromis is out questing after the ancestral beast which always kills the eldest male of his family, and when he finally finds it, this grotesque thing, it begins capering and dancing and turning into things like traffic lights. This is in the original publication. When he collected it in *Viriconium Nights* he rewrote the story entirely. When I read the original, I thought that the New Wave had finally reached fantasy. It did with that story, but nobody followed Harrison. He had to wait decades until the New Weird came along to have his influence. But it was a strong influence on me. I loved that surreal, contradictory anarchy of it. He'd taken dirt and rubbed it into the paint and he ruined that fine gloss of well-made fantasy in order to fashion something wilder and stranger. It was an enormous achievement, I think. Brilliant, brilliant work. I had been carrying that around with me for at least a decade. I kept waiting for someone to follow Harrison, and finally said, "To hell with it, I'll follow him."

Zinos-Amaro: You balance it with humor again. Rocket going through the *awen*: ". . . snatches of glossolalic nonsense floated out of him. 'The proletarians have nothing to lose but their chains,' he said. 'Lucky Strike Means Fine Tobacco.'"

Swanwick: Okay, that part was fun to write. The *awen* was always fun. Coming up with the names of the characters was fun too. Blugg, Skizzlecraw, Stilt, Smidgeon . . .

I should mention that in "The Changeling's Tale," which is coming up next, the river is also named the Awen. That was deliberate.

I'll also explain that the Baldwynn came from real life. I was visiting a distant relative with Marianne. We were sitting in the living room talking with the wife and her husband was in the room. It was almost immediately obvious that he was senile but she talked to him as if he weren't, as if he were going to give some sensible response to what she was saying. She would ask him questions and so on. He never said a word. He just glared at her with absolute hatred. It was a terrifying couple of hours that we spent there. Awful. So awful that I put it into the story and the novel. I rarely take things straight out of real life and plop then down unchanged, but this time I did. The Baldwynn ultimately became one of my best creations, I think.

There's a reference, when somebody dies, to Spiral Castle: "They've gone to Spiral Castle." That comes from Welsh, Sottish and Irish mythology. Spiral Castle is where you go when you die. If you go to Newgrange in Ireland, outside the great passage cairn there are some huge stones and they have spirals carved into them. I was tapping into something very old there.

Zinos-Amaro: Tell me about the last line of "Cold Iron": "They *soared.*"

Swanwick: That was swiped from Somtow Sucharitkul, from a story of his called "A Day In Mallworld." I'll confess, I didn't like it as much as I liked a lot of his other stuff because I'm fairly resistant to satire. When you have an enormous space mall, that's satire, there's no getting around it. But at the end of the story the young girl, a teenager or pre-adolescent, gets to leave the Mallworld on a spaceship and sees the stars for the first time. The end of the story was "It was *neat!*" with that "neat" in italics and an exclamation point. All fairness to you Somtow, I swiped your ending and I'm not giving it back.

Zinos-Amaro: You just mentioned "The Changeling's Tale"

(*Asimov's*, January 1994) a lovely, unusually autobiographical tribute to Tolkien.

Swanwick: When I was young, I ran away with the elves, like the young tavern boy abducted in the story, and I became a writer.

Zinos-Amaro: I recommend that everyone read your essay "The Changeling Returns," published in *Meditations on Middle-Earth*, edited by Karen Haber. *Interzone* called it "undoubtedly the best essay in the book" when they reviewed *Meditations*. In that piece you say, upon rereading *The Lord of the Rings*, that it's a "book sad with wisdom."

Swanwick: That was a meaningful essay for me. *The Lord of the Rings* really is sad. It's one of those books that changes as you age. Tolkien had of course not only been to World War I but lost most of his friends in the war. There was a sadness in him, but also a wisdom. It showed in little things. In one of his essays he mentioned that this old oak tree outside his office had been cut down and was mourned only by himself and a family of owls. During the "humanist-cyberpunk wars" one of the cyberpunks, I forget who, wrote something sneering at that as being sentimentality. But Tolkien was right. The loss of an oak tree is to be regretted. And he was right not to be ashamed of regretting it. I think a lot of what makes Tolkien so influential is that his heart was in the right place.

Zinos-Amaro: I've read "The Changeling's Tale" more than once, and a word that comes to mind is impressionistic. It sort of takes place in between the traditional beats of high fantasy narratives. You have giants, necromantic beasts, a dragon, and so on, but they're offstage.

Swanwick: I kind of left out all the good parts, and I left in the quiet, small bits. That's what the story asked of me. I started with the image of the bridge, a little like "Old" London Bridge and a little like the Rialto, which I'd actually been on. It was such a lovely image and I played around with that for months, doing bad drawings, stopping every time I crossed a river to lean on the railing and look out and imagine that bridge. I basically spent a lot of time creating the world, the quotidian feel of it. Then I saw that Marty Greenberg was editing an anthology of stories in honor of Tolkien called *After the King*. I emailed Marty and said, "Can I please write one?" He said, "Yes. Go to it." I tried writing it and it was one of those stories that could not be done in less than a couple of years. Eventually I knew I wasn't going to make the deadline and I wrote to him and apologized. He was very nice about it, I have to say.

When I went to write the story I wanted to do an homage but not a pastiche. I thought of "Smith of Wootton Major," which was a minor Tolkien work but had good stuff in it. That touched on a lot of that sadness, a lot of that wisdom. It also had alienation. The character keeps going off into fairyland and coming back. That brought the shape of the story to mind. Eventually I saw it as a story of somebody who's gone off with the elves and comes back. It's all being told in retrospect, so there were things that were lost and not remembered. Having those gaps, having those things lost, seemed essential. When you go off with the elves, there's a price to be paid. The price he pays is most of his memories being seared away magically. At first it looks like a failure, but it's only a failure in the way that van Gogh's life was a failure for example. He was mad, he couldn't sell paintings, and his life was in every way a failure—except for the end result. That's what I was getting at. When van Gogh went off to be a painter he made the right choice. So did my character, Will.

Zinos-Amaro: "The Changeling's Tale" strikes me as a story of dispossession along the axes of both space and time. Will is separated from his native culture, and his consciousness is up-rooted from time itself through the pipe smoking, through magic and the visions he experiences. At the end of the story he reaches a kind of acceptance. Do you feel like both of those separations were necessary for him to achieve that acceptance?

Swanwick: They were. I think in part that that ending came to me because when I was young I made the decision to be poor so that I could afford to be a writer. I met my wife Marianne in Henry R. Landis State Hospital, which is a tuberculosis asylum—you don't get much more romantic than that. I was a clerk-typist for the Bureau of Laboratories, and she was a rising young tech-nocrat, as she put it. I worked there for a number of years, and a lot of people there genially despised me, because I had very little money, and by my standards they had gobs of money. Because I married Marianne I would go back there every so often for social events. A funny thing happened around the time I turned forty. I noticed that some of the people who were still making gobs more money than I was envied me. They realized they'd made a deal with the devil. They'd gotten a job where they earned too much money to leave it, and at a certain age they realized that they were never going to run off and join the circus, but I had.

There was a memorial for Lucius Shepard at the KGB Bar in New York, and his son got up, one of many people who did, to say a few words. He said, "I lead a very ordinary life. Except that once or twice a year the circus comes to town." He was talking about the rest of us.

From the outside point of view, we really are the circus. We're the jugglers and trapeze artists and sword-swallowers. That's where the autobiographical part of "The Changeling's Tale" comes in.

Zinos-Amaro: Earlier in these conversations we talked a bit about how you think science fiction and fantasy are different. You were saying that the core of science fiction may be a belief in the ultimate knowability of the world. Your stories suggest that this backdrop lends itself well to an affirmation of identity, which may be the most knowable thing any given character can possess. The core world of fantasy, by contrast, is numinous, unknowable. This lends itself more naturally to wrestling with mortality, because death itself is unknowable.

Swanwick: Every word of that makes beautiful sense to me. At the heart of this story there's unknowability, because the elves leave what is essentially Middle Earth, and in what way they're leaving and going I don't know, except that they're headed toward the North, and something will happen and they'll disappear from the world. The world in their absence is falling into a science fiction world. There are pyroscaphs on the water and they're burning coal now, where before they were burning charcoal and wood. They've fallen into history. So in a way, as was the *Lord of the Rings*, this is about the loss of the fantastic too.

Zinos-Amaro: *The Ultimate Encyclopedia of Fantasy*, edited by David Pringle, mentioned "The Changeling's Tale" in its entry on you and included this phrase that stayed with me: "Swanwick's deep suspicion of the conventional consolations of popular fantasy . . ." I feel that with "The Changeling's Tale" you're trying to grasp *what* gave rise to fantasy on a fundamental level.

Swanwick: That's absolutely true. I came into writing via fantasy, as I've mentioned before, reading all the great fantasies, and there were not many not-great fantasies available at all. Those grappled with things that matter: life, death, beauty, transience. That seemed to me central to the enterprise. The exciting swordfights and dragon flights and encounters with giants—I left all of that out. I left out all the parts that C. S. Lewis would have left in! That's probably what that phrase in Pringle's book is referring to.

Zinos-Amaro: We should talk about some of the character names in this story: Krodasparasa, Tirathika (Will's adoptive name), Ratanavivicta, Cakaravartin, and so on. From what I can tell, these stem from Sanskrit origins and Hindu and Buddhist influences.

Swanwick: They came out of a glossary at the back of one of my books on Eastern religions. I took words like "great wheel turner" and "king" and put them together. Tolkien would have probably seen that I was getting the deep construction wrong, but I'd like to think that he would have appreciated me trying at least. I contrasted them with the human names like Becky, Dolly, Karl, and Eleanor. With Eleanor, by the way, I was remembering specifically Sam's daughter Elanor, who is named after the flower. Names mattered a great deal to Tolkien, so in an homage to him I thought it important that I get the names right, and that the names be grounded in their cultures.

I was careful not to reveal the gender of the child who's being addressed in this story. I didn't want a girl reading it to bounce off the story, or vice versa. This work was necessary not for the effect that it gives, as most fiction does, but for the effect that it doesn't give.

Also, I don't know if you noticed, but the humans in "The Changeling's Tale" are all dark-skinned. They're all brown or black. I did this in part because fantasy was and still is, though to a lesser degree, way too white. Everybody in fantasy was white, because they were at that time based on Medieval legends and such. I decided that either the humans or the elves should be dark-skinned. I went back and forth on it because when you look at it just in terms of race, no matter which way you go it sounds racist. If the elves are white-skinned, then their superior, more cerebral culture becomes identified with being white. If you do it the other way around, if the elves are black and the humans are white, then human beings are white and otherness becomes the black. I finally just went with what would make the better fantasy illustration. The elves with their white masks and icy affect would have made a good book cover, so I went that way. At least I gave it some thought.

Zinos-Amaro: Does Tolkien's deep knowledge of and affinity for philology resonate with you?

Swanwick: I loved it. At the same time, I myself would have been a really terrible philologist. For one thing I have no ear. I took a class in linguistics in college, probably in '71 or '72, and the only way that I managed to pass it was that I got a friend who had a good ear to do a transcription of something I had to analyze. It wasn't cheating, because we were being taught the linguistics. But afterwards I realized I had misread one of her symbols so that my analysis was completely wrong! It was one of those moments where you realize that there's an area that will be closed to you. But I can look at it from a distance with admiration. Like any other fantasy writer and most science fiction writers, I'm in love with old words and old dictionaries. *Brewer's Dictionary of Phrase & Fable*, that kind of thing. You can spend an afternoon wandering around in there.

Zinos-Amaro: "The Changeling's Tale" is steeped in melancholy and the acceptance of everything being finite and passing. I love how you embed the theme in your invented words: am'rta skandayaksa (the deathless elf-group), margakasaya (the path to extinction), parikasaya (final extinction).

Swanwick: These words were inspired by the same glossary I mentioned. Eastern religion deals with these things, and quite well.

It is funny that I find so much about death in my work, because I came to terms with it when I was like three. Mortality doesn't bother me much. It bothers me that I have less working time ahead of me with every year. But I'm not obsessed with death. Intellectually I acknowledge it as important, but emotionally it does not mean a lot to me. When I was three I visited my grandfather on his death bed, and I played my little ukulele for him. I can still see him in my mind, this beautiful old man, his hair as white as dandelion fluff, the sun setting it ablaze. I went home, and after my grandfather died I went to the wake, and afterwards my mother tells me I was walking around going, "What's going to become of me? Who's going to take care of me when you die?" It took her a while to find out that I'd made the connection between hair turning white and people dying. Her hair was turning grey, so I figured she was going to die soon. This gave her, I think, a welcome reason to dye her hair. She dyed it red, which suited her well. That cleared up my problem, and I haven't been bothered by death since!

Zinos-Amaro: In one of Will's early recollections in "The Changeling's Tale" he's thinking about a conversation with Dolly and Kate, and you use this interesting effect in the scene where he remembers their words just *before* they utter them.

Swanwick: That probably came from smoking lots of kief when I was young. I was trying hard to capture the effect of recreational drugs there. When I was young, I wasn't smoking to get high, I was smoking to explore. I really was. It sounds silly right now. But I wanted to explore and discover. I wanted a reminder in the story, periodically, that this was all being told through what might or might not be an elf drug hallucination. The drug undoes time-binding, so as he's smoking it and he's telling his tale, that's the effect that comes in.

Zinos-Amaro: You missed the deadline to submit to *After the King*, but after it was published did you go back to see what your peers had done with Tolkien?

Swanwick: No, I did not. I think it was out of guilt! I'm going to have to buy a copy. People had and still have such a strong emotional connection with him. He turned me into a writer, and I've always been grateful for that.

Zinos-Amaro: "Cold Iron" is structured like the start of a bildungsroman, while "The Changeling's Tale" is a kind of deconstructed, liminal high fantasy, but both of them, through their changeling characters, take us on journeys that expand and reimagine genre.

Swanwick: For both of these stories, I was working within the confines of fantasy. I'm not a rebel. I love this stuff. I'm not trying to destroy it. But when you spend literally years working on something and thinking about it you inevitably come up with something that's not going to be in the given structure. You find that to tell the truth you have to change how it's told.

Zinos-Amaro: In your essay "The Changeling Returns," you say the following about "The Changeling's Tale": "It was an honest story, I hope." I'd like to go deeper on what you mean by honesty in fiction.

Swanwick: Well, to quote Neil Gaiman again . . . He was being asked about *Neverwhere*, and he said he originally was approached about the possibility of writing a series about magical people in London disguised as the homeless. He said he couldn't have written that: he didn't want some teenager to run off with the homeless because he'd said that it would be cool. I feel that the ability to write is a set of tools, specifically a set of burglar tools, and you're not supposed to use them for trivial purposes. You're not supposed to use them to fix a leaking faucet or a squeak in the door. You're supposed to use them to break into the human heart and ransack its secrets. When you're a fiction writer, you've been given license to lie. You have to use this in the service of the truth. All the lies you tell have to add up to a larger truth. You can provide happy endings that are not going to happen to people, and readers will be perfectly delighted with them, but they're lies, and lies are not a healthy part of your diet. You can indulge a little bit in lying fiction like you can indulge a little bit in junk food. You can't make it central to what you're putting into yourself. For the writer, the responsibility is to be telling the truth about what the world is like and about what life is like and what your experience of these things is like and how you should best live. When you do that, when your refuse to take the shortcut to something that'll just be popular and empty, then you're telling an honest story.

Zinos-Amaro: Are there any stories you've written that you felt weren't honest at the time, but in hindsight encode some truths that you think are worthwhile? Or the opposite scenario? More generally, do you think that your perception of honesty in fiction changes with time?

Swanwick: All my published stories felt honest at the time. "U F O" did not turn out to be an honest story, but I was trying. How thinking of a work changes over time is a risk we all take. Especially since society changes. Right now I'm doing my best to understand all the changes in gender fluidity, in gender queering, and so on, not so that I can use it, but so that I don't put in something incredibly stupid in one of my stories. Kate Wilhelm is a very good writer. She wrote a story early in her career about a young man who washes out of the space academy and he gets a job on a space freighter. The big issue for him is that everybody has to use the services of the ship's whore. He refuses to because he's such a prig, and they explain to him why it's necessary. At the time, Wilhelm must have felt that this was bold and daring, but oh dear is it embarrassing to read today. We're all in danger from having the ground shift from under our feet. I think of a genre novel whose name I will not give out, written in the 70s, which had a great deal of sex, as so many novels written in the 70s had. Some of the speculation in it is very embarrassing today, and yet that was not at all visible at the time. I remember reading it and being impressed by the creativity of invention. You just write as well as you can, and you take your chances. Posterity is looking to save the stuff that still gives pleasure.

Zinos-Amaro: Speaking of posterity, we jump to an interesting future with "The Mask" (*Asimov's*, April 1994). Let's start by clarifying how many versions exactly there are of this story.

Swanwick: This one was fun too. The idea came from a trip to Italy with Marianne. One of the places we went to was Venice, and we told Gardner we were going to see Rome and Venice. Gardner, who was always looking for ways to trick writers into writing stories for him, pointed out that Stan Robinson had just written a very good story called "Venice Drowned," which Gardner knew that I admired. He said, "You should take notes when you're in Venice and write a story called 'Venice Rising.'" I thought that was a good idea, so when we were in Venice I *was* taking notes and imagining this future society in Venice. I noticed that all over Venice there used to be fountains, but they were capped to keep them from spreading cholera. I imagined a future where the fountains flowed again. Where essentially the left has won, capitalism is in retreat, and Venice is the last stronghold of capitalism. Everywhere else has got some vaguely defined eco-utopian socialist whatever. I constructed quite an elaborate structure for this society, what they were doing, and what they thought they were doing. Several times after I came back over the next couple of years I took swipes at writing that story, and I could never get very far into it. Eventually, I realized I was never going to write it.

Some time later I was reading a RE/Search book on J. G. Ballard, a big thing with interviews and articles and photographs of him. I came across this photograph of three potato-shaped white men sitting in chairs wearing suits. In front of them there was a young woman wearing a bikini bottom and a fishnet. The caption said, "Potato-shaped white man #1, potato-shaped white man #2, J. G. Ballard, and Miss Tempest Blaze, who in the early 60s put on a series of performances where she quoted from J. G. Ballard and select medical texts while removing her clothing." I felt like such a stick-in-the-mud. All I ever did was write stories and sell them to *Asimov's*. So I took a story idea I'd had for a novella and I made a two-hundred-and-fifty-seven word short short out of it, set in Venice 100, maybe 200, years from now. Then I took surgical gauze and made a life-mask out of Marianne's face. When that dried I painted it white, and then I cut the story into little strips and pasted it across the mask in a kind of demi-mask.

Marianne punched two holes in the back, threaded a red silk cord through them, and hung it on the wall. I felt better then. Of course, because I was, after all, a degraded hack, I did go on to expand it as much as I could and sold it to *Asimov's*. But the original impulse was good.

So the story exists in three forms. There's the original version on the mask. There's the expanded version that Gardner published, which was reprinted in *Tales of Old Earth*. And then for my collection *Cigar-Box Faust and Other Miniatures* I reconstructed the original story but I changed a few words, so that the mask would remain unique.

Zinos-Amaro: Do you have a preference between them? Do you think one works better than the other?

Swanwick: As a story, I think the longer one works better. As an event, the mask itself works best. It's just a magical thing to have done.

Zinos-Amaro: This story has a strong *commedia dell'arte* aesthetic.

Swanwick: A lot of that came from just having been to Venice. What an extraordinary experience it is to be in some place that is not like any other place you've ever been. When we first arrived there, we went to our pension, and I just sat in the open window on the third floor. A block away was the Grand Canal, and German tourists were surging along it with their boom-boxes. Nevertheless, it all felt silent. You could hear the sparrows hopping on the tile roof next door. Wandering through the city I had a sense that things didn't change. My big observation was how quiet Venice was because there was no wheeled motor traffic. When I got back home the next week I picked up a copy of John Evelyn's diaries. He was Samuel Pepys' coeval, so it's the second most famous diary of his time. He had been on a grand tour and had traveled to Venice, so I immediately went to that section to see what his reactions had been. His first observation is how quiet it was because there were no wheeled carriages. I saw then how little things had changed in this astonishing place in three hundred some years. I was trying to convey a sense of Venice not having changed a lot, still being run by ruthless people. I added the science fiction bits, and the element that the capitalists had decided that they had to be moral to survive, which is far more science fiction.

Zinos-Amaro: You pack a lot of world-building into this story, particularly in the flash version. Every line adds to the vision. It almost reminds me of one of those "condensed novels" by Ballard.

Swanwick: I put a lot of stuff into my stories because I write so slowly. When you write slowly there's time to add Easter Eggs. I believe that they work even if the reader doesn't notice them—they get a sense that *something* is going on. That's one of the things I'm trying for in most of my work: a sense of richness. In "The Mask" I was boiling a lot of ideation down into a page. It was strangely fun.

I loved Ballard's condensed novels. They were great. Quite possibly an influence on this, I have to say, in the short version. They were an inspiration. They were just so good, so fast. They also showed how much you can lean on the reader, how much you can trust the reader to do a lot of the work for you.

Zinos-Amaro: Can you say a little more about masks?

Swanwick: There are a lot of masks in my stories. If you come to my house you'll find lots of masks and lots of animal skulls mixed in with the art. Marianne the other day stopped, looked around, and said, "How did I end up in a wizard's den?"

CHAPTER FOUR
1995-1999

Alvaro Zinos-Amaro: We kick off the mid-90s with an unusually grim group of stories. The first one of these is "Walking Out" (*Asimov's*, February 1995).

Michael Swanwick: This was originally going to be a collaboration with Terry Bisson. I approached him and said, "We ought to do something together." He said, "Okay." He had some notes, this rudimentary idea for a story in which people were griping and grousing about how awful living in the city was, while all around them was what Terry called "a fucking utopia." I thought there was potential to that, so he gave me his notes and I started to work on it. I told Gardner Dozois that I was collaborating on a story with Terry. He said, "No you're not." And, as always, Gardner was right.

Zinos-Amaro: You ended up calling the protagonist Terry Bissel. How did Gardner know that the collaboration wouldn't work?

Swanwick: He just knew Terry well enough as a writer to know that Terry wasn't going to be able to collaborate with anybody. I wrote up the first part of the story and sent it to Terry with notes. He wrote back very apologetically saying that he couldn't do it, and that I could take the idea and do whatever I wanted with it. So I did, because by then I thought that there was a good story to be had here. It's based on the poem "She Doesn't Know He Thinks He's God" by Gregory Corso. I first read that poem when I was a teenager and loved it. It stayed with me. It gave me this rather dark story.

Zinos-Amaro: Ah, so the plot element of Kris being left with the baby is a direct import from the poem. The theme of denial is also a key aspect not only of this tale but the next two as well,

"North of Diddy-Wah-Diddy" and "Radio Waves." You seemed to be working in a very specific groove here. There's a line in "Walking Out" that sort of captures it: "We're none of us totally sane, you know."

Swanwick: Yeah, yeah. I started this story not really knowing where it was going to end. I knew that Terry was mad and that he couldn't go to New England because it didn't exist anymore. But I did not know what the story was about. This was another one of these that took rather a while to write. The character speaks truth to the people that he meets. I still don't know how I feel about the truths that he's telling. "You want to stop the next war? Burn the family albums"—he presents ethnicity as a bad thing. Being American Irish, I don't accept this. But this is one of those stories that I wrote because I really didn't know how I felt.

Zinos-Amaro: Going through the story a second time, I noticed the delicious irony of Terry calling out the watch salesman for denial.

Swanwick: Right from the beginning, everybody is a hypocrite!

Zinos-Amaro: Just as Terry himself is looking backward in the story, even if unconsciously, the style and narrative structure of "Walking Out" are themselves reminiscent of older, socially-minded science fiction from the 50s and 60s, relying on a series of scenes that draw on sociological extrapolation succinctly and build towards a surprise ending. Was that deliberate?

Swanwick: It's an old-fashioned type of science fiction. You have to be aware of what you're hiding when you start out, so you can mislead the reader. I was drawing from 50s social-commentary kind of fiction. I'm not sure if it was deliberate. I was not unconscious of it, but I wasn't also doing a pastiche. All these examples are there to draw upon.

Zinos-Amaro: This strikes me as a wonderful Philip K. Dick story not written by Dick.

Swanwick: It's a little like Philip K. Dick. I think it's more like Fred Pohl or even to a certain degree Robert Sheckley. There was that whole group of them that was doing the "comic inferno." "Walking Out" is a comic-inferno type of story. At the end the city is in pretty precarious shape, but then again, people have always been in pretty precarious shape. The people in the story are not necessarily in worse shape than we are.

Zinos-Amaro: The mention of an inferno takes us nicely to "North of Diddy-Wah-Diddy" (*Killing Me Softly: Erotic Tales of Unearthly Love*, edited by Gardner Dozois). This one's meaty.

Swanwick: This story started out because I picked up a magazine and among the incidental things it had was a reprint of Zora Neale Hurston's glossary of Harlem slang. Among the wonderful things it included was a line about Diddy-Wah-Diddy being several stops north of Hell. West Hell is where the people in Hell go for a high time on a Saturday night. I decided I wanted to do a train-to-Hell story. I carried this around with me for years, I'm not sure how long. It took me a long time to find the story. Anytime I went to New York on the train to visit editors I would stare out the window imagining giant centaurs out there struggling through the marshes, along with demons and such. After I finally wrote the story, the next time I went to New York it was a disappointing ride, because all of that magical spell of imagination was gone.

At the beginning I spent a fair amount of time trying to figure out what platform from Grand Central Station they would have left from. I was doing research, and there were no platforms that were right. Then I realized, it's a fantasy, I can add a platform at the tunnel that goes south! I was overthinking it.

I don't know at what point in the story I realized that most or all of the characters were black. Some of them had to be. I spent six years in Virginia and there was this strangeness of Southern culture all around me. There's a lot to like about it, because it's a very verbal culture. There's a lot to be terrified about it, because it's a very violent culture too. I wanted to use some of that, and this was my opportunity.

Zinos-Amaro: "North of Diddy-Wah-Diddy" surprised me in the context of the original anthology in which it appeared. It's not something I would have expected in this book.

Swanwick: It was a strange story to be picked up for this anthology. There were a lot of romance tropes in there that don't play out the way they're supposed to. Malcolm is gay and this desperado woman who comes in and hijacks the whole thing is obviously a lesbian, so they're not going to connect physically at all, but they do connect emotionally.

Zinos-Amaro: How do you feel now about your handling of Malcolm's sexuality? Our world is different from that of 1995.

Swanwick: It is, but I was thinking back to, oh, 1972 and even before that. I remember, at a diner my friends and I used to meet in, learning that there was a particular vacant lot in Williamsburg, Virginia where gay men went to hook up. Someplace obscure. Occasionally the police would go there, grab a couple of them and beat the crap out of them. It seemed so awful; even then, it was such a throwback world.

I'm happy with the gay aspect of the story because I'm happy with Malcolm. Malcolm is such a sweet character. For Malcolm, I have to go back a step. When I started writing this I wanted to write a Pullman porter, because if you read the history of the Pullman porters, you'll see they were really quite a remarkable crew of men. They were conscious of the fact that they were representing their "race," and served as an interface between the black and white worlds. They were all of them extraordinarily polite and extraordinarily helpful. Just admirable people. I wanted to write about one of these guys that was perfectly admirable in the way that apparently they were. So I created Malcolm, and he's making things as nice for people as he can. It's only when this woman tries to seduce him that I realized he was gay. It caught me by surprise, and it gave me a more interesting handle on him. Through the whole thing I was discovering the character. He turned out to be even kinder, even sweeter than I would have thought. He was a pleasant character to associate with. I really enjoyed writing about him.

Zinos-Amaro: As sweet as he is, though, at the end of "North of Diddy-Wah-Diddy" Malcolm is very clear about wanting to be excluded from the judgment or reprisal coming to everyone else. This is one instance of not being self-sacrificing. Of course, it doesn't work out the way we expect.

Swanwick: Well, he's afraid of going to Hell, and he's got good reason to be afraid. He has been left on the outside of the plot, because, I suspect, the others thought that he was a company man. His positions are all reasonable, it's just that the whole system is corrupt up and down. I really like the fact that the Stonewall Riots changed everything. After Stonewall, it was no longer a mortal sin to be gay. But then, the universe is unjust, so he doesn't get grandfathered into Heaven as he deserves to be!

Zinos-Amaro: That's a great detail. I have to say, for me the story's most remarkable element is the voice.

Swanwick: Malcolm had a good voice. So much of it was that he was a kind man who wanted nothing but good for other people. He was one of those characters that just falls into your lap, as it were, and they don't come along very often. He just popped up.

Zinos-Amaro: As much as I enjoyed Malcolm (and I'll note the silly coincidence that years later the lead of the series *Firefly* would also be named Malcolm Reynolds), the character that really caught my attention was Sugar.

Swanwick: He comes close to being a stereotype and I think not. He's a large, strong, inherently violent man, who nevertheless maintains control of himself, and loves his mother. That's an admirable person you're not supposed to admire.

Zinos-Amaro: Exactly. That made him more interesting.

Swanwick: With the character of Jackie, I was going back to Tolkien in a way, the idea of using a romantic trope while denying the possibility. "She led, I followed" was a deliberate gender role reversal. Then this mad woman has Malcolm dancing on top of the train; he gets into it and she says, "Okay, no more crawling." In romance fiction you used to see the swashbuckler that shows up in the woman's life and whisks her away and changes her sense of values. I did that here, except reversed. I found the idea that Malcolm and Jackie were not going to have sex strangely charming. It leaves romantic elements in place while confounding expectations. Jackie was not as real a character as the others were. She was more of a device.

Zinos-Amaro: Speaking of devices, in terms of the story structure, when did you figure out the big trial climax?

Swanwick: Oh, probably about five minutes before I started writing it. I wanted to have some of the great cosmic angels and demons there because that's half the pleasure of writing fantasy, writing about extraordinary, impossible things. I wanted to show that. You don't often have the chance to write something like that.

Zinos-Amaro: I can sense reading those scenes that you were enjoying flexing that imaginative muscle. We should talk about the story's influences. It's clearly in conversation with Robert Bloch's "That Hell-Bound Train."

Swanwick: The other story that "North of Diddy-Wah-Diddy" draws from is Fritz Leiber's "Gonna Roll the Bones."

Zinos-Amaro: I've not read it.

Swanwick: You would love that story. It is this American folktale fantasy. So short, so concise, so beautifully written. It's like a folktale, except a perfectly original one. At the center of the Leiber story, the hero, Joe Slattermill, is rolling craps with the devil. I wanted to write something that had the same folkloric, glossy feel to it. It's not an imitation of Fritz Leiber, but an attempt to live up to his example. There's also a streak of that wonderful American vulgarity in it, which I really wanted included in my story.

Zinos-Amaro: This story and "The Dead" are both more adult than the ones we've looked at so far.

Swanwick: It was needed. A train to hell doesn't carry good people. All the sins we really get to know anything about are based on sex. That's one set of sins we're not entirely sure that God got right!

Zinos-Amaro: We were talking about the theme of denial connecting this story with the previous one and the next. You have a beautiful line in "North of Diddy-Wah-Diddy": "People can fool themselves into believing anything."

Swanwick: Absolutely true.

Zinos-Amaro: You included this story in *The Best of Michael Swanwick*, so you obviously like it. But this was the one story in *Geography of Unknown Lands* that John Clute didn't particularly care for when he reviewed the book, saying "too much story cakewalking on ice much too thin for more than brief shenanigans."

Swanwick: I disagree. That was his take. He's a Canadian living in Britain, and as I say this was based on Southern folklore, so it wasn't anything that he'd be necessarily sympathetic to.

Zinos-Amaro: Readers were very sympathetic to "Radio Waves" (*Omni*, Winter 1995), a disturbing piece of work. The initial image is truly striking, and I think it's the best opening paragraph so far: "I was walking the telephone wires upside down, the sky underfoot cold and flat with a few hard bright stars sparsely scattered about it, when I thought how it would take only an instant's weakness to step off to the side and fall up forever into the night. A kind of wildness entered me then and I began to run."

Swanwick: This story is intensely personal. It began when I went to the corner to get a carton of milk. I was just walking along and looking up at the power lines overhead, and I imagined what it would be like to walk upside down on them. That was such a good, strong image that I played with that all the way to the corner and back. When I returned I wrote down the first paragraph. It's strong and unexpected. I wrote two or three paragraphs and stopped, for days or weeks, I'm not sure which. I could not find any way forward from that. So I sent the protagonist running.

Zinos-Amaro: You unleash the Corpsegrinder pretty quickly.

Swanwick: I threw in a monster to kick-start the story. I named it Corpsegrinder because it sounded monster-ish, and I threw in Charlie's Widow, Elizabeth, because I needed a second character, someone for Daniel to talk to and react against and so on. At that point I had no idea why there was a Corpsegrinder; I had no idea who the widow was; and who Charlie was. I kept on-and-off writing this, but it took a very long time to get it.

About three quarters of the way through, I had a breakthrough. I was at a train station, waiting for a cab, and a couple were arguing bitterly. The guy kept insisting that they had to go home, and talk about matters there, and the woman was saying, "No, we're going to settle it right here and now." It was intensely embarrassing. I turned my back on them and edged a little bit closer because I knew this was good material. And it was. It was strong enough that I could get away with including it twice.

"Radio Waves" takes place in my Philadelphia neighborhood, Roxborough. You can see the Seven Sisters from my front door. When Daniel goes running down the hill, he's running down Leverington Avenue, which I'm on. At that time there was an old abandoned movie theater called the Roxy at the corner. It was in the shape that I described it as being in. Things like the Hubcap Heaven, the car junkyard, a couple of diners and so on—they're all in my neighborhood. So there's a very strong sense of place here.

At one point, Daniel goes climbing down through a house. The inhabitants are described, including the poor bastard on the couch in front of the television set. That is my house, and I believe that is the only time I've actually put myself into one of my stories. I wanted to not be doing a bohemian sneer at people leading middle-class lives.

Zinos-Amaro: The plot of this story in a way made me think of Richard Matheson's *What Dreams May Come*. You have characters who have a pre-existing relationship, based on their physical lives, connecting in an afterlife, and they have to figure out that relationship on their journey. Had you read the novel?

Swanwick: I like Richard Matheson's stuff. I read a lot of it, but not that one. I think in some ways that this story is more like Theodore Sturgeon. He's done a couple of posthumous stories too. I knew pretty much immediately that this would be a story about dead people. The bit of cleverness was that gravity reverses itself and you fall off the planet, unless you're one of the few that manages to hang on.

Zinos-Amaro: The story is clearly supernatural, but I love how you give it this science fictional patina with the idea of the cosmic microwave background radiation. "Look hard, and the sky is full of the Dead" is a superb line.

Swanwick: I was so happy with that line. That line is about as deep into mystery as I've ever been able to get. I've always had a mystic streak, which of course is due to my religious upbringing. When I was seven, very often when I was going to sleep I would try to imagine infinity. I knew intellectually that I could not actually imagine infinity because it was explained to me, but I tried anyway just to see how close I could get.

I did the science-fiction flavored world-building very deliberately. I tried to make it all as logical as I could, given the premises. Every time that something new came along in this story, like when he remembers being in Times Square, came after months of waiting to have an idea that I could use to move the plot forward by another page or so, hopefully towards some understanding of what was going on. Times Square came from the observation that G. K. Chesterton made—Jim Morrow told this to me—about it: "How beautiful it would be for someone who could not read."

Zinos-Amaro: At one point in "Radio Waves" Daniel remembers that his dad used to navigate while driving by using the radio, turning it on and figuring out what city he was close to. Was that based on something you experienced?

Swanwick: That was based on the story my father told me about what it was like driving between cities when he was young. I always thought that was quite wonderful, and I finally got to use it. I'd say that about half of Daniel's memories are based on real things and half of them are made up. That was one of the real ones.

Zinos-Amaro: How did you decide on the idea that when two of these posthumous entities touch, memories are automatically transmitted between them?

Swanwick: That I simply made up because it was a convenient way to convey information, to have revelations, without slowing down the story. It's a story that needed to be in constant motion. They both needed to be learning more as they progress, until they get to the end and the reader understands what's going on. They have permission to die then and they can go away.

Zinos-Amaro: Daniel's arc reminded me a little bit of Will's in "The Changeling's Tale." You have two characters whose memories are being stripped away, and both of them have to get to a place of acceptance.

Swanwick: This was a very death-affirming story. As I look back, I can see that the loss of memories is a relatively new theme for me at this point in my career, and one that will pop up more and more. Especially as I start to grow old now. Back then, I was definitely anticipating. I was not having any trouble with memories.

Zinos-Amaro: You once said that ghost stories are hard to do without sentiment. In "Radio Waves" are we dealing with sentiment, nostalgia, or both?

Swanwick: We're dealing with people who refuse to admit that it's over. People who are not accepting the truth. Daniel, when he was alive, was not accepting that this affair he had was over. Charlie's Widow is not accepting that her husband is dead and gone. They both have to accept the facts, no matter how cold, no matter how unpleasant. At the end Daniel has to accept the fact that he can't redeem himself. It's too late. He was a bad man, he died, and there are no more second chances. The Seven Sisters are in there consciously as a Greek chorus. Their commenting on the action, usually sardonically. At the end, when they say, "Oh what a pity, just when he had achieved self-awareness" they go on to describe the kind of story that at this point the reader expects this to turn out to be. That was the story I didn't want to write. I'd written such a strange and, I hope, original story that I needed to have an ending that wasn't just what the reader had been taught to expect. I used the Seven Sisters to blunt any disappointment the reader might have at not getting that.

It does have a good ending. I know that because I had a reading of "Radio Waves" in San Francisco, I think, or it might have been Portland. You can feel when the audience locks in to the story. They locked in halfway down the first page, earlier than ever before. As I went along the story I began slowing it down, a little bit more, and a little bit more, and a little bit more. I was pausing between paragraphs, then between sentences, and by the time I got to the very end I was just dropping each word into this well of upturned faces, one at a time. That was really satisfying. When I got to the end I said, "I'm leaving . . . *now.*" And I took a step backwards away from the podium. Reading is a skill unrelated to writing, but occasionally you luck out and it works out.

Zinos-Amaro: Do you read your work out loud as part of your revision process?

Swanwick: I'm going to break this down into two parts. Writing my first draft is very different from what most people mean by drafts, because they usually mean "get to the end, then start from the beginning a second time." What I do is write as far as I can. Then when I stop I go back to the beginning. Then I write as far as I can again. That will move it on a paragraph or two. Then I go back to the beginning. At some point the first page is done—that's final draft. Then the next draft starts from page two. I only read parts out loud if I'm having a real problem with them, except when I've done what I hope is the final draft. Then I'll read the whole thing out loud, because any mistakes that you've made just pop out at you, especially if you've made a typo or grammatical error. For some reason the eye can go right over those things a dozen times, but if you say them out loud they're blatantly obvious.

Zinos-Amaro: "Radio Waves" won the World Fantasy Award for Best Novella in 1996. By now, you've won major awards and you've been nominated many, many times. I'm curious, were you reading your fellow nominees in your particular category?

Swanwick: That pleased and surprised me. I think my most popular stuff has always been stuff where I go, "This is awfully weird."

At that point I would have probably read all the other nominees already in the course of normal reading. I've slowed down in the last decade or so. I find it harder to keep up. In short fiction and novellas, I used to read pretty much everything of any substance in a given year. So I would have read the "competition."

Zinos-Amaro: The title of your next story, "The Dead" (*Starlight 1*, ed. Patrick Nielsen Hayden, 1996), seems like a clear reference to James Joyce.

Swanwick: When I had finished this story, I got a call from James Turner. I told him I'd just written a zombie story. He said, "Yeah, yeah, yeah, now let me get to the reason I called." I said, "It's a really good zombie story. Don't you want to know what it's called, Jim?" He says, "All right! What's your zombie story called?" I said, "'The Dead.'" Silence. Then he said, "You can't give a zombie story the title of the most famous short story ever written!" I said, "But it's a really *good* zombie story, Jim!"

So yeah, it was very cheeky to use that. Clearly, in a one-to-one competition, Joyce is going to win there.

Zinos-Amaro: Besides the cheekiness, some thematic and aesthetic choices overlap. In Joyce's story Gabriel Conroy's worldview is upended, and his attempts to control himself and his life fail. The same is true for Donald in your story. Both stories end in unease and irresolution.

Swanwick: I wasn't working from a Joyce template, but I have read that story several times with undiminished admiration and an analytical eye. At this point, if I claimed to have been influenced by it, I might well be bragging. I came up with the title "The Dead" relatively early on in the process. Originally it was called "Gravitas," because it was a story that I thought had to take itself deadly seriously in order to work.

Zinos-Amaro: Pun intended.

Swanwick: There's little bits of humor in it, but on the whole it's grimly serious. I was again inspired to write this by an art exhibit. I cannot tell you the name of the artist. A couple of decades ago I tried to look up who it was and couldn't find him. But it was a painter who did neo-realist paintings, and he was a hard lefty, so they were all satires of capitalism. You have Gilded Age barons in a coach, you have bombings of Wall Street and such, done up in a very moody, romantic way, and there was one painting of a young servitor in a red jacket with brass buttons and a dead, grey face, holding up a couple of strangled pheasants for the diner's approval. I thought, "That's wonderful. He's obviously got a boy zombie here. I'm going to write something starting from that." I started with that opening image and made it kind of contrarian. At the time, everybody was writing zombie stories in which they were the monsters. This story goes back to the original zombies, who were not monsters but victims. I could not name any of them, but there have been a lot of stories about zombies in the decades before this one where they were basically commodified corpses used as slave labor.

Zinos-Amaro: Kevin J. Anderson's debut novel, *Resurrection Inc.*, published in 1988, works this premise. Had you read it?

Swanwick: I may or may not have read it. But I was very familiar with that trope.

Zinos-Amaro: A very different work I wanted to ask about as possible precursor is Robert Silverberg's novella "Born with the Dead" (1974).

Swanwick: He was on fire back then, wasn't he? Doing great stuff again and again. Yes, I'll take him as an influence!

Zinos-Amaro: Your story "The Dead" has a beautifully dark connection between the literal dehumanization of bodies and the spiritual dehumanization of relationships, which have become purely transactional by the end of the story.

Swanwick: All deliberate. I made these people as awful as possible, partly because, well, this was a hard left communist story. This was about the triumph of capital and the death of labor. I read Karl Marx way back when. It's always horrified me. I felt that Marx was writing non-fiction horror, with his theoretics that capitalism always needs to have a moving frontier, and therefore it will keep getting worse and worse and worse. I would feel much better if somebody had disproved this. But apparently nobody has yet, or if they have, nobody's told me about it. I went with a Marxist reading. It's a warning, obviously. The protagonist is such a horrible person. I gave him an ending that even a person this horrible doesn't deserve. It's possible even to have a little bit of sympathy for him. Everything he says is a projection on Courtney of what he wants. She's not a good person, clearly, and she's in the service of a worse boss, but she's not the person he claims she is. He isn't really interested in *who* she is: he's just interested in manipulating her.

This is kind of my version of *American Psycho*, but without the physical gore. I did not read that novel. I went to the library, opened the book three quarters of the way through, read a page—and it took me a week to scrub that out of my mind. It was just disgust porn, really. So I didn't want to have that kind of physical stuff in "The Dead." The horror is not really what happens to Donald, either. The horror is what's happening to all of these people that he wouldn't nod to on the street. At the end I brought in the zombie prostitute because even that is taken away as labor. Bit by bit, everything gets taken away from the common people.

Zinos-Amaro: This is your most upbeat story so far Michael! For me the bleakness of the story is best captured by the following three words used to describe the zombie labor force: "Postanthropic biological resources."

Swanwick: Not only do they refer to them that way, but at the same time they're complaining how the poor are on their back. I've met people who felt this. And they were wrong. It wasn't the poor who were on their backs, they were on the backs of the poor. I'm not a Communist. I've never had the strength of character to be one. But the argument is strong here.

Zinos-Amaro: Besides being about denial, "North of Diddy-Wah-Diddy," "Radio Waves" and "The Dead" all explore life after death, and the power—and limitations—of love.

Swanwick: At one point I was working on these three stories at the same time and suddenly realized that in all three, the protagonist was dead before the story began. It was a spooky moment for me. I can remember thinking that it seemed particularly odd because I was feeling pretty happy in those days. But the hind brain throws out material for which there is no ready explanation.

Zinos-Amaro: Your creativity knows no bounds, in any case, as evidenced by the prolifically inventive "Abecedary of the Imagination" (*Disclave 1996 Program Book*).

Swanwick: I was Guest of Honor at that Disclave. They asked me if I could contribute something to the program book, maybe the reprint of a story that I thought was good but hadn't been reprinted. I was in the unusual position that everything of mine that was particularly good had been appreciated to hell and back. I didn't have unreprinted stories that were marvelous. I had a couple of unreprinted stories that were kind of lame. I did not want to put something lame in. But I had figured out by this time that I could do short shorts. So I put together an abecedary, in the tradition of Harlan Ellison and others. People expect so little from the form that you can do a lot with it. In "U is for Unicorn" I basically asked Marianne to come up with a recipe for a haunch of unicorn. It's not actually a story.

Zinos-Amaro: "Best served with sliced elf." It wouldn't make sense to go through all of these short shorts, but let me pick out a few I really enjoyed: "I is for Invaders," which has robot cats; "Q is for Queen," in which corporations tap the past in search of good leaders, and the thematically related "R is for Reality," in which reality itself becomes a corporate subsidiary owned by Murdoch; "W is for Werewolf," which has that delightful Lone Ranger twist.

Swanwick: I'm not as concerned with the workings of mega-corporations as most people of my literary generation were, but I caught a minor case of it here. Corporations make for good villains because they're anonymous. I was a kid in the fifties, so I loved the Lone Ranger, particularly Tonto, as played by the immortal Jay Silverheels. They're just such positive characters, they're fun to play with.

I'll mention that in "E is for Elba" the idea that the Earth is an asylum or prison is one that has been done by Ellison, Sturgeon and many others. "Z is for Zygote" is a riff on "A Momentary Taste of Being" by James Tiptree Jr. The advantage when you're doing lots and lots of short shorts is that you can ransack the science fiction treasury for ideas and you can just steal them. I ripped off James Tiptree Jr., but her story is undamaged, it's still great and anybody who sees this and goes, "I know where he got it from," no problem. I got degaussing iron from Poul Anderson's *Operation Chaos*, or rather "Operation Afreet," the first story in that series. It's not like writing a full-scale story and then passing the idea off as your own.

Zinos-Amaro: Obviously for each letter, a number of science fiction/fantasy terms are possible. Were there any alternate takes for a given letter that grew into openings of other stories you wrote later?

Swanwick: No. There may have been a few that I started and then threw out. For something like this, where there was a need for publication, I didn't feel like I could sit down and write a science fiction story and say, "I'll have this done in two weeks." For me, it could take two years. But I can sit down and write twenty-six short shorts in a few days. What I would do was that in the evening, when I was unwinding and sitting around with a glass of wine or watching television, I'd just take my notebook out and start writing short shorts. The next day I transferred them onto the computer, cleaned them up, and it was done.

Zinos-Amaro: Besides the ones we've mentioned, are there any others you want to single out?

Swanwick: I have a weird liking for the guy lost in alternate realities who comes up with an orange Oreo—this was written before there *were* such things! I think that every science fiction writer sooner or later comes to suspect that he or she drew something into existence. They'll write about it and then it'll pop up. It won't be some clever extrapolation, it'll be something like an orange Oreo.

Zinos-Amaro: When I was reading that one, "O is for Oreo," I imagined, based on our conversation about "The Overcoat," that he was going to reach in for the Oreo and then the Garfield the Cat cookie jar was going to bite off his hand.

Swanwick: That would have been good too!

Zinos-Amaro: Speaking of good, let's talk about "Mother Grasshopper" (*A Geography of Unknown Lands*, 1997). This incredibly memorable story was original to the collection.

Swanwick: I make sure to have an original story for every collection, and I try to make it a good one. That was important. "Mother Grasshopper" had a strange beginning. I believe this was back at that time when I was playing around on the GEnie bulletin board, which we talked about in connection with "In Concert." There was a story I liked by Michael Bishop called "Rogue Tomato." It had a giant grasshopper in it too. Jack Dann and I were having a conversation online, and I started busting his chops, explaining that everything that Jack wrote was about giant grasshoppers. Jack said something like, "I'll bet you think I couldn't do that." He produced a page of really beautiful, almost poetic prose. I took his prose and I rationalized it to at least twice the length. The opening sentence, for example, is entirely his. The line about not landing on the wings is mine. Creating the layer of limestone, and the hoedowns, was his. The new seasons, including Snows, was his. Everything else that rationalized it out was mine, so about fifty-fifty at that point. The next day I said, "Jack, here you go. Let's write a story." Jack was busy and he told me to take it and run with it, so I did.

This was one of those stories where it took forever for me to find out what it was about. It was a good, strong beginning. Within that past year I'd read Stephen King's *The Gunslinger*. I really loved what he did with it, the bravura anachronisms of it. I resolved to do something that was as good. The eel grass and dried buffalo chips in my story were taken from King's novel as an acknowledgement that, yes, I was stealing from him.

I brought in a magician to fire up the plot. They go off traveling from city to city. Except for the city they leave, New Auschwitz, all the city names are places in Pennsylvania. I thought that if I made it places from the Midwest or across the U.S. the internal logic of naming would be diluted by my choosing, but picking and choosing in Pennsylvania was closer to the original sources, so I did that. That was the fun part. But because I had no idea what was going on, this took me at least a year. He's chasing a magician across the chitin lands. Every new plot development made sense, but I didn't know what sense they made. I could see they were building to something. Then when Victoria comes in and seduces him, I figured it. When I finally saw that it was all about overpopulation and death that's when I could write the end of the story and finish it.

Zinos-Amaro: Victoria powerfully embodies the theme of mortality: she has a child with Daniel, and timescales are literally compressed. Also, Victoria has committed personality suicide before they meet, so in a way she's already died, and now lives again.

Swanwick: Yes, yes. She's not the person she was. The person she had been was unhappy. Victoria as she is in the story is very alive. She's much more alive than Daniel is. She brings him back to life, basically. Vengeance is not a valid way of life. He's crippled in more than one way.

Zinos-Amaro: Here's my brief take on "Mother Grasshopper." In the Greek myth of Tithonus, the declining immortal is turned into a cicada or grasshopper, his sound a constant pleading for death. Our protagonist Daniel, by being Death, is fated to bring an end to Tithonus' suffering. So I see this as a far-future extension of the myth, in which the aberration of Tithonus' greed for endless life is corrected and humanity gains an acceptance of mortality.

Swanwick: That's a good reading. I was thinking locusts, actually. When Victoria came along I realized that the grasshopper was a locust. But what you said is undeniable.

I stole a line in "Mother Grasshopper" from Tom Disch. It's when the magician says, "'God, don't they just break your heart?'" Before *On Wings of Song*, Tom Disch was writing a series of stories, including "Chanson Perpétuelle" and "The Pressure of Time," that were clearly going to be gathered into a novel, but then he decided against it. They were about a group of immortals who travel in a spaceship to another star system. Because they're immortal, spending a few thousand years on a spaceship is not a problem for them. In one of these stories one of these characters has an affair with a mortal; the affair does not end well, and the mortal goes off and joins a clown cult. One of the other immortals puts a hand on the protagonist's shoulder and says, "'God, don't they just break your heart?'" The immortals are all very cruel and petty. They're not using their immortality well. I loved that line and I said, "To hell with it, I'm just going to steal it outright. Anybody asks, I'll admit to it." After the magician says this in my story, that's when Daniel gives up his fantasies of revenge. That's when he grows up and becomes a real boy.

The Dark Tower series, which I mentioned, has a weakness, because after a while you realize it's never going to end. I did not in fact make it all the way to the last book, which doesn't end, but goes back to the beginning. I was determined that this story would have a strong ending.

Zinos-Amaro: You certainly delivered on that! Let's come back to Daniel for a moment. Was he always Death, and did the magician simply help him manifest his true inevitable nature, or could he have been something else, and ended up becoming Death *because* of his experiences with the magician?

Swanwick: He was a normal person. He behaved like a young man, thought like a young man. Fate came along and tapped him. He becomes Death through his apprenticeship and final testing. It's worth noting that the magician does not have a name. I got that from Robert Anton Wilson's *The Illuminatus Trilogy*. One of many good jokes in there is that a person makes several attempts to explain why a particular fictional character has no name and in the final attempt manages to get the whole explanation out: this character was Sergio Leone's Man With No Name, from the Italian Westerns. As Robert Anton Wilson explained, he has no name because he is death. This, I thought, was a really beautiful observation. I used the same thing in my novel *Stations of the Tide*. The bureaucrat has no name.

Zinos-Amaro: Speaking of names, in the Bible Daniel is essentially a heroic figure of wisdom—was making your Daniel Death a touch of irony? Or perhaps a way of saying that there's a kind of wisdom to passing on?

Swanwick: No, I named him before I found out that he was going to become Death. I just gave him a good name. It could have been anybody. He happened to be there when Death needed an apprentice. I think there is a kind of wisdom in him finally. As it turns out, a lot of my stories are death-affirming. When I was writing them I thought I was just being contrary, because everyone I knew, all the ambitious writers, were talking about writing a story that was life-affirming. But there may be more going on there that I know. I don't really look deep into myself, I have to admit. I'm not as interested in me as I am in the stories.

Zinos-Amaro: I think the story also subverts what one might associate with a grasshopper or locust; swiftness and a diminutive scale. Here it's vast. A whole world.

Swanwick: When I began writing this, I wanted to make it a hard science fiction story. I asked the hard SF writers I knew for advice. Charles Sheffield said, "This is very difficult. It's hard math." I said, "I know, I know. I'll brush up on my algebra and trigonometry. I'll get a copy of the software . . ." He said, "No, you don't understand, Michael. This is *very* difficult. It would be a lot easier if you just make it all up." I told him this was very disillusioning.

Zinos-Amaro: You paid tribute to him by having that sine wave that's named a Sheffield curve.

Swanwick: Next time I saw him, I told him I put it in the story and quoted him that line. He immediately said, "Oh, you mean like this," and moved his hand in a sine pattern. And I said, "Yeah, hand-waving!"

Zinos-Amaro: That's so great. Another aspect of "Mother Grasshopper" I wanted to touch on is how Daniel at one point feels similarly about his life to the protagonist of "The Changeling's Tale." He says: "It came to me then that being taken away from normal life young as I had been . . ."

Swanwick: A couple of things happened to me in life. Probably the biggest one is . . . When I was a junior in high school I came home one day and one of the panes in the window of the kitchen door was broken, and there was blood. Nobody would talk about what had happened. This was the first sign my father had contracted early-onset Alzheimer's. As you can see it's even hard now to talk about it. He very quickly went downhill. I got to watch this really, really beautiful and almost spiritual man whom I loved a great deal lose his self. That was a break point in life. That was when I gave up on becoming a scientist and decided I was going to be a writer. It happened right there. I like where I ended up a great deal. I value being a writer enormously, but it was not the life I originally planned for myself.

Zinos-Amaro: The theme of fearing a loss of self that we've seen crop up in a number of stories could well be connected to that experience. Subjectivity and the way you manipulate time in "Mother Grasshopper" is also very interesting. Right at the beginning we're told about "shaped temporal fields." Later, Victoria is "aging along her own exponential curve."

Swanwick: I was trying to write something set in the far, far future. Sufficient technology is not only not going to be recognizable, it's not going to be comprehensible. I put the incomprehensible stuff in the background and brought to the foreground this Americana, something that can hold your attention and you understand while the strangeness works underneath the surface. For me the important part of Victoria's journey is that when she starts out, when she first comes to, she has a kind of naïve wisdom. As she's growing along her own curve she grows much wiser than Daniel. That was for me the whole point: she was using life well, she was living a good life, however brief it seemed from the outside. I was also trying to do something where I had a wise woman who did not have "feminine intuition," which I think is a terrible, poisonous concept.

Zinos-Amaro: Talking about wisdom and its costs brings us nicely to "The Wisdom of Old Earth" (*Asimov's*, December 1997). David Hartwell said that this was your Jack London story.

Swanwick: In fact, it's my rip-off of Jack London. I read a story of his called "The Wisdom of the Trail," which is about an Alaskan native, who really worships the white man, considers him superior in every way. In the course of the story he unsurprisingly learns that this is not true. He's been serving a false god, as it were. I looked at that and thought that it would make for a great story about posthumans. Again, this was the contrary streak in me. A lot of people in science fiction at that time were talking about posthumanity as being a good thing. Campbellian supermen were superior in every way. I thought, "What if they're not superior? What if they just have more money?" They look pretty good from the outside, but they're not. I made the human character a woman, in part to get a fast distancing from Jack London's story, so I wouldn't be following too close to it. I had a lot of fun making them Canadians and therefore tapped into the ancient wisdom of Canada! There's a fair amount of observation about colonialism there.

Zinos-Amaro: I think that the ending of this story, particularly the last line, does a marvelous job of juxtaposing the inhuman with the posthuman. It provides quite a bite.

Swanwick: There's definitely that. This was a fast story to write. I did really carefully figure out where they were. The Flying Hills are real; you can find them on a map. The "Skookle River" in the story is the Schuylkill, which means "hidden river," so that the name in the story translates as "hidden river river." And of course I had fun with the "bell of liberty" they're looking for, one of those lost treasures where wandering a city in ruins isn't going to help you find it.

In a weird way, this is a conservative story. It says that there's value in being human, and that human values are worthy values. The women that Judith killed are behaving in a bestial fashion, they're sub-human or pre-human when they give in to their worst impulses.

Zinos-Amaro: That sequence felt reminiscent of H. G. Wells's *The Island of Doctor Moreau*, that kind of flavor.

Swanwick: Yeah, I think there's a little bit of that in my intention. It wasn't strong, but the influence of the great science fiction doesn't go away. It's pervasive.

Zinos-Amaro: There's a scene in "The Wisdom of Old Earth" where the posthuman off-worlder talks about his motivation for the trip: "I wanted to discover what I am in the natural state." Was there ever a time when you wanted to test yourself in a similar way?

Swanwick: I was a teenage boy, so ... I did a lot of rock scrambling when I was young. That will test you in that way. I don't know if you ever read *Deliverance* by James Dickey. He has a description of what it's like when you're climbing a cliff and you get to a point where you cannot go on. You reach around and there's nothing. You decide to go back down, you take one look down and you realize not only that it is a long fall that will kill you, but also that you cannot go down. Then *somehow* you go up. I have at various times tested myself, but not anymore than everybody else has. It's common to the human situation.

Zinos-Amaro: "Midnight Express" (*Sirens and Other Daemon Lovers*, ed. Ellen Datlow, Terri Windling, 1998) takes us back to fantasy but it speaks to core human desires.

Swanwick: It's a simple little story. I had two ambitions. One was to just tell a story in dialogue. No external descriptions. With the right story, that's a lot of fun. Obviously it can't be too long, or it's going to exhaust the reader, but this was short enough, and it moved fast enough, that I could get away with it. I also wanted to see just how smutty I could get without describing things explicitly. There's not a lot that's actually said, but you should be able to figure out most of what's going on. Ellen had a reading in the Village and several of her authors came to read their stories. Marianne and I read "Midnight Express" as a dialogue. I'm a pretty good reader, but Marianne just blew me out of the water. I mean, she was really, really good as the Sphinx. People were fanning themselves. It was funny because Ellen Kushner and Delia Sherman were there to read their stories, and each one read the story up until the sex began, and then said, "To find out what happens next you have to read the book," and slammed it shut and fled. Marianne was sitting next to me and said, "I was up there faking multiple orgasms." Boy, did it go over well. Everyone loved her reading.

Zinos-Amaro: For me your dialogue-only choice works well because we have two disembodied voices in a narrative that is precisely about the primal joining of bodies.

Swanwick: Yes, that's it.

Zinos-Amaro: The mention of night-lands made me think of William Hope Hodgson. Is he an influence, would you say, and do you have any favorite stories of his?

Swanwick: Probably *The Night Land*. He also had a sea adventure that was quite wonderful, *The Boats of the "Glen Carrig"*. It was in Lin Carter's adult fantasy series. There's this voyage, and they stop at island after island, and there are nightmarish things on the islands. But that was a long time ago. I don't have any specific influence from him, except that occasionally he reached a height of weirdness in his imagery. It sets a standard that I tried to see if I could reach or top.

Zinos-Amaro: Your story has a fun little reference to the dwarf-king Oberon when you mention "Oberon's court."

Swanwick: That's there to get a feeling of Faerie, to establish that they're moving through this magical, dark, *glamorous* land. I put in some signifiers to indicate that this was a railroad trip where a Sphinx would not be out of place. This is fantasy land. This is *Three Hearts and Three Lions* and *Land of Unreason* land. All those wonderful, old, light fantasies.

Zinos-Amaro: And yet your science fictional training still shows up with the phrase "chronologically liberated."

Swanwick: I've gotten pretty good at creating phrases like that that you don't have to explain. You can just drop them and move on.

Zinos-Amaro: I think from a storytelling perspective it's also savvy to keep the commercial traveler deliberately uncharacterized, because that draws us into the situation more viscerally, immersing us in what's happening instead of focusing on his particulars.

Swanwick: That was deliberate, yes. I wanted him to basically be a mask: an oval with a line for the mouth, two dots for the eyes, and another line for the nose. He really didn't have any purpose in there except as a convenient sex object for the Sphinx. That's, I guess, another wise woman, the Sphinx. It was Janet Kagan who, before she became a science fiction writer, wrote several porn movies. She said that in the first one that she wrote all the sexual encounters were initiated by the women, because in her experience this was how it worked out. The director/producer rewrote it so that all encounters were begun by the men. She said she didn't have a problem with that but asked why he made that change. He said, "Our viewers would be threatened." I thought, "Boy, what wimps these guys are." That really stuck in my mind. I suspect that most of the sexual encounters in my fiction have been initiated by the woman because I thought that was a pretty good observation on Janet's part. "Midnight Express" is another story that was written fairly fast and written with a great deal of gratitude towards women on the whole.

Zinos-Amaro: Maybe that carries over into "The Very Pulse of the Machine" (*Asimov's*, February 1998) too, whose only human characters are two women. I imagine the science research for this story was time-consuming.

Swanwick: You're right. This was a story that took a long time to write, and most of the time was in the research. I decided to write a hard science fiction story, so I went looking for a locale in the Solar System. Somebody had said to a friend of mine, who quoted it to me, that it was strange how NASA spent billions of dollars to send probes everywhere in the Solar System and bring back detailed information about all these alien places, and science fiction writers didn't bother to use it. That seemed to me to be a very wise observation. I chose Io because it looked interesting; it has volcanoes. I started downloading papers about Io from the Web. After I read a paper, I stapled the corner and dropped it in a cardboard box at the foot of my desk. At some point I also started downloading and reading information about the chemical properties of sulfur, because there's lots of it there. When the pile got to be about a foot and half, two feet high, it all came together. It told me a story. At some point I put all this information together and said, "It's a machine. Okay. There's the story." Then the writing went relatively quickly.

It's a very simple story. I stole the basic structure from Geoff Landis's "A Walk in the Sun." There's a woman on the Moon and she's crashed. She's isolated. Her radio doesn't work. She has to get back to the lunar base. Her suit has solar collectors on the back and night is approaching, so the terminator is coming, and when that passes over her she won't have anymore power for her suit and its cooling functions will cease and she will die. She has to keep walking, and she can walk just fast enough if she never stops to rest. At the same time, because Geoff Landis, engineer though he is, saw immediately that that's not enough of a plot to involve the reader, he had the woman working out her own personal problems with, I believe, her sister. It's an engaging story. Once you start reading it, you will not stop until you reach the end. I thought it was brilliantly done. For my protagonist, I made her problem her insecurities. Only woman on Earth who's ashamed of winning a bronze medal in the Olympics!

Zinos-Amaro: The Wordsworth poem from which the story "The Very Pulse of the Machine" takes its title appears to have been written by Wordsworth for his wife Mary Hutchinson. Our protagonist, Martha Kivelsen, has a somewhat similar-sounding name—was that deliberate?

Swanwick: That was a coincidence, alas. I read the poem to make sure it would be okay, but I did not read into the history of its creation. Most of the quotations were there simply because I needed Io to communicate in poetry, so I got out my big volume of favorite quotations and mined it furiously.

Zinos-Amaro: In a *Strange Horizons* interview, you talked about deliberately writing this story in pared-down prose. But you still get away with being "literary," because you quote Wordsworth, Tennyson, Dylan Thomas and so on.

Swanwick: I think it makes the hard SF guys happy when the protagonist can be an intellectual and still be a hard, tough engineering-type. When I was writing this story, I was thinking of Algis Budrys. He said that hard science fiction was not a subgenre, it was a flavor, and the flavor was toughness. This is one reason, again, why the protagonist had to be a woman, so that she could be tough and competent without me identifying with her.

I was brought up in the 1950s, which was a hyper-competitive time, and I was brought up to be competitive. I remember in second grade in St Paul's Grammar School in Schenectady they had an assembly and they gave out various prizes to the best students. I got a little gold pin for having an overall grade for the entire year of ninety-eight. It was better than anyone else got, by far. I took it home and hid it, because I was ashamed of not getting at least ninety-nine. So yet another reason to make the protagonist a woman and add a little distance between myself and her, so that I wouldn't corrupt the protagonist with my own faults.

Zinos-Amaro: The science in this story is really thought-pro-voking. The "sulfur flowers," for example, also brought to mind the world you created for "Trojan Horse" and *Vacuum Flowers*.

Swanwick: I was making notes and little drawings and such as I was creating the story, and I did as much invention as I could while keeping inside the hard science fiction universe. As Mar-tha's going along, she can be discovering new things and it's not going to just keep repeating itself.

Zinos-Amaro: Speaking of repetition, Landis won the Hugo for his story, and you did for yours. In that same interview for *Strange Horizons*, talking about "The Very Pulse of the Machine" you said that "the prestige of hard SF is so great that the fans wanted to reward me for essaying the form." This was some twenty years ago. Do you still feel that hard SF has this kind of prestige today?

Swanwick: I can't speak for the last few years because there is a kind of sea-change going on. More and more writers are refer-ring to stories as "fantastika," dissolving the boundaries between science fiction and fantasy. It would be hypocritical of me to dis-approve of this! But I think hard SF still has a lot of prestige. One time I went to visit Gardner Dozois at his house, when he lived in Society Hill, and as I was leaving he asked me what I was work-ing on. I told him I'd written a really good zombie story. He said, "Yeah, yeah, but what I want is hard science fiction. With space-ships." As I was leaving he stood out on the stoop and shouted, "Remember Michael, hard science fiction! None of this magic re-alism crap! None of this fantasy crap! Hard science fiction, with spaceships!" A few days later I went to New York and I visited El-len Datlow in her office. She asked me what I was working on, and I told her I just finished this really good zombie story. She looked disappointed and said, "That's nice Michael, but really what I'm looking for is hard science fiction with spaceships." The editors love an excuse to put spaceships on the cover. I think it still has a lot of prestige, but maybe less prestige than when science fiction was smaller and *Asimov's*, *Analog* and *F&SF* were at the center of everything. Hard science fiction gets you noticed.

"The Very Pulse of the Machine" was a very, very traditional story: an attractive protagonist with a Problem that she gets to solve, and then it fails, and then she comes up with a new solution. I wrote this for the purest of motives, and then when it went on to win the Hugo I thought, "Ah, so that's how you do it!"

Zinos-Amaro: Can you say a little more about the character development?

Swanwick: I had Martha dragging her friend Burton in part because she needed somebody to talk to, and in part because it's a metaphoric burden, and also in part to establish her character. She's a much better person than she thinks she is, and she subscribes to the traditional values—you don't leave somebody behind. Come to think of it, she was probably in the military before joining the Astronaut Corps.

Besides Martha, we have Julie, and we have Io. Now here's something that has been central to my understanding of story structure ever since I first heard it: John Kessel said that a story had to have a minimum of three characters. I've taken that very seriously ever since. Sometimes, of course, the planet becomes the character, or the locale becomes the character. I'm convinced that this is because if you have two characters, you can have conflict, but it's like a tug of war: one person wins, one person loses. That's not a story, that's a game. If you have three characters, then the protagonist can be pulled in two different directions and ends up in a place different from where he or she started, it's not either of the two poles. It's someplace else entirely, and *that's* the movement of the story.

Zinos-Amaro: I thought the way you blurred the boundaries between the living and the mechanical with science in this story was conceptually brilliant. It's what powers that third character.

Swanwick: It's harder to deal with the spiritual in science fiction than in fantasy because science fiction takes place, as we've discussed, in a knowable, almost atheistic universe. People don't go to church very often in science fiction stories, even in science fiction stories written by practicing Christians, for example.

Structurally, there was a point near the end of the story where it's established that the voice in her head is definitely real. It's not due to her stress and her overuse of drugs. Reading it over, I was struck that as soon as it's unquestionably real inside the universe of the story, that's when Io makes her this offer to make her immortal—maybe. I immediately restored uncertainty, because it's a story that needs uncertainty. If it's cut-and-dry at the end, then it loses all of its interest. Gene Wolfe once said that a story, to be useful, has to come close to saying the exact opposite of what it meant to say. I think this provides more insight into Gene than into literature as a whole, but I have found it to be an intriguing, and occasionally useful, observation.

Zinos-Amaro: That would be the ultimate act of misdirection.

Swanwick: Uh-huh. But also, there has to be something for the reader to do, not as part of the price of admission, but to make the experience more satisfying.

One of the things that made this hard to write is that I tried my best to make it clear to the reader what was going on before the protagonist knows. In my own reading, I like this quite a lot. If you look at *The Case of Charles Dexter Ward*, for example, the reader knows that Charles Dexter Ward has been possessed by a wizard from centuries before, and that very bad things lurk beneath the barn, but his friend doesn't and so down he goes. If you can let the reader know what's happening before the protagonist knows, you can build up a good bit of suspense, and the reader will like that.

Zinos-Amaro: You've referenced Stephen King a few times. It occurs to me that this is a technique he definitely likes to use.

Swanwick: He's a structurally brilliant writer. He *really* knows how to do that. And his son, "Joe Hill," does too. If you look at the *Locke & Key* comic books, for instance, it's almost like a skeleton key to plotting like Stephen King. It's notable that the plotting is primarily about character and personality. Beautifully done.

Zinos-Amaro: Character and personality are integral to the next story on hand, "Wild Minds" (*Asimov's*, May 1998).

Swanwick: I was in Glasgow for the Worldcon. I rented a room on Renfrew Street, which is up on the top of the city, in this very old, rather run-down section. Quite lovely. After breakfast with a lot of British fans—because they all knew where the cheap housing was they stayed in the same place, and we had lovely conversations—I would go off into the bright morning to the convention, about a mile walk, which was the perfect distance for walking. From its top, the city looked really beautiful, except where the M8 comes right into the city, and for about a block, on either side, it's just a blight. The buildings are shabby and have boarded-up windows—nobody wants to live there. Everywhere else in the city is far better. It was classic 1960s urban renewal that turned around and bit the well-intended politicians who paid for it. I was thinking about this a fair amount, and later in the convention I was on a panel on neural enhancement. For various reasons, it's coming, and it's going to be irresistible. When you can go into the human brain and make a few simple adjustments and cure schizophrenia nobody is going to turn away from that. At one point, to sum up, I said, "We should start thinking about these issues now, because it *is* irresistible and we want to be sure that we're not just taking and driving an M8 right through the center of the human brain." I thought that was a pretty good line. On the plane on the way home I said, "There's a story there."

I set "Wild Minds" in Glasgow, and I contrasted the shabby people, the alcoholics and losers that you see on the street, with the yuppies, basically, that's what the posthumans are, they're the winners in the new society and they believe they got there entirely by virtue alone. Then I combined that with Catholic teachings about guilt. I was on a panel with Gene Wolfe about Catholicism and learned a couple of good things. But I found out that he did not believe in Catholic guilt, he thought that was a myth. I said, "I disagree. I feel guilty about everything, and I feel guilty for feeling guilty about it." As has been established, I have mixed feelings about the Church. There are aspects of it I love, aspects that I respect enormously. I wanted to talk about those. That ties in to the value of humanity, and the value of being yourself when there's this great revolution going on. The old model of the brain was machinery, because machines were the most complex things we knew of. Now the model is computers, because *they're* the most complex things we know about. Obviously right now the human brain is still more complex. Some of the talk about the workings of the human brain was cold and artificial and seemed aimed at taking away agency and guilt, explaining everything away. In a way, then, this is me being a reactionary and a romantic, in the nineteenth century sense. But I really think it's just me being cautious. We shouldn't throw away something of value in our rush to improve ourselves.

Zinos-Amaro: To me "The Wisdom of Old Earth" and "Wild Minds" are the Swanwick take on singularity fiction. You're focusing on the transitional phases. Here in "Wild Minds" the narrator feels like he's "on the twilight lands between the cultivated fields and the wolf-haunted forests." He's in an in-between place. This is true of Judith Seize-the-Day in "The Wisdom of Old Earth" as well.

Swanwick: That's where you find the conflict, where you find a person torn in two different directions. And that's the essence of fiction.

Sheila Williams told me that normally when a story opens with a sex scene that means she's going to reject it within the first page. That's a useful thing, I think, for gonna-be writers to know. I had not known that at the time. But in this case it worked out well.

Zinos-Amaro: One of the best early moments in the story is when Hellene says, "The Church can't possibly approve of your attending orgies," and the protagonist says, "Well. It's winked at."

Swanwick: That's kind of like birth control. There's a lot more birth control happening among Catholics than the Pope is aware of.

Zinos-Amaro: Hellene doesn't need sleep. Was that a little nod to Nancy Kress's *Beggars in Spain*?

Swanwick: It might be. I do know that when I first came to college I was really interested in the idea of doing away with sleep so that I would have more time to study. I quickly found out that it was a bigger problem than I could solve myself. But it did seem like one of the first things that these posthumans would do away with, one of the things that makes them not human. They no longer dream, they no longer have access to the unconscious or subconscious or whatever it is that we're reading while we're asleep. They are totally rational in the way that totally rational villains in Ray Bradbury are. Bradbury is probably the first writer who showed me that the irrational and awful parts of the human psyche are valuable too.

Zinos-Amaro: If you had the option to "optimize" yourself, just as it's presented in this story, would you do it?

Swanwick: No. I would hold out because I'm perfectly content with my life right now. Now, you ask my twenty-year old self, he might well give a different answer. That would have allowed him to become a scientist *and* a writer.

Zinos-Amaro: What if Marianne optimized? Would you still resist it?

Swanwick: I think I would cry. There's a passage in the story about what happens when Sophia is optimized: "By seven she'd seen through God, prayer, and the Catholic Church. By eight she had discarded her plans to have children and a lifelong love of music. By nine she'd outgrown me." I couldn't optimize even if Marianne did, because that would mean no longer loving her. If I cannot have her love, at least I can mourn my lost love.

Zinos-Amaro: "Wild Minds" has a line that's perhaps the most explicit summation of a theme in your work that we've discussed a number of times: "I was afraid of losing myself." It also strikes me that this story is a kind of companion piece to "The Dead."

Swanwick: No question. Yet again, "Wild Minds" is a Marxist critique of capitalism. I'm not a Marxist, but in my nightmares I fear that Marx was right about the evolution of capitalism. This might be a theme in my work, people losing what they have. Not just identity, but jobs, self-respect, things like that.

Zinos-Amaro: In "120 is for Issues" (*The New York Review of Science Fiction*, August 1998), a fun piece of flash fiction, you yourself aren't exempt from bad treatment. I particularly enjoyed the line about your "motivational electroshock."

Swanwick: I wrote this one because the tenth-year anniversary of *The New York Review of Science Fiction* was coming up. I thought I should have something in it, but I didn't have any essay or such to write or anything comprehensive to say. So I wrote this piece of flash fiction, and because I'd been writing an abecedary for *NYRSF* it had application to the magazine itself. *NYRSF* was very useful to me. It provided something that I wanted from the beginning of my career: a place for which I could write up a non-fiction idea and have it published. I did not have to go hunting around for a market or fanzine that needed that particular thing.

Zinos-Amaro: David Hartwell, whose Dragon Press published *NYRSF* for over twenty years, said of the next story— "Radiant Doors" (*Asimov's*, September 1998)—that it was a "darker, painfully realistic, SF twist on C. M. Kornbluth's classic 'The Marching Morons.'"

Swanwick: Well, yes and no. The origin is actually a lot less glamorous than that. I read a review of an old Clifford Simak novel where doors open in the air all around the world, and refugees come pouring in from the future. It turns out that some time in the future aliens invade, and that's what they're refugees from, which I thought was a disappointing resolution. I read the book; it was not one of Simak's best. Then I had the thought, "What if they were fleeing from an unbearable future?" Followed by, "Oh God, now I have to write it." I had to live with this very painful idea for months while I worked out and wrote the story. It contains pretty much every awful thing I could think of. It may be the darkest story I've ever written. A friend dropped by one day with his fiancé, who is a rabbi, and she had read "Radiant Doors." At one point in the evening she took Marianne aside and asked how Marianne could sleep next to me, knowing that I had these things inside my head. And Marianne, God bless her, said, "They're not inside his head anymore, they're inside yours."

Zinos-Amaro: This is indeed a very dark story, but before getting into specifics, I wanted to ask, given Hartwell's comment above, what Kornbluth's work means to you, and if you have any Simak recommendations.

Swanwick: I admired Kornbluth enormously. He was a terrific writer. He had some great ideas. "Marching Morons," in spite of the fact that the science was not very good, was a great story. He was not afraid to look at some very dark places in there. For Simak, I would single out *City* most of all. It was a fix-up, but it was a series of brilliant stories, one after another. It flows wonderfully. He had such a kind, humane vision of the world, too, that was rare in science fiction back then.

Zinos-Amaro: Tell me how you prepared to write the refugee camp aspect of this story.

Swanwick: I did some research, but it was kind of generic, looking up articles and reading about life in refugee camps. The bureaucratic tent city at the top of the hill—the Tentagon, as they call it—was inspired by an event that the National Guard has once a year in Philadelphia in the summer. They set up a field hospital in Fairmount Park and they do free health screenings for anybody who wants it. A lot of poor people come out and get some free healthcare. It's beautifully thought through, because it gives them an exercise where they're dealing with real people doing real medicine and it benefits the people in the area. Probably saves a couple lives, too; a few people that show up are tested and told, "Go to the emergency room right now." One thing that impressed me was that the field hospital is made up of modular tents that are all zippered together, with air-conditioning units and canvas ducts moving the cold air through. It was a strange and wonderful locale to be in. I was doing some volunteer help for the Bureau of Laboratories, who did some screenings. When I encountered that, I said, "This is going into a story sooner or later," and carefully set it aside.

Zinos-Amaro: "Radiant Doors" seems to me to have a noir-ish ambiance. Some of the speech is hard-boiled in that way. You have a McGuffin, you have secret agents, you have people at the end of their rope. A few scenes gave me a *Casablanca* vibe.

Swanwick: The darkness in this story was deliberate. I saw from the beginning that everyone involved in this was essentially traumatized. The caregivers were not in terrifically good shape themselves. I think what you're picking up on is a kind of moral ambiguity, or a moral sickness. Everyone in it is morally compromised from the beginning, and aware of it. The only options they have to choose between are bad and worse—and even worse. I think that's the factor there. I wasn't specifically thinking of the noir genre.

Compassion fatigue, by the way, is part of a whole suite of problems that people working for charities have. There's a very famous one. When you're dealing with people whose problem is that they've been starving it can be very hard to keep yourself fed; you feel like a traitor eating food. On a smaller level, we know from experience that when you have friends who are very sick for years on end, after a while it's hard to keep caring. I'm thinking of a friend who was in various physical rehabs for years. Marianne and I would go and visit once a week. Other people went to visit periodically, but as time went by, one by one they dropped out. They couldn't keep doing it. But we're wonderful, so we did! Toward the end we were feeling a little annoyed at our friend for being so ill, but we applied our human rationality and did not mention this fact to them!

Zinos-Amaro: The combination of this story's set-pieces, setting and concept made it feel cinematic to me, so I wasn't entirely surprised to discover news from 2015 reporting that "Radiant Doors" was being adapted into a TV series. From what I can see, the 2015 series *The Refugees* used the exact same premise as your story, and so did the 2018 series *The Crossing*.

Swanwick: I had to wonder about that too. You look at Hollywood and you think, for example, about *Antz* and *Bugs* coming out at almost the same time. It doesn't feel like the most honest industry in the world. "Radiant Doors" *was* optioned. I had mixed feelings about it. On the one hand, having a movie made lends validity to your work, and the money would have been nice. On the other hand, I would have had to watch it. I think they were planning a television show based on this story. It was probably *The Walking Dead* that made them think they could do something this dark and have people watch it. I'm pretty sure I wouldn't have enjoyed it. I didn't watch *The Refugees* or *The Crossing*. As I say, I was unhappy I came up with the idea in the first place. I remember one time Bruce Sterling, in one of his Shaper/Mechanist stories, mentioned that on this particular space world they hadn't been able to get rid of cockroaches, so they genetically altered them to make them beautiful. I thought that was a great idea and was so very, very glad he had it instead of me.

Zinos-Amaro: You do some fun things with language in this story. The term Owners, for the future ruling humans, seems to continue that Marxist critique we were talking about. And "bippy" is an interesting word.

Swanwick: Owners is how I refer to the super-rich today. I do not have a very high opinion of the people who own most of the money in the world, I'm afraid. And it shows. The first thing you do in our country now, when you have a lot of money, is to distance yourself from those who don't. It's always easier to demonize people when you don't know them.

The word "bippy" came from the comedian Allan Sherman. I read his autobiography, and he invented a game show with a decoration that looked kind of like an asterisk that he referred to as a bippy because it had no other name. That stayed with me for about fifty years before I actually used it.

Zinos-Amaro: "Radiant Doors" and "Wild Minds" were both up for the Hugo in 1999, along with "The Very Pulse of the Machine," which ultimately won. What was it like to have *three* entries in the Best Short Story category? Did you consider withdrawing one or even two to try and focus more attention on the other?

Swanwick: It felt great, it really did. I had a five year period, from 1999 through 2003, where I was on a run with nominations. Back around 1990 when I won the Nebula for *Stations of the Tide* William Gibson called me long-distance from Vancouver and he burbled at me happily for a while. This was before cheap cell phone contracts, when something like that cost real money. He was a friend, but he wasn't so close a friend that I would have noticed if he hadn't called. He told me the most useful thing I've heard about awards: "Now that you have one, you need never want it again. They cannot take it away for bad behavior, and the tag of being a 'Nebula Award Winner,' which will follow you around the rest of your life like a little puppy, won't be any bigger if you win ten more." I remembered this after winning the Hugo the first time for "The Very Pulse of the Machine."

Everybody speculates that if you have more than one nomination it's better to refuse one. I decided to leave them all there and see how things worked out. Whenever one of my stories fell off the ballot, it tended to give its second-place votes to another one of my stories. So it turned out that having a batch on the same ballot was a good way to win. I'd been curious about this, and now I know. So my advice to young writers is, get four or five nominations on the ballot! Of course, it has to be honest. You can't go out like the Sad Puppies did and arrange for block voting. The fans don't like that. They're fond of their award, and they like the fact that it's an honest one.

Zinos-Amaro: John Berkey's illustration to "Microcosmic Dog" (*Science Fiction Age*, November 1998) is quite striking. The title of this story invokes Sturgeon, whom we talked about briefly when we discussed "Ice Age." Tell me about the original inspiration for this story.

Swanwick: There was a feminist science fiction story I read, with a sentient female space suit, and it was allegorical, in the sense of women being seen as an emptiness that needs to be filled. I could not for the life of me remember who wrote it or what the title was. I don't like allegory very much, and I started playing around with the notion of a woman in a space suit, until I came up with this idea of a woman who's been reconstructed into all of New York City. That's an old theme in science fiction, where the world is not what you think it is and one day it all begins to break down. Everything I wrote about New York City I wrote with enormous affection. It's where the O'Brien half of my family came from. Growing up I'd go there often to visit my grandmother. I still have relatives living in Queens. I always thought when I grew up that I'd eventually move to New York. It didn't happen, but I still retain great fondness for the city.

Zinos-Amaro: The phrase "singularity engine," first spoken by the titular dog, turns out to be the explanation for everything. That's a great phrase.

Swanwick: I just made that one up. There's a section in "Radiant Doors" which is this checklist of things they want more information on. I made all those up too. Some of them, I'll admit, I'm proud of, like "lepton soliloquies." It sounds like it means something very profound, whatever it is. Singularities were in the air at the time. "Singularity engine" sounded pretty good, and it could be used to explain away almost anything.

Zinos-Amaro: You made Tom Disch and Joyce Carol Oates characters in "Microcosmic Dog." By using real people, for me, maybe paradoxically, you reinforced the unreality of the situation.

Swanwick: The protagonist of "Microcosmic Dog" is not Ellen Datlow, but I did give her Ellen Datlow's voice. At one point she says, "Oh, that makes sense. I guess." Knowing Ellen Datlow, that's one of the things she says when she's confronted with something that she really doesn't think makes a lot of sense. She's said it to me many times. Disch and Oates both seemed to fit in well because they were both friends of Datlow. New York City needs to have some famous, glamorous people. But right from the beginning, I was dropping clues that this is not the real New York.

Zinos-Amaro: "Hell is no other people" was a fun riff on Sartre.

Swanwick: I have to say, *No Exit* is a great play, one of the ornaments of the twentieth century. That was just a fun line to write.

Zinos-Amaro: Through the 80s and 90s, were you watching science fiction TV shows and movies? I ask because the episode "Remember Me" of *Star Trek: The Next Generation* has a similar premise to this story and the narrative unravels along the same lines: people disappear and nobody remembers them, and at the end the protagonist is revealed to be trapped in a kind of warp singularity.

Swanwick: I watched the big science fiction movies when they came out. *Star Trek* gradually left me behind. And then *Star Wars* gradually left me behind. I hadn't seen that episode. But I certainly read the many, many books that the author of that episode read. We were neither of us the first to use either of those ideas.

This story was written relatively quickly. I did not have to do a lot of research for it. There's a description of a Bill Viola artwork in there which I loved. It's a faucet very slowly dripping, with the camera pointing at the drop of water and projected up on a screen, wrought enormous. You see this shape, and it quivers and forms, and then you realize what you're seeing is your own image upside down in the drop of water, and at the moment you realize this it falls and hits this tambourine, and it feels like the dissolution of ego. It's a lovely, profound piece, and it fit perfectly into the story. I *was* amused by the protagonist's horror at realizing that in real life she is blue collar.

Zinos-Amaro: When your next story, "Ancient Engines" (*Asimov's*, February 1999), was published, *Asimov's* was using little editorial taglines under cover stories, and yours said: "Want to Live Forever? Are You Willing to Pay the Price?"

Swanwick: The origin of this story is included in the story itself. My father-in-law, William Christian Porter, went to a science museum and was admiring this ancient locomotive when he discovered that he was older than it was. Since that time, I looked around to see how many machines there are that are older than me, and it turns out, not all that many. The automobiles that are older than me are all treasured and prized and only ridden on special occasions. There are older elevators, but you feel nervous riding them. At that time the whole cyberpunk thing was still going on, and there was a lot of talk about uploading into a machine and transcending the meat. Back then, there was a story I never got around to writing—which was probably just as well, because I wouldn't have enjoyed writing it—where somebody has himself uploaded into a machine, then comes back to Earth and finds that instead of his body being simultaneously killed the way it was supposed to be, somebody bought the rights to it and was going to make a snuff film using this person who still thought he was himself. The politics of that story were too ugly and they wouldn't form a nice artistic shape. But I was thinking a lot about the uploading-into-a-machine fallacy, and that got me thinking about what a robots' chances were. I was sorry that I came up with "Ancient Engines" after my father-in-law was dead. I think he would have gotten a kick out of it. He was a man I admired.

Zinos-Amaro: What was it you admired most about him?

Swanwick: He was, as he put it, an elder, distinguished lawyer. I watched as a younger relative went and asked him for advice on a business that she was starting. I knew nothing on the subject at all, so I was just sitting there listening. She explained her situation and I was almost quivering with the desire to express my opinion. My father-in-law asked her a question and then, with great reluctance, he offered an opinion that shed light on her problem. He was not anxious to offer opinions on things, or to tell people what to think. But what he had to say was always useful. I miss him around election times because we used to go to him and say, "Which of these judges should we be voting for, and which ones shouldn't we be voting for?" Reluctantly, he'd say, "Well, I suppose he's not so bad," or "You may not want to vote for him." He had that lack of desire to tell people what to think which is, I think, quite admirable, especially for someone like me, who's a talker. Every now and then I try to rein myself in by asking myself how he would respond.

Zinos-Amaro: When the central idea pops up in the story, I thought of church organs, and clocks, both of which can work well for several centuries. Since we've talked about General Electric a lot, I'll also mention that they've made refrigerators that have been working for some eighty-five years, which is pretty close to the human lifespan. Admittedly, these are machines with exceptional longevity.

Swanwick: Yeah. Really, "Ancient Engines" is a meditation on mortality. Gardner Dozois used to say that nobody could really live forever. Nobody would truly be an immortal, we would just be very long-lived. I agree with that. That's the whole point of the thought experiment: you get to the end of the Universe, and you ask yourself, "How do you survive this?" The young woman says, "Why be greedy? To live as long as the universe does is probably long enough." Science fiction writers tend to like immortality uncritically. They rarely deal with the fact that since everything is ultimately mortal, even the Universe, you're not going to get to avoid death at the end of it. You can just have more time to make your peace with the idea.

Zinos-Amaro: With TikTok, besides L. Frank Baum were you referencing John Sladek?

Swanwick: No, I was just thinking of *The Wizard of Oz*. I do admire Sladek enormously. I was talking with him once and I told him you could buy chi pants that had micro-crystals sown into the butt seam so that they could align your chakras, and he said that you could no longer write satire. Coming from Sladek, that was an extraordinary remark.

Speaking of *The Wizard of Oz*, by the way, did you know there's an entire other set of Oz books in Russian? At one point Lenin was trying to encourage Russian literature by banning almost all foreign literature, and the Oz books got banned. But they were so popular that one of the publishers found a writer, Alexander Volkov, and said, "Okay, write me new Oz books."

Zinos-Amaro: I was not aware of these, and should look them up, since I recently read all the originals by Baum. While we're on genre classics: "Ancient Engines" has an Asimovian flavor, in the way that a single concept is seriously extrapolated to its utmost limits.

Swanwick: Yes. And it's also basically just a couple of people sitting there talking about ideas, which feels particularly Asimovian. It's one of the things that made him so popular. The fans always loved that, because the people who read science fiction are drawn to ideas. I should mention, in this context, a reference to Univac. Univac was built here in Philadelphia and we were quite proud of it. When I worked at the Franklin Institute for the National Solar Heating and Cooling Information Center my boss had a box of vacuum tubes from Univac under his desk. I always wanted one of them so much, but I never had the chutzpah to ask! Asimov, of course, ended up "inventing" Multivac. Anyway, this story was a lot of fun to write. It came out nice and clean.

Zinos-Amaro: "Scherzo with Tyrannosaur" (*Asimov's*, July 1999) appeared the same year, and it's also a lot of fun.

Swanwick: I did it as a test piece for the mechanics of my novel *Bones of the Earth*. I had been researching the novel for rather a while, over a year. I was interviewing scientists, going to paleontological conferences, traveling to other cities to see specific fossils. I learned the language. By the end of that year I could sit in on any conversation with a paleontologist from anywhere in the world and understand everything. I could not contribute anything, but I could follow it perfectly. So the science in that story was about as good as you got at that time. Since then I think we've decided that *Tyrannosaurus* probably didn't run as fast as I had them running. Other than that the science holds. I put it together to see if I could make the mechanics of time travel work. I had the note-passing and the security apparatus to make sure that nobody creates any time paradoxes. By writing "Scherzo with Tyrannosaur" I put together the system for the novel.

This is set, I would argue, in an entirely different universe than the novel. I don't see any reason for it to be set in the same universe, and I didn't want to have to worry about making the novel consistent with the story. The name of the benefactors here, for example, is different from the novel. There's a reference to getting a message from one million years in the future, and in the novel it's something like one hundred or two hundred million years instead.

Zinos-Amaro: The opening line is tremendous: "A Keyboardist was playing a selection of Scarlatti's harpsichord sonatas, brief pieces one to three minutes long, very complex and refined, while the *Hadrosaurus* herd streamed by the window." Of course we eventually get to the Shostakovich piano quintet scherzo of the title.

Swanwick: I was listening to that while I wrote. I asked Tom Purdom for his advice. Tom is a Philadelphia writer who has been writing steadily since the late 1950s. He was also the music critic for one of the weekly papers here. He knows an enormous amount. I asked him what the best music to play would be while watching a *Tyrannosaurus*, and he provided me with the piece, and also talked me through the significance of it.

Zinos-Amaro: We've talked about the importance of rock and roll for you growing up, and I was curious about your relationship with classical music.

Swanwick: I've always liked it. Some pieces are important to me. Some odd things, like Quartet for the End of Time, are kind of a touchstone, for both Marianne and for me. I'm not as knowledgeable as I thought I would be by now, though. More of an appreciator.

Zinos-Amaro: Was there anything that inspired the setting for this story?

Swanwick: I was at the Borrowers' Ball, which is a big fund-raiser for the Free Library of Philadelphia. There was dinner in the stacks and dancing in the lobby of the main library. A really lovely evening. They had tables out, with really good catered food. You could buy a seat at the table for $5,000. Or, if you bought a table of six seats, they threw in a writer and spouse as a small perk for fun conversation. I was one of those small perks. It was a lot of fun. I got to chat with Joyce Carol Oates and then Marianne and I danced until they shut us down. I put a lot of that evening into the fundraiser in "Scherzo with Tyrannosaur."

Zinos-Amaro: The actual use of Tyrannosaur as an attraction is interesting too.

Zinos-Amaro: The boy shivering when the Tyrannosaur slams against the window came from something I observed at the Philadelphia Zoological Garden. They put in a polar bear exhibit with a pool that the bears swam in. One side of it was this extremely thick plexiglass, so you could see them swimming. When it was new the bears would sometimes come up to that window from below and rise up suddenly, snapping at whoever was there. The children would get as close to that as they could! The bears clawed at the plexi, trying to get at them and eat them. So I threw that into the story too.

Zinos-Amaro: Yes, little Philippe is memorable.

Swanwick: I like Philippe. He was a good character. He acted like a true little boy. I had a son myself, so I knew that intensity, that extreme emotional honesty that he shows.

Zinos-Amaro: Early on there's a reference to the Cadigans.

Swanwick: One of my first stories appeared in the same publication as one that Pat Cadigan wrote, and in it she had an awful couple called the Swanwicks. She was mortified when she saw my name on the contents page. This was the first she'd been aware of me, being in the same publication and appearing to make fun of me. It was just a strange coincidence. So here was my little joke back.

Zinos-Amaro: Speaking of references, in one of the publications of this time your forthcoming novel was called *The Jaws of Time*, clearly an earlier title for *Bones of the Earth*.

Swanwick: Wow, really? That's a terrible title! I have no memory of that at all. It might have been my agent's place-holder.

Zinos-Amaro: "Scherzo with Tyrannosaur" would end up in competition with your own "Ancient Engines" on the 2000 Hugo ballot for Best Short Story. Did you think one of these was more award-worthy than the other?

Swanwick: "Scherzo with Tyrannosaur" is a better story, there's no getting around it. "Ancient Engines" I have a fondness for because of Marianne's father, whom as I say I liked quite a lot. Good stories for different reasons.

Zinos-Amaro: We're hitting this period of your career where you are getting a lot of award attention. You win the Hugo for Best Short Story in two consecutive years. Do you feel that your work was becoming more accessible than in the early days of all those Nebula nominations, or do you think you were being just as literary as before but there was greater appetite at large for that kind of work?

Swanwick: Both. There's also a third thing. When I was starting out the Nebula was the award that an ambitious young writer wanted, more than the Hugo. The Hugo went to people like Robert Heinlein and Gordy Dickson. The Nebula went to people like Ursula K. Le Guin and Joanna Russ and Gene Wolfe. By 1989 or 1990 the voters for the Hugo got more literarily savvy. They were making some good choices by then, and sometimes better choices than the Nebulas were. It was a strange thing to discover. The award process is a mysterious one. I spent many years on the Nebula jury. We were charged with reading everything that was published, and could add up to one story per category. We could not, of course, read all the novels, but we came pretty close to reading all the short fiction. So year after year I would have read everything that was on the ballot. I would make my guesses as to what would win—and I was *never* right. Sometimes I'd be utterly cynical. Sometimes I made a list of what I believed was the absolute best. Sometimes I would analyze the political groups, and tried to figure out who would vote for what. No matter what I did, I always got it wrong. The awards go chaotic when you come right down to it. But if you're on the ballot, that usually, but not always, means that that story is pretty good.

Zinos-Amaro: I found your next story, "Riding the Giganoto-saur" (*Asimov's*, October-November 1999), unusually moralistic.

Swanwick: That was written just for fun. It's a much simpler story. A lot of it was the pleasure of describing dinosaur hunting strategies and dino-sex. Moving smut into areas where it had never gone before! If you've ever seen birds having sex, it's nasty, brutish, and short, as Hobbes said.

Zinos-Amaro: That phrase appears in the story. I got a strong sense of Dickens' "A Christmas Carol" from this tale, and maybe some Jekyll and Hyde too.

Swanwick: When I began, I wanted to write about somebody who was everything that I disliked. George Weskowski was so obnoxious that ending by punishing him would have called everything into doubt—why bother to write the story at all? Having to come to terms with the fact not just that he needed his humanity, but that maybe he wasn't ever as bad a man as he claimed to have been, that made the story work. The ending was pleasant and unambiguous.

Zinos-Amaro: I wondered if in developing the character of George you were doing one of your critiques of success in contemporary society, which rewards materialism and being cut-throat.

Swanwick: No question about it. There was an obituary in the *Wall Street Journal*, not so long ago, about a man who was a captain of industry and had amassed a huge sum of money, apparently perfectly honestly. In his old age he said he regretted having wasted his life earning money. He said he should have spent his time better. That just seemed to me the saddest thing imaginable. He had wasted his life *and knew it.*

Zinos-Amaro: There's a really clever idea in "Riding the Giganotosaur" that's almost a throw-away, about one of the ways that George builds his fortune with "lawsuit futures." Where did that come from?

Swanwick: I invented that. It just seemed to me something that would cause enormous amounts of mischief. Of course, at the resolution I have to walk it back a couple of steps, so he wasn't the sole inventor of this, but was in on it.

Zinos-Amaro: I love the sequence where the queens turn on him.

Swanwick: I like it too, and it felt right. He brings his human expectations into his life as a dinosaur. He wants to know why they would do this. That's not a dinosaur thought, that's a human being thought. He expects bad things not to happen to him. But in nature bad things happen, just because they do.

Zinos-Amaro: But the moralizing framework is strong. You tell us how George commits four of the seven deadly sins once he begins his misadventures, and then later we are quoted the "no man is an island" sermon by John Donne!

Swanwick: What can I say? I was brought up Catholic. Mother Church says give me your child until the age of ten and he's mine forever. I have my serious differences with the Church, but those are the morals I was brought up with. They're not going to go away.

Zinos-Amaro: Being trapped with the proto-rat, and then ultimately deciding to set it free for the heck of it, was wonderfully ironic.

Swanwick: I wrote that before the book on screenwriting called *Save the Cat!* was published. That book reduces screenplay writing to a formula, which helps to explain a lot of movies. One of the basic things is that the pet must be saved. If you look at *Independence Day*, there's a scene where the family is fleeing, and the aliens are attacking everywhere, and the family gets into a tunnel with a lot of other stopped cars, and the dog runs off, and the aliens are getting closer, and at the last minute the dog comes back and leaps into their arms and the aliens kill nine tenths out of everybody on Earth, but the dog has been saved, thank goodness. In my story, George saves this rat, and his life is redeemed. But there's truth to that too. He finally finds his true colors.

Zinos-Amaro: This brings us to the end of 1999.

Swanwick: Great, so we only have another twenty years to go! Then I can lay down my burden, and gracefully expire.

CHAPTER FIVE
2000-2004

Alvaro Zinos-Amaro: You wanted us to start our discussion of 2000 with the "The Madness of Gordon Van Gelder" (*The Magazine of Fantasy & Science Fiction*, March 2000), a cute piece of flash fiction. How much of this story is true?

Michael Swanwick: Everything from the beginning to Gordon holding out fifty cents and offering to buy it is true. Literally true. The story begins in Philcon, which is the local convention. I'm always there unless I'm a guest of honor somewhere else at the same time, which has happened a couple of times. That was a good Philcon. There were a lot of good people there, too many of whom are now dead, alas.

I was thinking about what happened with Nancy and Gordon afterwards, and I wrote it up. Then I sent it to Gordon without a self-addressed stamped envelope, and with a little note saying, "Here's a special treat for you. It's a story you don't have to reject, because I know you're not going to buy it in the first place. It's just sent for your amusement." After sending it to him, I forgot about it. On January 3rd, 2000, which was a Monday and the first mail delivery day of the year, I checked my post office box and there was an envelope in it, the very distinctive check envelope from *F&SF*. I thought, "I haven't sold anything to *F&SF*, why are they sending me money?" I opened it up, and there was a check that simply said, "For 'The Madness of Gordon Van Gelder'" down in the corner. I was filled with a moment of megalomania: "I can sell anything! This century belongs to me!"

Zinos-Amaro: And I'm sure the check was for more than fifty cents, so there you go.

Swanwick: It was a nice little bit of money for something that all told took maybe half an hour to write.

Zinos-Amaro: In the true part of this short short, you mention Nancy Kress and Charles Sheffield. Tell us a little about your relationship with their work.

Swanwick: I wrote my "User's Guide to the Postmoderns" because I thought attention was being given to writers who were not the best writers working then in short fiction, with the exception of Bill Gibson. But I wanted to bring attention to all these other writers I was very excited about, and in doing so I neglected to include Nancy. That was a mistake on my part. She was definitely part of the zeitgeist and was writing interesting stuff. She also knows more about the mechanics of fiction than anyone I know. She can create a character in fewer words, and get a story moving faster, than anyone else I can think of. Really a quite extraordinary writer. Somebody like her, who can write really good short fiction and then keeps doing it long after she's mastered the novel, is one of our secular saints. She got overlooked because she'd just published her first novel, *The Prince of Morning Bells*, which made me mis-categorize her as a fantasy writer.

Charles Sheffield—I like his stuff, but it's less to my taste. It's more *Analog*-ish. But a writer well worthy of respect, and I've enjoyed a lot of his work.

Zinos-Amaro: In the story Nancy says, "Promise me you won't sell this story to Gardner Dozois!" and you kept true to that.

Swanwick: I didn't mean to sell the story to Gordon, either!

Zinos-Amaro: I imagine that the next story, "The Raggle Taggle Gypsy-O" (*Tales of Old Earth*, 2000), was written in layers over time rather than in a quick burst.

Swanwick: You're right. Delia Sherman and Ellen Kushner were doing a reading at a Barnes and Noble on the Main Line, and so Marianne and I went to see them, of course, because they're friends. After the reading Ellen hit me up to make a contribution to an anthology she was pitching based on border ballads. I said, "Well, I don't really see any story ideas there, but if you could give me two things that nobody could possibly put in the same story, I'll give it a try." I find that kind of thing kick-starts the imagination. But she couldn't. She named a couple of ballads that didn't do anything for me. Driving home afterwards, I said to Marianne, "Okay, a truck full of *Deinonychus*. That's the first thing. What would the second thing be?" Instantly, she said, "A basket of dead puppies." To which I replied, "Oh, I can write this bastard!" So I started writing it from that. But it took me a long time, because I was writing without knowing what the story was going to be. Ultimately, the borderlands anthology did not come together, which was a pity, because even though this story took a long time to write, I think I would have had it finished in time for the anthology. When somebody gives me an idea, I feel obligated to them.

Zinos-Amaro: This story is packed with allusions.

Swanwick: Yes. Ted Hughes' *Crow: From the Life and Songs of the Crow*, which is a collection I loved to pieces ever since I discovered it, heavily influenced the story. The first line of "The Raggle Taggle Gypsy-O" is a swipe from Wallace Stevens' "Thirteen Ways of Looking at a Blackbird." The poem begins: "Among twenty snowy mountains, / The only moving thing / Was the eye of the blackbird." I changed "the blackbird" to "Crow." Throughout, because it was a story about ballads to a degree, I put a lot of balladic language into it. I also put in hidden references. For example, the martlet that takes off the box to be delivered at the end is a mythological bird that has no feet, and therefore can never land. One of those popped up in E. R. Eddison's Zimiamvian trilogy, I think in *Mistress of Mistresses*, and its eyes were two stars shining, and I swiped that line and put it in as well. When Annie is telling Crow to kill the gas station attendant, I was thinking of Marianne, who every now and then, if she thinks I'm not taking something seriously enough, will tell me to kill Claudio, a swipe from Shakespeare's *Much Ado About Nothing*. At one point I'm talking about how they can wander through the world, and people from older times forget their modern inventions because of "robust integrity," a little cosmology I made up. A physicist explains it to Crow, who doesn't understand it, and the physicist says "Live with it" and wanders off. Here I was thinking of James Tiptree, Jr.'s "Forever to a Hudson Bay Blanket," where time paradoxes are forbidden, but if one *does* happen, where do you go to complain? The line "'This here's my hog, goddammit!' he explained" is a swipe from James Thurber. In one of his stories there's an argument between a husband and wife, and he writes: "'Shut up,' he explained." That's a delightful line.

For this story, I needed a good rifle, and by chance Marianne and I went to an open house of a rod and gun club. I ended up talking to a man who was an Olympic shooter. He kept giving more and more and more information, until he was explaining how to pack your own bullets because the ones you can buy commercially won't be as consistently perfect. I wrote everything down, and he gave me the name of a rifle. I was going to use all this, but I was in correspondence with Gene Wolfe at this time, and I mentioned this conversation to him. He wrote back and said "You need a Savage 110 Tactical," and explained why. Well, he's Gene Wolfe, so I took his advice over the Olympic sharpshooter's.

Delivering the brother's heart in a box, by the way, was a reference to Nirvana's "Heart-Shaped Box."

Zinos-Amaro: We've talked about the importance for you while growing up of rock and roll, which worked its way into some of your stories, such as "When the Music's Over . . ." or "In Concert." I'm curious, were you keeping up with grunge music, alternative, postmodern rock, that kind of thing? Or were you aware of Nirvana more because it was such a massive, breakout band? Referencing that song is very clever, given the crows in the music video.

Swanwick: I had not been keeping up. Nirvana was in the last period when rock was particularly meaningful to me. Funnily enough, Lucius Shepard despised them, and all of grunge music. He was a self-described music snob.

Zinos-Amaro: From my secondhand knowledge, Shepard was prolific in his dislikes.

Besides the Hughes influence, "The Raggle Taggle Gypsy-O" strikes me as your covert Roger Zelazny story. Your have mythological creatures, a combination of diverse time periods, and linguistically you mash together slang and vulgarities with old, poetic words, the balladic terms you were mentioning.

Swanwick: It's definitely very Zelazny-esque. I swiped the highway through time from *Roadmarks*, there's no getting around that one. Also that bright, almost cartoonish kind of characterization that he did. Zelazny was certainly a huge influence on me. It's very sad to see that nowadays what people remember are the Amber books, which started out so well, and then slowly spiraled down into oblivion. Even in his later years, though, he would pull up every now and then. Zelazny had a strange problem with death. In a lot of his books, the protagonist ends up immortal and will never die, which is absurd of course. One of his best late works is "24 Views of Mt. Fuji, by Hokusai." It's a spectacular story. At the end of it the protagonist dies. By chance, I had the same book that Zelazny used for that story. It's not the complete set of the views of Mt. Fuji, it's a selection of them. When I realized this, I went over to my book, and with each view I turned to the next picture, which greatly enhanced the story. You come to the very end and the final view of Mt. Fuji is almost all red and black. It's a sunset. You turn to that and read the ending and it's an image of profound, deep and meaningful death. So yes, I will admit to being influenced by Zelazny as much as I possibly could.

Zinos-Amaro: You mentioned Jung when we discussed "Blind Minotaur," and I was wondering if you drew from his work for the ideas of the archetype characters and the collective unconscious in this story.

Swanwick: Not really. Once I had a trickster, I needed a pick-up mythology. I looked at the character and asked myself, "What kind of gods or powers do I need?" I took some care to make sure that they would be multi-ethnic and multi-cultural, from around the world, because the world is their bailiwick. It's not a carefully crafted pantheon, like Neil Gaiman's The Endless. It's there for the sake of the story, and afterwards they get to go their separate ways.

Accuracy can sometimes work against you. I've actually been to the Coliseum, for instance, and I knew there was no place for a garage underneath the Coliseum. When I went to write that scene, that knowledge almost stopped me. I reminded myself that it's a story, and you're allowed to make things up even though you know better. But the tyranny of fact really struck me.

Zinos-Amaro: You went through something similar with the non-existent train station in "North of Diddy-Wah-Diddy."

Swanwick: Right. Knowing better can stop you. This is related to the fact that I have to believe a story is possible in order to write it, at least on its own terms. If it starts feeling silly, it becomes unreadable.

Zinos-Amaro: Is there anything you can share about the story's reception?

Swanwick: I did a reading of this at Philcon, maybe even the same one where the Gordon Van Gelder story happened. The year before I had done a reading, and it was an incredibly depressing story—it might have been "The Dead." At the end I looked at the audience's faces and they were horrified. So this time I told them that to make up for it I would read a bright, colorful story with an upbeat, happy ending. Afterwards one of the people in the audience came up to me and said, "I'm really glad you said that because during the part of the story where he's beaten to death, I began to have my doubts." That tells you something about cheerful, upbeat, optimistic stories, I think: all the effect comes in at the end.

Zinos-Amaro: "Moon Dogs" (*Moon Dogs*, NESFA Press; *Asimov's Science Fiction*, March 2000), another Locus and Hugo finalist the following year, also has a powerful ending, but lets begin with its genesis.

Swanwick: I was driving through Germantown, which is a rather posh section of Philadelphia, and I noticed a little bit of woods between a house and a church. There was a circle of sycamore trees, and their white trunks stood out in the gloom. The other trees just sort of faded into the general darkness. I realized that this circle, that seemed almost magical, was because the trees grew around a pond. That image stayed with me, and I wrote up a description of what the trees looked like. From somewhere I got the words "drowning pool," which seemed to me very evocative. The description that begins with Nick being drowned as a form of therapy—which indicates what I think of pop cultural therapy ideas—is really horrifying for me as an asthmatic. I like that the black water, the drowning, the horrific nature of it, is just casually passed by.

I was pleased with the gundogs, the robot dogs in the story. They made it possible for Selene to be naked in front of a stranger and ask him to dry her off in absolute, perfect safety. I think they'd find a ready market in our world, and would make women's lives better. Anyway, when Nick finds her was the moment it became clear to me that the story was going to be based on the myth of Actaeon and Artemis. So from that point on, I knew it wasn't going to end well.

Zinos-Amaro: Besides this Ovidian framework, this story brought to mind your own "Snow Angels," which features a kind of similar male/female setup, and also deals with the theme of facing one's fears.

Swanwick: I've never made that connection before, but I think it's valid.

Zinos-Amaro: Tell me more about the background that informed the Sacred Vaccine cult—somewhat ironic, given our 2020 and 2021—, and Selene having been in this arranged marriage to Joshua when he's seven and she's five.

Swanwick: It seemed to me that with the entire world spiraling into disaster, and with it looking like most people are going to die, as most people do in fact in the background, there would be a lot of really bad behavior. If I was thinking of any specific cult, it would have been Jim Jones and the mass suicide of people drinking the Kool-Aid. I heard on the radio a recording of a cultist on the loudspeaker weeping as he gave everyone directions to come up and take the poisoned Kool-Aid. A terrifying thing. So irrational. That's what I was thinking of here. I made them as evil as possible.

Fortunately I was not very prophetic in how this was going to play out. Marianne spent thirty-six years in public health, working for the Pennsylvania Department of Health Bureau of Laboratories. I learned a great deal about emerging infectious diseases during that time. The thing about anybody who works in epidemiology is that they get happy about the strangest things. I could tell that some really horrible disease had broken out because Marianne would come home particularly cheerful. One time she said, "They've got a new disease that—get this!—only affects gay men and Haitians." That was the first I heard of AIDS, and I'm sure I heard about it before the President did. You want people who really care emotionally about these things on the job.

Zinos-Amaro: The following line from the story stood out to me, and I was wondering if it had a specific provenance: "You're afraid, so you take control by becoming what you fear."

Swanwick: I was thinking of G. Gordon Liddy there. After Watergate he was on the television rather a lot, explaining his very strange ideas. As a boy he was afraid of rats, so he caught one and killed it and roasted it and ate it. He was very proud of this fact. Afterwards, he was not afraid of rats. The whole speech that Selene gives about hunting down the buck that had gored her was inspired by G. Gordon Liddy.

The idea of Selene's position as a "plague heiress" came from

James Burke's documentary *Connections*. In that series he traced how one technological development leads to another. On the way to something like computers there was the Black Death. After the Black Death was over, the number of people in Europe was much smaller, and a lot of them had a lot of money, because they inherited it from the older people who had died and left it to their descendants. I took that straight from there. And that idea is what led to the thought that they had both lost their entire families.

Incidentally, I was at that Boskone when *Moon Dogs* came out, because NESFA published it. I had broken a toe, so I was hobbling around on a cane. I was telling people that this was one of three story collections that I had out that year. Marianne said, "You do realize you have the makings of a good mystery novel here. Tomorrow morning you're found beaten to death with your own cane. The detective says, 'Who had a motive for killing this man?' And every writer here is going to raise their hands.'"

Zinos-Amaro: I'm glad this is a mystery we didn't have to solve! Moving to decidedly lighter fare, we have "Letters to the Editor" (*Asimov's Science Fiction*, October-November 2001). Had you in fact been writing these humorous fake biographies between 1988 and 2000?

Swanwick: Yes, those are the genuine letters that I sent Sheila. I was doing this all along. Sheila would send me the Xerox form letter, and I'm going, "I don't have a life, I'm a writer. My big news this month is that I sold a story to *Asimov's*." So I just wrote a goofy letter, and kept doing it for my own amusement and Sheila's. She later on told me that she wouldn't have always sent me the Xerox form letter, except that she enjoyed my responses. So I was undercutting myself there. But it was fun to sit down and make up a riff. It didn't take any longer than writing a serious letter would have, really. After a while I decided to save them. Some time later there was a special issue of *Asimov's* and I didn't have any story to send that might make it into that issue. So I gathered up the letters, did a very light edit, added a final letter so that we had an ending, and sent it in. Afterwards I was very proud of the fact that I had sold *Asimov's* their own form letter.

Zinos-Amaro: My favorite line from all these, which made me laugh out loud, was your reference to writing "a penetrating series of monographs exploring the fiction of Lionel Fanthorpe."

Swanwick: I had this little paperback collection of excerpts from Lionel Fanthorpe, so it fit.

The technology has changed now, so Sheila sends an email asking for biographical information. I've been saving my responses. If *Asimov's* and I both last to another major anniversary, there will be, I hope, "E-mails to the Editor."

Zinos-Amaro: We turn now from this straightforward piece to something much less so, "Dirty Little War" (*In the Shadow of the Wall: An Anthology of Vietnam Stories That Might Have Been*, ed. Byron R. Tetrick, 2002).

Swanwick: I started trying to write a story about the Vietnam War while it was still going on, in the early 70s. I could not do it, for two reasons: one, I was not yet a good enough writer to be published, and two, when I thought of the war it just filled me with rage for sending American soldiers to a foreign country to die and to kill. The reason for why we were doing it kept shifting from month to month. They never really had a clear explanation for what it was all about. It wasn't until the year 2000 when I had enough distance and perspective that I could write about this. Byron Tetrick was a Vietnam War vet and a former student of mine at Clarion West. He came up to me at a convention and said he had this anthology that he'd sold and would love it if I contributed a story. I told him I'd been trying to write a Vietnam story for a long time, and that I probably wouldn't be able to do it, but if I did, I'd send it to him. As these things sometimes happen, the request knocked something loose and I was able to come up with an idea. I was thinking about a story that I either read or someone told me about—possibly Greg Frost—where there's a dinner party and everyone is chitchatting, saying the usual things, and ignoring the fact that there's a dead horse on the table. It was obviously metaphoric, the elephant in the room. I remembered that and thought, "Okay, I can see this now." I wanted to contrast the awfulness of war with the fact that back on the home front things were pretty good. Disney World opened during the Vietnam War, and the most we were ever asked to do was go out and spend a lot. That would help the economy and support our boys in Vietnam. The cognitive dissonance of the happy life back home and the misery for everyone in Vietnam gave me a way to write about that.

Zinos-Amaro: The way you literalize that dissonance through a surreal setup is really neat and creates a powerful effect.

Swanwick: In the first draft of "Dirty Little War" I had much more of a Lieutenant Calley feel to it, soldiers running through a village and torching it, and so on. I was thinking of Tim O'Brien's *The Things They Carried.* I'd done some research on what it was like being on a jungle patrol in Vietnam, but I wasn't really confident that I had it right, so I ran it past a friend of mine who was a Vietnam vet, Gene Olmstead. He read it and he spotted the influence right away. He said, "You know, O'Brien really had an axe to grind." I realized I was being unfair to these men. I revised the story and took that part out. I just left their suffering in. I told Gene I was doing this and he was horrified. Even though he was speaking for the soldiers he had been among, he didn't want to be censoring my work. But this change made the story so much better. It would have been mean-spirited and unfair the other way around.

The ending, where they reach the wall—on the one hand it's the wall of the house, but on the other hand, it's the Vietnam Memorial. There was a three-quarter replica of the Memorial that went on tour. It came near Philadelphia, so I went to see it. It looks like the real wall from one side, and the other side is all plywood. Even knowing that this was a replica, and a three-quarters replica at that, I walked along it and it was profoundly moving. It was unreal in so many ways, but the reality that it was a reflection of was so moving. It required that I tell this from the viewpoint of the soldiers.

Zinos-Amaro: Speaking of the wall, we have an image here that has been appearing every so often since your very early story "'Til Human Voices Wake Us"; "Death was a smooth and featureless black wall."

Swanwick: It's amazing how many times I've used that!

Zinos-Amaro: Lucius Shepard, whom we've mentioned a few times in these conversations, wrote a number of stories featuring Vietnam vets, jungle war settings, characters with PTSD, and so on. Did he read "Dirty Little War," and if so, what did he make of it?

Swanwick: No, no. I do know that he thought well of me. At one point, early on, I told him something about Fred Pohl, and he said very dismissively, "Oh, you're a much better writer than he is." I went, "Oooh, really?" My opinion was that Lucius was a Great American Writer, and I told him so to his face. He thought I was okay! I don't know what was with Lucius and Vietnam. The impression I got was that he wasn't actually a soldier. He might have been out there as a journalist, but maybe not. He wrote soldiers really well. I don't know what was going on there. He was a mysterious guy. I really wish somebody would write a biography of him. It would be tricky, because you'd have to gather up all these stories that he told, most of which were not true, and sort through them. He had one period where he said he was in Alaska, shacked up with a female Eskimo fur trapper. He'd be sending emails or such to people in New York, with long descriptions of his adventures, and yet somebody during that same period saw him on Staten Island!

Zinos-Amaro: It seems maybe he was his own unreliable narrator.

One of the things that makes the ending of this story so memorable for me is the linkage being generational. The scream turns out to be the mother's scream. Parents have sent their children to fight the War on the floor, while they have a dinner party.

Swanwick: That seemed to me to work because in the larger sense everyone who went off to Vietnam, well, they *were* the children of America. Speaking as an older adult now, they were all our children. Also, the mother's horrified reaction when she gets the news turns these awful people back into human beings. When I was writing that I was thinking of Cheever and Updike. I've never been a great fan of suburban short stories, but they could both do it well enough that they could make you like it.

Zinos-Amaro: Given "Dirty Little War," it seems apt to ask your thoughts about surrealism and science fiction generally.

Swanwick: I love surrealism. I think a lot of what I try to do with images is an attempt to bring surrealism into science fiction. Obviously I'm not the only one. Surrealism has had such a huge, broad influence. It's almost like Davy Crockett's buffalo that's so large that you need three men to see it all at once.

There's an influence which only I can spot on my work from black and white cartoons, things like *Eerie* and *Creepy* magazines. They had a disreputable air and really weird stories. I remember one that began with a cowboy in a wagon, and he's leaning back, shaded by a frilled parasol, playing "Oh! Susanna" on his banjo, and the wagon is being pulled by a dinosaur. There are a lot of very surreal images like that in black and white comics that I admired immensely and then tried to bring into science fiction prose. So sometimes the effect of surrealism is direct, and sometimes it's indirect.

Zinos-Amaro: There are obviously a lot of era-specific references in the story. Did your research turn up anything that surprised you?

Swanwick: I have a line in the story where the soldiers use bennies. I have heard people very authoritatively explain that American soldiers did *not* use speed during Vietnam. But I also talked to a vet who told me a story. He was in the middle of the Tet Offensive and his CO gave him a direct order to take the bennies. Six hours later, the officer said to him, "If I ever give you another order like that, shoot me." He'd spent all that time just talking his mouth off. So I believed him, because that's not a story you'd make up.

Zinos-Amaro: Speaking of war, when we discussed "A Midwinter's Tale" and "Griffin's Egg" you said that because you haven't served, you mostly try to avoid stories involving the military and/ or war. In "'Hello,' Said the Stick" (*Analog Science Fiction and Fact*, March 2002) you manage to come at it obliquely. I note that this was your first *Analog* credit.

Swanwick: I had long wanted to sell a story to *Analog*. When I wrote this, I thought it would fit nicely. That's all that that was. Once I had the idea for my story, I used Larry Niven's story "Night on Mispec Moor" as a model. It's a very short story about a soldier who's fleeing defeat on a planet where the people are limited to low-tech weapons. On this one particular, creepy moor he's caught out at night and there's a local fungus that inhabits the corpses of the soldiers who've died and they come back and attack as zombies. It was a very neat, efficient story, I think no longer than "'Hello,' Said the Stick." I didn't go back and re-read Niven's story or try to imitate it in any way. Niven also influenced a posthumous collaboration I did with Avram Davidson. I'm not ashamed of stealing with both hands from Larry Niven.

On the war aspect, there's a line where the stick says, "Is

this [radiation poisoning] crueler than hacking a man to death with a big knife? I don't see how." I got that from a chemical and biological warfare conference that I attended. At the end of the conference, the purpose of which was to help prevent the use of chemical and biological weapons, a woman got up and said, "I was over in [some particular country] just a couple of weeks ago, where there's an insurgency, and one side captured somebody from the other side, tied him up in chains and dragged him from a jeep for five miles. I don't see where that's any less cruel than what you're talking about." Everybody had to admit that simply limiting weapons to one type or another didn't necessarily make things better. It's one of those things that you find yourself thinking about off and on for the rest of your life.

Zinos-Amaro: You mentioned, in the context of "Picasso Deconstructed," that unlike most stories, "'Hello,' Said the Stick" was also a truly fun one to write.

Swanwick: I was at a reading that a friend was giving. It took about five minutes for me to realize two things. One was that I already knew the story, because my friend had run it past me for critique. And the other was that my friend was the single worst reader I've ever heard in my life. For a while there was some amusement to be had seeing if my friend would make a mistake in literally every sentence, and then stop and correct it, but after a time it became obvious that yes, this was going to happen, as it did. I had my notebook out and I started word-doodling, putting things down at random. "'Hello,' said the stick" sounded like a good beginning. So throughout the course of the reading I played around with the idea until I came up with the basic outline of the story. That night I went home and the next morning, a Saturday, I told Marianne I was going to go upstairs and work. I wrote the story, finished it, and put it in the mail to *Analog*. So from start to finish it was about seventeen hours, and I got to sleep late in between—it was a *very* satisfying experience. If I could write this efficiently all the time, what a monster of production I would be!

Zinos-Amaro: Was the economy of the prose in "'Hello,' Said the Stick" a deliberate choice to intensify the drama of the war? A function of the swift pace you wanted to create? Maybe both?

Swanwick: A combination of both. The story felt like it needed that kind of a voice: simple, clear, efficient. There was no reason to linger over anything.

Zinos-Amaro: Let us linger for a moment on your recognition. This story was a Locus finalist and a Hugo finalist in 2003, one of four pieces of fiction you had on that year's Hugo ballot (*Bones of the Earth*, "Slow Life," which we'll talk about shortly, and "The Little Cat Laughed to See Such Sport").

Swanwick: There is a tide in the affairs of men, and there's a time when you can get these awards nominations, and there are times when you cannot. If you look, for example, at Samuel R. Delany's awards, most of them are bunched in one period of eight or ten years, and afterward he's still writing wonderfully except that he does not get the awards. Part of that is being relatively well-known while still being relatively new.

Zinos-Amaro: Your next story, "Five British Dinosaurs" (*Interzone*, #177 March 2002), has some pretty outré scenes, even by your standards, maybe a little of the surrealism we talked about with "Dirty Little War."

Swanwick: This is the second story I wrote because of where I wanted to sell it, in this case *Interzone*.

Zinos-Amaro: You sure hit your target: it came out in the special 20th anniversary issue. Luck?

Swanwick: Yes. That knocked me out, quite frankly. The story is just five pieces of flash fiction. It also ended up being a finalist for the British Science Fiction Award, which also knocked me out. The five stories were simply these pleasant little entertainments. I guess it hit them correctly. Probably, all false modesty aside, "Five British Dinosaurs" made it into that issue because there were so many more serious stories in there, so you want something light and entertaining to break it up.

Zinos-Amaro: For me the through-line of this story is commentary or observations on British social protocols, ideas like respectability and status. How did you go about choosing which specific dinosaur to pair up with which specific story element?

Swanwick: To start with, there are not a lot of British dinosaurs. I decided to make it British dinosaurs because I wanted to sell this to a British magazine and hopefully make it more pleasant for British readers. The first one, *Iguanodon anglicus*, was the first dinosaur fossil that was discovered and acknowledged to be a dinosaur. So that was the best place to start. The others were simply the dinosaurs that would fit. *Altispinax dunkeri*, for example, was because of the appearance. It would make a good running dinosaur, and I was thinking of Ray Harryhausen for a couple of reasons. My friends Robert Walter and Tess Kissinger are dinosaur reconstruction artists, and they think the world of Harryhausen. He's like a god to them. So I gave Tess the opportunity to ride on a dinosaur along with her hero. Tess, when she was younger, had a job painting the Macy's balloons for the Thanksgiving Day parade in New York City, which is a job she hated. So she had the background for this particular position in the story. With the *Megalosaurus bucklandii* I was thinking of the first mention of a dinosaur in British literature, where in *Bleak House* Dickens is talking about a foggy day in London and how you wouldn't be surprised to see a *Megalosaurus* come wandering down the lane. So that was an absolutely necessary dinosaur to write about.

I threw in a few other jokes and references. The second story features Ralph Chapman and Michael K. Brett-Surman, scientists at the Smithsonian who gave me a great deal of help when I was researching my novel *Bones of the Earth*. The third story ends with the cutting remark, "The hallux is reversed." The hallux is the spur-like thing at the back of some dinosaurs' hind feet, which is essentially an evolution of what on the human being would be the big toe. For the cover for *Bones of the Earth* they got an artist who didn't know much about dinosaurs, and he did a skeletal dinosaur leg, and every time that a paleontologist would glance at the cover, they would immediately say, "The hallux is reversed." The first time they told me this I didn't even know what the hallux was, but I certainly learned! So putting this in the story was probably my little grumping, getting it out of my system. Benjamin Waterhouse Hawkins had to be in this piece, because he was the first person to do serious paintings of dinosaurs. He also built the models for the Crystal Palace—you don't get more British than that.

Zinos-Amaro: Both this story and the following one, "A Great Day for Brontosaurs" (*Asimov's Science Fiction*, May 2002), are firmly anchored in scientific detail. But in a way they're also fantasy, because you choose to have talking dinosaurs, with no explanation.

Swanwick: I had spent a lot of time researching *Bones of the Earth*, so I had all of this stuff down to my fingertips. When I went to write more dinosaur stories, all the science was right there. That was easy. I only had to look it up to make sure I hadn't misremembered it. The stories themselves were what they wanted to be. These are both light stories, and talking dinosaurs drinking tea are intrinsically fun! There's a beautiful power to *not* explaining something, as long as you do it front-on.

Zinos-Amaro: When we talked about "Walking Out" we commented that it was a kind of social commentary story with a 50s sf vibe; "A Great Day for Brontosaurs" is almost like a Golden Age story from the 40s, with updated science, but built on that classic double twist structure.

Swanwick: Late 40s or early 50s. Back then they were forever writing stories where ancient humans were being resurrected and outwitting their alien, so-called superiors. That's probably where I got this from. You can still read the better Golden Age stories today with complete pleasure—they still work.

"A Great Day for Brontosaurs" is a fast story, and a short story, because it's also an Adam-and-Eve story. Every science fiction writer tries to sell an Adam-and-Eve story at least once to prove that they can do it, because the editors are all so desperate to not buy them.

By the way, speaking of the science, in the story I say DNA is fragile, and in fact it's not, though at the time I wrote that everyone was talking about it being fragile. The *Jurassic Park* movies had come out, and they had the idea of using ancient dinosaur DNA to recreate dinosaurs, and it got into the popular imagination. If you wanted to get tenure in a respectable university you did not say anything good about dinosaur DNA. The paleontologist Mary Schweitzer found soft structures inside tyrannosaur fragments. I went to a secret lecture that she gave at Penn, one that dinosaur professionals and associated people were told about, but not the public. She did not want any journalists there because she didn't have tenure, and if certain words were put into her mouth, she'd never get it.

Zinos-Amaro: A lovely line in this story occurs when the Financial Officer is challenging the scientist about the purpose of his project, and the scientist finally says, "What is so beautiful and useless as a dinosaur?"

Swanwick: I think that line sums up dinosaurs wonderfully. There's really no need for them; we don't actually need to know them. We can understand evolution without dinosaurs. And yet we're so much better off with them.

Zinos-Amaro: I think that as humans we tend to take very seriously a lot of things that aren't necessary.

Swanwick: Yes. The story is also a comment on science, on what science feels like from the inside. People come up with uses for science, and they talk about these uses of science when they're looking for funding, but they're often in it simply because whatever they're into is cool. A good example of this was Ralph Chapman, who worked as a paleontologist but was technically an applied morphometrician. I once interviewed him in his office, and asked him, "If you couldn't do paleontology, what would you do?" He said, "Well, the FBI want to recruit me for their forensics department, because there's a lot of analysis of shapes that they do." And then he said in a small voice, as if he were admitting to something, "I really like shapes." I saw to the gist of him right there. So many good scientists could be making a lot more money using their skills elsewhere, but they're doing whatever they're doing because this is what they love working on. So "A Great Day for Brontosaurs" is an Adam-and-Eve story, but the point of the story was the beauty of science separated from its utility.

Zinos-Amaro: I want to come back to this in the next story. But one other thing I wanted to bring up here is the idea that these dinosaurs are acknowledged by the scientist not to be actually dinosaurs, but very convincing approximations. This theme—that we are preoccupied with copies or replicas—has cropped up in your work several times before, all the way back to "The Feast of Saint Janis."

Swanwick: That's all true, and it certainly feeds into the story. I also think it's a kind of honesty. There are people who want to recreate dinosaurs, or more practically or immediately mastodons—there are people working on that right now. At some point they have to admit that they're not recreating the real thing, but simulacra of mastodons. It's all embedded in the nature of our culture. We want whatever it is we can't have. And if we really cannot have it, we'll make something very much like it.

Zinos-Amaro: Your comment about science is a nice lead-in to "Slow Life" (*Analog Science Fiction and Fact*, December 2002). The crew, on Titan, has to answer questions from the folks back home via VoiceWeb, and as part of one such answer, Alan gives this little speech: "This is a voyage of discovery, and we're engaged in what's called 'pure science.' Now, time and time again, the purest research has turned out to be extremely profitable. But we're not looking that far ahead. We're just hoping to find something absolutely unexpected."

Swanwick: Absolutely true. There's also a social media question from a teacher named Mary Schroeder, by the way, who is named after one of our son's favorite English teachers in high school. She's our friend; we had her over here many times before she moved. Another hidden joke is in the line "I can kick it with my boot," about the beach. The first words from the Moon, after the Eagle had landed, were "That's one small step for man, one giant leap for mankind." When Neil Armstrong fully stepped down off the ladder, his first words were, "The surface is fine and powdery. I can kick it up loosely with my toe." So my line was a reference to that; I considered making it closer to what Armstrong said, but it was just too long and would have drawn attention to itself.

Zinos-Amaro: "Slow Life" feels like a spiritual sequel to "The Very Pulse of the Machine," with a female character whose life is at risk making first contact on an alien world. Just as you had researched Io heavily for that story, here I imagine you did the same for Titan. But the scientific detail is incredible. I mean, at one point you give us tables of hydrocarbon solutes and their mole fractions!

Swanwick: This is an odd story. There is a Philadelphia cartoonist named Matt Howarth, who did, and does, very edgy black-and-white comics. He had a great underground rep, and he's stayed true to his art, which has brought him up into poverty, really. Matt had an idea and reached out to me. He wanted to do a serial for Space.com. We'd do like one page a month; I'd write the script, and he'd cartoon it. I thought that that was a really great idea. I did some very fast, hard research and downloaded dozens of papers on Titan, and then wrote the first two pages. The first page would just be a series of panels with descriptions of the chemistry of a raindrop falling on Titan, which turns out would take several years, and what happens at each step of the way. The bottom of the page, when it's about to finally splash down, these hands would reach out with a baggie, catch it, and bag it. It then went on from there, and I imagined I'd be writing this on the fly while I was working on my other stuff, and I thought I could do that and do an interesting job of it. Matt tried really hard to sell it, and Space.com wanted it, but they didn't want to buy one-time use, they wanted it to be work for hire, where they would own the whole thing in perpetuity. That was not acceptable to either of us. Matt broke his heart trying to sell it to them. "Slow Life" went on to win a Hugo, which I think shows that Space.com was mistaken. They had the opportunity to have something really special and failed.

Zinos-Amaro: Ah. Yes, the story opening, though full of science, is very cinematic.

Swanwick: Again, we come back to Larry Niven. Niven's early short stories all had this great hard-science feel to them. I have all of the early collections. I thought, "How did he do that?" So I re-read some of these books. I realized that in a lot of them he began with a lecture about physics or space, like the physics of black holes or such. I thought, "I can do that." That's why I began the story as I did.

When I sent "Slow Life" to *Analog*, an *Analog* writer who's a friend said to me he had just talked to Stanley Schmidt, who said to him, "Michael Swanwick sent me a story, and it has real science in it!" My friend was greatly amused by that. When Stan sent me the acceptance letter he said that my story had a lot more technical detail than they usually allowed in *Analog*. I said, "I'm going to have *that* written on my tombstone!"

Zinos-Amaro: Thematically, I think a bit covertly this is a story where you're coming back to your perennial interest in identity and the struggle to hold on to it. But here you've rotated it ninety degrees, so that it's an alien life form, rather than a human being, who is struggling to retain, in the face of dramatic revelations, what it thought was its sense of self and its place in the cosmos.

Swanwick: There's definitely also a religious element there, in that Lizzie has come to drive them out of the Garden and into the larger universe. Her intentions are good, but it's a traumatic event for them.

Zinos-Amaro: She almost dies in the process, which fits into the religious redeemer archetype.

Swanwick: It's really hard to keep that out when you're dealing with certain issues. I tried not to play it up. I could have had her on the balloon on a cruciform harness!

Zinos-Amaro: I note that "Slow Life" has this really cool epigraph excerpted from *The Memoirs of Lizzie O'Brien*. Will we ever get more of that story?

Swanwick: That sound you heard in the background is my wife expressing her opinion that I should write my Lizzie O'Brien novel. If I do write the novel, the story will have to be set in an alternate universe.

Zinos-Amaro: Sure, you did that with "Scherzo with Tyrannosaur" and *Bones of the Earth*.

Swanwick: That's true, that's true. I'm just waiting for the right insight that will make the novel fly.

Zinos-Amaro: Towards the end of "Slow Life," the alien intelligence has this fantastic line: ". . . the chances of your destroying yourselves are well within the limits of acceptability." What do you think our chances are?

Swanwick: Yeah, that was pretty cold. But it had survived the same thing, so turnabout is fair play.

The very ending of the story, when she accepts the gift she's about to give the world, came from an incident I had when I was young. I went out to dinner with a girlfriend. We were driving back from a party or whatever in her pickup truck. She was driving down these dark country roads, and I gradually realized from the way she was driving that she was dead drunk. I also knew her well enough to know that if I tried to convince her of this fact it would simply decrease my chances of surviving. So I rolled down the window, stuck my head out in the air and laughed. I figured, "If I'm going to die, at least I'll have the pleasure of feeling the wind in my face first."

Regarding our chances as a species, I'm not optimistic, but I've been wrong before. I'm hoping that I'll continue to be wrong.

Zinos-Amaro: You think that humanity will likely destroy itself?

Swanwick: I think there's a good chance. But I also think there's a chance that we'll manage to survive. And if we survive then we'll have the tools to thrive. When I was twenty-one maybe I asked Will Jenkins, who wrote as Murray Leinster, if he was optimistic or pessimistic about the human race. He smiled and quoted James Branch Cabell: "I look upon it all with appropriate emotions." That turns out to be a pretty good answer.

Zinos-Amaro: This story was reprinted in a Hal Clement tribute anthology, which ironically didn't include anything by Larry Niven.

Swanwick: Larry was likely off on vacation somewhere at that time. As you probably noticed, I named the ship the *Clement*, and the lander the *Harry Stubbs*, in part because when I went to write this story I had recently read a story set on Titan which made it sound very dull and dreary. Then I read Hal Clement's *Half Life*, where it looks like the people of Earth are going to die of highly evolved diseases, so this group goes to Titan because if you're going to die you may as well do the most pleasurable thing you can, and what's more pleasurable than basic research? Clement really made Titan sound like an interesting, exciting place to visit. Shortly after I'd finished writing the story and it had been accepted, I went to a Worldcon and I happened to see Hal there. I told him I'd named the ship and lander after him and told him how much I'd loved *Half Life*. He said he was very happy to hear that, because it was nice to have one of his books other than *Mission of Gravity* being praised. A year later he was dead. I thought that was so typical of Harry, that he would stay alive long enough for me to tell him how much I liked his book. A lesser writer would die a month before I'd had the opportunity. But Harry had heart.

Zinos-Amaro: The next story, "King Dragon" (*The Dragon Quintet*, edited by Marvin Kaye, 2003), which would make up the opening to your novel *The Dragons of Babel*, certainly has a lot of heart. It's also a very dense undertaking.

Swanwick: Its origin is kind of anticlimactic. At a convention, Marvin Kaye told me he was doing an anthology of dragon stories, and he was hoping I would write a story for him, preferably with the dragons of *The Iron Dragon's Daughter*, though anything would be good. I told him I didn't have any ideas for dragon stories, but that if I had one, I'd write it up and send it to him. As sometimes happens, I came home from the convention, went to my machine the next morning and the idea for a story popped into my head. I knew from the start that it was in the same universe as *Iron Dragon's Daughter*. I swiped the key opening image from J. G. Ballard's *Empire of the Sun*. There's a scene where the young Jim is in the concentration camp and Japanese fighter planes fly low over the camp and he goes running out to see them and feel the hot wash of their engines over him in an ecstasy of technophilia. I thought that was such a great image, I stole it wholeheartedly. So I begin "King Dragon" with my character running up the hill to see the dragons pass over. He's in love with the idea of dragons, as everybody who has never met one is. When I started writing it, I named the hill Grannystone Hill, because it needed a name. When he gets up there, his Granny is there; she's obviously a Standing Stone, who normally does not take human form. That came from the legend of the Standing Stones of Brittany, who would periodically go down to the river to drink.

Zinos-Amaro: One of my all-time favorite lines in your work occurs in this story about a dozen pages in, when the dragon says, "You try my patience. Worse, you drain my batteries."

Swanwick: I was pleased with that. That's the clash of voices: the high fantasy voice and the Zelazny-esque contemporary voice.

Zinos-Amaro: It's also the fusion, again, of fantasy and science fiction.

Swanwick: Gardner liked the story enough to buy it for *Asimov's* and later put it in his *Best of the Year*, and Gardner didn't really like fantasy. But this is science-fiction flavored fantasy, so that got around his prejudices. This is a territory I inhabit a lot. I'm not sure exactly why. I tend to judge other people's stories as though they ought to be one or the other. Apparently I hold everybody else to a higher standard than I hold myself.

Zinos-Amaro: At one point Will learns from his mirror image that an explosion involving a basilisk "warped the world and the mesh of time in which it is caught" and that, as a result, he and his grandmother have been "thrown forward, halfway through the day." It's a slightly uncanny moment involving time travel. Did you consider other structural uses of time travel in the narrative, or was this incident clearly in your mind a one-off thing?

Swanwick: It was a one-off, but as I went into the series more, the warp and woof of time and space tended to congeal in odd ways. I didn't want to get too much into time travel because time travel tends to become very formal and stylized. It tends to turn into a logic puzzle, which is the opposite of what I want to do with fiction.

Zinos-Amaro: When we're being introduced to the green-shirties, the dragon gives this speech to Will: "Do not despise them because they are young. The young make excellent soldiers and better martyrs. They are easily dominated, quickly trained, and as ruthless as you command them to be. They kill without regret, and they go to their deaths readily, because they do not truly understand that death is possible, much less permanent." Beyond the literal meaning, I also think this ends up becoming a comment on the dragon's over-confidence in his own under-standing of how human beings work. From that hubris stems his downfall.

Swanwick: That's true, but there was another thing that was going into it too. When Will refers to the greenshirties as being "just kids," they're his age. They're his peers. But he feels that he's aged more than they have. I think the dragon was also spelling out his plans for him. The dragon, over the long term, is enacting a kind of seduction. He wants to turn Will into his creature. That's as close as he comes to spelling out his intentions.

Zinos-Amaro: I see the dragon as trying to unleash Will's id; he wants Will's primal impulses around violence, sex and death to be loosed and freed from morality, under the dragon's strict control of course. It's like he's tempting him with the drug of his own unconscious desires.

Swanwick: That's the dragon's worldview. When I started writing about dragons, the beaux ideal was Anne McCaffrey's dragons, which were positive forces that would love you and turn you into a better person. I always liked the traditional Western dragon, the dragon as devil, particularly the one in John Gard-ner's *Grendel*, one of the greatest dragons ever, I think so far unsurpassed. When I wrote this dragon, I was thinking of pure, malevolent evil. There was nothing good to be said about him, ex-cept that he was good at his job, which was destruction. As soon as the dragon decided to make Will his lieutenant, it was inevita-ble that Will had to kill him. There's no other way out. Will could not abandon his people even after they'd abandoned him, and the dragon could not be tamed. He could only be killed. Nobody else but Will was in a position to do so, not only in terms of plot accessibility, but in story terms of rightness. Like it or not, Will is the hero, and he has to do that. That is his role.

Zinos-Amaro: There's a powerful scene in "King Dragon" in which Will, having spent time serving the dragon, has scorn for his former friends. He'd developed an outsider's perspective.

Swanwick: You become whatever it is you pretend to be. Will has a role to play; he has no choice but to play it. His job is to be the one person who does not accept that role as being him. He manages to do that at a certain cost.

Zinos-Amaro: That cost involves the hag Bessie Applemere ending up with a "sterile womb and sightless eyes" because of her one untruth.

Swanwick: Yeah, and he makes that decision for her. That shows how much he's grown, and not entirely in a good way. I think I wanted to indicate that there's something you can't ever walk back. That's part of what he can't walk back.

The use of words like "crone" and "hag" in this story, by the way, comes from a very strange 1980s book called *Websters' First New Intergalactic Wickedary of the English Language*, which is a radical feminist Wiccan attempt to take all the negative words applied to women and redefine them. A "battle axe" is a bold and courageous woman fighting for the truth, and so on. "Crone" and "hag" are also words that are given the highest merit. When I first got this book, I thought, "This is ridiculous. You don't define words and put them into the dictionary *first*, so that people will use them that way. That's not the direction that it goes! Language starts with common usage." I gave the book away. But later on, when I was writing *The Dragons of Babel*, I realized I needed it and sought out a copy. A surprising amount of research goes into fantasy, and I cannot say why. When you can do anything at all, it somehow seems very important to have it rooted in actual things.

Zinos-Amaro: In the novella as originally published you end by hinting at this whole other adventure in store for Will. Obviously in the novel the story proceeds in a dramatized fashion. Did you know when you wrote "King Dragon" that this would be developed into a full novel?

Swanwick: Not on page one, but by the time I knew how this story was going to end, I knew it was also the beginning of a novel. At the end of it he goes back to his aunt, Blind Enna, and he's reconciled with her, and you realize that she loves him. In the novel, he goes back and she's terrified of him and drives him out. Some pretty harsh things happen in "King Dragon" and to end it with some reconciliation and love took the worst of that off. In the novel he's driven out of the village and redeemed elsewhere.

I will say, Will is literally the fair-haired, young country boy, but in "King Dragon" and the rest of the novel, I tried to make him a lot smarter than fantasy heroes usually are. Not as naïve, and not as clueless. He's actually quite smart. He sees what has to be done very quickly. That was a very deliberate choice. It was a reaction against lazy fantasies.

Zinos-Amaro: Right before he reunites with Blind Enna, he leaves Bessie Applemere, and you write: "There was no place to go now but home. It took him a moment to remember where that was." When I first read that, I thought that was a great ending line.

Swanwick: There needed to be a little more. That was just too harsh. Also, there's not always just one end to a story. In *Being Gardner Dozois*, Gardner told me that he once came to the end of one of his stories and came up with three last lines—so he just used one after the other!

Zinos-Amaro: Yours certainly works. When we talked about "A Midwinter's Tale" you said Van Vogt was the first writer whose name you committed to memory. Now, turning to "Legions in Time" (*Asimov's Science Fiction*, April 2003), you're doing a wild riff on Van Vogt's "Recruiting Station."

Swanwick: This story came about from teaching gigs at various Clarions. The most common sin amongst new writers is that they set the scene before the story begins, and usually it's three to six pages that can be easily removed. I was also struck that their writing tended to be very slow—they tended to over-describe everything, because they believe that that's what being literary is. So I decided to write a story that begins very slow and then deliberately, with each passing scene, gets faster and faster and faster. It goes up in an exponential curve, until at the end it just disappears in its own speed.

Zinos-Amaro: The story appropriately ends with a twist, one I didn't see coming, where the organization is comprised of thousands of instances of Eleanor Voigt. Did you know you were headed there all along, or did that just emerge from the conceptual scaffolding you were building on?

Swanwick: As I recall, I made it up as I went along. In each new section I needed something to bring in as a surprise, so I would surprise myself, and then follow the implications to *that*. When the young lady shows up, the Eleanor in disguise, I didn't know that she was Eleanor at the beginning of that scene. For me a lot of the fun of this story was this Depression-era woman judging what people of the early twenty-first-century must be like.

Zinos-Amaro: It sounds like you were paying tribute to not only Van Vogt's idea, but his working process as well, introducing new elements every several hundred words. Your title, "Legions in Time," also brings to mind Jack Williamson.

Swanwick: That's a hokey technique, but it still works. I'm always surprised by the more conservative writers who never take advantage of the old hokey stuff that still works. The title was a nod to Williamson, yes. Another influence on this story is Fritz Leiber's "Poor Superman." That was his parody of A. E. Van Vogt, in fact. In it he has a Van Vogtian superman who is outwitted and defeated by some normal people, because he isn't as clever as he thinks he is. That's Mr. Tarblecko in my story.

Zinos-Amaro: Not only did this all work—it earned you a Hugo for Best Novelette in 2004.

Swanwick: It came as a complete surprise to me when this won the Hugo. I was stunned. Afterwards Robert Silverberg came up to me and said, "Did the fans know what you were doing when they gave you the Hugo for this?" I had to admit I had no idea. I told the story to Gardner and he said, "They don't know, they really don't."

Zinos-Amaro: In this story and the next several, the trickster or deception theme plays a major role. Here Mr. Tarblecko keeps his real identity hidden from Eleanor Voigt, but then of course Nadine turns out to be a time-displaced Eleanor as well. In "Coyote at the End of History," the character is constantly putting on new identities. In "Deep in the Woods of Grammarie" there are various deceptions, like for example when the crow tricks the Hero into becoming a dragon. In "The Word That Sings the Scythe," Esme keeps her true nature and identity hidden until the end, and Will himself pretends to be someone he isn't at various points in the story.

Swanwick: That's all certainly there. I can't really explain it. I know that in my last novel, *The Iron Dragon's Mother*, a major theme of the novel was Caitlin of House Sans Merci learning how to lie convincingly, and the necessity of lying. Maybe as I get older I see the necessity for deceit more and more.

Once, I was at a convention and I was talking to Janet Kagan, who was good at spotting patterns in stories. She was upset because she looked at some of mine and saw betrayal in all of them! I said, "No, this is just something that works well in stories." But she thought she'd insulted me. So the next morning at breakfast I wrote a short short called "Like the Boiled Eggs in Isaac Asimov." In which Janet was being hunted down by SFWA's crack team of assassins, because she'd seen through the true themes in all these science fiction writers' stories. I gave it to her later in the day, and she liked it and it convinced her we were still friends, so that worked out well. The hotel was a distance from the conference center, so we had a little shuttle bus that went back and forth. After breakfast I was waiting for the shuttle and Allen Steele came up. He casually asked how I was doing, and I said, "Good. I wrote a story this morning," and he said, "Gah!" and spilled his coffee all over himself.

Zinos-Amaro: An astute reviewer online pointed out parallels between Van Vogt's novella and Madeleine L'Engle's *A Wrinkle In Time*. Did you ever read the latter, and if so what did you make of it?

Swanwick: I read it when I was a teenager, and I thought it was fantastic. I read it at the right time to appreciate all its virtues. I'm currently a little afraid to go back and read it now. A lot of the creativity of that sequence of stories stays with me. The mitochondria talking to the stars was just absolutely wonderful; the angels were quite charming; the fact that her mother was a working chemist, and would make stew on a Bunsen burner, and so on. The theme of enforced conformity was so fifties that I'm afraid to go back to it.

Zinos-Amaro: That conformity angle is one of the elements shared by Van Vogt's story, that lack of imagination and sameness in the evolutionary vision. But your story also has humorous elements, like the fact that everything becomes so insanely abstract at the end that we're essentially left with four talking heads in a kind of Socratic dialog, where the stakes are the fate of humanity and the universe.

Swanwick: Yes, that was pretty funny. I did something else that was deliberately comic, which is that Eleanor is constantly realizing things by logic that she couldn't *possibly* figure out. "Of course these people are from the very far future," and so on. I was certainly amused by that. On the comic side, I also stole something. Supposedly Allen Ginsberg, when he was young and obnoxious, once offered drugs to a famous female writer. They had lunch and tea, and he offered her some heroin. She said, "No thank you, I find it gives me spots."

Zinos-Amaro: The next story, "Coyote at the End of History" (*Asimov's Science Fiction*, October-November 2003), also has far-future elements. I'm curious if you were drawing on any specific reading or Native American text for inspiration for your story's five mini-fables?

Swanwick: Yep. At a used bookstore I found a book by A. L. Kroeber, the anthropologist who was the father of Ursula K. Le Guin. He had a collection of raven stories. He'd gone to a number of northwest Native people that he knew, asked them to tell him a raven story, and then recorded them. He put the stories down on the page exactly as they were said—he didn't improve them or clean them up. Some people are very rudimentary storytellers; others are born storytellers and their tales are complicated, elaborate. But the language in all of them was really good. There was something special about the rhythms of it. This combination of good storytelling and presenting the outrageous as a matter of fact was something I wanted to do. I went through the books in my library to see if I had any other trickster tales. I had an Iroquois collection by a man who lived in upstate New York who had a lot of Iroquois neighbors. He loved their stories and thought they should be written down lest they be forgotten. He *did* clean them up. There's a lot of references to fairies and witches, and it was really, really awful. I realized that with this kind of a story, everything extraneous is going to rot and go bad in a hundred years. I wanted to try and write something in this vein that would not go entirely bad. I was interested in that.

Coyote, in my story, stands for the United States. The other animals are emblematic of their countries: the bear is Russia, the dragon is China, and so on. As a personification of a country, I think a coyote works for the United States. There's always been a trickster element to this country at its very best moments—and worst too.

Zinos-Amaro: Was there a specific analog for the Mud People, or are they just people in general?

Swanwick: The Mud People represent humanity at large. This is also a slur that white racists use on other ethnicities. The whole purpose of this collection of stories, which has been curated and pruned and shaped by the aliens, the Star People, is to justify their really horrible and unforgivable actions. It's an exercise in narrative self-justification.

Zinos-Amaro: I had an interesting experience with this story. The first time I read it, I took Coyote as representing contemporary Americans, like you were saying. But on my second reading, I tried to invert the terms, and took the star people as the outgrowth of colonialist, expansionist humans, with Coyote as the trickster alien that we don't understand. And it works that way too.

Swanwick: Well, I was thinking of the experience of the American people when the Europeans came. On the whole, the action of the Europeans was genocidal. After it's all over and everything that can be taken has been taken, we get very sentimental about the noble Redskin. It goes both ways. I was picturing what happened to Native American people, mapping it on to the whole human race.

Zinos-Amaro: Did you always intend to end with Coyote's comeuppance, or did you consider a more subversive ending, like some of the micro-stories in "Deep in the Woods of Grammarie"?

Swanwick: It had to end with Coyote's comeuppance because that's just the way that colonial stories end.

Zinos-Amaro: "Coyote Changes His Sex" has probably accrued different meanings since the time you wrote it. What do you make of it now? In a way the reaction of the Mud People to the sex changes ("This is not right. People should be one thing and never change!") anticipates transphobia today.

Swanwick: It does. That was a bit of good luck for the story. When I was writing it I was thinking of all sorts of science fiction stories, for example by John Varley, where changing one's sex becomes extremely easy. I took it to a kind of extreme where they change every other day back and forth. The response to that was pretty much predictable.

Zinos-Amaro: This story was rewarded with the Number 1 spot on the *Asimov's* Reader's Poll. Since you mentioned Varley, can you tell me a little more about your response to his work?

Swanwick: Yes! It's a really dark story to be popular. Topping that poll was a bit of a shock.

When John Varley appeared on the scene, he just knocked everybody out, me included. He had all these new and fresh ideas, one after the other, in a very bright and colorful future. It looked for a while there like he was going to be the new Robert Heinlein. Then he went off to Hollywood and Hollywood did not treat him very well. I remember talking to him at a convention, and he'd just finished writing a novel. He described it to me in terms that made me think, "Wow, they've really done a number on you over there," because it was very much a revenge-on-Hollywood novel. They paid him a lot of money to write film scripts and not make them. One movie eventually got made, *Millennium*, and it was terrible—they did violence to his original story, "Air Raid." When he came back to the field, he was doing variants on the stories he'd already done. He no longer had the dazzling new ideas that nobody had seen before.

Zinos-Amaro: "Deep in the Woods of Grammarie" (*Realms of Fantasy*, October 2003) follows a similar structure to "Coyote at the End of History," with seven micro-pieces that riff off of and subvert fantasy tropes. "The Witch" is the standout for me, with those brilliant last lines: "The essence of a witch is wrongness. But sometimes, alas, that's what we crave."

Swanwick: I was able to be very smutty in that one without using any naughty words, too. I wrote these stories because I realized that I'd never had a story in *Realms of Fantasy*. I read it every month, thought of myself as a fantasy writer, and thought to myself, "I ought to have a story in this magazine." I didn't have any particular fantasy ideas at that time, so I wrote a number of short shorts designed to fit together. I sketched out ideas on a notepad and selected the best of them, and the ones that would give variety. It was done pretty much on pure craft. I was happy that the story was bought.

Zinos-Amaro: "The Hero" is memorable too, for the ending where the Hero's price for immortality turns out to be becoming a dragon. Do you remember what inspired that?

Swanwick: That would have been *Beowulf*. There's one reading of the dragon in *Beowulf* that it's the spirit of the king who was buried in that cairn with all his treasure, and turned into a dragon to protect it. So the king would have had a very unpleasant kind of immortality.

Zinos-Amaro: For me "The Village," with its striking image of a microcosm inside an abandoned shoe, is great meta-commentary for your own stories of this sort. They contain whole worlds nestled inside a larger narrative, and you always find new things in seemingly used-up tropes or ideas, like the abandoned shoe.

Swanwick: I remember trying to craft lovely images for "Deep in the Woods of Grammarie." Ever since I collaborated with Bill Gibson, who had told Gardner that he worked from images rather than ideas, I've been looking for images that I could turn into stories. It seems to me a productive way of coming up with something interesting. As we talked about when we discussed "'Til Human Voices Wake Us," I'm a very visual writer, and that certainly informed my approach here. Greer Gilman tells me she can't visualize things at all. She gets into her stories through music. There are nine and sixty ways of constructing tribal lays . . .

Zinos-Amaro: "The Last Geek" (*Crossroads: Tales of the Southern Literary Fantastic*, ed. F. Brett Cox, Andy Duncan, 2004) certainly benefits from a strong climactic image. What was the inspiration for this story?

Swanwick: I went to the College of William & Mary, which is in Virginia, so it's in the South. I'd only been in Virginia a year before then, and the South was a strange and sinister place to me. When Brett him me up for a story, I thought about it, and I realized that I didn't know most of the Southern Gothic stuff well enough to be able to use it. But I thought of when we'd have a visiting speaker at the College, John Barth for example, and he would speak to a privileged class. He would have this meeting and that meeting and the English Department would host one of their soirees, with their bottle of sherry which had been there since we first arrived and would be there when we were gone. I got to see how these celebrities were treated, what the formalities were. I thought, "Wouldn't it be funny if instead of a renowned poet or novelist it was a geek, someone who bites the heads off of chickens?" Carnivals are one of my enthusiasms, so I had read both fiction and non-fiction featuring geeks. They never played a big part, because usually in these stories they would find some broken-down alcoholic who was so desperate for a regular source of money for alcohol that they'd teach him the act of how to do it.

Zinos-Amaro: The story is written in the present tense, which you almost never do. You also have several scenes where you tell us the geek is thinking something, but you don't reveal what those thoughts are explicitly. You're holding us readers at bay.

Swanwick: Right. I dislike present tense because I find that it's a distancing technique. But this was a story where you needed the distance. You needed to watch it from afar for it to work. The same thing for the geek's thoughts not being revealed. That was all done for the same distancing purpose.

Zinos-Amaro: Was the moment where the geek balances a spoon on his nose an homage to Gardner Dozois?

Swanwick: Yes! Gardner taught all his friends how to do this. I can do this myself, as can my son Sean. I've seen him do four spoons at once, one from his nose, one from his chin, and two from his cheekbones. I was in London once, and somehow the subject of hanging a spoon from your nose came up while talking at John Clute's house. Sean showed him how to do it, but we could not talk John into doing it himself. He was fascinated but horrified; it was nothing he himself would do.

Zinos-Amaro: In this story you occasionally use words in a slightly poetic or literary way, as for example the word "slipstream" here: "He is eating a modest breakfast from the buffet in the lobby restaurant when the grad student reappears in the slipstream of a woman who pushes eagerly past the other diners." This creates a nice effect of sophistication that contrasts with the geek's core activity.

Swanwick: Yes. I was also trying to create a literary atmosphere around the event itself. It creeps out from the language into the real world.

Zinos-Amaro: Describing the geek "as American as John Wayne or Buzz Aldrin" was really inspired.

Swanwick: Oh, it's true, it's true! Terrifying but true. I did a reading of this story at a bookstore, and Jim Morrow's wife Kathryn was there. About halfway through the story she realized what kind of a geek this was, and she almost died laughing. She was the perfect audience for this story.

Zinos-Amaro: Turning to considerably grimmer material, "The Word That Sings the Scythe" (*Asimov's Science Fiction*, October-November 2004) makes up Chapter 4 and part of Chapter 5 of your novel *The Dragons of Babel*. This story is populated with a ton of fantastical creatures that we haven't seen in this universe before, such as centaurs, lubins, and the very ominous Year Eater. Did you work on developing the world for a while before continuing Will's story, or how did all this come about?

Swanwick: Once I realized that I was working on a novel, I was doing world-creation on the fly. The Year Eater is a god. He's one of the Seven, in fact, one of the big, important powers of this world, though you never get to see him/it/them directly. I also did a lot of research into folklore, looking for creatures that could serve as characters. I felt free to add a lot of my own creations. The stickfellas, for instance, I made up on the spot. I find them a charming invention.

Zinos-Amaro: The idea in this sequel, that the dragon left a bit of himself inside Will, is fascinating because on the one hand it's terrifying but on the other you can almost see it as a survival tool for Will.

Swanwick: I was thinking about survivors of abuse. Given the setup, this seemed to me an inescapable theme that had to be dealt with. It *is* terrifying, and he is rather smartly working with it, trying to defeat it. Will's intelligence made the story satisfying to write, because I did not have to let him fall into stupid situations. Anything he couldn't handle was too large for him to handle: it wasn't his fault.

Zinos-Amaro: The notion of "conservation of luck" was also intriguing. Esme is a luck attractor, but that means others have to be more unlucky for everything to balance out in the end.

Swanwick: This is an idea that I basically ripped off from Marianne. When Marianne was working she came up with this concept that you only have so much organization in your life. You can't increase the amount of organization you have by effort, you can just decide where it's going to go. She'd say, "I'm very organized at work. As a result, the house isn't going to be quite as tidy as my mother kept her house." I changed that to luck. When I introduced Esme, I thought that she'd last for a chapter or so, and then would be hustled offstage, but she moved in on the novel and took over. In fact, she pops up again in *The Iron Dragon's Mother*. I was at a big, noisy party in Edinburgh, and when I walked in a friend of mine who was talking to somebody lit up, ran over to me and said, "Michael! Rescue me from this hideous bore!" I gestured wildly and walked her to the opposite end of the room. That's what inspired Esme's sudden appearance in the story. Esme is unkillable and unstoppable. She's a demon-child. Little demon girls are always entertaining to read about!

Zinos-Amaro: Comparing the *Asimov's* version of this story with the novel version, there are some understandable changes in the sequence of events, but I also noticed a few subtle changes that I thought were interesting from a craft perspective. For example, the line "For hours they coursed over the countryside, straight as schooners and almost as fast" becomes "For hours they coursed over the countryside, straight as falcons and almost as fast" in the novel. Also, Anthea becomes Antiope, and so on.

Swanwick: In that first example, I just wanted it to be more of a fantasy-world, more faerie-like, so I tweaked some imagery to reinforce that. Regarding the name change, I originally got Campaspe and Anthea from E. R. Eddison's Zimiamvian cycle. And then of course there was the famous poem that started with "Cupid and my Campaspe play'd / At cards for kisses; Cupid paid." I think I changed Anthea to Antiope just to add a little separation from Eddison in the novel.

I should probably point out that the Scythe Song comes from the poem by Andrew Lang. Also, the giants who rise up into the sky and fight stem from Goya's painting "Fight with Cudgels." The confrontation depicted in that painting seems cosmic—it must be more than just a fight, and they look a lot like giants.

Thinking back on "The Word That Sings the Scythe" I remember how much fun it was to write. If there weren't a war going on, that world would be an extremely pleasant world to live in.

CHAPTER SIX
2005-2009

Zinos-Amaro: "Triceratops Summer" (*Amazon.com*, August 19, 2005) is a relaxed, gentle, almost folksy piece of work.

Swanwick: This is my love letter to Winooski, Vermont, where I lived from 1959 to 1967. At this time in my career I was good at writing dinosaur stories; you pick up the lore, and they're a pleasure to write. I hadn't yet written anything about *Triceratops*. So I picked up the idea and saw where it would take me. It was a story that allowed me to have a very positive, upbeat ending. My son, however, thinks that this is the most nihilistic, bleak story ever, because the summer these people have will come undone, float off and cease to exist. I said, "You know, when you get a little older and death seems like a real thing that might happen to you someday, you'll understand the value of transience."

Zinos-Amaro: Way to cheer him up! The story obviously celebrates being happy, and valuing what one has, over *pursuing* happiness. But I can also appreciate your son's reaction. Besides the loss at the end, you can argue that even unlimited possibilities are not enough to shake these characters out of their grooves.

Swanwick: Yes and no. For these particular people, they spend summer doing what gives them satisfaction. They're of an age and of a maturity where they value what they're doing, and do what they value. It was a pleasure to have a story to write about such people, because such people don't lend themselves naturally to drama. I spent my adolescence in Winooski, a small town, and it's an area that I know very, very well. The reference to people from out of state as "foreigners" is something that I heard quite a few times in Winooski. Winooski is an old factory town and I went to visit it once. Sean had seen where his mom came from, because his grandparents lived there, but he'd never seen Winooski. Both Marianne and Sean were appalled. Marianne said, "It must be sad to be the only small town in Vermont that has no small-town charm."

Zinos-Amaro: Was the name of the physicist Everett McCoughlan inspired by Hugh Everett, known for the many-worlds interpretation of quantum physics? Since the story involves an alternate timeline springing up from a single event, it seems a perfect fit.

Swanwick: No, I'm sorry. That's a pure coincidence. I can't start taking credit for stuff like this, or next thing you know I'll be cheating on my taxes. I will say, the line "Oh, they were funny, all right" was inspired by R. A. Lafferty; that was exactly his kind of diction.

Zinos-Amaro: At one point in this story, the narrator strokes the back of a *Triceratops* and observes: "It was the warmth that got to me. It made the experience real." Was that little moment inspired by something from real life?

Swanwick: It was, and such a small thing. When my son was young we took him down to Independence Hall. There was a guy feeding pigeons. At that age Sean liked to chase pigeons. I held him back and said, "No chasing pigeons today." The guy had pigeons landing all over him, and he handed one to Sean and let it stand on Sean's finger. Pigeon feet turn out to be very warm, almost hot. You don't expect this. So Sean was amazed and delighted. By no coincidence, dinosaurs were also warm-blooded—we're pretty sure. The Peter Dodson book I quote, by the way, *The Horned Dinosaurs*, is a real one. He's a world authority on *Triceratops*. The dinosaur colors on their frills being bright was a little joke on my part, because in paleontological circles there's a lot of debate about coloration in dinosaurs.

Zinos-Amaro: Was there anything else in this story based on experience?

Swanwick: Yes, one more item. At one point somebody blows a horn and the *Triceratops* piss themselves, hurry away and then come back. The first time that Marianne and I went to Ireland, in 1982, we stayed at a cinderblock building room that had been built as a bed-and-breakfast in the middle of a cow field. When we woke up in the morning there were cows with their noses pressed up against the window, peering in. We discovered that if we made a sudden noise or movement, they would piss themselves and trot away, and then come hurrying back to see what else we did. This seemed to me the kind of behavior that *Triceratops* might very well share with cows.

Zinos-Amaro: It also underlines the dinosaur's non-threatening presence.

Swanwick: Right. The whole thing is the Peaceable Kingdom. There are no villains in it. This story, incidentally, got me a Guest of Honor gig at a Toronto convention. I had a really wonderful time there; Canadian fans have always been exorbitantly kind to me.

Zinos-Amaro: Speaking of travel, in the story you mention Paris, London, Rome, Marrakech—and Disneyworld. That's a funny grouping.

Swanwick: When Sean was a child, people—including Marianne's parents—would always ask us when we were going to take him to Disneyworld. We would say, "Well, we took him to London instead." We were a little snobbish about this. We told his grandparents, "If you guys want to take him, it's fine."

Zinos-Amaro: From the clarity and sweetness of "Triceratops Summer" we turn to the grime and smut of "The Bordello in Faerie" (*Postscripts*, Autumn 2006).

Swanwick: I wrote this story because I wanted to see if I could write a serious literary story that was also pornographic. Lots and lots of genre writers have got something pornographic that they wrote on the side, either for money or as a jeu d'esprit. Very few of them are trying to do that as their own best work. There's a Mike Resnick book, *Tales of the Velvet Comet*, which may have inspired me. It's set in an orbital bordello, and there's lots of plot and absolutely no sex going on on-screen. Mike himself had written a lot of pornography when he was starting out, and he was very open about this. He did it strictly for money.

Zinos-Amaro: Yes, and he never revealed the pseudonyms he used.

Swanwick: Probably wisely, I think! I can see where he would have absolutely no interest in revisiting that territory again in his work, it representing the stuff that was done merely for money.

Zinos-Amaro: Your story strikes me as Farmer-esque, in the detail and outrageousness of some of the sex scenarios, and Delany-esque in the overall seriousness of the approach.

Swanwick: It's possible that those were influences too. I definitely wanted to take this seriously. We're in the twenty-first century, and it's not like this story is breaking any new grounds. Farmer's stuff was astonishing back when he wrote it. It was amazing work. I remember reading books like *A Feast Unknown* and *The Image of the Beast*. Farmer was trying to see how far he could go. My ambitions were a little less than that.

Zinos-Amaro: You still go quite far.

Swanwick: It fit the theme of a young man coming into his sexuality and seeing how far he can go, discovering a place that for him is the stopping point.

Zinos-Amaro: Talk a little about this notion of a bordello where human men end up being the prostitutes for other-worldly beings.

Swanwick: First of all, the idea for "The Bordello in Faerie" just seemed like a very nice reversal. It allowed me to write a story about someone who's a prostitute without all the usual baggage. In particular, when a man is writing about a female prostitute, it's often him writing out either his fantasies or his disgust, and the woman ends up disappearing. In my version the women are present but not known, they're just the customers, and our character only gets to see them as sexual beings. He has no idea about their lives outside the room with the green door. In fact, that was the whole point to the ending of the story. He goes and gets married, he no longer visits the bordello, he has a place in society, and he's learned a lot, he's grown up. He knows a lot more than he did at the beginning of this—but he still knows nothing at all about women! Ask Ned what his daughters did, and he has no idea.

Zinos-Amaro: Have you ever visited a brothel?

Swanwick: I have not. I was very careful to avoid them. In all my young reading as an adolescent I read carefully what writers had written about their own experiences in brothels, and it always turned out to be a bad thing. It was something, they wrote, that messes you up a bit and makes you not ready to have the kind of sex that you want to have. I took their advice. These writers collectively were for me the stand-in to a wise uncle, and I heeded his advice. I had a friend whose father had money, and when he came of a certain age his father took him to a tropical resort town and gave him a lot of money. Then he told all the prostitutes that his son had a ton of cash. That was how he educated his son into the sexual ways of adulthood. My friend, in retrospect, was not happy about that. It made him feel bad about himself.

Zinos-Amaro: I wanted to ask you about the names in this line: "They're sailors, raftswomen from the upper reaches of the Porpentine, where it flows out of Ultima Thule." Ultima Thule, which translates to the farthest of far places, has been used in genre more than once, but I wonder if you had Avram Davidson's novel *Ursus of Ultima Thule* in mind?

Swanwick: I really did enjoy that novel. But I was thinking more—this will sound very pretentious—of Nabokov's *Ada or Ardor*. At the beginning there's a description of the estate where they live, which is along a river, and the river rises in Russia and goes through Siberia and down through Canada and into New England, and there's just totally, absolutely bonkers geography there. I quite liked that. I was also thinking a little bit of the river Dapple in *Lud-in-the-Mist*, which rises in Fairyland and flows into the Dawl and thus into the sea.

The name of my river, the Porpentine, comes from a book called *The Amazing Vacation* by Dan Wickenden. It was published in the 1950s, and features a boy and a girl spending the summer at their uncle's place. He turns out to be a magician. There's a window, and sometimes, when it opens, you can go through into a magical land. It was a children's book, but quite an inventive one. To go through you had to bring something with you that you valued, and in the magic land that thing became a source of power, which others could steal from you, depriving you of your ability to return through the window. There was a character in the fantasy land, a guide for the children, called the "fretful Porpentine," which came from a line in *Hamlet*. I love the sound of Porpentine.

The town of Ironbeck in this story is, once again, Winooski. I also included a bar called the Bucket of Nails, which was a dive bar in Center City, when I first came to Philadelphia. It was a low, dark and violent place.

In the story there's also a lacquered Chinese bridge, and that's taken from William & Mary. They have a pond called Crim Dell, and there's a Chinese bridge over it. It's a central place for people living there.

Zinos-Amaro: What about the green door itself?

Swanwick: That's named for the song "Green Door," and then the work of pornography written by G. I.'s after World War II, and then the movie *Behind the Green Door*, all three of them only loosely based on each other.

You might appreciate that this is the only story I ever wrote using lucid dreaming. Most nights I'd try to visit the bordello in my dreams. In my dreams I'd go across a railroad bridge, across the Winooski River, and down the tracks until I came to one of those single red lights. I would follow a gravel path that sloped to one side, and I'd go down the third path and across the lacquered red bridge. Beyond that there was an old horse called Dobbin, and I would give Dobbin an apple, and he'd let me by. Past him I'd go out into the woods and break a twig, and all the leaves of the forest would turn incandescent bright. At that point I would be asleep and dreaming lucidly, and I could go to the bordello and imagine something to happen to my character. This process worked well for this story, and I was satisfied with it and didn't feel the need to do it again because there wasn't anything else I really felt would benefit from that technique.

Zinos-Amaro: I can see this successfully undergirding "The Bordello in Faerie," because you could exploit the freedom one has in dreams. When we discussed "Midnight Express" your goal was to be dirty without describing anything explicitly. Here the approach is almost diametrically opposite—with a single euphemistic exception.

Swanwick: That's right. It's the line "Slowly, slowly, then, ran the chariot-horses of night." That line was originally from Ovid's *The Amores*, "O lente, lente currite noctis equi!". Christopher Marlowe later picked that up for *Dr. Faustus* with the exact opposite meaning, crying out at night before the demons come to take him to Hell. I used it in its original meaning. It's one of these lines that will keep going back and forth in our culture.

The hag in the story is referred to as Mother of Goats. This is Shub-Niggurath, from H. P. Lovecraft. I did this as a joke, using this one phrase to turn the whole story into part of the Cthulhu mythos, and one that would appall Lovecraft.

Zinos-Amaro: Where did the Star Woman come from? She struck me as the most memorable customer.

Swanwick: Oh, her I made up. I was really pleased with her. I was thinking of all those Victorian and pulp naked women, the perfect and beautiful and utterly unconvincing characters with nothing interesting to say except "Choose the golden key when you go through the green door." I liked her a lot. I found her story mysterious. Aside from the fact that she's into being abased and degraded, you don't really get to know her. The women in the story have these other lives, far more interesting than what they're doing on their night off.

Zinos-Amaro: And I'm sure more interesting than Ned's own story when he's not there.

Swanwick: Yes, yes. I ran into Greer Gilman at Worldcon and I mentioned that I just finished this story. She asked if she could see it, and I said, "You have to understand, it's pretty rough stuff." She said she didn't care, so I gave her a copy. She came back the next day and said, "Sir!" And then she added, "You give good hag." High praise from Greer.

Zinos-Amaro: I was wondering if you got any kind of reader reaction outside of the usual because of the story's explicitness.

Swanwick: I saw someone on social media who posted that he was in an airport and he'd brought along a book with the story in it. He was partway through the story when he realized that, according to him, it was a) extremely graphic, and b) really good, a combination he was not expecting! Not necessarily a story you'd like to get caught reading in public.

Ned, by the way, goes on to make a cameo appearance in *The Iron Dragon's Mother*.

Zinos-Amaro: This raises an interesting point. This story is part of your Babelverse. The next story we're going to discuss, "An Episode of Stardust" (*Asimov's Science Fiction*, January 2006), takes place in Faerie Minor and was folded into Chapter 6 of *The Dragons of Babel*, so it's also set in the same world. The same is true of "Lord Weary's Empire," which we'll get to shortly, and "A Small Room in Koboldtown," which explicitly references Babel and features Will. So we have a cluster of stories set in a shared realm, not all of them sown up into the novels.

Swanwick: These stories are all interconnected because they take place, in large part, in a collective Faerie where all the mythologies are real, except that they've arrived in the late twentieth or twenty-first centuries. They've changed along with everything else in the world.

Zinos-Amaro: "An Episode of Stardust," set in this world, is framed as a club story, but its plot is based on a con, which brings to mind the Darger and Surplus sequence we'll discuss separately. What prompted you to use a club story framing device for this?

Swanwick: I follow a non-systematic history of fantasy, which I throw into my stories. A lot of short form fantasy was club stories. Fantasy as a genre tends to be overwhelmingly novels, whereas short stories have a much larger place in science fiction. My heart belongs to short fiction, so I felt the need to do a club story. I suppose it's a little indulgent to do that sort of thing, but it's fun. That's what this story was meant to be: just fun. It established a number of things that needed to be established in the novel: where Nat came from, how he went from being the King of Babylon to a con man, and why he would think that was a good idea. In our world, con people are just trying to take your money away dishonestly. I've met them and they're not very likeable. In Faerie, they're tricksters. Their job is not to optimize the flow of money to him or her, but to shake things up, to make the world a more interesting and dangerous place.

Zinos-Amaro: The placement of the story in the novel also serves to give the reader a bit of a reprieve from darker, more serious material. It's an escapist breather.

Swanwick: The problem with fiction is that if you take the world seriously it tends to be grim. Actually there's a lot of people having a perfectly fine time in this fantasy world, but they don't fit into the novel. William Gibson was once asked about *Neuromancer* and he said he figured there was a middle class out there somewhere in the novel, they just didn't interact with his particular characters.

The details of Whinny Moor Landfill were based on a long essay about landfills, which included the details of exploding garbage bags and so on. In the world of this story I mentioned the river Gihon, which is one of the rivers that flows out of Eden. There's also "Tir na bOg" written on a toilet door, a joke based on "Tír na nÓg," the Irish Land of Youth. In Ireland I saw a pinball arcade actually named "Tír na nÓg."

This was a simple, clean story, relatively fast to write. I was pleased by that.

Zinos-Amaro: We shift moods again, from the mischief of "An Episode of Stardust" to the harshness, both physical and psychological, of "Tin Marsh" (*Asimov's Science Fiction*, August 2006).

Swanwick: Oh yeah. This story came about because I went to a bookstore and found a one-volume collection of all of Hemingway's short fiction. I had most of it already, in shabby paperbacks, but the heft, size and look of this book were so good that I needed to have it. I went through it and binged on all the non-canonical stories. One thing I found out was that Hemingway was strongly influenced by genre: *Black Mask* magazine, fight stories, sea stories, and so on. He basically combined that with his deep reading into the great Russian writers. By putting them together he came up with Hemingway. When I finished reading this volume, I was enjoying the prose so much. It took me decades to learn to like Hemingway because he was forced on us in school, held up as being the best you could possibly be. Now I started to write a story in as close to that voice as I could write without doing a pastiche. I set it on Venus because I hadn't written anything set on Venus, and I'd like to have stories set on as many of the planets as I can. Also, Venus has marvelous names. They only mapped it relatively recently, and used a lot of names of goddesses, like Ishtar Terra and Artemis Chasma and Lakshmi Planum. I did a lot of research on what I could imagine finding on Venus that would be of interest.

The central idea is probably a swipe from Jack London, who did several stories about people in isolation who became partners and came to hate each other.

Zinos-Amaro: This story recalled for me, in terms of the overall aesthetic, your own "The Very Pulse of the Machine" and "Slow Life." You've mentioned Hemingway and London. In terms of the science fiction influences, I'll note that David Hartwell said of "Tin Marsh" that he thought it was "in the hard-boiled tradition of Leigh Brackett's stories."

Swanwick: I wouldn't deny an influence from Leigh Brackett. I wear that as a badge of honor! But I can't swear to it here.

For me this is basically an astronaut-in-peril story. You give them a problem, they have to deal with it and come up with solutions; then the solutions don't work, until they finally do. Except in this case they really don't, but they're lucky enough to hit pay-tin, as it were.

Zinos-Amaro: How would this story have played out, in your mind, if the characters didn't strike bounty right at the end?

Swanwick: They would have just gone on and on until they ran out of water and food and energy. They would have just gone plodding off, like something by Beckett. I value Beckett's darker works, but I did not see a particular reason to write one like that.

Zinos-Amaro: I like your riff on Asimov's Three Laws of Robotics with the Company's Three Rules: "No Violence. Protect Company Equipment. Protect Yourself."

Swanwick: This is the evil, capitalist version of Asimov's Laws. It's all about profit, with the saving of life as the lowest priority. Capitalism is the bad guy and has the moustache. "Tin Marsh" is definitely an anti-capitalist story, in the old school. It could have been written by a Wobbly. The Company is cheating them left and right, getting as much work out of them as possible, and with any luck not having to pay them the amount promised.

Zinos-Amaro: One thing that I wondered about was the use of humans to manually locate gold, tin and lead on Venus in a future that has AIs, neural implants that modify behavior, and suits advanced enough for humans to even exist on the Venusian surface. I would envision drones or something like that being used instead, but I understand such a technology wasn't pervasive in 2006 when you wrote it.

Swanwick: I really don't know. I really did do a kind of stripped-down world creation, and didn't get into those questions. I consider it possible, because the surface of Venus is so unfriendly—dark and hot, very high pressure—that human labor could be the cheapest possible solution. People are cheap.

In the end I think "Tin Marsh" doesn't work as well as I would like it to work for another reason. I did not go as deep into their complaints with each other or how they drove each other mad because I had made the mistake of making one male and one female. I did that because of the little bit of description about the moment they decide to become partners: the man picks up the woman, whirls her around, kisses her, and puts her down. I loved that, and it was autobiographical. So I made the leads male and

female but then I didn't want to go into "battle of the sexes" nasti-
ness, if you will. If I had made it two women, I might have been
able to go deeper into their specific arguments without evoking
the same nasty undertone I'm talking about. Anyway, it's a good
story, but it could have been better.

Zinos-Amaro: You return to Babel with the novella "Lord
Weary's Empire" (*Asimov's Science Fiction*, December 2006).

Swanwick: The title comes from Robert Lowell's *Lord Weary's
Castle*, obviously, but that's it for Lowell's influence on it.

Zinos-Amaro: Now, given that many of the events in this novella turn out to be not a dream per se but an illusion, I'm wondering if some readers felt lukewarm about the ending?

Swanwick: I'm sure some people had a mixed response to
that. The general response was more positive than I was expecting, actually, considering that this is from the middle novel of
a trilogy. *The Iron Dragon's Daughter* was received by a lot of
people as being an anti-fantasy. John Clute, for example, very
firmly states that as fact. But I was just writing a fantasy novel!
I wasn't trying to take down anybody. When I came up with
the idea for the second novel, I got in touch with John and said,
"Can you give me an outline of your theory of fantasy so I can
violate it?" He hadn't written it down anywhere; it's something
he would mention in talks. He very kindly shared it with me. I
kept a little synopsis of it next to my computer, and did my best
to subvert everything that he had said. "The King is missing and
therefore there's a thinning in the land," I would turn into "The
King is missing and therefore everybody's getting fat and the
land is prospering," and so on. The "proper" fantasy ends with
the restoration of the King; so I ended mine with the defenes-
tration of the King, to give it a happy ending. He literally goes
through the window.

Zinos-Amaro: Marvelous. Another way in which "Lord
Weary's Empire" might be a bit of an anti-fantasy is in its claus-
trophobia. It's set underground, in caverns, subways, sewers, and
it all feels very confined. There's none of the epic expansive sense
or scale of space associated with many fantasies.

Swanwick: That made it harder to write. The venue came
from a book called *The Mole People* by Jennifer Toth. It was about
the homeless people who live in the underground in New York

City. In a lot of these underground situations, people are impoverished, or addicted to drugs, or mentally ill. They're the people that nobody sees, and they flee to places where nobody can see them. There's a great deal of description in that book about what it's like there, in the tunnels, lair after lair. Nobody has a good map of all of them in New York City.

Zinos-Amaro: Did you happen upon Toth's book first, and that inspired the story, or did the story come first and Toth's book followed in the research?

Swanwick: I found the book in my research, but I would have bought it regardless, even if I didn't plan to use it for this story. Tunnels and darkness is one of the things my subconscious is fascinated by. So of course I would go there. I'm pretty sure it's popped up elsewhere in my fiction.

Zinos-Amaro: Rich Horton described this story as "a cynical but sad story, set in a sad but interesting world." How does the word "cynical" specifically sit with you?

Swanwick: I understand it. It's not the word I would use, but I don't have an objection to him using it. I don't think I am cynical in any of my work at all. Marianne, am I?

Marianne Porter: Oh God no. You're the most earnest thing out there!

Swanwick: Okay. This is one story of mine that is definitely nihilistic, I will admit that. But it also has heroic parts in it for Will. At one point he's riding a motorcycle through the sewers with glow-in-the-dark face paint. I tried to make that as much like anime as possible.

When I set out to overturn Clute's theory, I wasn't going against him, I was saying, "Let's try to actually write an anti-fantasy, and see what that would be." "Lord Weary's Empire" is the anti-fantasy part of the novel. It's like a critique of contemporary fantasy, which too often celebrates the wrong things. The celebration of war, in particular, and the fun of violence, the greatness of raising an army and sending it off to do damage to others I think is too often celebrated unthinkingly in our genre. I went after that and other things. I tried to subvert them, upend them, to show what things were creeping and crawling under the tropes. I'm surprised people weren't more angry about this. It hits against many things that are "fun" in fantasy.

It's fine to have fun, so long as you don't mistake that for learning something about the nature of the world.

Zinos-Amaro: With this story and others, you're not only commenting on the world—what is and should be—but on the stories that are attached to that world, and what they say about us.

Swanwick: Stories are the most powerful thing in our lives, and often in history. Ronald Regan, for example, ran across a story of a welfare queen who was riding around New York City in a Cadillac. Nobody could locate this welfare queen or even find out exactly where he heard the story. But he heard the story, and believed it, and that's where a lot of his economic policy came from.

A fact is a unit of truth, but a story is a unit of conviction. Once you attach a fact—or a lie—to a story, the fact or lie becomes much more powerful.

Zinos-Amaro: The world you create has mythological suggestions, like for instance Niflheim Station, named after the Norse world of the dead. But it's a unique blend, with a lot of your own inventions.

Swanwick: There's a certain amount of stuff about the emptiness of life that's based on Eastern Religion in this story, but it's bleaker than in Buddhism.

On the whole I picture this world as being a little like New York City. As they say, in some cases there are *more* people speaking this, that and the other language there than there are in the largest city of their own home country. So you've got everybody there, and it actually works. The diversity works. You get used to it, and you come to depend on it. Not just for things like food and music, but for presence.

Zinos-Amaro: Tell me more about Lord Weary's answer about how he came to rule an army. He starts by saying, "Carelessness."

Swanwick: That came from Bob Dylan. In the first *Playboy* interview with him, he was the most sullen interviewee ever. The interviewer asked him how he got into rock and roll, and he said, "Carelessness. I lost my one true love. I started drinking. The first thing I know, I'm in a card game. Then I'm in a crap game. I wake up under a pool table . . ." On and on, this amazing riff.

There's also a part of the story where Lord Weary says that when you die, you're melted down "like so many lead soldiers." That came from a book with essays by and about C. S. Lewis and J.

R. R. Tolkien. There was a conversation between the two of them, and they were talking about how wonderful E. R. Eddison was, though there were parts that they disliked. One part was Eddison's idea that when you die your soul joins the Godhead, which one of them characterized as being melted down like lead soldiers. Definitely a critique.

Zinos-Amaro: Just as you take on fantasy conventions in "Lord Weary's Empire," you have fun with the locked-room subgenre in "A Small Room in Koboldtown" (*Asimov's Science Fiction*, April-May 2007). While this is set in the same world, it has more pep to it, a different kind of energy. This one won the 2008 Locus award and was a finalist for the 2008 Hugo.

Swanwick: This was inspired by a story by Paul Laurence Dunbar, who is mostly remembered today for his poetry, but he wrote some fine short fiction too. The story was called "The Scapegoat." It's about a black politician in a mid-sized American town who's playing the game. He's no better than all the other politicians are, and no worse, but he's made the scapegoat for some crime that everyone else committed. He works a quiet game, and it takes him a few years, but he takes everyone down in revenge. I really liked that. I wanted to do two things with "A Small Room in Koboldtown." I had to grow up Will a bit. He needed to be older and have more experience. The other thing was that I really wanted to talk about American ward heeler politics, and specifically, African American culture. I'm not writing about African American culture because I have something specific to say about it, but because I want for them not to be excluded. You look at all the old classic fantasy, and there's nobody black in it. But writing today, if everyone is white, that makes me nervous. It feels like something bad has happened. Where are all the people of color? Similarly, with my fantasies, I want it to be acknowledged that people of color are present. In *The Iron Dragon's Daughter* the place held by black people was held by dwarves, because they're short and easy to discriminate against. Ultimately after the novel was out I wasn't really happy with that, because it was a Germanic culture, and I felt like I was denying African American culture, which is a terrible crime, really. Later I found out about haints from a friend of mine. His grandmother was from the South, and she used to tell him stories about them. That seemed to work a lot better.

Zinos-Amaro: I want to touch on character names. I'm guessing that Salem Toussaint's last name was based on the leader of the Haitian Revolution.

Swanwick: Absolutely. I wanted the last name to be black, and kind of grandiose. The first name comes from a lawyer named Salem Flack. My father-in-law, who was a lawyer, knew him. He used to tell stories about how Salem Flack was the last of the old-time lawyers. He vividly remembered at the summation of a trial Salem Flack getting down on his knees and praying to an almighty God to forgive the lying, perjuring eye-witnesses who had testified against his client! He was half-fraudulent and half-magnificent really. My character is a combination of the magnificent and the ludicrous. By the time you get to the end, you realize that the ludicrous part is really a put-on. It's a role that he's playing to make everyone underestimate him. He's really on top of things. You find out that he had figured it out all along, and just needed Will to be the one to deliver the news. In a similar way, I needed Will not to be the white savior of these haints of color. I had to make it clear that Will was not their superior.

Zinos-Amaro: A beautiful parallel between Toussaint and Ghostface: "I don't want him thinking I think I'm superior to him."

Swanwick: Ghostface was based on people I know. A disgruntled, angry man, but as he knows very well, he has good reason for that.

I think that through the entire novel *The Dragons of Babel*, and through this story, my impulses are democratic. The King is not a good thing. American patriots died to free us of a foreign tyrant.

Zinos-Amaro: One more note on names. Detective Xisuthros seems to reference the Sumerian Flood myth, as does Detective Shulpae, another minor Sumerian figure. Bobby Buggane alludes to an ogre-like creature native to the Isle of Man.

Swanwick: That's right. And they all come to live together in the city, and they all have to deal with the complex politics of ethnicity in practice, in a workable way. I wanted to touch on this, that this wasn't just black and white—in either sense.

Zinos-Amaro: This story contains a reference to the neighborhood of Diddy-Wah-Diddy—which would seem to connect your Babelverse to the supernatural realm of "North of Diddy-Wah-Diddy"!

Swanwick: Maybe. I hadn't thought of that connection, to be honest.

There's a moment, by the way, when Will says, "Oh, it's not about that, sir." That's an old salesman ploy. When somebody starts to say they're not interested in what you're selling, you say, "Oh, it's not about that." I learned this during my two weeks as the world's most perfect failure as a salesman. I could not sell you a glass of water if your hair was on fire.

Zinos-Amaro: Did your earnestness get in the way?

Swanwick: I think I have a dishonest face . . .

Zinos-Amaro: One might say that "A Small Room in Koboldtown" is a dishonest mystery.

Swanwick: As a locked-room mystery, I'm pretty sure that a reader would tell me that I cheated, because there's no way a reader could figure out the solution. I'm guilty, and I apologize for that! But it was a fun solution to the problem. It's dark around all the edges, but it's really a love letter to the city. For all its flaws, that city would be a fun place to live.

Zinos-Amaro: Speaking of fun, "Congratulations from the Future!" (*Asimov's Science Fiction*, July 2007) pops with inventive amusement.

Swanwick: This is a considerably lighter story, and probably has the least worthy origin of all of my stories. I heard that *Asimov's* was coming up on its thirty-fifth anniversary issue and I wanted to be a part of it, but I didn't have a really good story to sell them, so I made this up on the spot. I threw in as many references as I could to the writers who appeared regularly in the magazine at the time, most of them my friends, in a little piece that Sheila wouldn't be able to resist running. I got a big notice on the cover, so I ended up doing even better than I was expecting.

Zinos-Amaro: I think this one pairs nicely, thematically and technically, with "Letters to the Editor."

Swanwick: It's in the same spirit. It's all written quickly, and it's done with a deep knowledge of science fiction.

Zinos-Amaro: Also, there's the fictional Swanwick persona, which isn't the real Swanwick.

Swanwick: That's true. And the persona is rather egomaniacal!

Zinos-Amaro: Did the joke in which you describe folks like John Clute and Bruce Sterling speaking from exile, and then exile turns out to be the lowercase name of an actual place for former writers, have a specific source?

Swanwick: That joke is stolen from Gardner Dozois. Back in the early 80s, when cyberpunk was really hot, he said he could picture Bruce Sterling in his old age turning a little cranky and saying things like, "There hasn't been any good science fiction since William Gibson had himself uploaded to the orbital ashram!" It's a good joke, and it's not even mine.

Zinos-Amaro: You mention the Vinge-Stross Singularity in this piece, and I'm curious what your take on Singularity and post-Singularity fiction was back when this was a new and important part of the genre conversation.

Swanwick: I really liked the Singularity and post-Singularity as ideas. The Singularity originally meant that so many changes will take place in our future that you reach a point where you cannot predict things anymore. You can't see it coming; it's just going to be something entirely different. Of course, later that got changed into, "There's going to be this event that changes everything! We'll all be dismantling the Solar System and uploading ourselves and downloading ourselves!" and so on. Nobody did that better than Charlie Stross with his *Accelerando* series. This shows the virtue of science fiction: you come up with an idea like the Singularity, which posits something that cannot be imagined, and then you wait a year or so and a writer comes along who imagines it. Those kinds of ideas, those kinds of books and stories, were so much fun. They put a lot of energy into science fiction. They get people more excited about it, and thinking about it, which is the important part. Considering that I haven't really done any Singularity stuff myself, I couldn't be more happy with it.

Zinos-Amaro: Do you think anything in science fiction has the same kind of spotlight today that the Singularity had in the early to mid 2000s?

Swanwick: I'm feeling somewhat out of touch with science fiction today, so it's hard to say. One big thing that's happening in genre today is that there's a great deal of quality work written by people of color. I've been thinking about that. I think it's similar to the reason there was so much good mainstream fiction in the 1950s written by Jews. It was a time when a whole class of people who had been previously oppressed and held down artificially were coming into their own in society. I think that right now people of color, women, LGBTQ+, and generally any populations that share those qualities, are all producing exciting work. Beyond that, the question tends to be unanswerable until we have a retrospective view.

Zinos-Amaro: We switch from futuristic entertainment to a fairly serious alternate, or multi-alternate, history with "The Skysailor's Tale" (*The Dog Said Bow-Wow*, 2007). There's a lot of density in the conceits and the setting here.

Swanwick: This was originally going to be a novel. I reached a certain point in it and it was just not cohering. I put it away for several years and realized I wasn't going to do anything with it. So I changed it to a novella.

Zinos-Amaro: Remembering events that you've described on certain convention panels and in previous interviews, the opening third or so—essentially, all the scenes with the narrator's father and his dementia—struck me as deeply autobiographical, more so than any other story we've discussed.

Swanwick: The first line of the story is literally true. I was thinking back at some point and realized I could not remember burying my father. I know I was there. I remember being in the car with my mother and sisters and we were joking and laughing, and the limousine driver was really offended. He glared at us. But he did not know the situation, of course. I started thinking about my father and realized I find it very hard even to remember his face anymore. There are gaps in my memory. So I started to write a novel that would have gaps.

Considering how much of "The Skysailor's Tale" is made up, it is an astonishingly autobiographical work. The parts that aren't true to my life are true to other lives. I had picked up in a secondhand bookstore a big autobiographical work by a Philadelphia merchant. He was writing about his youth in the early 1820s in Philadelphia, what the people were like, who the various characters of the day were and what they were doing. The whole city seemed to be very alive then, so I wanted to write about Philadelphia at that time when it was still young and a little raffish around the edges, by the waterfront. It was a place of intellectual ferment, too. I did an enormous amount of research. Old Philadelphia is great fun to research. In the Library Company, for example, there's a statue of Benjamin Franklin which originally was in the Atheneum. It was the first statue of Franklin ever made. When it was put up the old people who knew him when he was alive joked that at night the statue would come alive, climb down, and visit the bars and brothels.

Will Keely's name, incidentally, comes from the Keely Motor Company. Keely was a con man at the turn of the century. He claimed to have discovered a series of harmonic convergences that allowed him to build an engine of unequalled power. He had wonderful, multi-colored charts of how it worked and gave demonstrations in his home in Philadelphia. He was always just months away from being able to commercialize this. I have an old issue of *Scientific American* with a report talking about how close he was to success. Finally he died and they found a big air compressor in his basement. It had all been a fraud from the beginning. He was one of the great, odd characters of Philadelphia, so I had to put this in the story.

I also got maps, and so on, so that every time that someone is walking in Philadelphia in the story they're following a real path that people would have taken. I was combining that with the notion of this fleet of airships that's metaphoric for my life-writing nonsense. That was also combined with the early history and the colonization of the Americas. It was a big topic, and looking back I'm not sure how it stopped working. I think at some point the disjunctures piled up too much. I was asking the reader to hold too much in her mind at one time. I came to a stop because I couldn't go any further. So I brought it into port a lot earlier than I originally intended. The ending with the sad man who believes that all the adventures of his life are over and the love of his life comes back to him was going to be the ending from the beginning.

Zinos-Amaro: Do you think that setting the story at a historical remove made it a bit easier to delve into the more personal material?

Swanwick: It made it bearable. I couldn't have written about it as a memoir, or set in contemporary time. I needed the remove. You'll notice that I framed the story as a conversation between a father and a child, who turns out to be his son at the end. That fireside chat aspect of it was to soften the dislocations for the reader, to make it seem less experimental, and more like the gaps that somebody with an imperfect memory telling a story would have.

There's another autobiographical element right at the end of the story. When Sean was born, they put him in my arms and I burst into tears. I looked down at him and I thought, "Someday, my son, you will be a man. You will grow up and by doing so turn me old, and then I will die. But that's all right. I don't mind. It's a small price to pay for your existence." I literally thought those words, which made it unchanged into this story. That was exactly what I felt, and I still stand by it.

Zinos-Amaro: Your framing device, the memory lapses, and even the title, made me think of "The Changeling's Tale."

Swanwick: I probably could have taken the very beginning of "The Changeling's Tale," made a couple of tiny little changes, and used that!

Zinos-Amaro: When developing "The Skysailor's Tale" did you realize this would be a multiverse story, with characters journeying across parallel realities?

Swanwick: Right from the beginning. It had to be because the idea that the British Empire would have dirigibles in 1820 was an alternate history, and if there's one alternate history, there's going to be many, at least as far as I'm concerned. There's a reference to the waterfront having a wall next to it along 2nd Street, and that came from the merchant's book. There *was* a proposal to build such a wall, to keep the unpleasant sights of the waterfront away from more distinguished people, and nothing ever came of it. This was part of my alternate history. Multiple universes just seemed right for this story. It just seemed like the engines powering the ships were blurring them across timelines, so it wouldn't merely be one alternate universe. They'd be wandering back and forth. He probably doesn't get back quite exactly to his own universe, but he manages to get close to it.

Zinos-Amaro: Did you read any of the *Long Earth* books by Terry Pratchett and Stephen Baxter? There's a central idea of this airship hopping across realities in the first volume.

Swanwick: I did read the first one. That was an odd book! It was not the seamless collaboration that Pratchett did with Neil Gaiman. I really think that for all Baxter is an excellent writer, he had problems with the fact that the basic notion was nonsense.

Terry Pratchett could get away with nonsense in a way that Baxter couldn't, I think. That said, that's no disrespect to either one. It was just an odd marriage of writer and idea. In terms of the concept, there's been a lot of airships in science fiction. Who knows who came up with the reality-hopping by dirigible first. I'm getting more and more cautious about claiming firsts as I get older.

Speaking of other writers, the part of the story where Will is talking to Tacey, and Tacey says, "Oh, I can see the happy crowds now . . ." and goes on like that for a while, that's a pastiche of Jamaica Kincaid. I discovered her short fiction and fell head over heels in love with it. And it fits the character perfectly.

Zinos-Amaro: Are there any specific Kincaid stories that stand out for you?

Swanwick: Two in particular, yes. "In the Night" is about all these nice, positive things that people never say about the narrator's father. In "Girl" there's a list of advice given by a mother to her daughter, like for example, "This is how you smile to an equal," or "This is how you prepare this particular fruit," but then occasionally she'll throw in things like, "You should do this, instead of growing up to be the slut I know you want to be" and other condescending lines. The language usage is so beautiful. *At the Bottom of the River* is the collection with these stories, and I highly recommend it, it's fabulous.

Zinos-Amaro: I'm going to look into it, thank you. In "Urdumheim" (*The Magazine of Fantasy & Science Fiction*, October-November 2007), which is rich with mythological import, language is a deeply humanizing force.

Swanwick: This story is largely about language. It comes from one of Jane Ellen Harrison's fellow classicists. Harrison was a mentor and companion to Hope Mirrlees. She was a major figure in classical studies, to such a degree that most people who haven't heard of her still take her ideas for granted. One of her friends wrote a paper about the rise of civilization out of primordial stupidity. The paper was in German, so primordial stupidity was Urdummheit. I thought that was such a great word, so I just changed it to Urdumheim, the home of primordial stupidity, which is what the characters escape from.

Zinos-Amaro: This story seems to be operating on at least three levels: creation myth, reinvention of the Biblical Tower of Babel story, and political satire of the Bush Jr. years.

Swanwick: I took a lot from Gilgamesh, obviously. Utnap-ishtim, for example, is the only survivor of the Great Flood. I was trying to take mythology and push it back into the times when we can't know it. Twentieth century satirists would always make a big deal of pre-Christian patterns that seemed to be what parts of the New Testament are based on. In "Urdumheim" I was trying to create a fictional pre-pre-Christian world that those earlier pre-Christian patterns could have been based on. So this is far before Gilgamesh. Gilgamesh is in fact a misunderstanding of these legends that came before it. I wanted to see how interesting I could make this notion.

It was not easy to write. I'd write a section and then have to stop while I figured out what came next. I think I had the closing lines when I started it, but not the plot, so I had to go into the story step by step. It took several months, all told. About ten years ago I was talking to a friend of mine who was one of my peers in the early eighties, and he said something like, "Remember how we used to spend months working on a single story?" I didn't say it out loud, but I thought, "I never stopped."

The element of all the inventions being made in a single generation is likely stolen from Samuel R. Delany, from his Neveryon books. There was a particularly brilliant woman who had invented bridges and money—she regretted the second one. But everything was new, everyone was inventing things. "I just invented the sword," and "I just invented clothing," and so on.

Zinos-Amaro: You definitely one-upped this. You just invented death itself, and murder!

Swanwick: I was very pleased with the invention of death. You go back to the first myth, and the first myth always asks "Why do we die?" Well, here's the explanation for it. It was inevitable that it would come into the story, because we had to get from there to here.

Zinos-Amaro: Because this story follows "The Skysailor's Tale," I wondered if the Igigi, the creatures who steal words, or logophages, can be read as a metaphor for dementia.

Swanwick: You know, it never occurred to me before now. But yes, they could obviously. Was that behind this story? I don't know. I really don't. I will admit that ever since it happened to my father, that has been one of my great worries, that it will happen to me. It's always in the back of my mind.

Zinos-Amaro: I think for a writer in general there's probably heightened sensitivity about retaining linguistic facility as one ages. I empathize with you on both fronts, as Alzheimer's is in my family.

Swanwick: Isaac Asimov used to brag that he didn't fear getting old because he could always just keep writing. Then he got AIDS from the blood transfusion and spent his last months in bed watching daytime TV. A very, very sad ending for him. As you say, all of us writers worry about that one.

Zinos-Amaro: I started to suspect that some of Nimrod's statements in "Urdumheim," when he's cognitively impaired, were references to Bush, but it was the line "Our enemies never stop thinking about new ways to harm our country and our people, and neither do we" that cinched it.

Swanwick: I was doing a mash-up of Bush and the nonsense language of our times. It's also a comment on the misuse of language. The thing I was most pleased with is when they make their original landing, draw a line in the sand meaning "We are here," and thus did history begin. That single opening paragraph is for me the justification for the entire story. And then when the protagonist has been deprived entirely of language he and the other oxen reinvent it using imitative sounds. This is a very old theory about the way language arose, I believe pretty much discredited. Nevertheless, it's one that doesn't go away.

Zinos-Amaro: That leads to the beautiful twist at the end of the story, where the multitude of languages is deliberately conceived as a way of protecting people from the Igigi. Rather than being a curse and leading to suffering, as in the original story, here it's salvation.

Swanwick: Also, today nobody really wishes we had just one language. In fact, we're concerned about losing languages, because every time you lose a language so much richness of expression and thought is gone forever, and you can't get it back. Every now and then you get a little window into another language, and you see how they're able to express things and perhaps even think of things that we can't, because their language is amenable to that.

Zinos-Amaro: The story, in celebrating linguistic diversity, celebrates imaginative diversity.

Swanwick: Oh yes. I hope so. It's funny, because I was trying to create a new mythology using old words. I was struck by how many references I had to later culture in there. The "Brekekekek koax koax" is from Aristophanes' *The Frogs*, the giant fish was from Hieronymus Bosch, and the elephant with spider legs is from Salvador Dali.

Zinos-Amaro: Following the story's logic, our versions of these things are simply the distant echoes of the long-forgotten originals . . . "Urdumheim" is such a powerful piece of work, I'm wondering if you considered it for inclusion in *The Best of Michael Swanwick*?

Swanwick: It may well be that it was in a grey area from a rights perspective for reprinting. I placed the stories in *The Best of* in chronological order. However, I'm pleased that there's a second *Best of* volume coming, to be published in 2023, and "Urdumheim" will be included in this second volume.

Zinos-Amaro: Fantastic news. In addition to everything else this story has going for it, filtering it through the mind of a character suffering progressive language loss is an impressive technical accomplishment.

Swanwick: I'm beginning to understand why you see it as a strong possibility that it's all about dementia! For all that I'm borrowing from everywhere in "Urdumheim," it's not an imitation of someone else's story. I think it's original, which is important.

Zinos-Amaro: At one point in "Urdumheim," the narrator hears a cluster of words, and you vary the typography to suggest that effect. You also use an interesting typographical technique in "From Babel's Fall'n Glory We Fled . . ." (*Asimov's Science Fiction*, February 2008) to represent how the alien millies speak.

Swanwick: That kind of typographical trick is something that they did a lot in science fiction back in the 70s, at a time when I was intensely studying the work of my superiors to try and figure out how they did it. For the most part I always enjoyed those examples of concrete poetry, as it were. I've kept them and I'm very fond of them. I think they work well on the page.

Zinos-Amaro: "From Babel's Fall'n Glory We Fled . . ." offers up a very unique mix of economics and biology. The alien world creation and biological angles are superb.

Swanwick: This one took me a long time to write, and it was another busted novel, I'm afraid. It was going to be a first contact novel. I had worked out the whole history of *Europa*, the ship that was sent from Earth. Essentially what they did is dump a lot of people on it with a lot of raw material and tools and then say, "Build or die." So it's not entirely built at the time they send it. I had worked out the two economic systems, which are both based on the Marxist critique of capitalism, the moving frontier leading inevitably to collapse. One economic system is based on knowledge, or information, and the other economic system is based on trust. They can't really bring knowledge and trust together, try though they might.

I was building the stellar system that the planet's in, which is in the last stages of planetary formation, which is why there are so many meteor strikes. It seemed to me an interesting locale for a novel. I did all my research on the system, built the planet, built the aliens, I worked out what the steam jungles would be like, what kind of creatures would be in there, and at some point I stopped and thought, "I have been working on this for a year non-stop and I don't have any characters or plot yet. Okay, time to write something else!" I set it aside. Then, of course, being a frugal person, I came up with an idea for a story and decided to use as much of that material as I could, which was only a fraction of what I created.

Zinos-Amaro: Have you considered setting other stories in this venue?

Swanwick: I have, but I was never inspired to. The humans are really caught in a forked stick. They are born into debt, paying off a debt that keeps growing because they need information from Earth. The information they send back helps to pay off some of it, but not enough to be clear. "From Babel's Fall'n Glory We Fled . . ." is really a kind of J. G. Ballard story dressed up as a planetary adventure. A couple of times I tried giving a whack at a story on *Europa* midway through the journey, but it was just too depressing.

Zinos-Amaro: I would want a sequel with Carlos Quivera.

Swanwick: That's hard to imagine. Like a sequel to "The Ones Who Walk Away from Omelas."

Zinos-Amaro: I'd read that too—so now you have two challenges! Speaking of other stories, "From Babel's Fall'n Glory We Fled . . ." recalls, at least in the setup, Barry B. Longyear's famous "Enemy Mine."

Swanwick: I *was* thinking of that story, and of course it's in a long tradition of stories where you have two enemies who have to work together to survive, and ultimately form a bond of friendship.

Zinos-Amaro: You make fun of that explicitly in the story.

Swanwick: I do, I do! I wanted to do a lot of complicated formal things with this. The alien language is just a part of it. There's this whole other tale of infidelity and revenge that occurs before the story opens, and is only referred to. And there's the discontinuities of narrative, and so on. I wanted to create as chewy a story as possible, one full of things, including lists at one point. So for the central action, I needed something simple. I stole that from Barry and those who came before him, and then had the characters refuse to go along with the plot.

Zinos-Amaro: Also, this story is told from the point of view of the sentient suit Rosamund, which adds another layer of innovation and complexity. Particularly since she had the relationship with Carlos.

Swanwick: That's in part inspired by *Empire Star* by Samuel R. Delany, which is narrated by a sentient jewel named Jewel who, as is revealed at the end, is cheerfully talking about itself. I thought that was a delightful idea and used it here. I tried to make "From Babel's Fall'n Glory We Fled . . ." so pleasurable for the science fiction reader that they would overlook how bleak and despairing it is.

Zinos-Amaro: This is a lovely line spoken by the suit: "All machines know that humans are happiest when they think least."

Swanwick: What a nihilistic line! And I can't deny it. It's quite possibly true. But I added the "all machines know" so that we wouldn't be certain that in *our* terms it's true.

Zinos-Amaro: I think part of the reason the story is dark is also that you're suggesting that the Marxist alternatives to capitalism eventually end up degrading and collapsing back into the capitalist model.

Swanwick: Yes. Yes. Maybe we'll come up with something better down the road. If we do I'm hoping it's after I'm gone. The last time we came up with something better it was Communism, and that ultimately caused a lot of pain, some of it to people I consider to be friends.

Zinos-Amaro: Friendship is one of the themes informing our next story, "The Scarecrow's Boy" (*The Magazine of Fantasy & Science Fiction*, October-November 2008), which also happens to feature sentient non-human narration.

Swanwick: This is one of my favorite stories. The bots in this world do the work and take on the responsibility, and they allow human beings to behave very badly in the absence of meaningful work. This could be my class envy of the rich speaking, it's entirely possible! I realize that this is ironic. Many times Marianne and I have traveled to countries like China and Russia where we're astonishingly rich compared to the average citizen.

This is also one of Marianne's favorite stories of mine. She loves the relationship with the boy, and how it's told sparingly. You're convinced that the scarecrow has made a commitment to this child, and is capable of following through on it. As a parent, this resonates with her. Also, there's the funny moments, like the interaction with the vending machine.

Zinos-Amaro: I'd like to touch on a specific question raised by this story: "Do you think that good and evil are hardwired into the universe? As opposed to being just part of our programming, I mean. Do you think they have some kind of objective reality?" When we discussed "The Dragon Line," you described yourself as a moralistic writer. You've also talked about the influence of Catholicism on your worldview. So I'm curious, do you personally believe in the objective existence of good and evil?

Swanwick: As far as the moralistic aspect, there's no getting around that one. From my personal experience with good and evil, I tend to believe they exist objectively. But on an elevated, philosophical plain, I honestly don't know. I know what it feels like when it happens to you, and I know whose side I'm on in such a clash of values. I'm down with the robot in this one.

Zinos-Amaro: There's a very funny line in "The Scarecrow's Boy," which besides possessing great surface wit, seems to imply that there will always be a combination of the unknowable and the predetermined in life. I'm referring to this: "We are as God and Sony made us."

Swanwick: One of my favorite lines ever. The robot is simply doing his best to navigate a morally confusing world. I really think that the difference here is between those who take responsibility for their actions—the robot does so, as well as for the actions of others—and those who refuse to. They use nihilism as an excuse to behave however badly they want to behave.

Zinos-Amaro: All of that resonates with me as a reader. It also struck me that the story could be seen as a comment, again, on the father-son dynamic. In this case you remove the parent and show what the negative consequences are of such an absence. The boy references his dad having been in a car accident, and the other boy with whom Sally and scarecrow Jack were familiar lacked an obvious parental figure and grew up to be nihilistic.

Swanwick: I don't know whether he lost his parents or they just neglected to raise him, but pretty clearly he was raised by machines, and he was aware of the fact that they were possessions.

Zinos-Amaro: He treats them that way—until his encounter with the screwdriver.

Swanwick: The story began with me trying to think of a Halloween story. I came up with the image of a scarecrow in the field who was alive, and I sent a little boy across the field to see what would happen, and the scarecrow turned out to be a robot. From that point on basically the logic of the story took over. Each step implied the next step. Sally the car, by the way, is obviously a Mustang!

Zinos-Amaro: You elegantly sidestep the details of the political asylum, the nature of the conflict, and so on. It keeps the story nicely focused.

Swanwick: Yes. I didn't want it to be a satire of the right wing or of the left wing. It's a story about emergent morality, and the politics are uncertain. Even the robots don't understand them. They're the politics of the future, and on one side they appear to have curdled. When I originally started this, I pictured the lake being like Lake Memphremagog, which is half in Vermont and half in Quebec. Then when I looked it up I found it was a north-south lake, so that the lake crossing I needed wouldn't be happening in reality. So I had to be vague about where this is set. It's set in Vermont or a place rather like it. On the whole the story was written relatively quickly for me, and came out nice and clean. It said what it needed to say.

Zinos-Amaro: Stylistically, for me it recalls "Hello, Said the Stick," which also spotlights a non-human consciousness.

Swanwick: Yeah. It's the same kind of prose. Clear, spare, not-showing-off prose.

Zinos-Amaro: Those words can't be applied to William Hope Hodgson, from whose work your flash story "Hush and Hark" (*The Drabblecast*, #84) takes its title.

Swanwick: The Hodgson-inspired title isn't originally from me, but from the illustrator Jason Van Hollander. Jason has won the World Fantasy Award twice as an artist. He is a very interesting, very smart person with a sly, wry sense of humor and a psychological inability to get more than a mile from his house. He can't go to conventions. Darrell Schweitzer once got him to a Philcon, but that was long ago. Jason is a big fan of Lovecraft and the Arkham House writers. He shared one of his images called "Hush and Hark" with me. You can find it online easily enough. Something about it spoke to me. It's creepy and dark, but the little peasant non-human woman is kind of cute and fairy-tale-ish at the same time. Thinking about Jason, I made it cosmic horror, about the fear and dread of the large spaces of the universe, combined with this mole-like woman.

Zinos-Amaro: Mrs. Underhill.

Swanwick: Yes. "There was an old woman lived under the hill, / And if she's not gone she lives there still." She is a cosmic power, but on a very, very, very small scale. She organizes the workers of the soil and keeps things going. Her other half is a nihilistic presence that can undo everything. It's not death, but it's a Thing.

Zinos-Amaro: She misses her husband and is actually looking forward to the reunion. "That cold, implacable hand closing about me" makes for a nice image. This leads us to several other of your uncollected non-series flash pieces, starting with the very funny "Metasciencefiction" (*The Drabblecast*, #84). "It's only the first sentence, and already the story's in trouble."

Swanwick: This is one that I wrote one sentence at a time, meaning that when I wrote the first sentence, I had no idea what the second sentence would be. I bootstrapped my way through the story. The only thing I knew is that things would just keep getting worse for the poor writer.

Zinos-Amaro: The essence of dramatic fiction.

Swanwick: It is. Sometimes when people object to a particular story, you have to remind them that fiction is about bad things happening to people.

Zinos-Amaro: In this story you reference, among others, Hemingway, Cordwainer Smith and Joanna Russ. We've talked a bit about the first two. Tell me about Russ.

Swanwick: I'm an admirer of her work. She was a magnificent writer. I was actually in correspondence with Joanna Russ for a while. Contrary to her public image, she was the warmest, kindest person imaginable, very generous with stories about the early days of science fiction when she was just starting out and very generous with her memories of those involved. If you go through her *F&SF* reviews of books, you can see her generosity in them too. There was an Avram Davidson review, for example, where she began by saying, "This book *is* very sexist, but it's so good that that doesn't matter." She loved science fiction, and if it was good science fiction she'd forgive you almost anything. I have very fond memories of corresponding with her. Never met her.

Zinos-Amaro: How did the correspondence start?

Swanwick: She wrote me. She saw something by me that she liked and told some women friends of hers on the West Coast that she'd like to correspond with me, and they convinced her that it would be okay. I remember when I got her letter, I was walking around the house, holding it aloft and saying, "Joanna Russ wrote to me! Joanna Russ!" It was out of the blue. She also had a long correspondence with Chip Delany, which I believe she considered to be the best and most meaningful correspondence she ever had. Apparently, they went very deep into theory. That's a collection that I'd like to see printed.

Zinos-Amaro: I couldn't agree more! It would be interesting to investigate your own material along these lines, and possibly distill some of it for publication. Did you preserve your correspondence with her?

Swanwick: Yes, I have all the letters, and I could probably find them.

Zinos-Amaro: Excellent. What stands out to you from her body of work?

Swanwick: Goodness. I like pretty much all of it, but I keep going back to the Alyx stories. Those stories were very important to me. When I was unpublished and unpublishable, one of my ambitions was to write an adventure story with a woman adventure hero. At that time it seemed something very difficult to do. Now, probably not half but a strong percentage of genre fiction has strong heroines in it. It was reassuring back then to read Joanna on how difficult it was to create Alyx. She had that wonderful moment where she described starting to write Alyx as being beautiful, and Alyx looked up from the page at her and said, "Oh, come on." She also wrote a story called "The Zanzibar Cat" about *Lud-in-the-Mist*, a metafictional work where at the end the author takes the entire story and shoves it up her vagina, because she's the author and can do anything. I asked her about that story, and she explained that in *Lud-in-the-Mist* you're promised that things are going to be wonderful in Fairyland, but you don't get to see it, of course, because Hope Mirrlees was promising something that could not be seen. That story might be my favorite metafiction of all time.

Zinos-Amaro: I thought *Picnic on Paradise* was extremely well done.

Swanwick: Oh, there's so much in that. I first read it, I think, in my early twenties, and found a lot of wisdom in it. There's a bit, for example, where she makes love with Machine a second time, and realizes he's doing the exact same things as before. They have an argument, and he says, "Look, if you do something, you do as well as you absolutely can, right?" And she says, "No." He stomps off. I thought, "She's right. Trying all the time to do everything as well as you can is not human." Which took a lot of pressure off me. Such a warm and wise story in which the incredibly competent heroine actually acts like a recognizable human being.

Zinos-Amaro: Joanna Russ certainly paved the way for many.

Swanwick: She led the way for everyone else.

Zinos-Amaro: At the end of "Metasciencefiction" the writer muses something like, "If it sucks, it sucks, but it will still have dinosaurs with guns."

Swanwick: Yes! That's kind of my judgment on science fiction. Even in the bad stuff, there's something there. Dinosaurs with guns. It can't be *all* bad. I was teaching at Clarion West once and a student turned in a story full of painful, forced sodomy. When the time came to critique it I said, "What this story needs is more dinosaurs." I explained that Joe Haldeman had written one of his intergalactic spy stories, which were collected in *All My Sins Remembered*. He'd been selling them to *Analog*, which bounced this one story. Joe showed it to Gardner Dozois and said, "What's wrong with the story?" Gardner replied, "It needs more dinosaurs." Anybody else would have just gone sulking off, but Joe said "Good idea." If you read the story, the protagonist is walking along a beach, thinking about all his troubles, when all of a sudden he's attacked by a dinosaur, he pulls out his ray gun, they have an exciting battle and he kills the dinosaur and he goes walking back to the hotel thinking about his problems. *Analog* bought it and published it. So what I was saying in my critique was that this story needed more excitement, more color. It was too bleak. Later on someone submitted a story that was all brightness and color and action and fun. I said, "This doesn't really work," and the student replied, "It has lots of dinosaurs!" To which I said, "Well, it needs more sodomy." I explained that writing fiction is all about finding the balance between dinosaurs and sodomy. I thought I'd come up with a good metaphor. Gardner Dozois was teaching the following week and he said, "What the hell did you tell this class?" They're all submitting these stories with dinosaurs and sodomy, and they said you told them to write them. I didn't mean it literally, of course!

Zinos-Amaro: The black humor continues in "Errata Slip Found in a Copy of the Arkham University Press Trade Paperback Reissue of the Necronomicon" (*Weird Tales*, Fall 2009). Let me say upfront that it's a really bad idea for them to be reissuing this text as a trade paperback. Of course, you end the story midway through a sentence, in the Lovecraftian tradition of an implied and highly unpleasant narrative interruption.

Swanwick: It's almost inevitable that that's how it would end!

Zinos-Amaro: Even though this story is only a page long, it can be read as a commentary on style (the first errata correction) as well as horror and fantasy tropes (the second item).

Swanwick: It's all commentary on Lovecraft, really. It's either impossible or next to impossible to do satire of something that you don't like or respect. I see people try it. Parodies of people they cannot stand are really awful. They will not concede that there are virtues to the work. Mostly, I wrote this story because I wanted to be published in *Weird Tales*. It was one of those things I'd never done.

Zinos-Amaro: In its own way, "The Magaracs: A Family Saga, in Fragments" (*World Fantasy Convention Book 2009*) may be a first for you too, since the story is structured around a series of photographs that are integral to the text. What's the background here?

Swanwick: There was a place called The Resettlers only a couple of miles from us, which sold the leftover dribs and drabs from estates. Marianne and I would go there occasionally. It was like a museum of American physical culture. Just fascinating to wander through. For only a couple of bucks I found a plastic bag of photographs. It was all one family from the twenties or thirties, no notations as to who any of the people were. They were not a very usual family. They were an interesting and odd batch of people. I looked at them and thought, "These need a story. A rationale." So I made one up. I wrote the story for its own sake, and then the opportunity to have it published came up after. A lovely, timely opportunity to do something different. Where else could I have published such a thing, with the pictures? The prose was different from my usual prose, too, and that's always fun to do. How flat-faced can you be, jotting down insane claims about this family? It was a delight to write.

Zinos-Amaro: There's a lot of great beats in "The Magaracs: A Family Saga, in Fragments," like the casual mention of the resurrected Edgar Allan Poe, but my favorite moment is in fragment 3, where we learn that nothing could be worse than marrying a feminist: "At last he married a feminist, and the family cut him off entirely."

Swanwick: I was thinking about how today people like to claim that their female ancestors were feminists, but back then all the men and certainly most of the women would have been horrified at the idea. If you read Woolf's *A Room of One's Own* in it she says that the essay runs the risk of being written off as being feminist. You look at it now and it's gloriously feminist. Back then that possibility was viewed with horror and fear.

The Edgar Allan Poe joke may have been taken from a small detail in John Crowley's *Little, Big*. Somebody is looking through a book of photographs of the house and it has a caption that reads, "Name, Name, Name, and Elf." The man reading it goes "Elf?" There's no explanation given.

I think underneath everything this is a story about the disappearance of family history, which is similar to the disappearance of ethnicity in our country. People come here and become more and more American and eventually forget where they came from. "The Magaracs" is connected with the immigrant experience in a subtle way. I named the family after Joe Magarac and set it in Pittsburgh to establish their Slavic background. The implication was that their strangeness was brought into America from the old country. And clearly they've been successful in the new one. So, categorically, this story would be slipstream urban fantasy (not in the original Leiberesque meaning of the term or the current romance-and-supernatural meaning, but the middle meaning epitomized by Emma Bull and Will Shetterly).

Zinos-Amaro: There's also a slipstream-ish vibe in "Last Drink Bird Head" (*Last Drink Bird Head: Flash Fiction for Charity*, ed. Ann VanderMeer & Jeff VanderMeer, 2009), where you come up with a cute bar situation. I imagine this story was solicited for this charity project.

Swanwick: It was. I wanted to write an actual science fiction story. I knew that the VanderMeers encouraged sort of metaphoric, *Weird Tales*-ish sort of stuff. I wanted to have something that would stand out from the others. The theme, I believe, was inspired by those glass-bodied toy birds that bob their heads into a glass of water. They're a heat engine. It was an extremely arbitrary challenge to set to a writer. I managed to end my story with the four words, though that was not a requirement.

Zinos-Amaro: We end our survey of this phase of your career with one more standalone piece of flash fiction, "Invisibility for Beginners" (*The Drabblecast*, #140). It's a sort of ironic title, given how visible your work had become by the 2000s. This one feels like it's written in the format of an advertisement. I enjoyed the bite in the line that starts with, "Even a spiritual moron . . ."

Swanwick: There's a certain amount of New Age fraud going on in the background here. I'm just having fun with what a humiliating thing this would be if you followed the instructions. A night out on the town, indeed.

CHAPTER SEVEN
2010-2014

Zinos-Amaro: "Goblin Lake" (*Stories: All-New Tales*, ed. Neil Gaiman and Al Sarrantonio, 2010) starts out as an exercise in inspired historical whimsy and then plunges us into the deep waters of truth vs. artifice, reality vs. fiction. This is a fascinating piece of work, explicitly indebted to Hans Jakob Christoffel von Grimmelshausen's *Simplicius Simplicissimus*. Was that the main inspiration?

Swanwick: This is one of my favorite stories. Yes, it came mostly from *Simplicissimus*, but I had also done a fair amount of research into that general era when I wrote my novel *Jack Faust*. I already had a feel for the times. *Simplicissimus* is a really fascinating book. Von Grimmelshausen is a pseudonym; we don't even know the author's real name. All we know is that when he was twelve or maybe fourteen some soldiers came through his parents' farm and requisitioned horses and food—and *him*. He grew up in the army, at war. Later on he got a job basically as a secretary for his former commanding officer. When he wrote *Simplicissimus* it was such a big hit that somebody pirated it and added some more chapters to the end. He pirated the pirated edition, kept the chapters he hadn't written, and added some more at the end of the book! So, he was definitely one of us.

The serious parts of it are terrifying. It is a fantastic book. It has great satire in it and in the last quarter of the novel it suddenly takes this break and goes into fantasy. I stole rather a lot from those chapters.

Zinos-Amaro: "Goblin Lake" in a way reverses this, by starting out with fantasy elements and then transitioning into so-called reality, or a fictional version thereof.

Swanwick: So much fantasy is about fantasy, when you parse it all down, and of course it always comes down on the side of fantasy, because it's the home team. It's justifying itself. With this story I thought I'd place fantasy and reality against each other and have a more thought-through conflict.

Zinos-Amaro: My impression is that the fantasy in this story, that part of the equation, is a proxy for all of fiction. It goes beyond genre.

Swanwick: That's definitely there, and was intended. Every now and then you have to bite the hand that loves you! This story has one of my favorite jokes ever, by the way, when the King explains that characters in books do not read books, so if you've read a book this year, it will tell you whether you're a real person or not.

Zinos-Amaro: Lucky for me, then, that I've been reading all your fiction! In "Goblin Lake" you again pay homage to E. R. Eddison: you use the names Doctor Vandermast and Zayana, which appear in Eddison's *Mistress of Mistresses* and *A Fish Dinner in Memison*.

Swanwick: I was originally going to have Doctor Vandermast as Eddison's character, explaining the nature of the world. But that would have been dragging in another character, and the King was already explaining things. It was simpler to stay with him. Also, I found him a charming old duffer. I liked him as a character. Another reference in "Goblin Lake" is to James Branch Cabell. The hero-as-trickster is very Cabell. I had my character nicknamed Jack, which is the English equivalent of Jurgen, after Cabell's *Jurgen, A Comedy of Justice*. I was going to have him called Jurgen, but I couldn't come up with an explanation that the readers would accept naturally and go along with. Jack is probably just as well, because while I borrowed a lot from Cabell, it wasn't really about Cabell. It would have been a different story if it had been about Cabell's fiction.

The naming of Jack is really a nod to my younger brother. He was a very, very beautiful young man. Very smart and clever. In the late 80s he was killed by a drunk driver in Florida. He had been hitchhiking and the car got a flat tire. They pulled off to the side and were fixing the tire when this drunk driver killed both of them, my brother and the driver. He then fled, and somebody who witnessed the event chased after him, and as a result he was arrested. It turns out that he didn't have any money and his driver's license had already been taken away from him because he'd killed someone else driving previously. So they decided there was nothing to be done and they released him.

Zinos-Amaro: I'm really sorry for your loss, Michael. What a terrible turn of events. It's shocking and mind-boggling to me that the culprit was even released after the first incident.

Swanwick: The laws about vehicular homicide in Florida are really lax, in large part because they have so many old people there. Marianne's father, the lawyer, looked into this case and got all the court documents. He was appalled that the driver was let off. Anyway, when you see a character named Jack in my work, it's often a reference to my little brother, to give him a bit more life.

Zinos-Amaro: I understand. That's very sweet. Coming back to "Goblin Lake," I assume that it was commissioned by either Neil Gaiman or Al Sarrantonio for their anthology. Did knowing that you were going to submit a story for them specifically inform your choice of story? I ask because, thinking about some stories in Neil Gaiman's body of work, I can see ideas in "Goblin Lake," like interrogating the nature of fiction within a fictional structure, and just generally the idea of a meta-fantasy, that might have resonated with him personally.

Swanwick: I think Sarrantonio got in touch with me. But yes, I was approached, and I asked myself what story I had that I could write on deadline. I had this idea that was brewing, and figured I could force myself to write it quickly enough to make it in. I wrote it, submitted it and they published it. I'll admit that when I decided on this particular story, it did seem to me that it would fit well with Neil Gaiman. For all that I'm absolutely sure that Neil wasn't deliberately doing this, I think that the definition of good fiction might have been implicitly defined by the best of Neil's own work. If you look at the finished book, there are stories on this side of it, and that side of it, but if you ask where the center of all of this fiction would be, it would probably be in one of Neil's stories.

I should mention that in "Goblin Lake" I included a description of a horse falling into the Mummelsee and rising out of it with two legs and wings and so on. That is the Jersey Devil. It's a fascinating piece of folklore, with no resolution. It's the beginning of a story, and the rest of the story isn't there. So I was commenting on fiction in other ways too.

Zinos-Amaro: The meta-element takes the form of a fundamental choice: remain immortal, and exist inside a fictional realm with a certain built-in simplicity, or aspire to a greater authenticity and complexity at the cost of mortality. Is there any piece of fiction rich and alluring enough to tempt you out of our reality and *into* that fictional world?

Swanwick: There was a time when *Lord of the Rings* would have done it for me. But not now, I don't think. No. The beginning of *Ada* would be close, maybe, when they're young, and having hot sex, and being rich. But of course that world sours on them as they grow up. It's a novel where time goes backward and all the magic goes away. There are flying carpets at the beginning, and by the end it's a world very much like the one Nabokov found himself in.

In Jack's life in so-called reality it's cold, he has to pick up the spilled pig slops by hand, chop wood, and so on. In a weird way, that's a comforting world. He's complaining about the children never writing, but he's had children, and a wife who loves him, with whom he's obviously had a good relationship. It's not a bad life he's opted for. Did he make the right choice? I think that the entire story is really a lead-up to the last line: if there's no God, we will never know what the right choice was. There's the Catholic boy at work.

Zinos-Amaro: Indeed. The next story, "Steadfast Castle" (*The Magazine of Fantasy & Science Fiction*, September-October 2010), offers an excursion into the detective subgenre, especially the locked-room, or in this case, the locked-house, mystery. You have fun with some tropes, like the femme fatale. Who are some of your favorite fictional detectives?

Swanwick: Father Brown, obviously. Sherlock Holmes. I've read all the original Doyle stories, and a great deal of peripheral Holmes material over the decades. Mary Jane Latsis and Martha Henissart, under the pen name Emma Lathen, wrote a series of novels where the detective was a banker, because all the crimes were financially motivated. He could figure out where the money led to. It wasn't so much the detective I liked, as it was the authors' writing and thinking. If we're going to bring in television, I'll add Columbo. That was just such an engaging character.

Regarding "Steadfast Castle," I'd been carrying around an idea for many decades of a house that basically corrupts the owner by telling them whatever they want to hear, by encouraging them in all their unspoken desires. That's what I set out to write when I began, but it very quickly changed into the story of a house that had fallen in love with its owner, who was not a worthy man. Love knows that, and doesn't care. Once you have a detective asking questions, it turns the story into a mystery because the form demands it. And there is, as you say, a detective-specific type of narrative: how did this guy disappear? Why did he disappear? And so on. But for me this is all secondary to the emotional story.

Zinos-Amaro: Like "Midnight Express," this story is all conversation. When did you figure out it would be all dialogue?

Swanwick: As you know, there's a formula for how much dialogue to put into a story relative to description for a desired pace. The more dialogue, the faster it reads. That was definitely part of the thinking here. It had to be short, and it had to be fast, because I didn't think it would bear up under close examination. I did a pretty good job creating the technology behind this world so that you could have close to ubiquitous surveillance and yet a clever person could still manage to escape. But it wasn't a big enough idea to support a lot of description. I do like the fact that I sent him down into the basement with a flashlight!

Zinos-Amaro: You paid homage to three hundred and seventy-nine horror films with that one beat. There's a great moment around that time when the detective says, "I'm not afraid," and the house replies, "You should be."

Swanwick: I think this story would be good for a half-hour television play. There have been a couple of series of good Ray Bradbury story adaptations; something like that.

Zinos-Amaro: Given that the house can represent itself through a body unit, or avatar, and the whole general creepy vibe, I'd nominate this for the *Black Mirror* treatment.

Swanwick: That would work. Dark as it is, people like "Steadfast Castle" a lot, and I'm always a little puzzled by that.

Zinos-Amaro: Your next story, "Spirits in the Night" (*Abyss & Apex*, 4th Quarter 2010), has a title suggestive of dark affairs, but it turns out to be a charming flash spoof of "Icehenge" by Kim Stanley Robinson.

Swanwick: I quite enjoyed Robinson's story, and one day I just sat down and wrote this piece. I could have called it "Gin-henge," but it would have given away the central image too immediately. Wendy S. Delmater asked me if I'd sell her a piece of flash fiction, and I said, "Sure." I chose the three or four best pieces of unpublished flash fiction I had on my computer, and I sent them to her and said, "If you like one of these, it's yours." This is the one she picked. If it weren't for her, it would exist only on my harddrive. I should probably make more of an effort to market my flash stories, but I don't.

Zinos-Amaro: You devise some great names here, like Gin-henge, or the archaeomixologists. And then of course you reference Robinson himself with Tristram Lee Robinson.

Swanwick: You can't get away with these things at greater length.

Zinos-Amaro: It's unclear who committed the prank in "Spirits in the Night," but I think it's significant that everyone is nonplussed *that* it happened. This implies that irreverence will be normal, to some extent, in near future space exploration, which in science fiction is often handled, if you'll forgive the pun, more soberly.

Swanwick: I'm absolutely, one hundred percent convinced of that. People are still going to be people, and people are very eccentric.

Zinos-Amaro: Even though this is a very short piece, you still get some science in it, like the freezing point of ethanol.

Swanwick: True. At the time I wrote this story, it was an accurate portrayal of Pluto as we thought it to be. What's funny is that we thought it was the dullest planet in the Solar System. Now we know it's anything but. It has mountains of ice, and plains of frozen nitrogen, and a great variety of terrain. If the images from the latest probe had come back before the classification decision was made, I think it would still be called a planet.

Zinos-Amaro: We turn to a different kind of mostly desolate terrain in "Libertarian Russia" (*Asimov's Science Fiction*, December 2010).

Swanwick: This is one of three stories I got from my first trip to Yekaterinburg, which is in the Ural mountains, two time zones east of Moscow. The second story was "Pushkin the American," which we'll get to soon, and the third one I decided not to write. It was going to be based on a Russian-Ukranian artist, named Ilya Kabakov, who turned his apartment into a piece of art, as they did in Moscow in the Soviet Union at that time. The work was called "The Man Who Flew into Space From His Apartment," and it featured an enormous slingshot in the kitchen, and bits of fallen plaster from the ceiling. I plotted out a story about a drunken engineer who nobody likes—he's very loud and vulgar—working for Uralmash, the Urals heavy machinery factory. In private he builds himself a spaceship and blasts himself into orbit, drunk and singing obscene songs into the radio. I realized this story was a satire on Soviet life, and I don't have the right to write it, that's *their* story to do. So that one never got written, and I don't think it ever will.

After I'd been in Russia for about a week, I found myself obsessively making up theories about why the Russians are the way they are. I've never done this in other places. I've been in Finland, which is also Slavic, and didn't do that; I've been to China, which is even more different from our culture, and didn't do that; and so on. My tentative theory is that the Russians are a lot like Americans, so much like Americans in some ways, that Americans have a hard time understanding why they're not like us the rest of the way. Americans and Russians are like twin brothers separated at birth: one of them got all the good luck, one of them got all the bad luck, and neither one deserved it.

I carried trying to understand Russians home. A year or two or three later I started wondering why Russians didn't have their own cowboy stories. Siberia is so much like the Old West, inhospitable, sparsely populated and so on. You travel around in our West, where cowboy stories happened, and you can see that they're almost entirely a myth. Life there was not exciting and full of gun fights. It was mostly dullness and hard work. So I decided to create a story about a young Russian who wants to be an American cowboy while still being a Russian. That seemed to me a good starting point. I figured he was a libertarian, and I asked my Russian friends by email, "How do you say 'libertarian Russia' in Russian?" They said, "No, no, you don't understand. Such a thing is not possible." I told them it was fiction, but they kept saying it wasn't possible anyway. Finally, I said, "Fine, how do you say 'libertarian Chicago'?" They replied right away. This ended up on the cutting room floor, but I think it told me that I was on the right track, asking a question that was meaningful.

Zinos-Amaro: When you were growing up, were you a reader of Westerns?

Swanwick: Sure, but mostly I saw the movies, which I think are better depictions of the myth.

Zinos-Amaro: When I read "Libertarian Russia" the version of the Western myth that came to my mind was Jack Kerouac's *On the Road.*

Swanwick: It's the same underlying myth, yes. The Kerouac myth has grown and mutated into looking for America, and my character is looking for Russia. Kerouac was influential on me when I was young. I wanted to be like that. I wanted to be Dean Moriarty. When Victor in my story walks away at the end, he begins to grow up. He's giving up on becoming Jack Kerouac, but for a brief instance he *is* Kerouac. The image of him going off on his motorcycle while the money blows in the wind like leaves is straight out of *Treasure of Sierra Madre*. He doesn't look back. At the end of the Western, the cowboy never looks back. Victor has outgrown the myth, but for one moment he *was* it.

Zinos-Amaro: I expect that a number of elements in this story are based directly on your travel experiences.

Swanwick: I put in a lot of things that I had seen in Russia. The bar/restaurant they go to, for example, was a place I had been in. On my last day in Moscow, during my second visit to Russia, a friend gave me a ride to the airport, and as we were driving through traffic in this golden smog, a young guy on a motorcycle went "alpine skiing" back and forth through the cars. That all made it into "Libertarian Russia." I had trouble with the language for the OMON characters, because they would have been speaking Mat, which is a Russian set of obscenities. Their profanity starts where ours leaves off. It's much cruder and more offensive than ours. One of the reviewers complained about the cursing in the story, but I was already toning it down. The OMON slogan in the story—"We Know No Mercy And Do Not Ask For Any"—is in fact true as well. When I was in Moscow, I got up one morning, went out on the street, and there were OMON thugs in baby blue camouflage on every street corner. They were hanging out, hitting on young ladies, and no one could explain to me exactly why they were there. Russia has more flavors of police than anyone. It's alarming at times. That's why I had a fictional depopulation occur, to make my story possible.

Zinos-Amaro: Did you hear from your Russian fans and friends?

Swanwick: Yes. I had more than one come up to me and say, "What did you mean by this?" Some people found it kind of upsetting, as if it were an attack on Russians. On the other hand, a Russian living in America told me that I had nailed it. He's outnumbered, but I choose to believe him.

Zinos-Amaro: In "Libertarian Russia" you cite Vladimir Visotsky's song "Skittish Horses." I found a version online, and it really brought the ambiance of the story to life. Where did you come across this song?

Swanwick: On my trip I discovered that Russians are way more into song than we are. As I was writing the story I hit YouTube and went searching for songs that would be meaningful to a Russian. It seemed to me that "Skittish Horses" would have made for a good song in a Russian cowboy movie, and at the same time it wasn't a cowboy song, it was something very Russian. It's about moving out. Victor is moving away from his callow youth. He starts out sure that he knows all the answers, and one by one questions them, becomes disillusioned. At the end of the story he has a far better grip on reality than when he started.

I have to say, there are strange things out in wild Siberia. I came back to my hotel one time and there was a shaman waiting for me there. He was a little guy with a neatly trimmed beard and a tweed jacket and tie. He gave me a plastic bottle of vodka and a devil stone. He told me I had power in me, but it wasn't unlocked, and the devil stone would help. I did not know what to make of that, but I keep the stone near my computer. Some days, if I don't feel like writing at all, I hold it for a while and say, "You can do this."

Zinos-Amaro: And you *have* been doing this, with great results. "Cold Reading" (*Flurb: A Webzine of Astonishing Tales*, Issue #11, Spring-Summer, 2011) continues to explore the dividing line between fiction and reality we were just talking about. "Oh, don't be so existential" is a terrific line.

Swanwick: This story is an example of what craft can do. As I recall it, I was thinking about a very 60s thing—I'd seen a number of plays where somebody's stuck inside a play and hasn't been warned or given a script and has to thrash about. For some reason I started writing this story, and continued until it ended, writing it in one evening. I did a little bit of acting in high school and was never very good at it. I love the milieu of the theater far more than I do the thought of acting. When I was in college, for a semester I worked as a stagehand for the college theater. A lot of the majors in the theater department were annoyed because they had a star system, and a small number of people got all the good roles. When I was working backstage, Glenny Wade was the female star, playing Sally Bowles in *Cabaret*. They put on really, really professional-level theater. It was a terrific version of *Cabaret*. When she graduated, Wade changed her name to Glenn Close. Working backstage with people of that caliber was really quite wonderful. I really loved it, and the only reason I did not continue doing that was that I couldn't afford to give up the time and still keep up the grades. That would have been a job I would have been perfectly content doing all my life. To this day, I really love watching actors. The Canadian television show *Slings and Arrows*, by the way, is the most astonishingly funny and accurate portrayal of actors ever. It's just fantastic.

Zinos-Amaro: Thank you for that recommendation; I'd never heard of it. You mention a 60s vibe. The opening of your story is very similar to an original *Twilight Zone* episode called "A World of Difference." It also recalls work by writers like Borges, Pirandello, Calvino, and so on.

Swanwick: I'm not sure if I ever saw that specific episode. There was a version of this idea in a story by Theodore Sturgeon, who may have been one of the first to tackle it. There's a nifty little story by Damon Knight, called "You're Another," where somebody finds out that he's the comic relief! I did read the writers you mention and admired them. If we stipulate that their work is infinitely better, then we might speak of this story in the same breath as theirs. I was talking online with Eileen Gunn one day, and I told her I had this story and didn't know what to do with it. She asked to see it, and she recommended I send it to *Flurb*, where Rudy Rucker would publish it and it would get some publicity. So I did, and it ended up being in an issue that Eileen guest-edited.

As far as I can tell, it got me no attention whatsoever. This story is far from a major story. It just kind of exists.

Zinos-Amaro: To me is shows continuity with "Goblin Lake" through its meta-fictional quality. Also, like "Steadfast Castle," this is stripped down into essentially all dialogue.

Swanwick: Yeah, yeah, in a larger sense that awareness is there. You're right about the dialogue choice. This story needs to move fast. If it slows down, it will stall and crash.

Zinos-Amaro: "An Empty House With Many Doors" (*Asimov's Science Fiction*, April-May 2011) may not be meta-fictional, but it nevertheless continues to relativize the self, this time by means of the multiverse. As with "Steadfast Castle," it feels like the high concept is really a tool in the service of an emotional reflection.

Swanwick: It is. This story is my love letter to Marianne. I was sitting around one day and thought, "What would I do if Marianne died?" I wouldn't commit suicide, but I thought I might well drink myself to death. That would take a while. It would take discipline! I was thinking also of a neighbor who lost his wife to cancer. One thing he did was simplify. He threw out a lot of stuff. He ended up with maybe half the possessions he had before. He got rid of not only everything that reminded him specifically of her, but also normal, ordinary things that reminded him of *their* life. So I had the opening of the story, where the man is manically cleaning up, he's got the rugs all vacuumed, he rolls them up and throws them away. But after that it was slow going. This was as slow a story as any I've written. I know it took years. I kept coming to a point and stopping. In the first attempt I got the protagonist down to the bottom of the hill and didn't know where it would go from there. At some point I came up with the parallel worlds traveler, and when he reaches up to try and help the guy, bam, he ends up in another world. From there I wrote relatively quickly until the parallel husband comes home. It takes our character a while to realize they look identical, because people don't really know what they look like. I'm always amazed to look in the mirror and see how funny-looking I am! The obvious places to go from there were either for him to kill his other self and take his place, or for the three of them to set up house together. I didn't like either of these resolutions, so again I had to wait. I should mention that "An Empty House With Many Doors" is set in my house and my neighborhood.

Zinos-Amaro: I'm glad you said that, because there's a story of yours I wanted to bring up, "Radio Waves," that also features your house and street, and feels connected to this piece. Both stories deal with loss and slippage across realities. Also, both stories begin with an inversion: in "Radio Waves," we begin by walking the telephone wires upside down, and in "An Empty House With Many Doors" the television set is upside down. The normal state of affairs, as it were, has been flipped.

Swanwick: I hadn't made the connection of the upside down element, but yeah, that's what's going on. He has the television upside down because the television is the most normal thing and normalcy has been turned upside down. He's no longer watching it to get pleasure out of it. He's just watching it to help him pass the time while he paces his drinking. The woodpecker ad in the story, by the way, was a real one. Surreal and totally banal. When I finally saw how to end this story, I went to the backyard one evening, sat there in the dark with a glass of scotch, and worked on the last paragraph in my head. I built it up sentence by sentence, that little monologue that he gives, and as it got stronger I began saying it out loud. When it was all done, when every word was, in my estimation, in a state where I could not improve upon it, I went inside and wrote it down.

Zinos-Amaro: This is certainly one of your most heartfelt stories. How did you share it with Marianne?

Swanwick: It was sincerely meant. There's no postmodern irony here at all. When it was finished and complete, I handed it to Marianne, and said "Read this." And she did and she kissed me. Marianne can read subtext. She's fluent in subtext.

Zinos-Amaro: "An Empty House With Many Doors" was liked by reviewers. I'm curious if you heard from anyone who was moved by it.

Swanwick: Some young filmmakers asked for permission to make a short film of this story for non-commercial purposes. We got a contract drawn up, and they filmed the outdoor parts in my neighborhood. The guy who played the main character was really quite good. He looked like a decent person who was heartbroken. There's a scene where he's walking along the canal, and the filmmakers threw in a cameo of Marianne and me. We walk past him and nod, and then I put my arm on Marianne's shoulder. That represented everything the character didn't have. The film isn't quite finished yet, because it needs CGI, but I'm anxious to see it. As a writer this is one of those strange little perks you get, one of the odd things that don't happen to real people.

Zinos-Amaro: Speaking of real people, and the theater experiences you mentioned related to "Cold Reading," let's talk about "The Man in Grey" (*Eclipse Four*, ed. Jonathan Strahan, 2011). This one—pun-intended—is hard-hitting.

Swanwick: There's a whole sub-genre of world-as-stage stories. Damon Knight, Theodore Sturgeon, Paul Park, and so on, have written them. In these stories the focus is always on the person who discovers that the world is a stage and they hadn't expected it. I wanted to reverse that and look at that story with the focus on the people who are the stagehands, the people who keep the world going. In all these stories these people are always very sure of themselves. They know exactly what they're doing and are rather arrogant in fact. I wanted to change that. I wanted to humanize them, to make them unsure of themselves.

Zinos-Amaro: Fritz Leiber also came to mind when reading this.

Swanwick: He was great at that kind of story.

Zinos-Amaro: There was a specific Sturgeon piece that "The Man in Grey" made me think of, called "Yesterday Was Monday" (*Unknown Fantasy Fiction*, June 1941). I re-read it recently and was impressed by how he handled the concept of our reality being built out discretely to give the illusion of sequential time.

Swanwick: I think that's one of the ones I had in mind, yes. Definitely an influence. Sturgeon was one of our best writers, and that was one of the best stories of this type. This sub-genre probably wouldn't be possible without Sturgeon.

Zinos-Amaro: You've played in this wheelhouse before. Reality is not as it appears in "Walking Out," and the deconstruction of everything powers "Microcosmic Dog."

Swanwick: We all have these thoughts sooner or later. Especially on a foggy day, if you're alone. That's why these stories work, because people are familiar with the thought, even if they've forgotten that they had it.

Zinos-Amaro: You've mentioned one reversal, the humanizing focus on the stagehands. I think your tale introduces another, even more dramatic inversion. Usually in these stories, the protagonist for whom the veil is lifted *likes* reality and wants to get back to it. Your story begins with a protagonist who wants to *escape* reality.

Swanwick: She's young, and she's in a terrible fix, and doesn't have the perspective to know that she can live through it. I quite like her, for the same reasons that the Man in Grey does. I used Martha because that was the most ordinary-sounding name I could come up with. She has an ordinary name, and she's caught up in a very ordinary tragedy, but she herself is extraordinary.

Zinos-Amaro: I want to ask you about the last line of this story. For me, the "I love you all" is chilling, given Martha's fate. It feels like an inhuman intelligence who doesn't understand humans projecting onto them. But I'm wondering if you meant it as genuine affection?

Swanwick: Your reading is perfectly valid, and I won't deny it, but that wasn't how I intended it. If you read the story on a metafictional level, the Man in Grey is me. In fact, Marianne tends to buy me grey clothing! She feels that it works best with my appearance. Nobody has made this connection, but it is how I think of myself and I do, in my way, love all of my characters. I don't visit suffering and pain upon them unnecessarily.

Zinos-Amaro: In this reading, the Man's comment about our reality being a game would be you reflecting on the game of literature.

Swanwick: Yes.

Zinos-Amaro: It strikes me that this is not how you intended the story, but I thought than an interesting way to read "The Man in Grey" is as a study on the hallucinatory power of terminal depression. In this view, everything Martha experiences is the result of her own internal suffering.

Swanwick: Oh, I like that one. That hadn't occurred to me. Depression is what she's suffering from. So the Man in Grey being her depression would make sense. He would be the literalization of her depression. Again, a perfectly valid interpretation.

Zinos-Amaro: The way that "The Man in Grey" handles the theme of free will, which you've explored in your work going all the way back to "Walden Three" and "Trojan Horse," is something else that I think sets it apart from similarly-premised pieces. Martha affirms her free will by liberating herself from what the beings like the Man call The Great Game.

Swanwick: She has made this choice herself. It was a difficult choice, and those standing out in the Grey applaud her for making her decision, whichever way she goes. That's what the story is all about. Free will is the most valuable thing in the world, in this specific thought experiment anyway. This was part of the reversal I was mentioning before. I wanted only the actors to have real agency, to be truly free agents. The people behind the scenes can't do anything but what they're doing. They're functionaries. All they can do is appreciate. That's the only freedom they have.

Zinos-Amaro: You're saying they're like literary critics.

Swanwick: I try not to make cheap jokes at the expense of critics!

Zinos-Amaro: I'm happy to do it on your behalf! Speaking of analysis, I compared the version of this story as it appeared in *Eclipse Four* with the reprint in your collection *Not So Much, Said the Cat*. The original version contains the line: "You'd have to talk to him for an hour to realize he wasn't human." In the reprint, you made a subtle change: "You'd have to talk to him for an hour to realize he was only a prop." Was this to soften the otherness and make it less suggestive of aliens, so that readers wouldn't be distracted by a possible alien angle?

Swanwick: Absolutely. On re-re-reading it jumped out at me that the not human comment could be interpreted as alien, and that was one interpretation I really didn't want.

Zinos-Amaro: I loved your description of the reality underneath what we think of as reality: ". . . the roiling, churning emptiness that underlies the world we constantly make and unmake in the service of our duty. The colorless, formless negation of negatives that is Nothing and Nowhere and Nowhen. The calm horror of nonbeing. The grey." Was there any particular inspiration for this? For me it was a bit evocative of The Nothing from Michael Ende's *The Neverending Story*.

Swanwick: This had to really be nothing you'd want. It's not an alternative to give up reality and then get a job behind the scenes. I've seen the film adaptation of *The Neverending Story* and

I own the novel in hardcover, with three colors of print. It's on my enormous pile of books to be read. The idea as shown in the film could have been an influence on me easily but I would've gotten there without it.

Zinos-Amaro: Earlier in your career, you were preoccupied with characters trying to retain their personal sense of identity. After that you interrogated identity through the lenses of deceit and transformation. In this phase of your work, it seems to me that you're engaging with the identity of reality itself. "The Man In Grey" continues to pursue the ontological destabilization we've seen in recent pieces like "Goblin Lake" and "Cold Reading."

Swanwick: It's all done in service of the story. There's a documentary film on Andy Goldsworthy, the artist. At one point he's setting out to the woods to do something artistic, and his wife asks what he's going to do today. "What have you done with my wife? I'm an intuitive artist, you know that!" I saw that and I thought, "That's what I am. I go into these stories blind." Sometimes I have an idea and I know what I'm going to do with it, but usually I just go in what seems like a productive area to explore mentally. I go in knowing that I don't know, knowing what I'm trying to figure out. Then the process of figuring it out comes quickly or slowly, depending on the story.

Zinos-Amaro: "The Man In Grey" feels like one of the stories that probably didn't take as long to write.

Swanwick: That's true. When I went to write it I did go down into an industrial area in South Philadelphia and made notes, walked around and absorbed it. A train went by very slowly. I think I scared the conductor! Somebody being there who shouldn't have been there . . . If so, I'm sorry. He may have thought I was considering suicide—I wasn't. There's a moment in the story when the Man in Grey says that having free will is "an extraordinary privilege and it's one I don't have." There are a lot of stories that set out deliberately to be life-affirming and I think that they simply affirm that life is worth living, rather than establishing it. I wanted to present the idea that life, even an unhappy life, is an extraordinary privilege, and I'm hoping that the story earned it. The story being so bleak and dark, surrounding Martha's extraordinary character, hopefully undoes any Hallmark aspect to the observation, but it doesn't make it any less true. The very last line, which you mentioned earlier, is supposed to be a surprise. I presume nobody saw that one coming.

Zinos-Amaro: For all its darkness, there's a bit of humor in the suggestion that there are really only forty-five or fifty thousand real people in the world.

Swanwick: This would explain a lot of coincidences! You're abroad somewhere and you run into someone you know. If there were billions of people it doesn't seem possible that you'd have these coincidences all the time.

Zinos-Amaro: In "The Man in Grey" you peel back reality, but in our next story, "The Dala Horse" (*Tor.com*, Wed Jul 13, 2011), you dress up reality as kind of fairytale.

Swanwick: This one was fun to write. I was a Guest of Honor at Swecon once, and after the convention they had a pub meeting. Marianne and I were invited to it on the same day, which we realized meant we had been good guests and they liked us. If we had behaved badly they wouldn't have wanted me to be there, so that they could talk *about* me. And oh my goodness, those young Swedish fans can drink! When it was time to settle up they all grabbed their cell phones, because Sweden is the most wired country on Earth, and were squirting information back and forth, but they were having a hard time because there were all these empty beer bottles in between breaking up the signals. At one point I pulled out a little wooden dala horse, which I'd bought as a souvenir, and there was this embarrassed silence. One of the people on the con committee said, "Oh, my parents have one of those." So it's the essence of not-cool, if you're Swedish. I thought it would be nice to write a story about it. There's no mythos, or backstory, to the dala horse. It's just a little carved wooden horse that somebody painted in Dala, Sweden, that caught on and became a national symbol. So I created one.

Zinos-Amaro: You evoke Svea, the personification of Sweden.

Swanwick: When I was wondering about in Sweden I saw a statue of Svea, which I could not find when I tried Googling it. It was a really good sculpture. It wasn't like the Victorian things. I was quite positively impressed. There's as much stuff from my one visit to Sweden as I could cram into the story. The little girl herself is an actual person. A couple of the fans had a daughter whom the mother called her "tiger girl," because she was very small and fierce and definite. She wasn't at all bratty; they were all positive qualities that warmed the feminist cockles of the mother's heart. I threw her in, hoof to tail. She's a lot younger than you can usually manage to make a protagonist. Of course, since the world is being seen through her eyes, it becomes a fairytale.

Zinos-Amaro: You called the girl Linnea, and a reader named Linnéa Anglemark commented on "The Dala Horse" online.

Swanwick: Yes. I borrowed her name for my protagonist. She and her husband are friends. I thought that a little nod to her wouldn't hurt.

Zinos-Amaro: You wrote online that you were thinking of two specific little Swedish girls when you wrote this story. You've told us about one. Who was the other?

Swanwick: We were in a park, Marianne and I. There was a school class of kindergartners, maybe even pre-K, these beautiful children, who were feeding the ducks. One little girl came over to Marianne. She didn't speak any English, and Marianne didn't speak any Swedish, but the girl took it on herself to explain to this poor woman how you feed ducks. There was this wonderful self-assurance and kindness to her that both of us had to admire. That informed part of the character of Linnea. She's a good girl, and a practical one.

Zinos-Amaro: The differences between our world and the future world of the story are suggested rather than spelled out. You mention things like the Coffin People, or the Strange Folk. Those details do a lot of the lifting for you.

Swanwick: The way that I pictured it is that we're the Coffin People, of course. After us come the Strange Folk. For these artificial intelligences, basically, I used the idea that I set out to use and failed to use in "Steadfast Castle." What if our technology encouraged us to do anything we wanted? In the course of that, we'd be corrupted. Sweden is the last good place. The people there did not work together with Svea to corrupt themselves, but pretty much all of Europa, or the rest of Europe, has consumed itself in an orgy of violence, sexual excess and self-destruction. All of these horrible things I implied without actually telling the reader what they were. That's the best way of making it hideous. Europa now desires to get into Sweden and to corrupt it as well, just out of spite, because that's what it's picked up from its people. A little moralistic, but I put that on the backburner.

Zinos-Amaro: The fact that Linnea doesn't understand those implications helps them to be more understated.

Swanwick: She doesn't understand them at all. She sees the world in simple terms. Günther is not a bad man, he's a troll, and that's just the way trolls are. Really her innocence is the reason she survives. I was really happy with that part. You can't always do that.

Zinos-Amaro: You manage a tricky feat. She survives because of her innocence, but in the process she loses her naïveté because of all the information downloaded into her.

Swanwick: She's going to be a very strange child.

Zinos-Amaro: One of the saddest moments in all of your fiction thus far, Michael, was the almost offhand scene in which both the intelligent knapsack and map are thrown into the flames. They were so loyal. How dare you!

Swanwick: I agree. All I can say is that the plot demanded it. You had to see that though Günther wanted to be a good man, he wasn't. Poor knapsack and poor map. This is a story, in the end, about redemption. Günther is going to have to rebuild himself from scratch, but he's a nice guy again, which is what he wanted.

Zinos-Amaro: The implied history is very dark, but the story itself has touches of lightness.

Swanwick: The Santa Lucia song means that this is secretly a Christmas story! I'll also point out that when Svea and Europa are having their standoff, Svea says, "I prefer the one about the little girl as strong as ten policemen who can lift up a horse in one hand." That's a reference to Pippi Longstocking, who is basically a national hero.

Zinos-Amaro: Have you thought of doing more with this universe? It hits that future-as-past sweet spot, combining advanced tech with a feeling of mythology.

Swanwick: Science fiction does that thing really well, doesn't it? It's one of the reasons I love it so much. "The Dala Horse" is out on option, and the guy who optioned it hopes to turn it into a television series. There's a lot that can be done with that world, as you say.

Zinos-Amaro: Great news. I hope something comes of it. The past and the future also play a role in "For I Have Lain Me Down on the Stone of Loneliness and I'll Not Be Back Again" (*Asimov's Science Fiction*, August 2011). The Irish American protagonist is looking back to perhaps a romanticized view of his Irish roots while being pulled forward by the promise of space exploration.

Swanwick: This story came about because Janis Ian put together an original anthology of stories based on her songs, *Stars*. She asked if I'd contribute one, and I knew immediately which song I wanted to write about. It's a song called "Mary's Eyes." She wrote it as an homage to Mary Black, an Irish singer. She did not know that she was singing about Deirdre of the Sorrows, but everyone Irish immediately saw that. She's standing on the bones of Ireland's past, there's no getting around it. So I wanted to write a story about my Irish heritage and what it means to be Irish American, about the tension between the realities of Ireland and the mythologies that the American Irish have about it. By the time I finished writing the story, the book had already been published, so I sold it elsewhere, and sent Janis a copy. When she did the audiobook version, she bought the reprint rights and put my story in as a kind of bonus. While doing the audiobook, she asked if she could write a song for the snatches of lyrics I included for "Deirdre's Lament." I said, "Yes, of course." She told me she was going to register it with ASCAP under our names. I told her the lyrics were actually from a nineteenth-century Dublin solicitor named Samuel Ferguson. She explained that under ASCAP rules that didn't matter; I was now the author of the lyrics. So I have a writing credit with Janis Ian! I'm absolutely amazed. She did a very beautiful job with it.

Zinos-Amaro: The first edition of her anthology appeared in 2003 and your story was published in 2011, so you must have been at it for a while.

Swanwick: It was a long and difficult story. It stalled out several times. Each time I tried to figure out where it would go from there honestly. It started with the title. I could have called it "The Stone of Loneliness," which is a good title. But I had been reading a lot of fiction by new writers with titles like "The Gift," "The Event," "Roadkill," that kind of thing. I taught during this period and told my students it was best to have an interesting title, like "I Have No Mouth and I Must Scream" or "Time Considered as a Helix of Semi-Precious Stones." Back in the 70s and early 80s plenty of stories had long, colorful titles, and they died off. I think editors didn't like them as much.I wanted to put one out there as an example!

In the story, the character's great-great-grandfather is standing on O'Connell Street on Easter morning of 1996 when Gerry Adams walks by. I was there on that day, outside a virtual reality parlor, when Marianne pointed to a man who looked like Gerry Adams. Next to him was another man with the broadest shoulders I've ever seen in my life, which meant he was a bodyguard and that was in fact Gerry Adams. It was the anniversary of the uprising, and I could see the post office, which still has the bullet scars. It was an amazing experience. I realized Irish history was not dead yet.

A lot of other things in "For I Have Lain Me Down . . ." are autobiographical. The old man dying with the white dandelion hair was my grandfather, as we talked about during "The Changeling's Tale." The Fiddler's Elbow was a real place we discovered on our first visit. We had a long talk with a dairy farmer there. The Stone of Loneliness is real, and as I described it. When I lay down on it, I felt all the sorrow of the world pouring into me. I'd been carrying that around for eight or ten years, meaning to write about the experience.

Zinos-Amaro: With this story you make the historical personal, and vice versa, with family as the unifying knot.

Swanwick: "Mary's Eyes" is one of the few songs that will make me cry and they are all about Ireland. Those few songs are all about Ireland. The only things that can make me cry are Ireland, and my family. That is it. One time Janis was performing at this coffeehouse as a favor for a friend and I'm sure she was surprised to see an old man weeping there. It's the Irish sadness.

Zinos-Amaro: These two lines from the story stayed with me: "The thing that sits like a demon in the dark pit of the soul. That Irish darkness."

Swanwick: The story is about the cruelties of history visited upon Ireland. It also explain why Irish rock is the way it is. You listen for example to a song by Black 47 cursing out Queen Victoria and many of her advisors by name. No one but the Irish would hold a grudge in such vivid detail for a hundred and fifty years.

Zinos-Amaro: The protagonist in the story gets played by

Mary and her organization, but he decides not to comply. He affirms that he's his own creature, and he can't be made to do things purely out of loyalty or a sense of national heritage. He doesn't feel the need to prove that he's the wolf inside the sheep.

Swanwick: It was an immoral act to plant a bomb that's going to kill people. I wanted it to be a morally difficult situation that he's in. Earth is still occupied by invaders, it's still a subject world. There's no easy way to choose sides. But he could not embrace the darkness and the violence. In the end, it's about loss and love. There's love of country, and there's love of family, and to get a little pretentious, love of humanity. He's off to a bright new future, but he's lost everything, including the woman he loved, his country, and his world.

Zinos-Amaro: An interesting point of linkage between this story and the next one, "Pushkin the American" (*Unfit for Eden: Postscripts 26/27*, ed. Peter Crowther & Nick Gevers, 2012), which also concerns itself with historical forces, is the sense of finality when the characters part. Mary says "I never want to see you or think of you again," a scene which is reminiscent of Elena and Pushkin going their separate ways.

Swanwick: People do part and usually the thought that they'll reunite is a fantasy. Life is real, life is earnest! We forget that too easily.

Zinos-Amaro: That seriousness helps to ground what is in essence a secret origins alternate history. Your story "Urdumheim" explored, among other things, how language can shape the external world. In a sense, the infatuation of your Pushkin with language follows up on this, showing that language can also be used to reinvent the inner self.

Swanwick: Who among us wouldn't like to be able to? I got this story from my first visit to Russia. I had been there a couple of weeks, and I felt the presence of the Russian language. It was all around me and I couldn't understand it. It was almost a physical pressure. The last day in Yekaterinburg I was on my way with a friend to a museum that had some Kandinsky pieces in it I really wanted to see. I had been pushing myself hard for about two weeks to see and do everything I could, experience Russia as fully as possible. On that last day I just collapsed. I sat down by the river Iset. I couldn't go on. I had to pause and regain my strength.

I thought, "What if I couldn't go home? What if I was stuck here? What would I do?" The only kind of job I could get would be one that didn't require any language. I'd try to learn Russian as fast as I could. My goal would be to try to learn it so well that I could become a writer again. As I thought through it, I realized nobody would want to read a story about Michael Swanwick becoming a Russian. So I chose someone more interesting. There is in the esteem of most Russians no writer greater or better than Pushkin, and I thought it would be an outrageous claim to make him an American. I started writing from there. The last paragraph of the story does all the work of addressing its counter-factuality. It's one of my favorite jokes.

Zinos-Amaro: Who are some of your favorite Russian writers? Where does Pushkin fit in?

Swanwick: Pushkin would be up near the top for me. I gather the translations do not do him justice. The translation problem is very difficult because Russian is so different. The poet Vladimir Mayakovsky wrote a poem about his Soviet passport and how the world envied him having it. If you read it in English, it's a good poem. But you don't understand why they've got a statue of Maya-kovsky in Mayakovsky Square in Moscow. In Yekaterinburg I was in the apartment of a Russian poet who gave me a copy of a book. One of his poems had a line in it about the *Iron Dragon*'s children. I felt like I was in the center of the world. His apartment was small and book-crammed like a Russian poet's apartment should be. I mentioned Mayakovsky and he recited the famous poem from memory. Listening to it, even without being able to understand a word, you could hear the greatness of the poem from the roll and thunder of sounds. Everything I know about Russian writers is second-hand, alas. Nabokov, when asked who the greatest Russian writer was, said, "Tolstoyevski." True. I'm also a big fan of Victor Pelevin, an author of many books, among them the novel *Generation "П"*, also known in English as *Babylon*. It is set in the early times of perestroika, where everything is really desperate and the hero is a young man who's wandering through this dystopia, taking drugs, thinking about Eastern religions, and coming up with parodies of advertisements. It's a fantastic novel. It summed up the times.

But my favorite Russian writer is Mikhail Bulgakov. When

Marianne and I came to Moscow we got an apartment on the Garden Ring, and as we explored the area I think we saw every site mentioned in *The Master and Margarita*. In Novodevichy Cemetery, Bulgakov's grave had flowers on it, while those of famous politicians and generals were bare. There are many other fine writers, like Chekhov, or Turgenev, but my heart belongs to Bulgakov, who was a fantasist, and admirable as hell. I'm also nuts about the work of Isaac Babel, particularly the *Red Cavalry* stories. It's about a war that can only be experienced in a fragmentary way. At first it looks like a collection of anecdotes, but it's really a splintered novel; a work of sheer brilliance.

Zinos-Amaro: I can see "Pushkin the American" proceeding pretty smoothly from the thought experiment you described.

Swanwick: I did write it relatively quickly. I used some real details. The Ryazanovs, for instance, were actual people. The English Club existed. The children's rhymes are Russian. There's a little nod to Zelazny's *Lord of Light* as well, in the line "Nobody writes poems to air," and a subtle reference to Nabokov, who once wrote about "a firework display of festive thoughts on the velvet background of Pushkin," in the simile "as if it were but a velvet background."

I set this story in nineteenth century Yekaterinburg because it's an interesting place. It couldn't be Moscow. Russians are famous for their jokes, and the first joke I ever heard in Russia was, "Have you heard that Russia is opening an embassy in Moscow?" Non-Russians set things in Moscow, but not setting something in Moscow automatically makes it more Russian. The protagonist of my story is a young fool, the type of character Pushkin liked to write about. Since I was, once a upon a time, a young fool myself, it's an area with which I'm very familiar. I know how young fools think.

Zinos-Amaro: Elena, however, is no fool. You write: "Theirs was an old, old story and even an innocent like Elena knew exactly how such stories went, and how they must end."

Swanwick: She's living in reality. There's no future for them.

Zinos-Amaro: Despite his affinity for the language and ability to make a name for himself, your Pushkin misjudges the culture, and more specifically her character.

Swanwick: Yeah, he doesn't understand her. He has this image of her: they're lovers and perfect for each other. This same story is happening today. I was pleased that I managed to portray Elena as a person rather than an object of love. In a way she has more of a personality than the protagonist.

Zinos-Amaro: Mariella Coudy in "The Woman Who Shook the World-Tree" (*Tor.com*) is an equally compelling character. The story delves perhaps more deeply into the portrayal of physicists and mathematicians—the academic community—than any other piece by you. What prompted you to go down this path?

Swanwick: David Hartwell had bought a painting for a Tor cover, and after they decided not to use it, he then solicited various writers to think up stories around it. It was very evocative, clearly based on Andrew Wyeth's painting "Christina's World." I looked at it and said, "I know why we don't see her face."

It's established in my story that she's very homely, and also very brilliant. When I was working as church secretary at the Tabernacle United Church in West Philadelphia they came up with the money to complete some repairs, so for a while there was a glass cutter working at the church. She was very homely and I found myself rather drawn to her. If I hadn't already been madly in love with Marianne at the time, I would have asked her if she was single. I knew that her being extremely plain meant that my attraction wasn't merely to a pretty face, which is something that Richard ends up saying in the story. That experience is what inspired the central part of the romance. The other thing is that I wanted to write about somebody that was much smarter than me, an actual genius. I wanted to inhabit her brain. It's possible that I was inspired in part by Disch's *Camp Concentration*. Trying to depict a superior kind of intelligence made it an interesting challenge. In this story, nobody really understands what Mariella is saying. Richard can dumb it down with metaphors, so that people can fool themselves into thinking they sort of understand it, but it's ultimately too radical a change in the perception of reality.

Zinos-Amaro: Speaking of that, the story contains the following lines: "The world's the same as it ever was. The only thing that'll be different is our understanding of it." In "The Man in Grey" you hit on something very similar: ". . . the world's the same as it's always been. It's only your understanding of it that's changed."

Swanwick: Oh my goodness. I had not noticed that similarity.

Zinos-Amaro: I think this speaks to the preoccupation of your fiction from this period with preserving some notion of reality. In your own life, what would be a moment or an experience you had where somebody could have sat you down afterwards and said, "Michael, it's just your understanding of reality that's different now"?

Swanwick: I think you could make the argument that when Second Wave feminism came along it did that. People look back today and see the feminists as being angry, and they *were* angry at certain things, at certain policies and such. But in person they were all very kind, and they were simply explaining what the world was like. You look back and think, "Why was it so hard to understand?" But it was, because it was contrary to everything I had ever been taught. I could hear the truth in the voices of feminists, but it was hard to understand what they meant. I think something analogous is happening now, with gender fluidity and gender indeterminism and so forth. I'm trying to listen in modesty. My son Sean helps.

Zinos-Amaro: "The Woman Who Shook the World-Tree" contains a lovely line: "There is no such thing as time. There's only the accumulation of consequences."

Swanwick: I was proud of that one. I think it captured the enigma of the discovery. In my original version of the story I set up the experiment to indicate the non-chronological nature of time, to prove that you could have something happen before it was caused to happen. I wasn't sure if it made sense, so I asked John Cramer, who's a science fiction writer and a physicist (and also Kathryn Cramer's father), a man who is approachable and generous with his time, if I'd gotten it right. He said, "You know Michael, you created an experiment that could have been run in the nineteenth century." He told me how to update it to a more contemporary setup involving lasers and such. In the end, I wanted to write about the passionate pursuit of science, and I think I achieved that. As a footnote, I'll say that there is a Michael Swanwick, who is a physicist, at MIT, and I keep getting notices of his papers. I can't even follow the titles. I think this is the alternate world where I went and had the future I thought I was going to have.

Zinos-Amaro: As someone with a physics background, one of my favorite observations in this story was the following: "Almost nobody could think about even the most complex equation for more than three days straight without growing weary of it." It's kind of Mariella's test to see how smart people really are.

Swanwick: Yes! She's operating on a different level than most of us. For her to think about a problem like this for three or five or seven days would be normal. Richard Zhang is based on several very handsome men I've known who rather wish that they weren't. It turns out that good looks just got in their way. When Richard says he wants to work with Mariella, and she asks why she should let him work with her, I love the arrogance of that moment.

The "What's all this?" line was taken from Doris Lessing's reaction to a bunch of reporters who had gathered to tell her she had won the Nobel Prize. They told her she had won and she said, "Oh, crap." At one point in the story, after hearing Richard out, Mariella says, "That won't work." That was based on Jack Dann. Early on when I was working on a collaboration with Jack and Gardner, he came into town and asked how it was going. I said, "It's going really great. I just made a change that will surprise you." He looked at me for a second and said, "I know what you did, and it won't work. You're going to have to put it back." He was right. In the case of "The Woman Who Shook the World-Tree," it has a romantic ending, and I'm always happy when I can do that.

Zinos-Amaro: If there were a means by which you yourself could recover a person, or a moment in time, but it would entail the destruction of you both, as it does in this story, who or when would you pick?

Swanwick: My kid brother Jack is as close as I'd come. If I could see him for a minute to tell him I love him, that would mean a lot to me. But I wouldn't want him to be back for just a second and then be dead again. And I wouldn't be willing to die myself. I have quite a good life right now.

Zinos-Amaro: I'm glad you would resist the temptation. The same can't be said of the characters in "The Year of the Three Monarchs" (*The Sword & Sorcery Anthology*, ed. David G. Hartwell and Jacob Weisman, 2012). This story has an unusual structure. It's made up of three short connected narratives, but feels like one cohesive piece, because the ending of each section hooks directly into the start of the next, including the last one, which loops back as well.

Swanwick: Some charity—I believe this happened at Clarion West—asked me to contribute a story for an auction, and I wanted to do something interesting, so I said I'd write three flash fictions to order. Specifying that whoever bought them could do whatever they wished for five years except take my name off them. They were won by Jacob Weisman. Jacob asked for three sword-and-sorcery shorts because he had a S&S anthology coming out with David Hartwell. Afterward, he very graciously gave me the copyright back. I tried to make it the best triptych I could. Sword-and-sorcery needs to be, in my opinion, pretty polished, and that's what I tried for. Whenever you write at shorter lengths, anything that doesn't work really stands out. For this story I took three great archetypes from fantasy: the wizard, here Xingool the Sorcerer, who is supposed to evoke Clark Ashton Smith, the warrior, here Kangor the Swordsman, who's supposed to evoke Robert E. Howard, and Slythe the Thief, possibly in honor of Fritz Leiber. Nowadays there would be a lot of pressure to include an assassin, but I don't really approve of assassins!

Zinos-Amaro: One way I think that the story can be read is that all three archetypes relate back to the pursuit of power, which in sword-and-sorcery often seems to lead to Pyrrhic victories. There's no long-term stability or promise of a better tomorrow.

Swanwick: I was on a panel of appreciation of Fritz Leiber once, and he was in the audience. This was shortly before he died. He was in a wheelchair. I had a theory, which I asked him about, that the Fafhrd and the Gray Mouser stories were actually horror, but that this is disguised by the fact that *they* always get away at the end. There's a happy ending, but meanwhile behind them cities are in flames and people are being eaten by rats. Fritz Leiber replied, "Everything I've ever written is horror." That insight of his gave me my way into this triptych. It doesn't read as horror because it's clever and fun!

Zinos-Amaro: It moves quickly, but it did leave me with that sense of ultimate defeat that emerges from your take on the tropes. I appreciated your name choices, like the Riphean Mountains, which I take it was inspired by ancient ideas about the northern boundary of the world.

Swanwick: That was my intention. Mencius, the character with a Greek-sounding name, was in fact named after a Chinese philosopher. Choosing those types of names is in the great tradition of modern fantasy in its early decades. You can read somebody like E. R. Eddison and get a good idea of who he was reading. That was back when there were natural fantasists and natural fantasy readers, but there wasn't anything for them to read. These fantasists would go into the far reaches of the library, where the old books of legends and Eddas and Sagas were. They didn't have fantasy novelists to take in, so they absorbed classical mythologies instead. We are the richer for their poverty as children.

Zinos-Amaro: We shift now from the Leiberesque to your very elegant Gene Wolfe tribute story, "The She-Wolf's Hidden Grin" (*Shadows of the New Sun: Stories in Honor of Gene Wolfe*, ed. Bill Fawcett and J. E. Mooney, 2013).

Swanwick: I figured that since the book the story was appearing in was a festschrift I could get away with taking "The Fifth Head of Cerberus" and inverting everything. I wanted to write a feminist Gene Wolfe story.

Zinos-Amaro: Gene Wolfe has a large body of work, with many deeply interconnected narratives. What made you pick Cerberus?

Swanwick: I read it when I was young, eighteen or nineteen. It was such a wonderful, wonderful story, most specifically the opening novella of the book. Wolfe's story knocked out Gardner and Jack Dann. Just knocked them out. It showed them what an utterly brilliant writer Wolfe was. For years after that, anytime any of us were going to New York, we enthused to editors who didn't want to hear about what a genius Gene Wolfe was. It is such a rich and complex novella. There's a key to it. Gene Wolfe wrote a very short essay, called "What I Know About Writing (in no particular order)", and the most interesting thing he said in it—which I alluded to when we discussed "The Very Pulse of the Machine"—was: "Almost any interesting work of art comes close to saying the opposite of what it really says." If you look at "The Fifth Head of Cerberus" it has two different levels. There's the hard science reading of the story, which is that we're dealing with a colony planet that is failing for not-well-understood genetic reasons. The other reading of it is that it's set in Hell. That explains why no one behaves at all well. Each reading precludes the other, but they're both clearly there, and intentional. It's as rich and deep a story as Gene has ever written.

Zinos-Amaro: Your story knocked *me* out. I decided, as a little experiment, to not re-read the Wolfe ahead of your story. I was interested in how well your piece might work for someone with no knowledge of "Cerberus," or at best a vague recollection of it. And I think it really does work, in an admirable way.

I find that your story also has two readings, possibly more. One interpretation—let's call it the more realistic, or hard reading, to continue with your terminology—would be that the character at the end is trapped in a world that has to do with the alternate realities created by the perfumes in the laboratory. You set that up, for example, by mentioning the truffle smell twice before getting to the final devastating line, along with the implications of the word "canvas."

Another reading stems from the story recalled when the character was younger and, during her debate with Amélie, had to hold the position that interbreeding with the aboriginals happened during colonization. There's a genetic remnant of interbreeding that can be reactivated; the imagery of the wolf suggests that possibility as well. In this view, the internal aborigine has been unleashed and is out to possibly join with others who have undergone this same metamorphosis.

With these two interpretations, I'm thinking you were paying homage to Wolfe's ambiguity on purpose.

Swanwick: I was. On the other hand, when I wrote it, in my mind I was going with that idea of the reversion to the aborigine being triggered. When I got to the ending, however, I said, "This is bleak. But it could be made worse!"

Zinos-Amaro: You succeeded! This could be about someone who simply *believes* that they're reclaiming themselves, as part of an elaborate fantasy within a decaying society.

Swanwick: I thought that the feminist Gene Wolfe would not stick with an easy answer or an easy conclusion. The ending should be disturbing.

Zinos-Amaro: After reading your story, going back to Wolfe's revealed a lot of fun connections. For instance, he gives an address as 666 Saltimbanque St.; your story features 999 Rue d'Astarte, not only a numerical inversion, but an interesting mythological allusion. You reference Veil's Hypothesis. To mention just one more. In "Cerberus," Wolfe writes: "He turned and saw Eastwind, who pushed past him and stalked away with the quick-kneed hair-heron gait." Meanwhile, in your story, you describe how "she studied us as a heron might some dubious species of bait fish."

Swanwick: When I started to work on this story, the first thing I did was to go back to "Cerberus." I re-read it several times with great care. It's extraordinary how much is packed into that story. If I had had time to write a full novella, it would have contained even more such things. For example, in my story I mention St. Dymphna, who is the patron of madness and incest. I do feature madness, but not incest. If I had written a longer work, that would have also appeared.

Zinos-Amaro: When Susanna conceives of her passion for theater, you mention *Riders to the Sea*, *Madame Butterfly*, *Antony and Cleopatra* and several others. I think in almost all of the stories you quote there's a motif of a powerful female character who comes to a bad end by suicide. This suggests a dark fate for Susanna.

Swanwick: In the story, she is self-destructive. She does destroy herself. But really her death is done to her by her world, her society. There's no place for her in that world that ends well.

Zinos-Amaro: Indeed. Maitresse tells them that they are the failed result of trying to create males. Not only are they clones, but they're defective.

Swanwick: I was thinking of the Catholic Church here. Maitresse says, "It was your responsibility to anticipate his action and forestall it without giving him offense." That's the Catholic Church teaching that a woman is an occasion of sin if a man behaves badly toward them. This always struck me as astonishingly unjust. As downtrodden as the nuns made me feel, they did a worse number on the girls. Of course, Maitresse is there as a woman who is nevertheless acting as an agent of the patriarchy.

Zinos-Amaro: The inversions in this story are so good. What kind of response did you get to this piece?

Swanwick: I didn't get much. I had the satisfaction of having written the story. I was really happy.

Zinos-Amaro: Did you read the other tribute stories that appeared in *Shadows of the New Sun: Stories in Honor of Gene Wolfe*?

Swanwick: I did. There were a couple I liked quite a bit. Most, I thought, were not as good as they should have been. I think mine was the best!

Zinos-Amaro: I haven't read all the others, but I wouldn't find that hard to believe. As I said, I specifically approached this from the point of view of someone who didn't have Wolfe's precursor in mind. It worked beautifully, and was only enriched after the fact by additional knowledge of the original. More than that, you evoke the tone and sensibility of Wolfe's writing, but you're not mimicking it. Rather, sort of channeling it. A subtle example is when you start a scene by writing: "The components for a disaster had been assembled. All that was needed was a spark." The construction of that sentence is perfect: somewhat detached, ironic, engineering-like, foretelling bad things. And there's the theme of not knowing who you are, which you tackled for years in your own work before getting to this point, making you ideally equipped to engage with "Cerberus."

Swanwick: Thank you for that. I went into this as an enormous admirer of Gene's genius, but not wanting to write a pastiche, which is setting yourself up for failure. I had before me his story, proof that it could be done. Starting where I started was far easier than without knowing what Gene had accomplished. I was trying to see if I could write as good a Gene Wolfe story as Gene Wolfe could, but including something he *wouldn't* have written. I do find the theme you mentioned satisfying. In the end, his story was better, but mine still came out pretty good.

Zinos-Amaro: Wolfe tapped into a number of mythologies through his career, and you also move into the realm of myth with "Of Finest Scarlet Was Her Gown" (*Asimov's Science Fiction*, April-May 2014).

Swanwick: This was another story that took a long while to write. What came first here was a little bit of verse, which I made up many years ago: "Of finest scarlet was her gown; / It rustled when it touched the ground./ Even the Devil, with all her wealth, / Had no such silks to clothe herself." Sometimes when I autographed books I would use part of it for the inscription. I thought it sounded evocative. I am not a poet, alas. Like so many writers, I have to acknowledge the superiority of really good poetry. Anyway, I was remembering this one time when I was maybe twenty-three and a friend of mine let me read her diary. I read a page and then she changed her mind and took it back. The page I read described an incident that happened while she was on a date that was awful, with a strange emotional construction. That stayed with me for decades until I decided to write the story. I started with the image of the Devil coming to take somebody's soul and the young teenage daughter witnessing it. I proceeded from there, making it up as I went along. It was hard, slow work.

Zinos-Amaro: "Ten Dates So Bad They Could Only Have Happened in Hell" seems like an apt working title for this one. In a way, I think the story can be read as a postmodern version of Orpheus and Eurydice.

Swanwick: When I knew that's what the story was, I went online and found several websites where women consoled each other over bad dates. There was a *lot* of material. Unlike in the classical myth, here our protagonist gets away at the end. The story was so dark that I needed her to make it out, with her boyfriend in the trunk to make it bearable.

Zinos-Amaro: She does survive, but she fails the Devil's test and she fails to save her father. The notion that you can't get *everything* you want seems in line with the myth—desires have costs. Unlike Orpheus, Su-yin is quite pragmatic.

Swanwick: The ending turns her failure into a kind of victory. She was never going to win because the Devil had justice on her side. The father acknowledges that he's in Hell because he truly deserves to be. He also gives his daughter good advice. In an early scene he submits to the Devil, and Su-yin watches this in shock. I was thinking of a friend I had who was telling me about her father, who had died far too young, and how it had always shocked her to see him kneeling in church. She felt that this was an abasement of him that should not be made. I took her view of her father and gave it to Su-yin.

I do like the fact that at the beginning and at the end she's driving her car very badly. I am a big fan of establishing someone's character by how they drive. It tells a lot about people, but we usually never comment on it except when they cut us off on the Interstate.

Zinos-Amaro: I remember that was a technique you used to great effect in "The Dragon Line."

It strikes me that a significant narrative element in "Of Finest Scarlet Was Her Gown" is reminiscent of "U F 0". That story also presented a situation in which a character faces a test of sexual temptation and in the end gives in. You rebirthed a story you weren't crazy about in a completely different guise.

Swanwick: Ah, this hadn't occurred to me! I finally made good use of that!

Zinos-Amaro: There's some throwaway details besides the driving that I think work very well to establish character. You tell us that some of Su-yin's favorite things are "a carton of Virginia Slims, *Mastering the Art of French Cooking*, a stuffed toy that had somehow survived from her childhood in rural Sichuan." This is another simple way of giving us great insight into the personality of this young woman.

Swanwick: My brother-in-law is Chinese. I was living at his house briefly when his father died in Taiwan. He built a shrine for his father and wept in front of it. The shrine had things like his father's favorite carton of cigarettes, his favorite whiskey, things like that. That was something that stayed with me, and I thought this was a reasonable use of the memory.

Another memory: when I first came to Philadelphia, now and then my friends would take off to stay with their relatives elsewhere and I'd be all alone. Usually it was winter and I'd go to a diner where the waitresses called you "Hon," which would always cheer me up! The ladies working there were always so pleasant and matter-of-fact. They always made me feel happy again. I ended up using this for the Greasy Spoon.

Beelzebub is my favorite character in the story, and his name was inspired by Behemoth in Bulgakov's *The Master and Margarita*.

Zinos-Amaro: Near the end "Of Finest Scarlet Was Her Gown," Su-yin is drinking a moonflower cocktail—she's gained a certain level of sophistication. I quite enjoyed the conclusion, with her sailing off into adulthood. It's a nice arc.

A very different kind of hellish visitation occurs in "Passage of Earth" (*Clarkesworld Magazine*, April 2014). This was a gut punch for me. It starts as a hard sf story, full of technical detail, yet with an *X-Files*-ish vibe, and then leaps into utterly macabre territory.

Swanwick: Another story that was really, really difficult to write. In a used bookstore I found a manual on dissection. That informed the opening of the story. It was wonderfully satisfying to create an alien's physiognomy through its dissection. Then I asked what this could tell about the psychology of an alien creature that looks like a giant worm, and clearly doesn't think the way humans think.

Zinos-Amaro: Nietzsche's idea that "if you gaze into the abyss, the abyss gazes also into you" seems particularly apt for this story.

Swanwick: Oh, that's great. Everything happens in the story in the order in which it's presented, but of course from the very beginning, this is in fact the worm reading the protagonist's memories. The worm is doing this over and over and over, trying to digest the protagonist's memories, and finding itself unable to. I made the other agent his ex, because them having broken up quite vituperatively pumps some emotional energy into the story when it was at its driest.

Zinos-Amaro: The way it shifts gears and tones is fascinating. That early banter, almost rom-com-ish, makes the start very accessible. But then that drops away and we plunge into layers of damage and loss.

Swanwick: They were two people that never should have married. When she first pops up, she seems to be the evil ex-wife. But in fact I was trying to depict a realistic relationship beyond the dichotomy of good and evil. I was trying to push beyond that dichotomy more broadly. Are the aliens good or are they evil? Neither. They are what they are, and that's completely different. So many of the models for this kind of fiction do trade in the dichotomy that it made it difficult to transcend.

Zinos-Amaro: You appear to be giving us a scene showing humans dissecting an alien. But in fact what's really happening is that an alien is dissecting a human. That reversal really helps to shatter the conventional models of something like this.

Swanwick: I don't know if I knew that from the start or if I figured it out after Hank eats the little wafer. After that I cut to where he's driving the car and his hands are sticking to the steering wheel with blood. I remember that's where I stopped for a long time. In the driving scene, when the ghost of Evelyn appears and he starts having a conversation with her, I knew he was being digested. Later, after a flash-forward within a flashback, I stopped for months again. After I picked it up again, I could only see two endings for the story. One was, he goes on being digested forever and ever and ever. It's hell for him. The other is that he realizes what's happening and uses that to take over the worm's consciousness, and then he's in command of a spaceship traveling to the stars. Both of those were so trite, I couldn't stand them. At last, I came up with the final paragraph. I think it ends up with a weird kind of hope. His final thoughts are a metaphor for our lives, "blindly burrowing forward through the darkness, learning what we can and suffering what we must." That ending made it possible for me not to throw away all the hard work that came before it.

Zinos-Amaro: For me as a reader, this ending didn't so much imbue hell with a bit of hope, as it did bring hell into life.

Swanwick: Maybe so. I'm done with the story, and now it belongs to the readers.

Zinos-Amaro: There were lines leading up to the ending that suggested a deeper darkness for me. For example, "Why are all your memories so ugly?"

Swanwick: That's a good question! That's the worm speaking trying to establish some rapport with him.

Zinos-Amaro: Moments before, he asks Evelyn to help him, and the response is: "Scornful laughter. 'Can you even *imagine* me helping you?'" There's a pervading sense of disconnection throughout the story.

Swanwick: That was sad. If he could imagine her helping him, then she would. I admit, it's a pretty bleak story.

Zinos-Amaro: On a metaphorical level, I think the whole narrative works as a comment on getting stuck in the processing of trauma. I understand that within the narrative the worms and the spaceships actually exist, but we can imagine an interpretation where they are merely signifiers of elements within the human mind trying to assimilate its own pain.

Swanwick: I think that's a fair reading. I like it.

Zinos-Amaro: Our next story, "Six Untitled Tales Written in Mark Twain's Library" (*The New York Review of Science Fiction*, June 2014), is considerably lighter fare. What's the importance of Mark Twain to Michael Swanwick?

Swanwick: When I was in seventh grade I was for a time in a

Catholic school that had just started to accept boys. There was one class—hygiene, or gym, or something—that was for girls only. It was at the beginning of the day, and during this time they'd let me sit in the library and read for an hour. They had a complete set of Twain's works. I read deep into him. I read his writings on Hawaii and such. I just love him. I like the breadth and joy of his vision. Also, the darkness. And he was a science fiction writer. "Captain Stormfield's Visit to Heaven" is a fantasy written by a science fiction writer, there's no getting around it.

Zinos-Amaro: How much of the introduction in this story is true?

Swanwick: Every word is literally true. A friend sent me a notice that you could sign up to write inside Mark Twain's library. That sounded cool. Marianne and I put together an agenda for a trip: we went from Philadelphia to Boston in ten days, blogging all the while (I called it "Geek Highways"). We were visiting all the science and tech and science fiction and fantasy writer sites between Philadelphia and Boston. For example, we visited several places where Poe wrote "The Raven." We visited Thomas Edison's laboratories, which was a great experience. We went to Grovers Mill, the town where Orson Welles first landed the Martians in his *War of the Worlds* radio broadcast. Places like that. At Mark Twain's house there were a number of writers, mostly youngish, almost all astonishingly introverted. I was the most outgoing person there, which was a remarkable experience for me. We sat in Twain's library for several hours. I did imagine Mark Twain's ghost coming up, looking over my shoulder and saying, "Interesting. Do you also masturbate in groups?" Comparing writing to masturbation is a very Twain/Clemens thing to do. I started a number of stories but the six in the final piece were the ones I finished. I liked them. They're worth reading, and they're amusing, but they're not substantive, so I wrote the introduction to make the whole thing a non-fiction-fiction-hybrid, and sent it into the *New York Review of Science Fiction*, which took it.

Zinos-Amaro: You're clearly having fun with these. I thought it was audacious that your protagonist—your fictional persona—turns out to be the secret author of "The Celebrated Jumping Frog of Calaveras County."

Swanwick: That little story was the making of him. Overnight he went from nobody to famous. Luckily, he knew what to do with that.

Zinos-Amaro: Until I read your story I didn't realize that Twain thought *Personal Recollections of Joan of Arc* was his best work.

Swanwick: He did. He set out to write a debunking of her and became a convert.

Twain felt pretty clearly that he had a minor gift. He could spin out tall tales, humor, satire. But I think he would have preferred to be able to write Serious Novels, like Sir Walter Scott was doing. Clearly, though, he knew what to do with his talent. He worked it hard.

Zinos-Amaro: The twist in the final story, in which a writer is hired to act as a vessel programmed with the emulation of Twain, and then generates *The Adventures of "Becky" Thatcher*, was wonderful. The reference you make to *Highlander*—"There can only be one!"—was also funny.

Swanwick: We can imagine Tom Sawyer grown up—he's *Babbitt*. I enjoyed writing that. But it's hard to imagine Huck Finn grown up.

Zinos-Amaro: For a late-night closeout to our chapter, we turn to "3 A. M. in the Mesozoic Bar" (*Far Voyager*, ed. Nick Gevers, 2014). I wonder if Robert Silverberg's *Hawksbill Station* fed into this story?

Swanwick: I did read *Hawksbill Station* a long time ago and enjoyed it, but it's hard to say what effect it had. This story had a very strange beginning. A friend of mine named Neil Varrone, who is not in the science fiction community but who reads it casually, said, "I've got a title for you," and gave me it. People usually try and give you ideas, which are not worth anything. I wasn't expecting much from a title, but from it came a story. Never say never! When the story was eventually done, I gave him the original typescript. I have no idea if he kept it or not, but at least he knew I was grateful.

The photographer taking pictures of everyone, by the way, came from a throwaway panel in a comic book by Matt Howarth. He had an alien race driven by the desire to have a picture of everything. The fact that the photographer can do this also tells you how many people there are in this research station.

Zinos-Amaro: The comic book panel image brings to mind the overall flow of the story; it moves swiftly from start to finish.

Swanwick: Most of "3 A. M. in the Mesozoic Bar" takes the form of withholding information and letting the reader know that it's being withheld. The title is kind of sinister, and then you follow it up with this manic cheerfulness that lets you know *something* is wrong. By gradual steps you find out first that everyone is going to die in the morning, then *why*, and so on. When you fully understand the situation, the story is at an end. It's a one-idea, "tumble-down-the-stairs" narrative that was written relatively quickly.

I enjoyed them discovering that in this scenario money is useless, except as a comic device. Also, they find out there's really only a couple of things you can do when you just have a few hours left to live. This is as bleak as anything I've ever written.

Zinos-Amaro: I'm not sure I see it that way. I think the story contains a belief in the fundamental goodness of life, and a recognition that one of our failings is that we don't appreciate that goodness enough. The story wouldn't really work without that observation. For me, however, that's the opposite of bleakness, which would be to believe that there's something inherently wrong with being alive in the first place, that there's a wrongness to existence itself.

Swanwick: I agree with that, actually. I was just trying to say that life isn't a means to an end. The acquisition of money or sexual conquests or even love isn't the point of it. Life is an extraordinary gift to have. Most of the potential people in the universe have never had it.

Zinos-Amaro: You phrasing things this way makes me think that "3 A. M. in the Mesozoic Bar" is a cousin story to "Triceratops Summer." Vacationing in Europe isn't the point—enjoying what you have right now, even if it's an "extra" summer you're going to forget—is the point.

Swanwick: A lot of people, when they realize they're going to die sooner rather than later, grasp that many things they thought were important actually aren't.

Zinos-Amaro: That said, let's focus on something truly important. Tell me about Sazerac cocktails.

Swanwick: Oh, I love them. Rye and cognac with an absinthe wash, basically. With bitters and a twist. It's a good bar that can serve you a Sazerac. They are great. Marianne likes them too. Now—I can tell from her face—we both want one. In fact, we have the ingredients at home—and we've just decided we're going to have some tonight.

CHAPTER EIGHT
2015-2022

Zinos-Amaro: We've reached the phase of your career where more of your stories seem to end on quiet, introspective notes. I wouldn't say morose, but certainly reflective. Your outing into serialized fiction, "A Week Without Magic" (2016), is more grounded than the surrounding entries in the series by other authors. This story was "episode" 6 in *The Witch Who Came in from the Cold*, conceived by Max Gladstone and Lindsay Smith. The title evokes John le Carré; a meeting of witchcraft and tradecraft.

Swanwick: They contacted me and asked if I would be a guest writer. It was going to be work for hire. I thought that the whole setup was pretty good. You could pitch this as being a good television series. It had the same virtues. I'd never done anything like that before, so I thought it would be valuable for me to see if I could do it or not.

They did an interesting thing. They had a whole outline for how the season went and what had to happen in each episode. They allowed a great deal of creativity in what actually happened, but certain plot developments had to occur at specific parts of the series. I noticed that the synopsis for my episode was plotted in such a way that if I couldn't deliver it they could just skip to the next work. I figured that since my episode was operating in a different mental space than the other episodes, I'd make it a week without magic; the incidents that happened would advance the characters. It was surprisingly fun to do. If I were young, I'd probably have tried to talk my way into becoming one of the regular writers. The only problem I had was that they had a non-hierarchic method of reviewing the text. I remember a lot of back-and-forth in the corrections about whether an item was spelled "duct tape" or "duck tape." Nobody could agree.

Zinos-Amaro: Had you read the earlier episodes? How free or constrained did you feel in developing Tanya?

Swanwick: Yes, I had read the preceding installments. They gave me a surprisingly free hand to do almost anything. They knew they could always take it out in rewrites. That was part of the fun. I really liked their character. Tanya was a hoot to play with. You can see aspects of her that are implicit but aren't actually said. For example, the fact that she has no idea that she has no sense of humor whatsoever. They also provided files of information with background for that period of time, since the story is set in the 70s. I said, "I remember all of this."

In my original version I had an additional subplot with a young Russian lothario, but, alas, space constraints were such that I had to drop that storyline. Tanya and Gabe were given to me; the minor characters were my creation. I remember, they had Zoom meetings where they talked through the plot, and—as I've demonstrated with you on our call today—I don't have the warmest relationship with technology, and so I was able to get on the Zoom calls and see them and hear them, but I was unable to communicate! I found out later on that the software being used back then didn't work well with Apple. But the writers obviously all liked each other and had fun plotting things out.

Zinos-Amaro: Were you a fan of le Carré, or spy novels in general?

Swanwick: Big fan of le Carré. I read *The Spy Who Came in from the Cold* when it was a new book. My mother recommended it to me, back in the 60s. I read all his spy books. I think for le Carré, generally the later into the series he got, the better the books. I'm also a big fan of Len Deighton, particularly the Harry Palmer novels.

Zinos-Amaro: Speaking of fun, next we turn to the madcap "Universe Box" (*Asimov's Science Fiction*, September-October 2017), which in my notes I summarized as a romantic screwball comedy reimagined by Dali.

Swanwick: That's close, that's close.

Zinos-Amaro: I picked up some Lafferty in there, and Sheckley too. One of your characters comes from the epic of Gilgamesh.

Swanwick: It does. This one has a lot of everybody in there. It had a very strange origin. At a pop-up remaindered bookstore

Marianne and I found a stack of coffee-table books of artwork by one of the great dinosaur artists, Charles R. Knight. We grabbed one. I have a thing about cigar boxes, and Marianne, who got another copy of the book, harvested the illustrations and lined the inside of thirteen cigar boxes with these Knight illustrations and star-maps. She started gathering things to put in there, like pieces of coral, antique German glass taxidermy eyes, all manner of things. Then she asked me to write something for a chapbook to go inside.

"Universe Box," began with a trickster stealing the universe and hiding it in a cigar box. Then I proceeded to see how entertaining I could make it. I like the idea of a protagonist who doesn't realize he's the most boring man in the Universe. That's essentially comic.

Zinos-Amaro: The story combines many modes: a be-careful-what-you-wish-for yarn, a cosmic romp, a con heist thriller. Besides this fusion, you also drew on some real-life experiences, is that right?

Swanwick: There's an early scene where a car crashes into a wall, barely missing the protagonists. I was with Gardner and Susan one evening, and we were walking back to their place on 13th Street. There was no traffic on the street so I jaywalked to the other side, thinking they would be right behind me. But when I looked back they were still on the other side. At that moment a car came roaring down the street and sped on to the sidewalk and tried to hit them. They flattened against the wall, so the driver missed them, and then drove away.

I think the screwball element is the most important in this story. The high goofiness. At the end Mimi goes off to become a giraffe wrangler! It's a romantic comedy where the girl doesn't have to marry the dull guy, she can escape him. I've done that a couple of times—just thought, "The woman deserves better than him." In *Stations of the Tide*, for example, the Bureaucrat falls in love with a witch. Near the end she tells him that if he follows his duty and goes off to capture the escaped wizard she won't wait for him. He has to choose one or the other, and he chooses duty. As a result, he never gets to see her again. I did that as a reaction to all these stories where the man chooses duty and then he gets the girl anyway. This one had enough self-respect to walk.

Zinos-Amaro: Speaking of realism, the most memorable part of this story for me is the stunning last paragraph. You give us this beautiful closing image of Howard walking around the city at 3 am, soberly reflecting on the smallness of human beings and the great cosmic flow of which they're a minuscule part. It transforms the whole experience into something far more serious and existential, not only thematically, but also stylistically. You dial back the hyperbole and render the scene in a mainstream literary way.

Swanwick: He has a glimpse of reality. For a brief moment, Howard comprehends the universe. He achieves an instant of transcendence. He's touched by grace. I didn't originally know it would end like this. I was just making it up as I went along, following the logic of the story. Luckily the story was fast-paced enough that it kept throwing itself headlong into something new.

Zinos-Amaro: The ending of "Universe Box" segues nicely into the next story, "Starlight Express" (*The Magazine of Fantasy & Science Fiction*, September-October 2017), which has a melancholy feel from start to finish.

Swanwick: The first couple of pages of this story were done in about a day, really fast for me. I spent a lot of time imagining this world. I knew from the beginning that what happened was that the woman who emerged from the transmitter was a blip, a copy, a remnant of an earlier age. I worked out a lot of where the plot had to go, but I couldn't figure out an ending for it literally for years. Gardner told me that Flaminio had to fall in love with Szette and be heartbroken at the end. The problem I had with that ending was that it was the same ending that everybody uses. I enjoyed the world creation for this story so much that I didn't want to throw it away. I kept waiting until I found that ending where he gets to travel all over the Solar System, in ways we can't even begin to imagine right now, and has to admit to himself that he's never gone anywhere or done anything. He becomes emblematic of the whole culture he's in. That worked, I think, but it took me forever to find it.

Zinos-Amaro: Yet in a way the ending is consistent with Gardner's vision too, because his inability to move past the events of the story, as it were, despite his literal displacement by vast distances, can be read as heartbreak. At first Flaminio is an unwitting prisoner of her bracelet, but his life ends up with deeply unrequited love.

Swanwick: Yes. Also that.

Zinos-Amaro: The Great Albino is a memorable secondary character.

Swanwick: He came from Hieronymus Bosch. At the center of his painting *Garden of Earthly Delights* you have the giant and people climbing up into him with ladders. Despite the monstrous quality, he has a very human face.

Zinos-Amaro: I was wondering if your phrase "the woman in white" was a reference to Wilkie Collins' famous novel, which has a similar setup involving the appearance of disoriented woman.

Swanwick: I'm afraid not. That novel is on my list of books to be read one of these days. Marianne speaks well of it.

I should say that Maurizio Manzieri, the artist who did the cover for this issue of *F&SF*, really did a wonderful job. He makes Szette beautiful in a cosmic, science fictional way, with her Milky Way galaxy earring and so on. If you read the story and go back to the cover again, though, you realize she looks a little vapid. I think this is one of his best covers, but then I would think that!

Zinos-Amaro: Part of this story's power comes from its fine juxtaposition of a very far future with an ancient Roman setting, which made me think of your earlier story "The Mask."

Swanwick: I've been to Rome, of course, and the contrast between these very ancient things and cars going by hits you strongly. But I'm also indebted to Robert Silverberg's *Nightwings*, set in a future Rome with a profound misunderstanding of its own past. Their reading of ancient history is off, which makes you stop and think that our view of the past is probably just as bad a misreading. So kudos to you, Bob.

Zinos-Amaro: He achieves a similar effect in the far-future recreations of the masterful "Sailing to Byzantium."

Swanwick: Yes. And of course he did a lot of traveling and visited ancient sites, because he's a history and archaeology buff. The contrast of epochs must have probably struck him everywhere he went.

Zinos-Amaro: Gardner and Rich Horton both selected this story for their yearly best-of collections, and for the reasons mentioned above I agree that it's a remarkable piece.

Swanwick: Overall, it's a sorrowful situation. This civilization had access to the whole universe and managed to lose it. The weight of history keeps them from rebuilding.

Zinos-Amaro: In a way, I think the very same thing could be said of the next story, "Eighteen Songs by Debussy" (*Asimov's Science Fiction*, March-April 2019), which continues a fine thread of wistfulness. In the introduction you mention attending a recital of the Academy of Vocal Arts with Tom Purdom.

Swanwick: They provided one of those sets of lyrics that are stapled in the upper left hand corner, so you hear a little rustling in between each song. I found it all very evocative and very romantic. I think the sadness is there, but was provided by the music itself, which is about lost love, yearning and so on. While I was listening I started writing on the sheet. I created a vignette for each song, though I didn't use all of them. When I got home I cleaned up the draft and had a story.

Zinos-Amaro: I listened to the songs and I think it's worth doing to better appreciate the story. I agree that the sadness exists in the source material. But you deepen and amplify these fin de siècle blues with concepts like biochips, virtual worlds, the ability to ride bodies, swap genders and so forth. Even with these abilities, the characters are trapped in a kind of endless reenactment and remixing of the past. Despite all of our technology, we can't evolve.

Swanwick: On the one hand that's melancholy, but on the other hand it's realistic. You can't get much real evolution in the course of a few centuries, or even millennia. It takes serious time to do that. We're going to be human for the foreseeable future.

Zinos-Amaro: One of the story's magnificent lines is: "What are the pleasures of joy compared to the terrible dark pleasures of despair?"

Swanwick: We've all felt that way at some point, when we feel really, really, really sorry for ourselves!

Zinos-Amaro: The story also returns to one of your oldest themes, the malleability of memories and identity, and the blurry line between artifice and reality. It's a miniature, impressionistic thematic homecoming of sorts.

Swanwick: That is indeed a major theme through my career, as we've seen time and again. But also, at the end, one of the characters actually manages to become human. But then, that's sad too, like Peter Pan growing up. You can have so much fun behaving badly, but then when you grow up and become human you have to take on responsibilities. The story ultimately tries to remain true to human nature.

Zinos-Amaro: The very next story, "Ghost Ships" (*The Magazine of Fantasy & Science Fiction*, September/October 2019) ends on a reflective, existential note much like that of "Universe Box," except here it's possibly even darker. You explain that everything you wrote is true, save the names, and that when Marianne first read this she thought it was an essay.

Swanwick: That's right. I remember when she said that, I looked up and said, "What?" The ghost story was told me, as I wrote it, and it always struck me as very spooky because it happened in broad daylight. There was no reason for it, no explanation for it. It was just there. And it didn't seem like a story the kids had the imagination to invent.

Zinos-Amaro: So you went to the memorial, and they showed the pictures and told the stories, just as you described?

Swanwick: Exactly. We were countercultural when I was in college, and we joked that we were going to have counterreunions after we graduated. I lost touch with the group, but they found me thirty-some years later, and it turned out that they had indeed started having their own unofficial reunions. Everything I put in the story happened. I may have saved a life by being too cheap to lend a friend a quarter. Walking around during my forty-second college reunion, which was the first one I went to, put me into an autumnal mood. I realized how little I had ever belonged there. I was greatly moved by everything that happened. I was happy to see how well my friends had done. We were the druggies in college and we were all supposed to end up badly. It turned out that, with one exception, all of us made quite decent lives for ourselves. It was a profound experience, and I put it all together fairly fast, considering it was a complex story with a great deal of emotion behind it.

Zinos-Amaro: These lines certainly convey that: "It came to me that everything was provisional. Or perhaps the better word was temporary. [. . .] Everything we are and do and care about will in time be undone."

Swanwick: It really hit me hard that the kid that my friend had saved had died. His life being saved was an accomplishment that should endure. It did force me to think about the temporary nature of all things.

Zinos-Amaro: "We are, all of us, involuntary passengers on fragile ships."

Swanwick: No question about it. I'm proud of the ending of "Ghost Ships." It's a good set of images. The story is also a reaction to stories where an author claimed something happened to them but you know it's not true, only a fictional device. I thought there was something pure about telling a ghost story that really happened and knowing that nobody would believe it. What is the mystery of a ghost ship, as compared to the mystery of life, of just being alive? This was one of those times where you stop and consider the whole thing at once.

Zinos-Amaro: Like Howard's moment of transcendence in "Universe Box."

Swanwick: True. Catholics can never really escape; they can't get very far.

Zinos-Amaro: *Nobody* can escape in "Cloud" (*Asimov's Science Fiction*, November-December 2019), one of the most quiet and despairing end-of-the-world-stories I've ever read.

Swanwick: It *is* quiet. I wrote it as mainstream. You can probably tell. My only attempt to market it as mainstream was to send it to *The New Yorker*, but they didn't take it, so I sent it to Sheila. I knew *Asimov's* would be a good place for it. Incidentally, "The Man Who Met Picasso" was the only other story I submitted to *The New Yorker*.

The origin of this story lies in real life. When I was twenty-two, my girlfriend took me to a family gathering at her aunt's house. This was outside Richmond, and she was FFV—one of the First Families of Virginia. If you're in Virginia, they're very aristocratic, and at least a bit moneyed. For me the party was an interesting and alienating experience. My girlfriend told me going in that there was a good chance that her aunt would hit on me, just like in the story. Apparently her aunt hit on all of her better boyfriends! She did get a little drunk through the course of the party, and at the end she suggested I come back and visit her sometime without my girlfriend, who was standing right there with me. My girlfriend was quite pleased with me, because I'd passed this test.

Zinos-Amaro: This is one of your stories that's highly aware of, and critically interrogative, of class. We've talked about that angle of your fiction going all the way back to "Griffin's Egg." What brought up the one percenter element here?

Swanwick: As you say, I'm hyper-aware of class. I always am. I put in everything I could in "Cloud" from my tiny, fleeting, sparse encounters with these people. The Issey Miyake gown, incidentally, was contributed by Jack Womack, who knows enormous amounts about fashion. There was a SFWA editors/publishers get-together where Buzz Aldrin showed up once. I got to meet him, which I'm sure made a much bigger impression on me than it did on him. I threw aspects of that event in as well. I just felt I wanted to include the wealthy elite in the discussion. My characters are the worst examples of the one percent of the one percent, but at least, unlike a lot of other American science fiction writers, I haven't pretended that they don't exist.

One thing that inspired "Cloud" was years of staring at clouds from airplane windows and trying to figure out how to use them as a setting. The basic idea, though, came from John Cheever's "The Swimmer," which recapitulates a man's life through one long and pointless stunt. It's a fantastic story, which I love up and down. That's what I was doing when Wolfgang gets to the dinner party. In a sort of little Möbius strip, he gets to see the rest of his own life, as expressed by the older, successful real estate magnate, Radford Anderson, who's older and older and older every time he meets him, until he finally realizes he's looking at himself.

Zinos-Amaro: That was a wonderful name for the character, too.

Swanwick: I was trying to make him sound as gilt-edged as possible.

Zinos-Amaro: The Cheever influence shows up in the mainstream aesthetic.

Swanwick: If I had written it as science fiction, I think it would play out as allegory, and it's not meant to be allegory, it's meant to be metaphor. The story hasn't gotten a lot of attention from science fiction.

Zinos-Amaro: I'm glad at least it made it into Rich Horton's *The Year's Best Science Fiction & Fantasy 2020* anthology. I found this story very well done in a variety of ways, and it's one of my favorites by you, but as soon as I got into it I suspected many might find it too oblique and downbeat. It doesn't have much of a plot, which I don't think is generally favored in genre, and none of the characters are sympathetic, though I do think they're interesting.

Swanwick: It was not an easy story. Marianne had that same response you're talking about. There's nobody to root for in "Cloud" and there's nothing obviously at stake on a literal level.

Zinos-Amaro: You're flirting with nihilism here. You're right on the cusp of it. As the end of the world approaches and Judith seeks succor in Wolfgang, you have him fail. He can't accomplish the one positive thing he might conceivably do, which is to help another human being in need: "He wanted to be more comforting but for the life of him he couldn't remember how." Beautiful.

Swanwick: Judith has had her own dark night of the soul, and he hasn't even noticed. He has the opportunity here to actually confront himself, and to realize that he needs to change, and to try to do so. He fails the test.

Part of the reason that I named her Judith, by the way, was that I was trying to hint that part of the family is Jewish. I had a line in the story that Sheila had me take out. When Radford, who isn't Jewish, shows Wolfgang his watch, the Breitling—a watch suggested by Bill Gibson—, he tells Wolfgang that it was once owned by Joseph Goebbels. Originally I had him saying, "I never met a Jew who wouldn't swap his grandmother for it." I wanted to make clear what a horrible, horrible person he is, but the line was too strong for a science fiction audience, who in context tend to believe what you say literally. As Gardner Dozois said, "Irony is a really dangerous tool to use in SF."

A little ironic touch occurs near the end of the story, when the old Radford has lost the use of an eye, and the page before I've compared him to Odin. Unlike Odin, he hasn't gained any wisdom.

Zinos-Amaro: The story's underlying sense of failure brings to mind "The Edge of the World."

Swanwick: I can see that. Like that story, this one was very difficult to write. I'm not a nihilist, but you write about things that are important, and things that scare you. I think that that nihilistic bleakness is one of the things I'm afraid of.

Zinos-Amaro: Part of the reason I think "Clouds" is so powerful is that it records your own disquieting response to that bleakness. At one point Anderson tells Wolfgang, "Now the game is over and it seems I won," but rather than being able to derive any satisfaction from his material success, he wonders how long it would take to hit the ground from the skyscraper they're on.

Swanwick: Right. These characters are at a stage where they don't need anything. They have enough money to take off the afternoon for the rest of their lives. Everything has become a game; it's all about winning. Trying to win is probably the single worst possible way to approach life. This is an evening in which Wolfgang comes to understand that he's not a good person.

Zinos-Amaro: "We're good people, aren't we?" Judith asks. I think you perform a wonderfully savage reversal of expectations early on in the story. You've set up the fact that Judith's aunt, according to her, is going to hit on Wolfgang, so we as readers are waiting for that to either happen or not happen. But instead, almost immediately upon arriving, it's Wolfgang who begins fantasizing about Judith's aunt and her breasts, going as far as thinking to himself that "it was easy to see why her late husband had been moved to acquire her."

Swanwick: I wanted to let the reader know early on that you can't possibly empathize with Wolfgang. He thinks that his thoughts are rational thoughts to be having. He's everything that I dislike.

Zinos-Amaro: From a technical perspective, another element I appreciate is how several of your physical descriptions suggest a confusion of up and down. This adds to the sense of disorientation, but more importantly externalizes the characters' lack of ethical compass.

Swanwick: That's right. There's no moral compass. The outer world reflects their inner world. Things are relative and immaterial. The world is about to change, and nothing they do is going to matter. There's a line in the story about the glory and misery of Manhattan. As talked about when we covered "Microcosmic Dog," I really love Manhattan. When I was eleven or twelve I remember visiting my grandmother. It was evening and I was standing out on the sidewalk, looking at all these tall buildings with bright lights. I remember thinking if you could lift them up, turn them and shake them, all the misery within would come pouring out, all the different kinds of unhappiness.

Zinos-Amaro: From these ruthless players in a fast-dissolving reality we turn to "Dragon Slayer" (*The Book of Dragons*, ed. Jonathan Strahan, 2020), which at least in the beginning is much more whimsical in tone. Give these two stories, without a byline, to any reader and I'm sure they'd bet they were by different writers.

Swanwick: I wrote the first page of "Dragon Slayer" quickly, and then when I got to the lines "To the south it was summer. It seemed to be always summer there" I stalled and spent several years trying to figure out where it would go next. At one point Greg Frost and I tried to see if we could do it as a collaboration, and that didn't work. It took a long time to find the center of the story.

Zinos-Amaro: I'm curious if that center included the time travel aspect, or if that came later.

Swanwick: That came later. I managed over several years to write two more paragraphs. It was only when Nahal spoke that the story came alive for me again, and in the conversation that they have, before they're first attacked by the dragon, was when I realized that Nahal was actually Nahala. Even though it was a rather trite trope, him being a girl in disguise gave the story a purpose.

Zinos-Amaro: In the first half or so, you're approaching it like a picaresque adventure.

Swanwick: It was a blast. I love sword-and-sorcery, and yet I almost never write it. I wanted to create a world that offered, for us readers, the pleasures of sword-and-sorcery, but for whose characters it was a completely real place. Therefore they would react to events in this world like real people of *their* times would, not like, say, Conan the Barbarian. Olav doesn't have a fantasy hero name because he's not a hero; he's just a very strong, very capable guy.

Zinos-Amaro: The section that begins with the description of the port of Kheshem is a lovely, classically-wrought example of painting that world in for us. And then you populate it with believable, everyday folks.

Swanwick: I like the characters. I like them as people. You'll notice that when they reach Kheshem I flip the narrative and Nahala becomes the protagonist. From that point on we see the story through her eyes. I'm surprised at how easily that worked.

Olav didn't have anywhere interesting to go in his development, whereas Nahala had a lot of growing up to do, really fast. She gets her period at least in part because characters in high fantasy never tend to get their periods at an inconvenient time. I can only think of one Michael Moorcock Jerry Cornelius story where this happens, and *They Fly at Çiron* by Chip Delany. The character is on an adventure, she misses her period, and the adventure stops. The local women basically set her up to be the town prostitute, and it's only after she gets her period again, and she knows she's not pregnant, that she can go back into the adventure.

I like the fact that Nahala's idea of what a grown woman should be involves lots and lots and lots of jewelry, along with killing people! Now, *that's* a successful life! It really drives me nuts whenever I read a book or see a movie set in a different era and the hero or heroine has exactly our contemporary, liberal views on everything. For example, in this story at the end the character grows fat because in that culture that would have been seen as a positive—he's so wealthy, he never goes hungry, what a fortunate man, and so on. I also liked the idea that knowing how to cook, mend, and clean, are seen as manly chores. That's not a stretch; I was in Boy Scouts. The throwing knives in the story, by the way, are based on real throwing knives that Marianne had as a girl and still owns. They look quite lethal.

Zinos-Amaro: We touched on your use of time travel in fantasy before when we discussed "King Dragon." In "Dragon Slayer" you again quite elegantly constrain the time travel element so that it doesn't give the story a science-fictional vibe.

Swanwick: That was important. The time travel here was a game. I'm sure I thought up most of the bits—killing somebody, going back and letting them see themselves die, and then offering to prevent this from happening for a fee—decades ago, over the course of playing with science fiction ideas. It was a matter of pulling everything in as tightly as possible, and it took care of the question of what to do with Sliv. He was too nasty to let him live, and too much a child to kill him. So he gets to escape and live a long life that will eventually lead to him being killed on the mountainside. The time travel was the fun aspect of writing this, as opposed to the literary aspect. Keeping it from becoming too much like science fiction was mostly achieved by having it look the way that it would to the characters in their own society.

Zinos-Amaro: It also enhances the opening line, "Every road and open doorway is a constant danger to a man of wandering disposition," because now that becomes an active observation by the narrator, as opposed to simply a way into the narrative. It's an acknowledged opinion.

You take a very different approach in your next story, "Artificial People" (*Clarkesworld*, July 2020), which explores ideas covered many times before by other sf writers. How consciously important was it for you to try and make this material fresh? Or were you just happy to follow the story wherever it took you?

Swanwick: I was trying to make it fresh. If you think about sapient robots and take the idea seriously, the interest is all in how different *and* how similar they are to humans, and how that comes together. Trying to imagine that blend of familiar and unfamiliar abilities was the whole charm of the story for me.

Zinos-Amaro: I appreciate how you use the passage of time as a narrative strategy to differentiate your uniquely non-human character from everyone else. You don't have to state things explicitly; time does it for you. That reminded me a bit of Asimov's "The Bicentennial Man."

Swanwick: I certainly read that novella. I read everything by Asimov—except the non-fiction, nobody's read *all* of that! All the great treasure lode of robot fiction, including that story by Asimov, and an awareness of it, sits in the background of this story. And an awareness that everybody else has been playing with that body of work, and borrowing from each other, so it's okay. You don't have to leave signifiers behind.

Zinos-Amaro: Speaking of signifiers, can you say a little about *Misty of Chincoteague* and the image of horses in "Artificial People"?

Swanwick: I just put that in, but I've actually never read *Misty*. I've been to Chincoteague and seen a statue of Misty. It's part of our culture; it was there, so I used it.

Zinos-Amaro: I think that a nice bit of linkage between several recent stories, made explicit in both "Cloud" and this one, is the examination of whether one has used one's life wisely. In "Cloud" the answer for the characters is an emphatic "No." Here the question, when applied to Leonidas Erdmann, also yields a

"No," but if we think about it in terms of the non-human protagonist, Raphael, the answer would be "Yes."

Swanwick: Well, where this story came from was that I went
to another concert by the Academy of Vocal Arts. It was called
"Sparks and Embers." The program description read: "Imaginative song pairings to ponder the spark of new life, new seasons and new love, with the embers of endings." That tells you
something about the themes and reflecting on life. Again, as with
"Eighteen Songs by Debussy," they handed out sheets with all the
lyrics, but unlike with that story, I didn't write out my piece during the concert itself. I did write outlines and parts of each section
on the lyric sheet. It probably took me about a week to turn it
into a finished story. The songs, as the description suggested, were
mostly about love and loss. One of the songs featured an incident
from World War II that I stole and used directly.

I think it's pretty clear that the robots *are* people, just not our
people. The whole story is a bildungsroman; it's a sentimental education. I like the idea of the narrator falling in love with an older
woman, although because he's brand new at the start, *any* woman
would be older. I was thinking of Maggie Kuhn, whom we discussed all the way back in "Walden Three." As I mentioned, I met
her a few times, and she once said somewhere in print that one
thing nobody ever talks about is younger men and older women.
I thought, "I should make sure to include that in my fiction sometime." I like the way it came out.

Zinos-Amaro: Tell me about the name choice of Erdmann.

Swanwick: I went for the German of "earth-man." Suggests a
kind of aloneness to him. A simple pun.

Zinos-Amaro: Your use of pared-down prose is very effective, especially in moments of heightened emotion. You keep the
writing crisp and restrained, creating more space for the reader's
experience.

Swanwick: It *is* about the emotions, and it had to move fast,
or else it would have moved really chunkily. There's an emotive
moment I took from real life. Misty becomes a toddler in order
to chase after a butterfly. That comes from a little home movie
we have somewhere, which Sean's grandfather filmed of him
chasing a butterfly when he was a toddler. I loved that image.
I think we have a projector, so I suppose I could find the actual

image, but I don't need to—it's enough to know that it exists.

Zinos-Amaro: Though Raphael would probably not describe himself as a poet, sometimes the language becomes so minimalistic that it gets compressed into poetry. For instance, when he notes, "She was aging away from me." Beautiful turn of phrase.

Swanwick: That just seemed to say it. It's a very sad thought. It accomplished a lot, in terms of the story. It's important to show that even though we're in his perspective, it's not just about him. And the utilitarian aspects of this artificial life-form, with the various failed projects, take a backstage. They're not the most interesting element. Dr. Lange is on a sad path. She's fallen in love with this young person, whom she can't have, and she knows it even though he doesn't. At the end she dies and the question is left unresolved: has her life been a tragedy, or has her love for him been a grace note? I don't know. You can get so close to judging lives, but you don't ultimately have the authority to do so.

In turn, when he's considering whether to use his newfound love to fund the extinction of the human race, at a low point in his life, he thinks, "It was a terrible thing to contemplate depriving an entire species of it. Still . . . it was not as if any of them were much good at it." Humor keeps creeping in, even at the grimmest moments, which provides some balance.

Zinos-Amaro: "The Last Days of Old Night" (*Clarkesworld*, December 2020) also explores a sea change in the history of humanity, this time in the far past. I understand this story was inspired by a trip to Iceland.

Swanwick: Marianne and I went to Iceland in 2018 because Eleanor Arnason had written about what positive experiences she'd had there, with the SF community at Icecon and with the country as a whole. She was absolutely right. Near the beginning of our visit, we stood on the black sands of Reynisfjara and admired the basalt sea stacks there. Our tour book said that legend had it they were two giants pulling a boat ashore when the sun came up and turned them to stone. But so far as I could find out, that was it. I thought the stacks deserved a whole story and I kept thinking about them until I found one.

We visited Snorri Sturluson's homestead, which was an astonishing experience for a writer, and saw the remains of his hot bath and the spiral staircase—the only one in Iceland at the time—leading down to it. We saw Geyser, after which every other geyser is named. On the way to an evening Icecon event, we saw the Northern Lights over Reykjavik. One of the con organizers hurried out to meet us and make sure we didn't miss it. We visited Thingvellir where, geologically, Europe and North America are splitting apart and where the Thing, one of the of the primal sources of democracy was held. And Reykjavik is a lovely and culturally engaging city. We had a favorite cafe there, where we ate a small order of rotted shark. "We only offer it so we can see your expressions when you taste it," the server warned us. It was a memorable trip.

Zinos-Amaro: It sounds like you had a great experience with the Icelandic science fiction community. Any words on Icelandic literature or art in general—anything that has stayed with you?

Swanwick: Iceland is the most literate nation on earth. One out of ten Icelanders will publish a book in their lifetime—not just write but publish! The yearly literary festival is always front-page news. But Icecon, their national science fiction convention can't get a mention. SF is still below the country's literary radar. Nevertheless, the community there is warm and supportive, aspirational, and even in a way heroic in their efforts to win recognition for science fiction and fantasy. I think the world of them.

Zinos-Amaro: In parts of this tale I felt like you were channeling the spirit of Poul Anderson. A reviewer online noted an R. A. Lafferty influence.

Swanwick: I am proud to acknowledge both of these. There's a touch of Michael Moorcock's Chaos Lords in the mix as well.

Zinos-Amaro: At one point, you write: "Like the popcorn machine and the microwave, it had come into existence in tandem with the knowledge in her head of its location." Later: "A singularity called the monoblock." These are delightfully anachronistic subversions, which hybridize science and myth, resonating with the very name of the character, Mischling.

Swanwick: As I've mentioned before, in our genre history there were plenty of natural fantasy writers who, finding no reliable markets for fantasy, wrote SF that was secretly fantasy or else a hybrid of SF and fantasy. Their example made all that come easily. But I should acknowledge my borrowing from Gregory Frost. In his *Shadowbridge* world, there are spiral piers occasionally jutting off from the pylons of his world-spanning bridges at the center of which new things occasionally appear, such as a vacuum cleaner or a pachinko machine. Sometimes the knowledge of their use also appears in the minds of those nearby and pachinko machines proliferate. Sometimes they don't, so the vacuum cleaner has to be put in a museum of modern art. *Shadowbridge* and *Lord Tophet* are wonderful books from a fantastic writer.

Zinos-Amaro: The description culminating in "[. . .] counterintuitive manner, the boat could be turned in the same direction as the wheel," could be read as a literalization of the plot, in which three giants, counter-intuitively, wish to save themselves from a great change through a tiny creature. And the change is wrought through the spinning of the world.

Swanwick: This shows you how much can be packed into a story if it's slow in the coming and has to be periodically set aside to mature and ripen.

Zinos-Amaro: The line "The most heroic deeds are often drab and boring" strikes me as part of your ongoing meta-commentary on fantasy *through* fantasy.

Swanwick: Most serious fantasy, from *The King of Elfland's Daughter* to *Little, Big* (choosing examples almost at random), is essentially about the relationship of fantasy and reality. In my fantasy, I'm trying to move beyond that. Which makes it ironic that, yes, nevertheless so much is exactly that meta-commentary.

Zinos-Amaro: Your next story, "Dream Atlas" (*Asimov's Science Fiction*, March-April 2021), moves very quickly. It has the same kind of single-mindedness as a flash piece, with just a bit more room to elaborate the central idea.

Swanwick: It was quick to write. I got the idea and could see where it was going from the beginning, so I could start it, head to the end, and stop when I arrived. As the title of the story suggests, it was inspired by *Cloud Atlas*, not the novel, but the actual *Cloud Atlas* compiled in 1890. I thought that one could similarly compile a dream atlas. It seemed within the realm of possibility. We do have a complicated relationship with our dreams.

Zinos-Amaro: You do acknowledge in the story, though, that this project could never really be completed. It's an infinite undertaking.

Swanwick: It's also not a very remunerative business! Eleanor, the protagonist, manages to get funding for it, but she's not getting rich off of it.

The red-and-white bird in this story, by the way, comes from all my research into paleontology and the Cretaceous. It seems like the kind of thing you might see in a dream, but it's deliberately not splashy enough to take attention away from the plot.

Zinos-Amaro: The focus on dreams, and the time travel element which introduces a kind of precognitive knowledge, take us all the way back to "'Til Human Voices Wake Us." I think there's an interesting resonance here with that early story. Another piece of linkage exists with "Clouds." There Wolfgang sees an older version of himself, just like Eleanor does here. That suggests a kind of third-act reflection to me.

Swanwick: Of course, the future self that Eleanor sees is someone admirable. Not only someone successful and well-dressed, but someone who unlike future Wolfgang has accomplished something with her life. She's made a serious contribution to science.

Zinos-Amaro: Her casually rummaging around to find her Nobel prize was delightful.

Swanwick: Wouldn't that be great? It's a little bit like science fiction awards. You want them desperately, and you're really, really grateful to get one, but afterwards you have this thing you actually have to put somewhere. Marianne advises not to leave your Nebula award in the sun, or it will blow up.

Eleanor has a mentor who says, "The Imagination is always right." One of Marianne's professors, when she was at Florida Atlantic University studying biology, said, "The organism is always right." I thought that was a profound observation.

I have to say, I think the ending of "Dream Atlas" works, but I was not entirely happy with it. That's the reason that not long after I wrote "The Beast of Tara," which posed the exact same problem, only this time the protagonist chooses the opposite direction.

Zinos-Amaro: In a sense those stories belong together, then. We'll get to "Tara" soon. I'll admit I also wasn't crazy about the ending of "Dream Atlas," because it comes down to the old there-are-things-we-shouldn't-know trope.

Swanwick: A minor story, alas.

Zinos-Amaro: "Annie Without Crow" (*Tor.com*, April 7,

2021) is certainly less minor. What made you want to return to the characters of "The Raggle Taggle Gypsy-O"?

Swanwick: This one is one of my favorites. It gives me warm feelings to contemplate it. It was fun to write, and probably got written at exactly the right pace.

I really, really liked the characters of that earlier story, and I saw instantly that they *could* be series characters. I was thinking about this off and on. In "The Raggle Taggle Gypsy-O" it's Crow who's acting and doing things and making things happen. Annie, through no fault of her own—she's not actually a passive woman—doesn't get to move the plot herself. So I thought I would like to let her strut her stuff without Crow.

Zinos-Amaro: This story has a lot of fun, bouncy moments and clever repartee between the characters. Did you know from the start that the poet Annie meets would be Shakespeare?

Swanwick: I did. She comes from Elizabethan England. When she goes home she has to encounter Elizabeth and she has to encounter Shakespeare. I kind of wish I could have come up with someone else. But the character I created for him is a little full of himself—at least that made me happy! It wasn't your usual Shakespeare story.

Zinos-Amaro: This was no *Shakespeare in Love*.

Swanwick: Funny you should mention that. I own the DVD of that movie and watch it every so often. It's like porn for writers, I think.

Zinos-Amaro: That should have been the blurb on the movie poster!

Swanwick: I did use a lot of Elizabethan Lite language in "Annie Without Crow," which is of course copped from Zelazny, along with the anachronistic, contemporary slang. For something that's light and frothy like this, if you use *real* Elizabethan language you slow down the reader too much. I was proud to throw in Sonnet 130 with the "your eyes are nothing like the sun" line. The part where she says to Shakespeare, "I really should castrate you. [. . .] Alas, I was always a sucker for a gaudy line of patter," was inspired by the line "The cheaper the crook, the gaudier the patter" from *The Maltese Falcon*.

Of course the climax of the whole thing, the justification for it, is the moment where she rips open her bodice and gives her little non-Romantic speech. Romance is not pretty, it's not tidy, it's not cute. It can be very, very destructive, as we've all seen. She makes her case before all these avatars that outrank her for Romance being as strong an impulse as any.

Zinos-Amaro: "It invades the heart like a conquering army and it takes no prisoners." This story, while comical, speaks seriously to the power of Eros, as established in the very first image.

Swanwick: Yes. And at the very end, Crow pops up again, and they are perfectly made for one another and they go off to have more adventures, which I have no interest in writing about! I prefer to leave those adventures implied.

Zinos-Amaro: Much is implied in "Huginn and Muninn—and What Came After" (*Asimov's Science Fiction*, July-August 2021), which strikes me as a very strong piece of work.

Swanwick: This was my James Tiptree Jr./Alice Sheldon story. In retrospect, I think it was too subtle to call my protagonist Alyssa rather than Alice, and I'll probably change this if the story is reprinted. Anyway, Tiptree once told Gardner that for years she had lived with two vultures perched on her shoulders. That was her depression. Eventually one of them stirred, flapped its wings and flew away. The other one did the same some time later. Unfortunately, apparently they came back, which is an enormous pity.

I wrote this story because Tiptree had published a story called "In Midst of Life," in which she was obviously picturing her own afterlife. It's one of her weaker stories. It really doesn't come to grips with her own obsession. I thought that her obsession lent itself to more exploration.

Zinos-Amaro: The magazine publication of this story includes a warning that uses the word "despair." For me, this is rather a story about deep, simmering rage and other unexpressed emotions than it is about despair per se.

In the second paragraph, you write: "As a young woman she [Alyssa] had sometimes dropped clues leading like a trail of breadcrumbs into the dark forest of her being. But nobody had ever followed them all the way in." To me, this suggests the behavior of someone very hesitant to let others inside. When this person does make an attempt, however feeble, to invite someone in, it's unsuccessful, which could plausibly lead to feelings of rejection and frustration. Hence, the anger angle.

Later, in a telling moment, she flings a crowbar as hard as she can. That action seems to come from a deep place.

Swanwick: That sounds like a fair reading. She *is* angry. Truthfully, it's not really about despair. We don't know what's in her mind. As she says, she's the only one who knows. And she chooses not to share it. Deep unhappiness I can see in there, and rage as you say, but not despair. But the warning you're referencing is really about suicide, so it makes sense that it's linked up to despair, because suicide is something that's very difficult to discuss frankly when what we want to do is convince people not to commit that act. A friend of mine tried to kill herself and almost succeeded but failed—she did not take enough pills. She woke up in the hospital. Later, she told me that that had been the bravest thing she had ever done in her life. But you don't want to say that in print, necessarily, in a magazine where a teenager going through a bad stretch may run across it. The ethics can get tricky sometimes. I myself have never been suicidal. It's a horrifying, scary thought to me.

I think that Julie Phillips' biography of Tiptree is the best biography of a science fiction writer ever written. David Hartwell said it was the best biography of *any* writer. He may be right.

She was such a complicated and private woman at the same time. I based the characterization, and much of the plot of this story, on an observation that Farah Mendlesohn made, which got a lot of people angry with her. Mendlesohn suggested that Tiptree was not really a lesbian, but rather an un-transitioned man. I thought that was a rather deep observation, and "Huginn and Muninn—and What Came After" was a way of grappling with it. I was aware of the fact that I was stepping in dangerous waters here because of my age. But it was an interesting idea to put into practice, and I hope I learned something from it.

Zinos-Amaro: One of the few glimpses we get into Alyssa's history pre-story is her relationship with her mother, now deceased, and later resuscitated in the pocket universe. Alyssa's mother took her to war-torn countries, where she witnessed an execution, saw a horse-cart full of corpses, and so on. Those things could easily be trauma-inducing.

Swanwick: Oh, yes. You see that in Tiptree's life. The circumstances were different, but the trauma was equally there.

The restaurant in the story being called Mueller's, I should mention, is a nod to the name Sylvester Mule, which Tiptree had toyed with as a pseudonym.

Zinos-Amaro: Structurally, I think this story has some similarity with "The Man in Grey." In both pieces we begin with a character in a dark place, who through the course of the narrative is shown a new reality beneath our own, can't unsee it—as the character of Mistral explicitly states—and once back in our ordinary reality, chooses to kill herself.

Swanwick: I can see that. I wanted to give Alyssa a hard choice, and how she responds to it is, I think, the only thing that gives us a clue as to what and who she is.

Zinos-Amaro: This is how she reacts when she's given the choice: "A shadow play? False friends, imaginary enemies, elaborate scripts to keep me dancing for your amusement? The opportunity to sit in the dark talking to myself for all eternity? Better to die in reality than live forever here." Those alternatives—immortality within fiction vs. mortality in reality—strongly recall "Goblin Lake."

Swanwick: Yeah. What can I say, I'm very fond of reality! It has its problems, but on the whole I enjoy it enormously. I think Alyssa makes the choice that Tiptree would make. Oh, and "the glorious, rapacious, loving, destructive, yearning human race!" is the line right before what you quoted, and I threw that in to make it clear what was at stake with her decision.

Zinos-Amaro: I'd like to offer up one more view of "Huginn and Muninn—and What Came After." Alyssa is shown a pocket universe, but really that universe is about *her*. It's not truly engaging, and can never be, because it ultimately derives from her own desires, memories and experiences. In a sense, to me this literalizes the idea that depression equals solipsism. If she had escaped into an alien universe, say, this might have offered the genuine possibility of relief from her loneliness and unknowability, but this is just her falling back into herself.

Swanwick: I like that quite a lot. You know, I can't claim to understand Tiptree, and therefore I can't claim to understand Alyssa, but it seems to me that we tend to make Alice Sheldon into the person we need her to be. Really, at the very core of her murder-suicide, is mystery. It's the unknowable. That unknowable quality had to remain. It can't be budged, it can't be understood, it can't be moved off-center, it can't be manipulated into something *useful*. If we're going to think at all about Alice Sheldon, we have to come to grips with that fact.

Zinos-Amaro: The New Wave, which we talked about a bit when we discussed "Ginungagap" and the start of your career, dealt with subjects like suicide quite fearlessly. Your story "The White Leopard" (*New Worlds*, ed. Peter Crowther and Nick Gevers, 2022) appeared in a new incarnation of a famous New Wave publication. Had you been a reader of the original *New Worlds*?

Swanwick: Oh yes, oh yes. All the British New Wave back then. A lot of it came to me secondhand, obviously. I'd pick up the occasional original magazine copy at a convention, but a lot of the stories I read were reprints. That was an exciting time in science fiction. Ballard, and Moorcock, and all the rest—it was a circus.

Zinos-Amaro: Was there ever any New Wave material that transgressed too much for you personally, material that you thought was successfully executed from a technical perspective but seemed to go too far in whatever direction?

Swanwick: In the second *Dangerous Visions* anthology edited by Harlan Ellison there was a story by Piers Anthony called "In the Barn." It's an astonishingly offensive story about an alternate world where women are lower-intelligence creatures kept in barns, like cattle. It was offensive on so many grounds that even someone who enjoyed *Naked Lunch* could find no pleasure in it. I've read a little bit about Piers Anthony, and it's my understanding that he believes that men are essentially helpless before their lust. He has a terribly warped view of sexuality. The story reflects that, and it was badly written too, so it's not really an example of what you were asking, it was just awful and nasty.

I can't really think of good stories that were too much for me back then. I was very young when the New Wave came around. I was in my early twenties, and that's an age where you welcome transgression, because you want to show your intellectual courage. Brian Aldiss, who was one of my heroes when I was unpublished, equally successful at novel and short story lengths, pushed boundaries more than once. *The Dark Light Years*, for example, is all about excrement. But it didn't offend me.

Zinos-Amaro: Tell me about ending up in this new version of *New Worlds*. I assume Peter or Nick reached out.

Swanwick: They did. I had a story which I had just finished that day. I thought, "This isn't very *New Worlds*," but sent it to them anyway because it was what I had. It kind of stands out in that volume as not fitting in that well. But they liked it well enough to buy. I don't think Moorcock, for example, would have considered it New Wave! Though he did buy conventional stories when he was editing the magazine, simply because he couldn't get an entire issue full of New Wave stuff every month.

Zinos-Amaro: The very last line of "The White Leopard" does something interesting and in a way subversive, which we'll talk about in a minute. But I could see this story being published in, say, *Asimov's*.

Swanwick: Yes. In truth it's a pretty conventional story, and would have likely ended up there if Nick and Peter hadn't requested something from me.

Back in the 50s there was almost this genre unto itself that consisted of stories about married couples who couldn't stand each other. They literally hated each other. These stories popped up across all genres, except romance I suspect. It went away as divorce became more acceptable. I didn't have any interest in writing one of those stories, partially because I have a very happy, satisfying marriage, so I don't have anything to draw from there. But a while back Marianne and I were on a long train trip, and there was an old couple having a bitter argument. The woman had purchased the tickets and she had failed to buy the sleeper car. They argued steadily and bitterly. At one point the man lay down in the middle of the aisle and said, "This is where I'll have to sleep because you couldn't get a sleeper car!" She replied, "Get up, you damned fool, you're making a fool of yourself!" They were pacing themselves so that they could keep this up for hours, which they did. I was fascinated by the fact that all that they had was their hatred. They somehow valued this hatred. This was what kept their marriage together—despising each other so much.

Now, separate to this, an occasional pastime that Marianne and I share is going to estate sales. You get to snoop in other people's houses. Sometimes you find really strange, interesting items there. I came up with the idea of finding a land drone, which is an obvious next step in military operations, and fixing it. I was thinking along the model of Heinlein's *Have Spacesuit, Will Travel*. The first half of the novel is the boy fixing the spacesuit, and the second half he has adventures. The second half, which has tons of plot, is nowhere near as fun as the first half. I was thinking about that, and the joy of repairing such a thing when you have the skills.

I attached the couple who hated each other to the drone concept, and those two sources together made the story. Neither source by itself was enough for a story, but together they worked.

Zinos-Amaro: The prose exploring the forest via drone is full of memorable imagery.

Swanwick: A lot of what I like about "The White Leopard" is the evocations via the sensorium. When I was a kid, I spent my summers in the woods. In the morning I'd throw a couple of peanut butter and jelly sandwiches into a knapsack, fill a canteen with water, and disappear. I spent a lot of time there.

When the protagonist is seeing through the leopard and looks up and the sky is swarming with satellites, that was based on an experience I had at Launch Pad, a week-long course on astronomy. Mike Brotherton, who is an astronomer and science fiction writer, brought along with him a pair of night-vision glasses that he had bought on eBay. I tried them on. The sun hadn't set, and there was a hazy sky, but with them you could see the stars and satellites going by. It was amazing. One of my ambitions is to own a pair of glasses like that. I threw that into the story, and the leopard has an even better set of night-vision goggles than he did there.

Zinos-Amaro: To me, this is a story about characters whose traumatic experiences have left them stuck in the past. They're frozen in time. Anything that provides an escape from their untenable present, no matter how dangerous or wicked, is welcomed. That's why I find the closing line so powerful. He's going to die, but he's happy to have re-experienced the wife of his memories one last time before succumbing to his fate.

Swanwick: At one point the protagonist marvels at how it's possible for two people to hate each other so much. Again, this is based on something I'd been saving up for years. I had a friend whose marriage broke up, and one day he went to where his ex-wife was living with her new boyfriend to get something or other.

The boyfriend came out and beat him up, because she had told the boyfriend he had done certain things which he hadn't. When he told me the story, he wasn't looking for sympathy. He just wondered, "How can one person hate another that much?" It seemed a profound question, and this story gave me a chance to use it.

Originally the ending of the story was more conventional. The protagonist and his new girlfriend drive the wife into the woods, track her down and kill her. It wasn't an interesting ending; it just sat there being predictable. I changed it so that the wife gets the last laugh, but what I like about it is the line you mentioned. It adds a moment of grace. He doesn't die in vain. For that one moment, it's all worth it. The future he's throwing away has nothing for him.

Zinos-Amaro: There was another line I wanted to touch on: "Night after night, Ray explored the forest, interested in everything and caring about nothing but pure sensation." To me this hedonism signals his moral decline, and in a way I think the line could double as your critique of our own society's increasing pursuit of pleasure and sensation at the expense of all else.

Swanwick: He's alone in the woods, and even there manages to behave badly: he terrorizes a raccoon just for his own amusement. It shows that he's rotted through. I'm afraid, as I've said a few times, that I'm a moralist. I would rather not be one, but you're mostly stuck with the values your parents give you.

Zinos-Amaro: Morality also informs "The Beast of Tara" (*Asimov's Science Fiction*, January-February 2022), a story we mentioned in connection with "Dream Atlas." Here I found the resolution more satisfying. There's a freedom of choice that's ensured by cross-temporal checks and balances.

Swanwick: I liked this outcome more as well. We have to imagine that if time travel were possible, there would be competing interests at work. Partway through the story, my son Sean pointed out to me that this was all about colonialism. I said, "Ooh, right. That works much better, and gives it interior substance."

Zinos-Amaro: The character development is richer here as well.

Swanwick: There was a complicated little ecology of emotions within the camp. I worked out how everybody felt about everybody else. That was very pleasurable, especially since the woman scientist who was in charge of the whole thing was oblivious to most of that. The dynamics were pleasant to figure out and put together. "Dream Atlas" was more of a sketch.

Incidentally, the name Gallagher was a reference to the story "Gallegher" by Richard Harding Davis. He was a big newspaper writer during the Spanish-American War. He was a very glamorous figure; very handsome and worldly. He wrote some fiction along with the non-fiction he was best known for. "Gallegher" is about a newsboy who manages to solve a crime and capture a criminal, the quintessential scrappy, young slum kid. Davis is buried in Leverington Cemetery, which is about five blocks from here. We drop by every now and then and leave a flower.

Zinos-Amaro: The Irish element here brought to mind "For I Have Lain Me Down on the Stone of Loneliness and I'll Not Be Back Again," where you also made use of the Stone of Destiny. And the basic high concept is fun, similar to the idea in Bob Shaw's "Light of Other Days" but applied to sound rather than light.

Swanwick: As an Irish American, writing about that specific place is a unique pleasure.

This was another COVID story, where I was casting about what to write next. The basic idea of reading the vibrations in the stone and hearing the heart of Tara was something that was presented to me as fact in 1978. Somebody told me that scientists were working on a way to listen to the deep vibrations inside rocks and hear into the past. It sounded really good, but if you stopped to think about it, it didn't seem likely. It doesn't stand up to scientific scrutiny. I did some handwaving in the story about how much math would be required to understand it. This is fine; the idea was just an enabling device for the story.

Zinos-Amaro: Speaking of tools, what was the inspiration for the wonderfully-titled "Nirvana or Bust" (*Analog Science Fiction and Fact*, March-April 2022)?

Swanwick: Some friends went to the Grand Canyon. When they came back they talked about what it was like to be sitting on the edge of the Grand Canyon at midnight, with millions of years of history below them and millions of years of light coming down above them from the Milky Way. Marianne and I both liked that, so we went to the Grand Canyon and did it. I thought it would make for a good story opening. I also had a conversation with a friend; she's short, and she was talking about things that people do because she's short that annoy her. I decided to have a character who is short, but to not make it much of a factor. I began the story with the basic chase scenario and then figured out the rest step by step. This was one of those tales that just grows into creation; it crystallizes.

Zinos-Amaro: You've used the idea of smart or even sentient suits before, but here you take it to the next level, with the merging of disparate consciousnesses to create something new.

Swanwick: Yes. We come back to my fascination with the differences between natural intelligence and artificial intelligence. I came up with the idea you mention as a way of continuing that series of thoughts without making it all schematic. The opposition of humans and machines has been done so many times. Here I created humans and machines gearing up toward a war. I did what I could to introduce a machine that would be different from the standard one. I gave him a Savile Row suit and made him suave, as a way of avoiding the triteness of robots. Also, I made him a mantisform, which I think looks cool! When the assassin appears, his first words are "Pardon my intrusion," which are the first words spoken by the creature to another human being in *Frankenstein*. That's a bit of a joke.

Zinos-Amaro: In a way, with this story you're returning to one of your very early themes, namely different modes of consciousness and the possibility of transitioning between them, as explored, for instance, in "Trojan Horse."

Swanwick: This has to be from growing up Catholic. The emphasis is on transcendence, in which I've been interested since forever. Writing is probably the closest I'll get to experiencing this.

Zinos-Amaro: Considering how most of your stories turn out, I think that's a good thing!

Swanwick: Right! I *am* a pessimist, but then again, I could be wrong.

"Nirvana or Bust" is another one of those stories where the last paragraph pulls back to the long view, and by doing so does half the work of the story.

Zinos-Amaro: It's certainly a memorable last line. In my notes for "Reservoir Ice" (*Asimov's Science Fiction*, July-August 2022) I described it as "'Needle in a Timestack' on steroids."

Swanwick: I probably read that story, because I was reading all of Silverberg's short fiction back then. "Reservoir Ice" is in reality a COVID-19 story, one where I went back to old fictions I never got around to writing. I have about forty stories partially written, but that doesn't mean I ever know what I'm going to do next. The original idea came when I was back in college—which means, fifty or more years ago!—thinking of my friends' romantic entanglements and the possibility of time travel. I thought the first thing you'd do is go back in time and *not* say that stupid thing that got your girlfriend so angry at you that she walked out. You'd use your superior knowledge of somebody's life and likes to go back in time and try to win her over. But then I figured by the time you got there, she'd be gone, because she would be trying to win over an earlier love that she had failed to get. I was wise enough to know at that time that I wasn't writer enough to handle the idea. This idea was waiting for me on a back shelf. I thought, "I can do that. That could be fun."

Zinos-Amaro: The fun is in the rom-com type setup, which quickly gives way to more serious ideas.

Swanwick: It sets itself up to be about sex, but it's really about love and romance. As I wrote it I discovered the characters were all awful people, with the exception of the department head, Dr. Nabirye, a stodgy, not-very-expressive black man, an introverted intellectual. Him I like a lot. He's a decent man, trying very hard to do the right thing. Everybody else is just after results that make *them* happy.

Zinos-Amaro: In a sense this ties back to "The White Leopard"'s implied critique of the selfish pursuit of sensations. In this case, the very fabric of reality is at stake.

Swanwick: Yes. They want what they want but they don't really *care*. He may love his wives but he doesn't really care about them. It's all terribly, terribly selfish behavior. He doesn't realize that he's stalking a woman until she sends him a card telling him to stop doing it.

Zinos-Amaro: Was the closing scene, and the description of the muskrats and the ice that give the story its title, based on your own life?

Swanwick: Literally so. In the essay "The Changeling Returns," which we discussed in the context of "The Changeling's

Tale," I talk about how Tolkien was the writer who turned me into a writer. At one point in the essay I say, "Well, we don't tell our parents everything." I mention how I didn't tell my parents that we used to have races across the used car lot, running over the tops of the cars. I didn't tell them how we used to go to this fishing spot, and to get to it we had to go through an abandoned power station where we had to jump over this gap with jagged metal ten feet down below. I certainly didn't tell them about this episode in the reservoir, which is as described in the story. My big sister Patty told me that my sister Mary bought a copy of the book and read that section to my mother! I had no idea. By then my mother was in her late 80s or early 90s, and she didn't say anything to me about it. My follies were no longer her responsibility.

Zinos-Amaro: From the last nine stories we've discussed, five of them ("Dragon Slayer," "Dream Atlas," "Annie Without Crow," "Beast of Tara," and the current "Reservoir Ice") involve time travel or a temporal dislocation of some manner. Is this current preoccupation with time travel the result of a particular life stage? Just a natural extension of always having been interested in time travel? Something else?

Swanwick: This is the kind of pattern that your subconscious will throw up and you don't know yourself what it means. My theory would be that this actually comes from the COVID years when I spent a lot of time wishing things were otherwise. Other than that, it might be coincidence, or it might be something at work. I'm not sure which it is.

If you think back to your college years, and look at all your friends, you realize that the events of "Reservoir Ice" are no more messy than what was going on back then. Everybody was young, had lots of energy, and things were changing very fast.

Zinos-Amaro: That's an interesting point. You could interpret the time travel metaphorically, as capturing the ferment of youth. This story, along with "Cloud," "Huginn and Muninn—and What Came After" and "The White Leopard," seem to have more of a mainstream sensibility than we've seen in other clusters of your work.

Swanwick: These are more character-oriented pieces in a way. Perhaps I'm more capable of balancing this now with the science fiction elements.

Zinos-Amaro: We've gone through over one hundred of your short stories in detail, essentially everything you've published solo that isn't flash fiction or part of a series. When you look at this long bibliography, and assess where you are now in your writing career compared to where you started, what are your ambitions? Are there specific things pertaining to short fiction that you feel you have yet to accomplish, or do you just want to continue to do more of what you've been doing?

Swanwick: I don't think that I've yet written anything that will be around five hundred years from now, and that's really what I'd like to do. I'm just eaten away by ambition. But I've never been really good about career planning or any of that stuff. I just write whatever I have on hand that's best to write.

Zinos-Amaro: What do you think is the story or stories of yours that might have the biggest chance at longevity? Some have already been reprinted regularly for several decades.

Swanwick: Artistically, "The Edge of the World" is one of my favorites, which is ironic because when I wrote it I thought, "This is a good, second-rank Michael Swanwick story." Other people began chiming in about how much they liked it, so I promoted it to first-rank.

To be honest, I mostly don't look back at my career. Doing so, I cannot see or feel any progression in my short fiction over the last forty-two years other than the fact that as I've acquired more craft the stories tend to grow shorter. I mentioned this when we talked about the first five stories, which were novelettes. Most of my short stories now come in under 5,000 words.

Zinos-Amaro: Do you ever deprioritize certain ideas?

Swanwick: Not really. Writing is difficult for me. I spend a lot of time not getting anywhere with my fiction. So if I have a good idea, there's room to play with it, so there's no reason to strategically put off anything. I have a lot of pieces underway. I have forty or so partially-written stories and when no new ideas come, I start opening files and see if I can coax one to life. If I can't, I'll mope around the house. As you know, writing is not a very glamorous life.

Zinos-Amaro: Despite these difficulties, you continue to publish a half-dozen stories per year.

Swanwick: I'm glad I can do that. I'm going to continue to write until the end. If I come to a point where my fiction isn't any good anymore, I'll write essays. And if I can't write essays, I'll write reviews. I'll find something to do that is worthwhile and that I can keep doing. Right now, for instance, I've been writing introductions for reprints of Philip K. Dick novels by Centipede Press. I wrote introductions to the first three—*The Cosmic Puppets, Dr. Futurity*, and *Vulcan's Hammer*—and they liked them and asked me to do the next four. Eventually, theoretically, I'll have done thirty-three of them! The game is to see if I can say something different and interesting about Dick in each introduction. I think it's possible, because he led a rich, and involved, and sometimes contradictory life.

Zinos-Amaro: You've written introductions to reprints of many interesting authors and works over the years, including a recent one to *Dune*. Do you see yourself ever assembling this material into a nonfiction book? It's been a little over a decade since your books on James Branch Cabell and Hope Mirrlees came out, and about twenty years since the interview volume with Gardner Dozois that inspired this project.

Swanwick: The recent *Dune* reprint, also from Centipede, I actually have lying flat on a shelf, because I don't have any shelf tall enough for it!

At some point, yes, I could see myself assembling some of this material. I'd like to have a collection of my best nonfiction. But since I haven't made any efforts towards that end, it will be a while. Someday when I don't have any stories demanding my attention, I'll look into it.

Most of the introductions I've written pay very well for a short essay, and I put a lot of work into them. I'm doing my best to make them unprofitable by doing far too much research!

I read a fair amount of collections of essays, and literary figures tend to write Introductions and essays about people who don't really need the publicity. Henry James doesn't need another essay explaining why he's so good, thank you. On the other hand, any time I write about R. A. Lafferty, I feel like that's doing some good, because that's somebody who actually needs attention. If I do all the Philip K. Dick book introductions, that could make for a not terribly long stand-alone volume, and maybe one of the publishers who does paperback originals would want it.

It might sell a few hundred copies. It would be pleasant to have, but not important. My nonfiction can eventually all disappear, and that's fine.

Zinos-Amaro: The ambition you mentioned for your work to endure is specific to your fiction then?

Swanwick: No question. I think my nonfiction is useful and helpful, but not important. The one exception might be my volume on Hope Mirrlees. It was important to get that information out there. Marianne believes it continues to be important, and I will defer to my wife's opinion.

Zinos-Amaro: *Being Gardner Dozois*, the project that instigated this volume, I would say also continues to be important.

Swanwick: I hope so. Gardner deserves all the attention he can get. He was able to talk about his work in a way that other people can't. Gardner was an analytical writer and I am an intuitive writer. I wish I were analytical, particularly in the present case, but there you are. I think *Being Gardner Dozois* would be a useful book for an aspiring writer to read. Or somebody who has made a sale or two, and is looking to up his game.

Zinos-Amaro: That's my hope for this set of conversations as well. This brings us full circle, so I'm wondering if you have any closing thoughts.

Swanwick: I would like to live as long as George Bernard Shaw and keep writing all the while. When he was in his sixties, he said he was the world's first immortal man, and they laughed. In his seventies, they were still laughing. In his eighties, they were laughing, but not as loudly. In his nineties, they started getting worried.

Looking back, I can safely say I've never tried to manage my public persona. I was never afraid to write a small, funny, not-very-important story. Some writers—I won't mention names, because some people take this as a criticism, though I don't intend it as such—only write "important" stories. I've always just written the best thing I could write at that particular moment. Sometimes the best thing I could write was a pretty minor story.

When I started out as a writer forty-two years ago, a number of my friends were among the best short fiction writers in the field. As they learned to write novels, for the most part their loyalties shifted and they gave up writing short fiction. I think in almost every case it was a sad thing.

I believe in the beauty of short fiction, in the purity of it, and the fact that it can do things that long fiction simply cannot. Writing short fiction isn't profitable, but it's incredibly satisfying. I would hate to lose that ability. That would be very sad indeed. For a year or two, that happened to Stephen King. So he accepted a job as the editor of a volume in an important short fiction best-of-the-year series, and instead of simply relying on the pre-vetted fifty or however many stories they were going to have him choose from, he went out and looked for short stories himself and read furiously. At the end of that process, he had re-taught himself how to write short stories. At his best, he's a very fine short fiction writer, so it would have been an enormous pity to lose him. Clearly, he feels about short fiction the way I do: it's a value in and of itself.

In a way, at seventy-one years of age I feel like I'm now truly getting a grip on the craft of stories. The longer I can manage to hold on, the better the chance I have to write something really good.

CHAPTER NINE
CAPRICHOS & SERIES

Zinos-Amaro: You've been an incredibly prolific flash fiction author.

Swanwick: At some point I acquired the ability to write short shorts. It was very convenient for me, because I could write them in the evenings, while watching television, without losing any of my regular writing time. It was efficient. As I wrote more and more flash fiction, I learned more and more about the form.

I've now rendered it virtually impossible to determine exactly how many pieces of flash fiction I've written. "An Abecedary of the Imagination"—is that twenty-six pieces of flash fiction? Well, one of them is just a recipe for unicorn. It has a little joke at the end, but is it actually a story? By most definitions, not. I've written several stories that were made up of flash fictions. Do they count as one story or several? I've also, a couple of times, taken a piece of previously written flash fiction that appeared in a fairly obscure place and plunked it down into a new abecedary I was writing. So does that count as one story or two?

I do know I've written several hundred of them. I have a batch of them on my hard drive that I've never made any effort to sell. If a project comes along, I can just dip into them and see what will fit in.

It's an interesting form, because by itself a piece of flash fiction is basically a joke, not necessarily funny but the same kind of structure as a joke. Even the famous ones are not very literary. They don't have the complexity and ambiguity that you go to fiction for. But if you write two dozen flash fictions on a theme after a while they begin to interact with each other. If there are enough of them, in their interactions they can acquire the complexity and interest that proper literary fiction has.

Zinos-Amaro: I'd like to talk a bit about some of your major flash fiction series. The first was "Writing in My Sleep," made up of a dozen plus flash pieces that appeared in *The New York Review of Science Fiction* in 1991. These were later reprinted in *Cigar-Box Faust and Other Miniatures* (2003).

Swanwick: These were literally stories that I wrote while asleep. In my senior year of high school, my creative writing teacher, and a friend of mine also in the class, got into a discussion about writing stories in their sleep. I had never heard of this before. But they both did this, and they both agreed that this was more common than people knew. I thought that was interesting. Decades later, I started doing it myself. I was very curious as to whether what I was writing was brilliant or incredibly stupid. Your dreams flee quickly, so I kept a notebook by my bed. Anytime I had a dream in which I wrote something, I taught myself to wake up, and I would touch the wall so that the coolness of the plaster would anchor me to reality, and then I would repeat the story to myself, so that I would remember it. In the morning I'd write it down, first thing. I kept this dream writing diary for over a year and didn't look at it. When I finally did, I found the pieces you mentioned, which are somewhere between stupid and brilliant. Very strange, enigmatic little writings, I think. I like them quite a lot. From there it evolved until I had the ability to write flash fiction on demand. Marianne will occasionally say something like, "Swanwick, I need five stories about eclipses." And I'll get to work.

Zinos-Amaro: Let's jump ten years, to 2001, where over the course of two years you wrote 118 flash stories comprising *The Periodic Table of Science Fiction*. That's a remarkable feat by any measure. In the introduction of the book Theodore Gray mentions Primo Levi and Oliver Sacks.

Swanwick: I had read Levi's book with great admiration long before this project. For context, by 2001 I had done the abecedary of short shorts for the Disclave 1996 Program Book that we talked about, and *Puck Aleshire's Abecedary* of flash stories, so I was very comfortable with the form. Eileen Gunn had a new magazine, called *The Infinite Matrix*. She asked me if I could do an abecedary for them, and since I'd already done that twice, I knew I could, and that it would be boring for me. Instead, I came up with the idea of *The Periodic Table of Science Fiction*. I wrote the first piece, corresponding to Hydrogen, for Eileen. There was then a blip in the sponsorship, and the magazine ceased to be. So, feeling a little responsible for depriving me of a source of income, she got in touch with Ellen Datlow. Ellen thought that that was an interesting project, so she took it up for *SciFiction*, an interim project she edited between sponsorships. I wrote a new "Hydrogen" entry for her and went on from there, writing a new piece every week. These stories required a fair amount of research. Mostly, they were easy to write. For example, Helium—oh, okay, the capital city of Barsoom. And so on. It was going well until I came up against vanadium, as I recount in the book, which seemed to be only of note because it was an essential element in the diet of chickens. I wrote about vanadium being the couch potato of the periodic table, and, boy, did I get letters! People were angry at me, because as it turns out my series was being used by chemistry teachers to help interest kids in chemistry. If I had been in communication with these people, some of the stories would have probably been more interesting!

About a month or two after I started this series, Eileen's magazine came back into existence, and she asked if I could do something else for her. I looked for something more difficult.

Zinos-Amaro: Right. This brings us to a very intriguing series, from 2001-2003, overlapping with your periodic table of science fiction. You worked on eighty stories that were essentially your interpretations of the etchings by Goya called *Los Caprichos*.

Swanwick: During this period, besides these two series, and besides all my regular short story and novel writing activities, I was writing a new story per month and posting it on my blog, to try and draw attention to it. By all appearances, I was madly prolific. I would walk into a room at a convention and writers would turn pale and hold up crucifixes and strings of garlic! I was, back then, a terrifying figure to them.

I've always loved Goya as an artist. Well, he was two artists. He was a commercial artist who could make you look really handsome and show off all the details of your clothing. This wasn't interesting to me at all. But the second artist was full of darkness—the Irish darkness in me resonates with this work.

A lot of the descriptions of Goya's *Los Caprichos* etchings were apparently Spanish folk sayings from the time, and translated into twentieth-century English made no sense whatsoever. But the pictures made enormous sense. I thought they deserved much better stories underneath them. That was my purpose writing these flash stories. Like with *The Periodic Table of Science Fiction*, as the Goya-inspired series of flash stories went on characters started to recur, in this case almost immediately. Prick the Donkey was the first one, since a number of etchings involved a donkey being a student or doctor or whatever. I followed his moral progress, or lack thereof. I didn't use the original numbering, so that I could separate out character appearances. Elena the Man-Hearted, who is absolutely ruthless and without conscience, and a great deal of fun, eventually meets up with Grace, who is the eternal victim and has nothing but bad luck. They become friends and in time part again. While I was writing the story of their first meeting, I had a blinding insight, came downstairs, where Marianne and Sean were sitting talking, and said, "I just realized that Elena and Grace are two aspects of the same woman!" They looked at me and said, "Well, duh." This had been obvious to them for a long time and had gone right past me. It was a continuing series of discoveries for me, which made it an adventure to write, considering how dark the etchings are. It was difficult to structure, though. I remember I had complicated charts, with different colors for each—witches, Prick, Elena, and so on, so they wouldn't get lumped together and could continue to coevolve through the stories.

Henry Wessells once invited me to come to New York to James Cummins Bookseller where he was working because they were about to ship out a bound copy of the original etchings. I got to actually hold them in my hands and see the etchings themselves. They are so much more complex than their reproductions. He did subtleties of murkiness that I suspect are physically not yet possible to be reproduced on paper without the original copper plates. I remember there was one that had figures in the darkness not shown in any of the reproductions. If I had seen that, I would have probably written an entirely different story for that particular etching. I was working very hard to write stories that were in sympathy with what Goya was trying to do.

Zinos-Amaro: These "Sleep of Reason" flash stories haven't been reprinted, have they?

Swanwick: They have not, but they are going to be, in 2023. Back when I wrote them, my agent was unable to sell them. About a year or so ago, I thought, "I know all these people at small presses. I should talk to one of them." I approached PS Publishing and asked if they would be interested in doing the series as a book. We went through my agent and negotiated, because John Berry, who is a very big name in the font community, had expressed an interest in doing the design, and so he will be involved in the process.

I was at a Worldcon with John and Eileen Gunn when Gardner's most recent collection had just come out. I had a copy and John asked if he could see it. He flipped through it and said, "Not bad. I would have used a different weight paper, but other than that, not bad." I told this to the publisher and he almost melted with joy. John Berry had said his book was "not bad"! So John will be doing the design of my book. I'm extremely pleased with that.

Zinos-Amaro: Since 2010 or so, the bulk of your flash fiction has been appearing through the micro-press Dragonstairs.

Swanwick: I'm going to let Marianne say a bit about this, since it's her press. People tend to confuse me with Dragonstairs, but this is her undertaking.

Marianne Porter: I am literally sitting over there at that table stitching together a chapbook right now.

A little background. For thirty-six years, I worked for the Commonwealth of Pennsylvania. I had a briefcase, I had an office, I had a business card. I would walk through the door of a commercial laboratory and people would stare in horror, which was great. But thirty-six years of that was quite enough, and I decided to retire, young, fully vested, good pension, medical coverage up to my eyebrows. I toyed with the idea of being a voluntary arts administrator for musical groups, per Tom Purdom's suggestion. It was an attractive notion. Meanwhile, I think Henry Wessells, just mentioned by Michael, had encouraged me with my first chapbook, which was a reprint of "A Midwinter's Tale" in 2010. Later, as the Darger and Surplus stories were coming out, Michael wrote four short pieces that taken together were interrelated. Michael would go around and give these small chapbooks to people at conventions as a publicity thing, but you'd have to find him at four different events to get all four stories. I had some left over, and offered to sell them. Several people placed an order.

It's been down the rabbit hole ever since. I will say, I've done a few other things, like a book of essays by Tom Purdom, an essay that Gardner had written—to his shock and horror—, and one of Susan Casper's stories after she died. But mostly the content of Dragonstairs Press is Michael's work, partly because he's cheap, and partly because I like working with him on these projects. You play around with these things. The papers I use are gorgeous. A lot of the chapbooks are giveaways at conventions, but I've established relationships with two book dealers who get a volume discount for their own purposes. For me, it's mostly fun.

Swanwick: Every now and then Marianne comes up with the notion of something we haven't done before. I once wrote a hard sf short short called "Tumbling." Each scene fit on one page exactly. That one was a challenge. The chap book was a 3" x 3" accordion folded story.

2020 was a big year for Dragonstairs, because of COVID. All that isolation led to more flash pieces. I was able to write a lot of them quickly. For example, "The Devil's Bestiary" series, probably inspired by Ambrose Bierce's sarcastic, snarky work, is longer than the usual Dragonstairs book.

Zinos-Amaro: Looking back over the hundreds and hundreds of flash stories you've published, are there any particular favorites that stand out? Any pieces that capture specific moments in time particularly vividly for you?

Swanwick: When I began telling them, some of the Christmas stories were pretty dark. As time went on I decided that that was inappropriate for a solstice card, at a time when people need warmth and cheer. So they've gotten kinder and more sentimental over the years. My favorite one of those is "Manger Animals" (2011). I used the legend that on Christmas Eve and on Christmas day animals could talk, and specified that only the animals that were at the manger can talk. Because baby Jesus, like any other little kid, loved animals, the manger animals are still alive, and once a year they reminisce about this day they have no real comprehension of. "I remember somebody fed me straw," or "You can't get good hay anymore, that's a fact," and so on. It's sentimental as anything, but I love that story.

"The Mousewife's Tale" is also fun and sentimental. Two other favorites, which we've already discussed in their rightful chronological places, are my Stephen King parody, "The Overcoat," and the later "The Madness of Gordon Van Gelder." Ditto for "Five British Dinosaurs" and "Coyote at the End of History."

Once I ran into Andy Duncan at a convention and he had acquired a notebook, because he knows I always carry them around and scribble in them. He was doing an imitation of me. I asked him if I could borrow it for a minute, and then wrote a story inside it, called "Unfinished Notebooks." I said, "Here. It's yours to do with as you wish." He was horrified. About a year or so later they made him Guest of Honor at Trinoc*coN, and he sent it to them for publication in the Program Book, so he made use of it, as I thought he would.

Zinos-Amaro: As a reader, do you have a favorite writer of short shorts?

Swanwick: Oh yes, oh yes. Julio Cortázar and his *Historias de cronopios y de famas*. Those are really wonderful, and they do that thing where some are standalones and some are connected series which interact and grow. In one of the standalones, there's a definition of fear which is a short short in itself: "In a small town in Scotland they sell books with one blank page hidden someplace in the volume. If the reader opens to that page and it's three o'clock in the afternoon, he dies." Kafka's short stories are really condensed, but his fables are often even shorter and just as wonderful. "The Great Wall of China," for instance, is fantastic. Within science fiction, Frederic Brown was great at very short lengths. He didn't write as many short shorts as I would have wished, but he was a busy man with a lot on his mind.

As a reader I have a particular fondness for minor literary oddities, so it gives me great pleasure to have created some of my own. Sometimes I think I'd like to go through my bookshelves and assemble *Michael Swanwick's Six Inch Bookshelf of Short Short Writers*. Flash fiction is a much more interesting area than most people realize. I'm afraid it's a minority taste, within the already minority taste of short fiction. But there's a small number of people who discover and appreciate small, perfect things.

Zinos-Amaro: I'd like to switch gears now and talk about your two non-flash fiction series, the Darger and Surplus stories and the Mongolian Wizard tales. What was the genesis of Darger and Surplus?

Swanwick: I was reading Thomas Pynchon's *Mason & Dixon*, and they have a quite wonderful talking dog in that. The two of them go to a variety show and the talking dog is part of the act. They get excited about this and go to talk to the handlers backstage. "You have quite a wonderful dog there, sir," one says, and a handler nervously replies, "We don't think of that dog as being ours." The dog then growls, "Damn me, they better not!" I decided I wanted to write about a talking dog, but I didn't want to do the same kind of dog. I sat down and wrote a description of a dog standing up on two legs, a rather anthropomorphic dog, dressed like a dog in a Mother Goose Nursery Rhyme book would be dressed. I put him down in the docks of London in a future that I played with off and on, which is less technologically oriented than our own but no less thriving, so that was my setting. Because I needed to have someone for him to talk to, I created Aubrey Darger, who came by and struck up a conversation. His name obviously comes from Henry Darger, the outsider artist. Incidentally, I've actually touched the manuscript for Darger's fifteen-thousand page novel, The Story of the Vivian Girls. There was an event at the American Folk Art Museum in New York and I got to be one of the readers of the original work.

When I started the first Darger and Surplus story, I wrote one page and had no idea where it was going. Obviously the man approaching the dog had to be a con man. Together these two just ran off with the plot. They were always one step ahead of me. They knew what was going on, and I did not! The entire story became a process of discovering the basics of it. Until they found the remains of the old world electrical system in the palace, in Buckingham Labyrinth, I had no idea that existed. Same thing with the conjuring of demons. I had no idea there would be any demons in the Internet. It was all a process of discovering things, almost by accident.

Zinos-Amaro: That's interesting. From your many, many stories, I think that the Darger and Surplus romps have your most sophisticated plotting. They seem to owe as much to the crime and mystery genres as they do science fiction.

Swanwick: So much science fiction was written by really talented hack writers who were forever writing in other genres in order to make money. Harlan Ellison, for instance, won the Edgar

Allen Poe Award twice, as well as the American Mystery Award. So there was this long-standing tradition before me that it was easy to fall into. And of course con man plots are very, very old. Once you write about con men you have to be clever. You can't be sincere.

Zinos-Amaro: How did the Mongolian Wizard series come about?

Swanwick: It was important to me that this series be different in kind from Darger and Surplus—otherwise there wouldn't have been any point to it. Here I was more consciously trying to write a *type* of story. I was thinking of the Lord Darcy stories by Randall Garrett. In fact, after I wrote the first story, I went back and reread all of Lord Darcy. I was surprised that the world of these stories was really very shallow. He hadn't bothered to do research on Victorian forms of address and so on. He just made it up as he went along. Another influence on these stories was Poul Anderson, with his Operation Chaos series. Anderson made the mistake of beginning his series, which had a great setup, by writing what should have been the climactic last story. The sequel or two that he wrote, which were set in academia, were nowhere near as interesting. Regardless, I loved both those series, and wanted to write something like them.

With my first story, I again started with an image. The wizard arrived and made himself extravagantly underestimated. Because I had to have somebody react to that, I came up with Franz-Karl Ritter. Then he took over. Every step of the way I had things happen, and then I had to figure out what they meant. When the soldiers disappear into the wainscoting, for example, Ritter realizes there's been a major breach of security. I followed up on the implications and figured out what was going on based on that. I don't think readers could see what was coming, because I certainly couldn't! This kind of story is a lot more work, but a lot more fun also, than the other ones.

Zinos-Amaro: When did you know both of these would be series? "The Dog Said Bow-Wow" (*Asimov's Science Fiction*, October-November 2001), the first Darger and Surplus escapade, won the Hugo, and was a finalist for the Nebula and Locus awards. Did that contribute to making it a series, or would you have done more with both of these worlds regardless of the reception to the first story?

Swanwick: I would have done more of both regardless. Both stories really resonated with me, and that was enough. I knew when I finished each story that it would turn into a series, though I did not know that when I began them. With Darger and Surplus, it wasn't until the extreme end of that story, when they're in a boat leaving London burning behind them, that I realized there would be more. When Surplus looks back and says sadly, "I can't help but feel in part responsible," that was a line I stole from an episode of *The Simpsons* called "Bart the Lover," in which Bart writes a series of love letters to his teacher as a prank, and when she's supposed to meet her dream man at the café and starts weeping when he doesn't show up, Bart says, "I can't help but feel partly responsible." It was entirely his doing! It was such a great line that I stole it outright. At this moment Darger tells Surplus to lift up his spirits, because they're headed to new lands and will make their way to Russia and the Duke of Muscovy. It was only then that I realized they were going to have more adventures.

In my early career I tried to come up with ideas for series characters because editors loved them and were asking for them. I couldn't come up with any. I realized the secret to Darger and Surplus being a series is that these two characters themselves don't change. It's like the original *Star Trek*. At the end of each episode, the needle has gone back to zero and you're exactly where you were before. They all remain friends and they're aboard the same ship, off to explore brave new worlds. So it doesn't really matter what setting you put them in. I love the fact that Darger and Surplus are real con men, who operate genuine scams. They think that they're good people, having a good time—and they're totally deluded in this! They're terrible people and awful things happen to them! But this never penetrates through their basic optimism; they always believe they're five days away from a life of infinite wealth and leisure. Their way of being never changes.

Zinos-Amaro: Their lack of self-awareness, their ability to gloriously self-deceive, is for me definitely part of what makes the series endearing. They themselves are not exempt from their own conning, and they're impermeable to psychic damage. You have their stories set in a post-utopia, but even if it were an outright dystopia, I think the same lighthearted sensibility would emerge from who *they* are, regardless of the world around them.

Swanwick: That's right. We've talked about Leiber's Fafhrd and the Gray Mouser stories before, which were also a partial model for Darger and Surplus. As I said, Leiber acknowledged to me that the world in which they're set is actually a horror world. But up until the last book, they remain optimists. Something similar is going on here.

Zinos-Amaro: This series is different from the Mongolian Wizard sequence in the fact that you've also written novels featuring Darger and Surplus: *Dancing with Bears* (2011) and *Chasing the Phoenix* (2015).

Swanwick: At the end of each story, they set out of a certain destination, but at the beginning of the next story, they're inevitably somewhere *else*, because they're so distractable. They can't hold to a long-term plan. But for me they were always making their way to Moscow, and I always thought that if they *did* reach Moscow, that story would deserve a novel, because it was such a big, important part of their lives. That's when I wrote *Dancing with Bears*. It's a light novel, even though the background is dark. Moscow burns behind them!

Zinos-Amaro: Do you see a Mongolian Wizard novel in the future?

Swanwick: No. The plan is to write a series that, all put together, will chronicle the wizard war from its beginning to its end. I think of this war as beginning, technologically, in the late eighteenth century, and continuing up through the First and Second World Wars. The end of the conflict will be followed by a coda showing what becomes of Ritter. Nine stories have been published so far, and I've sent two more to Patrick Nielsen Hayden for *Tor.com*. I've been really happy with how *Tor.com* has published and treated the Mongolian Wizard. The illustrations by Greg Manchess are exactly how I pictured Ritter. I'm currently working on the twelfth story, which I pick up and put down every now and then. This story deals with the changes brought upon Europe, the destabilization of reality. I'm rather wishing now that I'd put that off for a while! The eleven stories that are finished represent half of what I have in mind—twenty-one or twenty-two stories in all. Since they're about five thousand words each, that adds up to about a novel's length. I have hope that they'll be published collected in this way.

In terms of the overall arc, Ritter's moral development is at stake. These stories track the battle for his soul. Will he manage to survive as a decent human being or not? His job puts a lot of strain on him to do things which are not good. He's a particularly interesting character. I pictured him as being a proto-Nazi. If he were in Austria when Hitler came along, he would just fall into that at the beginning. He's very slowly learning better—or is he? In the second story, "The Fire Gown" (*Tor.com*, August 15, 2012), he's running an investigation and he interviews a Jewess, and, boy, that took my breath away. In "Day of the Kraken" (*Tor.com*, September 26, 2012), which followed, he thinks that the mining of a port with Kraken eggs is a terrible war crime, something he would never do. As one of the later stories begins, he's just returned from taking those exact same eggs and mining an enemy port with them. He's a conflicted man. Morally, he's being drawn in both directions. Sir Toby is perfectly amoral and is trying to cure Ritter of any morality whatever so that they can get on with winning the war. He's a practical, ruthless man.

Zinos-Amaro: In the same way, do you have an overarching shape in mind for the Darger and Surplus series?

Swanwick: Oh yeah. Two things are going on there. One is that they're on an accidental voyage around the world. They don't have a plan for this, but at the end of each tale they always have reasons to get out of town quickly. They're always heading east. After *Chasing the Phoenix*—which is the first time they didn't burn the capital down—it's possible that they'll pop up in Japan, but they're probably going to go to San Francisco. I have an idea for a novel set in San Francisco and I know what the big con is that they would be running. I know some interesting facts about it, so that could well happen. I've written one story set in New Orleans. I know they also have to go to Vermont to explain the secret behind Surplus's birth. Eventually, if I get around to writing all these stories, they will end up back in London.

This brings us to the second thing: they will find London utterly transformed, because even though they're not aware of it, they're catalysts, and everywhere they go they are rousing up the remains of the demons of the Internet, the AIs and such. Europe has been completely changed by them. London will be the original steampunk London my publishers wanted me to have. If I don't end up writing the rest of the Darger and Surplus saga, at least my comments here will provide a ghost narrative of what might have been.

Zinos-Amaro: What's the best entry point that you recommend for readers who want to explore these two series?

Swanwick: In both cases, it's the first published story, "The Dog Said Bow-Wow" and "The Mongolian Wizard" (*Tor.com*, July 4, 2012) respectively. These stories set up the rules, establish the characters, and you don't need to know anything to enter them. The other stories, maybe yes, maybe no. I try to make them all easy for someone to come to new, but the opening ones are the best choice.

Zinos-Amaro: Can you say a little about toggling between these series, and any relationship that might have with your overall writing productivity?

Swanwick: I have found that the times I have been most productive have been when I have had a bright and cheerful story, like the Darger and Surplus ones, and a dark and grim story, like the Mongolian Wizard stories have become, going at the same time. I can alternate between them. I'll get to the point where maybe I can't take another festering radioactive corpse and then I'll switch over to the cheerful story until I can't stand another capering, giggling Smurf, and then I'll go back to the dark one. So during those times when I've had two stories like that going, there's been no waste time at all. Switching projects can really help your productivity. It keeps you from getting bogged down in one line of thought.

There's one more thing I want to say. The wolf in the Mongolian Wizard stories is a character people have really come to care about. It makes me sorry that he might have to die. He is a soldier in a war, and soldiers die. I will decide that later on. Talking with Gardner about *Lord of the Rings*, one of the things we agreed upon was that Tolkien had missed a bet. That one of the hobbits, either Pippin or Meriadoc, should have died. We agreed that Tolkien came to care too much about them. Having lost a lot of his friends in the First World War, he probably just couldn't do it. I don't have that problem. I've had the privilege of not being to war.

Back when I used to teach occasionally, one of the things that was hardest to make a new writer understand is that it's okay to do cruel things to fictional characters. They're not real. They don't hurt, they don't feel anything. Sometimes it's necessary. People try to let their characters off more easily than would happen in the world. That's fine, if it makes your work more entertaining. If not, you have to revert back to reality.

CHAPTER TEN
COLLABORATIONS

Zinos-Amaro: Your collection *Moon Dogs* (2000) contains a number of interesting collaborations and non-fiction pieces. Throughout your career you've collaborated with many notable writers, including William Gibson, Tim Sullivan, Gardner Dozois, Jack Dann, Eileen Gunn, Andy Duncan, Pat Murphy and Gregory Frost. Your list of collaborators is long and illustrious to say the least.

Swanwick: Most of these stories I wrote to learn. That started with the very first collaboration, "Touring" (*Penthouse*, April 1981), written with Jack Dann and Gardner Dozois. As I've recounted, when Jack was in town visiting, Gardner would call me up and invite me over. We would spend the evening talking about everything. Gardner and Jack were usually planning a collaborative anthology and they would hack the beginnings of that together. Jack would also bring over whatever he was working on and get Gardner's advice. Every now and then one of us would say, "There's a story idea," and we'd work it up into a story. Sometimes I was not involved, sometimes I was. Our idea for "Touring" was a posthumous rock concert with Janis Joplin and Elvis Presley and Buddy Holly. We talked it through until we had the entire plot from beginning to end. I took down copious notes. I went off and wrote the first draft. I sent it to Jack, who revised it, and then he sent it to Gardner, who completed the final draft. I was obviously the low man on the totem pole, but I had the advantage that Jack and I agreed that Gardner was the alpha male here. He was the one we both acknowledged as the better stylist than ourselves. Gardner had final say, and that worked well, because it meant you couldn't have arguments. That was pretty much the pattern for most of the collaborations with Gardner.

Generally, I did collaborations with people to challenge myself. Collaboration is really as much work as writing a full story, except you only get one half or one third of the money. But there's a great deal of satisfaction in learning how to become a better writer, from observing what the other writers involved do. That's what I was in it for, almost always.

Zinos-Amaro: In the Afterword to *City Under the Stars* you talk a little bit about the process of writing with Jack and Gardner. You said it was "much like the folktale about making stone soup. Add salt! Paprika! A wizard! Invisible cats! We called ourselves the Fiction Factory. We wrote some wonderful stuff and sold it all, often to the slicks." Jack Dann went on to publish a collection of these collaborations and he did in fact call it *The Fiction Factory* (2005).

Swanwick: That wasn't published until our run of collaborations was over. During the time we were writing these stories and selling them to the slick markets, Gardner said, "We must never breathe a word of this to anybody else, because if word gets out that we call this the Fiction Factory they'll use it as a hammer against us." By 2005 enough time had passed.

Zinos-Amaro: Tell me a little about your work with Eileen Gunn. You two have collaborated on four stories.

Swanwick: Eileen Gunn is a writer I admire immensely, and a good friend. She doesn't write enough. She writes very slowly. I keep trying to convince her that she is naturally a fast writer, if only she could turn off that voice that says "No" and sit down and write it out. "Shed That Guilt! Double Your Productivity Overnight!" (*The Magazine of Fantasy & Science Fiction*, September 2008) was our first collaboration. I'm proud of that one. I basically tricked her into it! We were on this bulletin board where people talked back and forth in support of Clarion West. Eileen was going, "I'm such a slow writer, and I feel guilty," and I told her, "The Guilt Eaters of Philadelphia has a program for you!" My point was, don't think, just write, don't look at what you've written until you're done, and *then* you can feel guilty about it and revise all you want. She fought back, of course. We went back and forth in a joking fashion, until the exchange came to a natural end. I took all of our comments, revised them very slightly, sent them back to her and said, "Congratulations Eileen, you've finished a new story." She gave it a new and better ending, and there it was. It was very satisfying to con her into writing a story.

Now and then over the years I wouldn't propose to her that we write a story, I just told her that's what we were doing. For "Zeppelin City" (*Tor.com*, October 6, 2009) I gave her the first section, asked her to write the next block, and so on. That one took forever. We argued vehemently about everything. But it's one of my favorite stories. It was a pinata filled with delightful inventions.

"The Trains That Climb the Winter Tree" (*Tor.com*, December 21, 2010) came from "Shed that Guilt!" She'd jokingly described the SF dekalogy she couldn't write: "elves, mirrors, electric trains, trees that extend into the stratosphere and rain gold on those below, and Dick Cheney's evil twin." So I told her we were going to write that, and gave her the opening paragraphs. Which she immediately changed into something absolutely different. I said, "Eileen, you've short-circuited the entire process. Now we have to write two stories!" Her opening became "The Armies of Elfland" (*Asimov's Science Fiction*, April-May 2009). We wrote those two pretty much simultaneously, swapping manuscripts back and forth. Making those stories happen is an example of mastery of craft. But "Zeppelin City" was one that I think we both put our hearts into.

Zinos-Amaro: In these cases, you were the initiator of a collaboration. Have you ever been on the other side?

Swanwick: Yes, in "Green Fire" (*Event Horizon Online*, January 1999), written with Andy Duncan, Pat Murphy and Eileen. Ellen Datlow was the editor of that magazine. She would recruit four people and say, "Okay, you're going to do a round-robin story." The rule was that one writer starts it, passes it off to the next, and so on until you get to the end. The installments were published weekly, and the writers weren't supposed to talk to each other about where the story was going. Susan Casper had done this before, so I went to her and said, "What's your advice?" She said, "Cheat. We played by the rules and it was terrible. One of the writers always took things off in a random direction, and the whole thing became chaos."

I got in touch with Eileen, who had been chosen by Ellen, and asked her, "How are we going to do this?" She brought up an idea I had had that she liked. There had been an *F&SF* competition where you had to make up an urban legend based on true facts involving science fiction writers, and you had to add one telling detail. My idea was to start with the true fact that Isaac Asimov, Robert Heinlein and L. Sprague de Camp had all worked at the Philadelphia Navy Yard during World War II; the urban legend part was that they all became involved in the Philadelphia Experiment, teleporting battleships; and the telling detail was going to be that they had all written stories about teleportation before the war, but they didn't write any *after* the war. I had no idea if that was true or not, but it didn't matter. We had a start. Eileen threw in Grace Hopper. We sat together and roughed out the entire story. We decided that each one of the four writers would get one of the characters, so that they only had to research one person. We held de Camp in reserve in case we needed him. For my parts of the story, I would throw in something random and pulpish. So you'd have these well thought-out, researched sections with Asimov, Heinlein and Hopper, and then I'd introduce a pirate ship on the horizon. That collaboration was as much fun as one has ever been—for *me* at least!

I should say that my collaboration with William Gibson on "Dogfight" (*Omni*, July 1985) was also a lot of fun. As we were going back and forth, we used the "hot typewriter" method. Each person gets the story for a month, during which he can do anything, or nothing at all. At the end of the month he sends back the story with any changes. The other person can then do anything at all with that story, and then sends it along. Bill Gibson would take something out, and I would put it back in, and he would take it out again—quite rightly, he was from the beginning a very, very good writer. I think I was happier with the end result than he was, but I cannot speak for him.

Zinos-Amaro: It sounds like many of your collaborations relied on either the "hot typewriter" or "round-robin" methods. What about the story "Archaic Planets: Nine Excerpts from the Encyclopedia Galactica" (*Asimov's Science Fiction*, December 1998), a collaboration with your son Sean?

Swanwick: What happened there was that I had written up this little story where I had one section for each planet in the Solar System. Sean was either fourteen or fifteen at the time. He was amused when I showed it to him and said, "Can I write one?"

Very quickly—he might have even sat down and done it on the spot—he wrote a piece for Jupiter. I looked at it and said, "Well, this is better than *my* Jupiter piece, so I'm tossing mine out and putting yours in." I corrected the spelling and that was it. That was a different method of collaboration.

I also had two unusual collaborations with Sheila Williams. One is "Letters to the Editor," which we discussed, where I assembled all these ludicrous biographical responses I'd been sending in when asked for updated information. Much later, she had an editorial where she explained why she would never publish a story with the title "The Time Wife from Earth Shot the Last Man on Death World." I wrote a short short, saying at the start that the title would only be revealed in the last line, and the last line was that title. She published the short short as part of an editorial called "Never Say 'Rather Unlikely' Again" (*Asimov's Science Fiction*, November-December 2018). So I have a fiction/non-fiction collaboration with Sheila. I think I have done my bit to blur the lines of what is fiction and what is not.

Zinos-Amaro: We can infer yet another different approach for your posthumous collaborations. You share author credit for stories with Avram Davidson, H. G. Wells and Anthony Trollope.

Swanwick: As I like to say, the only way I could have collaborated with Avram was over his dead body!

For the Wells and Trollope, we have to take a step back. I wrote a piece called "A Nettlesome Term that has Long Outlived its Welcome" (*The New York Review of Science Fiction*, July 2007) about fix-up novels. I'd gotten very tired of having my novels called fix-ups. The first one, *In the Drift*, was a fix-up; there was no getting around it. But the other novels were not. They were episodic, and I would carve out sections and rework them as standalone stories to generate interest and publicity in the novels. I had learned how to do this by watching Jack Dann when he wrote *The Man Who Melted*. He would bring his latest section of the novel to Gardner, who would advise him on how to turn it into a self-contained story. He did pretty well, garnering some Nebula nominations that way. How Jack was able to do this, for example with a story called "Going Under," in which he basically changed the ending and meaning of the text, really struck me. It was a wonderful skill. When I did this with my novels, people claimed that they were fix-ups because the definition they were using at that point was that *any* narrative whose parts could be taken and published independently was a fix-up, whether the author had conceived of the original idea as a novel or not. It was a way of dismissing good work out of hand and it annoyed me. So I said, "Okay, I'm going to do this with Wells' *The Time Machine*." I took out a section and made it into a standalone story. Then I asked, "Does that make that novel a fix-up?" I did the same by excerpting a book by Trollope. Did he write fix-ups too? And if so, how? So those two posthumous collaborations were written with the full force of malice. It seems to have worked. David Hartwell and I fought a war against that term, and I think ultimately we won. You don't see "fix-up" thrown around as liberally anymore.

Zinos-Amaro: If you could collaborate with anyone, past or present, who would it be?

Swanwick: From past writers, I would love to collaborate with Hope Mirrlees. Also Italo Calvino. Maybe Roger Zelazny (though his collaboration with Dick was pretty limp; I'd have to take the lead there). Russ and Le Guin and Delany, whom I admire this side of adolatry, would probably not have responded well to my interference. For someone still around, it would be A. S. Byatt. I love Byatt's work. It would be a delight to collaborate with her. At one point, I had a plan to collaborate with Gene Wolfe. It just never gelled. We were going to collaborate on a story set in Egypt, and we exchanged a couple of letters about it. I proposed one possible ending, and he said, "Well, we can't use that because I just did it in my last *Soldier in the Mist* novel."

There have been a couple of times where I tried to collaborate with someone, but we didn't click. The chemistry was just not there. I've mentioned Janet Kagan before, who was a good friend and died far too young. She was a very popular, squeaky-clean writer who got her start writing porn movies. I came up with an idea for a unicorn on a porn movie set and told her we were going to collaborate on a story. We tried. We exchanged one or two bits of prose. She finally said, "I can't do this your way." I replied, "I can't be as upbeat about this whole thing as you are." So she went and wrote an upbeat unicorn-on-a-porn-set story and I wrote a downbeat unicorn-on-a-porn-set story with Tim Sullivan, called "Fantasies" (*Amazing Stories*, August 1991). That turned out to be a minor story, but you have to write all the stories out to find out whether they're going to be great or not.

Zinos-Amaro: Absolutely. On that note, what collaborations are you proudest of?

Swanwick: The novella I wrote with Gardner, "The City of God" (*Omni Online*, December 1995), which I later expanded into *City Under the Stars*, would be one. I've already mentioned "Zeppelin City."

I'm extremely proud of "Vergil Magus: King Without Country" (*Asimov's Science Fiction*, July 1998), with Avram Davidson. Toward the end of his life Avram was having trouble plotting, I believe. He tried to make up for that by doubling down on the prose. The writing became very intense, thoroughly worked and ornate, sometimes to the detriment of the story. "Vergil Magus: King Without Country" was beautifully written. It sounded like the most intelligent man on Earth nattering on about whatever entered his head. It was all fascinating, but you didn't realize there was a story there until the final paragraph, when it all came together. Then you realized the whole thing was as well constructed as a Swiss watch. But then, in the same sentence you realized this was a story, it was over!

Grania Davis had sent it in to *Asimov's*, and Gardner very much wanted to publish it, but he knew that the readers wouldn't like it for those reasons. He handed it over to me, with permission from Grania, and asked if I could do something with it. This was Avram's prose at its finest; I couldn't counterfeit that. So what I did was break it into chunks and after each of his sections I cut away to an exciting event involving Vergil Magus working his magic, then went back to Avram's description. I took all these elements from Avram's story and made a larger, far more pulpy story out of them. I think I got almost every reference he had buried in that story and expanded it. The finished story now fully made sense and had a happy ending. When it was published, Gregory Feeley said in a review that he couldn't tell where Avram left off and I began, which I was extremely flattered by. With this exercise I felt that I had achieved my mastery in the basics of fiction.

Zinos-Amaro: I'm fascinated by these exercises in craft.

Swanwick: I'll give you one more. Jack and Gardner and I wrote a ten thousand word story called "Golden Apples of the Sun," which *Penthouse* really liked. They were going to pay us thousands of dollars for it—*if* we could cut it down to five thousand words. That is, *one half* the original length. Jack was out of town, so Gardner and I sat down and cut out a couple of comic scenes. Then we went through it a second time and removed several paragraphs of description and such. On the third go we started removing individual sentences. Fourth revision, we were down to cutting out phrases. We did a fifth round where we removed every single adverb we could find! The sixth time we changed all the instances of "did not" and "was not" to "didn't" and "wasn't." By this time we were knee-deep in blood. Gardner lost the will to live. He sat there, hunched over, shaking his head, like a great shaggy buffalo, saying, "I don't know, I don't know..." I drove on. At the end of that I was the one who pushed it to the finish line, rephrasing things from three words to two words, from seven to six, until finally it was at four thousand nine hundred and ninety-nine words—I counted. The story was published as "Virgin Territory" (*Penthouse*, March 1984). Later, the full novelette appeared in a *Year's Best Fantasy* volume with the original title. This exercise showed me how ruthless I could be with prose. That ruthlessness has never left me. It's been a great comfort, and of great use, many times.

Zinos-Amaro: How do you think of voice as it relates to collaborations?

Swanwick: One time at a convention I ran into Howard Waldrop and Andy Duncan and took a picture of them. They put their heads together and smiled. I said, "Geez, these guys look like two Dust Bowl-era grifters." For about a month I kept looking at the picture, and I knew my hindbrain was trying to tell me something. I had this notion on the back burner of two con men in a fantasy version of America, and I started to write a story about that. I came up against the problem that Andy and Howard both have very specific voices. Howard is from Oklahoma, which was a voice I couldn't do, and I wasn't terribly confident in my Andy Duncan voice either. But I knew that Gregory Frost was really good with voices, so I suggested to him that we collaborate. We met several times. I was really, really happy with the outcome, "Lock Up Your Chickens and Daughters—H'ard and Andy are

Come to Town" (*Asimov's Science Fiction*, April-May 2015).

Someday, Greg and I may collaborate again. We have a story that we made copious notes for many years ago. During the lockdown we were both talking about getting back to it, but we couldn't find the notes. I'm hoping that we do eventually return to it though. I esteem Greg very highly as a writer. He has not received a fraction of the acknowledgment that he should have, but he's as good as anyone in my generation.

Zinos-Amaro: What other insights have you gleaned from collaboration?

Swanwick: One of these evenings with Jack and Gardner, Gardner had acquired a new typewriter and was a little suspicious of it. His old one had a platen that was slightly loose, so that as he typed, the words went down and then up again in a kind of wave across the page. He would type on onionskin because it was the cheapest paper you could get, and he had practically no margins. This was his lucky typewriter. The new device was nice and crisp and clean. Every now and then Jack would walk over and try out the action on it. Jack had an idea for a story about an old man sitting on a park bench and growing young. Gardner said, "That's great. What's the story?" Jack said, "I think it'll be very sensitive." We couldn't finagle a plot out of him. Jack typed the opening line of the story. We talked about other things, and sometime later I went to it and I wrote the line, "Pterodactyls picked their way through the gutter, their legs lifting storklike as they daintily nipped at random pieces of refuse." Jack asked what I was doing, and Gardner said, "He's writing our story for us!" I replied, "No Jack, I'm making fun of you." Again Jack said, "This is very sensitive!" When I came back the next day Gardner said, "We've finished your dinosaur story." He showed it to me. It was very simple. This guy sees all these dinosaurs on a walk, then goes back home to his old depressing wife and his old depressing apartment. He hears a clattering sound and it's more dinosaurs falling from the sky. He says, "At least it's not raining cats and dogs anymore." That was it. Gardner said, "You can put your name on this, you'll get one third of whatever we make." I said, "No. You'll be lucky to sell it to George Scithers." He asked if I was sure and I told him I didn't want anything to do with it. Two weeks later Gardner calls me up and says, "We sold that story to *Playboy*, you putz!" The story was called "A Change in the Weather" (*Playboy*, June 1981). That experience taught me a lesson in not being arrogant. It was a fast, funny story, which of course people would like, and I had been too "high art" for it.

Zinos-Amaro: Jack might have said you were too sensitive.

Swanwick: Ha! Jack loved the story and did think it was very sensitive.

Every collaboration I've done has made me a better writer. I got what I wanted out of it—I don't know about the other people!

AFTERWORD

BY
MARIANNE PORTER

I met Michael Swanwick in a tuberculosis hospital in Philadelphia.

I was a rising young technocrat on the sixth floor, and he was
a hard-working, serious, underpaid clerk-typist on the fifth.

He was bright, funny, articulate. Clearly well educated and
interesting. I was fascinated. He was going be a writer, and he
had made a deal with his supervisor to use the office Selectric
(he typed so fast he could jam it) at lunchtime and after work.
He wrote All The Time, and he never finished anything. He left
behind him a trail of fragments of prose, crumpled sheets of
typescript, inventive screeds of passion, romance, and adventure.
They had no endings.

I thought he might be crazy.

We both lived in the vibrant heart of Center City, in the bat-
tered apartments that had been carved out of stately old townhous-
es and were offered to the young and impecunious. Michael had
grown up in smaller places in the Northeast and was excited to
live in the big city, with its culture, its art, its hordes of new people.

Among those people were Susan Casper and Gardner Dozois.
Michael became friends with first Susan, who was always sure he
would be a writer, and then Gardner, who was terrified Michael
would thrust one of his unfinished orphans on him and ask for
advice. He met Tom Purdom, writer, and Sara Purdom, who introduced him to the joys of city society. Artists Bob Walters and
Tess Kissinger showed him the challenges of scientific illustration
and let him hobnob with scientists. George Scithers, first editor of
Asimov's, and his colleague Darrell Schweitzer revealed the inner
mysteries of publishing, although it was a while before Michael
was published in the magazine.

Philadelphia was a hotbed of creativity and Michael thrived there. He got a job in that TB hospital and then at the Franklin Institute in a solar energy information center. He volunteered at the Wilma Theater, when it was a women's collective. He went to art galleries. He walked the streets at all hours. And always, always, he wrote. Until, finally, he finished something. The rest is a series of brilliant stories, short and long, and a trail of awards, Hugo, Nebula, World Fantasy, Roscon, Aelita, Theodore Sturgeon.

Somewhere along the way, I fell in love with him, for all that hard work and intelligence and passion. I married him when I realized that with him I would never, ever, be bored.

Michael is widely regarded as a master of the short form. Most writers like to talk about their work. A chance to revisit and reconsider their written career is clearly irresistible. But not my husband. Reviewing the final copy has led to a couple of weeks rambling around the house, muttering "Did I say that?" And, "What did that mean?" And, "Do I really start every sentence with 'So'!"

Michael wrote *Being Gardner Dozois* in part because he valued Gardner's analytical understanding of his own writing. I think Michael was genuinely surprised to realize how intuitive his own approach is. And now you can share these insights. I truly think you will be fascinated, just as I was, all those years ago.

—*Marianne Porter, May 2023*

ABOUT THE AUTHOR

Alvaro Zinos-Amaro is a Hugo- and Locus-award finalist who has published over fifty stories and one hundred essays, reviews, and interviews in professional markets. These include *Analog, Lightspeed, Beneath Ceaseless Skies, Galaxy's Edge, Nature, The Los Angeles Review of Books, Locus, Tor.com, Strange Horizons, Clarkesworld, The Year's Best Science Fiction & Fantasy, Cyber World, Nox Pareidolia, Multiverses: An Anthology of Alternate Realities*, and many others. *Traveler of Worlds: Conversations with Robert Silverberg* was published in 2016 to critical acclaim. *Being Michael Swanwick* is Alvaro's second book of interviews. His debut novel, *Equimedian*, is forthcoming in 2024.

OTHER TITLES FROM FAIRWOOD PRESS

Hellhounds
by David Sandner & Jacob Weisman
small paperback $9.00
ISBN: 978-1-933846-19-4

Embrace of the Wolf
by Jack Cady & Carol Orlock
trade paper $18.99
ISBN: 978-1-958880-06-7

The Whole Mess
by Jack Skillingstead
trade paper $20.95
ISBN: 978-1-958880-12-8

Geometries of Belonging
by R.B. Lemberg
trade paper $18.99
ISBN: 978-1-958880-01-2

After the Tide
by Jessie Kwak
small paperback $9.00
ISBN: 978-1-958880-11-1

Liberty's Daughter
by Naomi Kritzer
trade paper $18.99
ISBN: 978-1-958880-16-6

The Ultra Big Sleep
by Patrick Swenson
HC & trade paper reprint
$19.99 / $31
ISBNs: 978-1-958880-07-4
978-1-958880-08-1

Whispering Wood
by Sharon Shinn
trade paper $19.99
ISBN: 978-1-958880-13-5

Find us at:
www.fairwoodpress.com
Bonney Lake, Washington

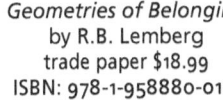

www.ingramcontent.com/pod-product-compliance
Lightning Source LLC
Chambersburg PA
CBHW020842020726
47497CB00005B/1213